SLEEPING IN EDEN

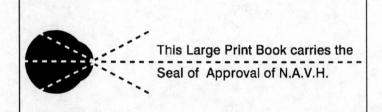

This Large Print Book carries the
Seal of Approval of N.A.V.H.

SLEEPING IN EDEN

NICOLE BAART

THORNDIKE PRESS
A part of Gale, Cengage Learning

GALE
CENGAGE Learning·

Detroit • New York • San Francisco • New Haven, Conn • Waterville, Maine • London

GALE
CENGAGE Learning®

LIBRARY OF CONGRESS CATALOGING-IN-PUBLICATION DATA

Baart, Nicole.
    Sleeping in eden / by Nicole Baart. — Large print edition.
        pages ; cm. — (Thorndike Press large print Christian mystery)
    ISBN-13: 978-1-4104-6341-8 (hardcover)
    ISBN-10: 1-4104-6341-9 (hardcover)
        1. Physicians—Fiction. 2. Young women—Fiction. 3. Women—Crimes against—Fiction. 4. Large type books. I. Title.
    PS3602.A22S54 2013b
    813'.6—dc23
                                                                    2013033740

Published in 2013 by arrangement with Howard Books, a division of Simon & Schuster, Inc.

Printed in Mexico
1 2 3 4 5 6 7 17 16 15 14 13

To the ones I lost and the ones I hold.
May I never be caught sleeping in Eden.

1
Lucas

On the day the leaves began to fall, Jim
Sparks hung himself from a rafter in his
condemned barn. The sun was warm but
the air was cool; a prophecy of winter in the
breeze that shook the first honey-colored
leaves from branches that would soon stand
naked, all angles and lines, snow-draped
modern art adorning the prairies.

Morning dawned sudden and crisp, robed
in fog that crowned the fields with ribbons
of silver and left geometric patterns of shimmering frost reflecting light like diamonds.
But by the time the clock passed twelve, the
afternoon had melted into a reluctant
autumn warmth. It was the sort of day when
you could not help but turn your face
toward the sun; a day that could not be
duplicated in a year of days.

And he killed himself.

The wind sighed audibly through the barn
when Lucas Hudson stepped out of his tiny

import, a rusty blue thing that had become a sort of inside joke in a town staunchly dedicated to everything domestic. Gravel crunched beneath his tattered sneakers, and he shielded his eyes with strong, surgeon's hands as he surveyed the scene before him.

Jim's property was a graveyard of gutted engines and frozen pizza boxes that seemed incapable of finding their way into the dented, metallic garbage can that lay half buried in the weeds beside his front step. The disarray stretched across five acres of unkempt lawn and sagging buildings bordered by an aging farmhouse against the eastern fence, and a grayish barn with peeling paint along a northwest line of poplars.

Lucas stood on the driveway and looked past it all. He leaned into the slight breeze, absorbing warmth through his sweatshirt, and watched the golden cornfields dance.

Everyone hated Jim Sparks, and the phone call that had summoned Lucas didn't inspire the quintessential emotions of pity, regret, or even shock. Instead, he felt numb. Cold. It wasn't surprising that the man who seemed to resent every aspect of his existence in this small town had finally done what many had always expected him to do. Truth be told, most people thought he'd simply leave rather than take the more permanent way out. But suicide accomplished the deed: Jim would never face another insidious rumor.

"Lucas!"

The sound of his name made Lucas start, but of course it was Alex. His friend had summoned him here, had torn him away from Jenna when they had actually been having a conversation — words exchanged that meant something. But it was impossible to say no to Alex Kennedy. He was a force of nature, a grown man with the soul of a child. It didn't hurt that he was also the police chief, even if the title seemed a bit presumptuous for a village as small and sleepy as Blackhawk, Iowa. Lucas had often thought the decorous, hardworking citizens of his hometown would likely do just fine regulating themselves.

Alex loped across the sloping lawn, his usually grinning mouth set in a serious half smile to convey the gravity, the tragedy of the situation.

"Hey." Lucas shortened the distance between them in a few long strides. He tried to return Alex's wan smile, but it came out lopsided and faded the moment his mouth managed to take shape. Lucas knew he looked like he had tangled with shadows in some rough back alley, and he ran his hands through his thick, dark hair before stuffing them in the pockets of his gray hoodie.

"Thanks for coming," Alex said, lifting an eyebrow but apparently choosing to ignore Lucas's uncharacteristic dishevelment. He offered his own brand of sympathy in a quick thump to the back. "I know this is usually your only day off."

"And I don't usually act as coroner," Lucas reminded him. But Alex didn't bother to respond.

They walked in silence to the barn, a leaning affair with broken windows that snarled at the world through shards of glass clinging fanglike to the rotten frames. The mid-afternoon sunlight poured through wide cracks between each and every board and sprinkled dust across the shaded east-facing entrance. Though Alex called it a barn, the building in question had once been a stable, and the wide, high doors seemed to frame the past. Lucas could almost imagine the carriages, buggies, and sleighs that had long ago passed through the now sagging arches. It was surprisingly charming in its age and fragility. Never mind the squad cars, the haphazard yellow tape, the sounds of people talking gravely within.

"Why didn't you call Elliot?" Lucas finally

asked, pausing in the shadow of the hay-mow.

"Out of town. Vacation."

"So who's taking care of the morgue?"

"Someone croaks, we gotta send them to Fairfield," Alex explained.

Lucas sighed. "You know, there are other doctors in town."

"I think the Townsend brothers got their licenses in Mexico."

Lucas's laugh was a soft snort, but at least he laughed. "Oh, you owe me big, Kennedy. This is hardly in my job description."

"Yeah, well, you know." Alex lifted the heavy latch and pushed the door open, stooping to secure it with a rock the size of a small melon. The action didn't necessarily shed light into the barn.

Lucas stepped tentatively into the shadow of the old building and gave his eyes a moment to adjust to the dusty, filtered light. The two town cops called to the scene were talking in hushed tones out of Lucas's range of vision, but a quick scan of the inside of the slanted barn revealed as much clutter as could be expected from Jim Sparks. There was junk everywhere — piles of old firewood, small farm machinery, moldy hay bales.

And yet, a few reminders of the former

glory of the Timmer Ranch clung to the landscape like artifacts from some era beyond memory. There was a brass plate with the name *Philadelphia* etched in sweeping strokes above a corner stall. And two long, curved bale hooks, covered in rust that could be mistaken for ancient blood in the dying light. Reaching to touch a lone harness that was draped from a nail near the door, Lucas caught a whiff of leather. And then he made out a clearing. Between an old tractor and the first animal stall, a body hung limp and motionless only two feet off the ground.

Lucas maneuvered around an abandoned axle and surveyed the scene before him. Jim had knotted a pretty handy noose; the spine traveled across the front of his throat and tossed his head back at a grotesque angle. His face was a cruel shade of bluish purple, and his tongue lolled thick and offensive out of blood-speckled lips. A rickety wooden chair lay upturned and off to one side of the body that swung almost imperceptibly like a broken, bloated pendulum. And the beam itself, the rafter that held Jim Sparks in death, ran bent but sturdy from one end of the barn to the other, cutting a crooked line that seemed to say, "At least I can do this." Lucas suddenly felt tired. He was

expecting horror of nightmarish proportions. What he got was something altogether
pathetic and horribly, wretchedly sad.

"How did they find him?"

Alex made his way past Lucas and stood
with his forearms on the half wall of the
stall in which Jim dangled. He looked like a
spectator at a county fair, examining the
qualifications of a late entrant. "He didn't
show up for work last night. You know he
works the late shift at the plant in Fairfield?
Well, some guy that splits his hours got
ticked that he didn't show and decided to
come by and give Jim hell. The barn door
was open, swinging in the wind . . ." Alex
looked over his shoulder at Lucas. "He
called the city office from his cell phone and
took off. Can you believe that? Called the
city office, not 911."

Lucas smiled faintly, aware that in spite of
his seemingly gruff disposition, Alex was a
teddy bear in disguise. Lucas had it on good
authority that his best friend got choked up
watching Disney movies with his daughters,
and he didn't believe for a second that Alex
was as nonchalant about the grisly scene
before him as he tried so hard to convey.
"You okay?" Lucas asked him, dropping his
voice conspiratorially.

"Fine." Alex shrugged.

13

"Seems like a bit of a cold thing to say." Lucas sloped an eyebrow. "There's a dead man hanging a few feet from your nose."

"I don't see you crying," Alex huffed.

"Fair enough." Lucas sighed. They obviously weren't going to have a brotherly heart-to-heart, and since he didn't know what else to say, the clock ticked off a few seconds of awkward silence. Finally Lucas passed a hand over the five o'clock shadow along his jaw and swallowed a groan. "Let's get this over with so that I can go home."

"My thoughts exactly," Alex muttered.

Lucas still felt hesitant but joined Alex at the stall. "Was there a suicide note?"

"Not that we've found. There's not much in here and we went through the house already. Couldn't find a thing of value. You know, I think we're going to have to torch the whole place. Jim Sparks lived like an animal. Honestly, you should see the shit he has in there. Garbage piled high . . ."

"Signs of a struggle? You know, unusual scratches, flesh under his fingernails, extra footprints in the barn?"

Alex snorted and indicated the numbered red tags that littered the barn floor like macabre confetti. "You telling me how to do my job, Hudson?"

Lucas held up his hands in defense.

"Never. I'm just saying, I think it's pretty obvious it was a suicide."

"Look, it's my job to treat the entire farm like it's a crime scene right now. This is a homicide until we can prove otherwise. Do I have to bag the hands for a forensic team? Or are you going to do your job?"

Lucas never got a chance to respond. As if on cue, two cops emerged from the darkened tack room that was half hidden behind a sagging row of whitewashed bee boxes. They held out a camera to Alex. "We took pictures. But only because Kennedy made us," the younger one said, winking at Lucas. "I think it was a waste of time. Nice to meet you, Dr. Hudson."

They shook hands, and Lucas smiled even though he could tell Alex was irritated by the cavalier way his cops insisted on handling the situation. Blackhawk was a small town, but Alex took his job very seriously, following the letter of the law with admirable diligence and an almost old-world sense of honor. Well, to a point. It seemed there was sometimes a little wiggle room within the defined code. But it took a veteran to know when to bend and when to stand firm. The two young men who rounded out the police force were nothing but rookies. Kids, really. Two boys who grew up within Blackhawk city limits and knew little more than the character and quirks of the 2,587 people who called their wooded corner of northwest Iowa home. Their world was finely bordered.

Alex's frustration was understandable, but Lucas didn't feel like hearing a speech. Before the police chief had a chance to lay into the uniformed boys, Lucas said: "Let's get this over with. I'm documenting, you guys have to take him down."

"You might want to take a few moments to investigate the circumstances and, seemingly obvious or not, try to determine cause of death," Alex prompted with a grunt. "And, of course, you'll want to confirm that he is, in fact, deceased. I can't do that, you know. The coroner has to."

Lucas felt his shoulders stiffen. "Get me something to stand on," he said, his words sharp and just a little too hard. He had acted as coroner on only a handful of occasions, and they had all been run-of-the-mill, small-town stuff. An elderly lady who died in her sleep. A middle-aged man who died of a withering cancer in hospice care. Lucas was an excellent doctor, arguably wasted on the monotony of rural life, but this was unprecedented. Jim had knocked him a bit off his game.

16

It took awhile to find something that would work for him to stand on. There were no ladders, no boxes that looked even remotely sturdy. All that was available was the same chair that Jim had used, and after a few moments, with a heavy sigh, Alex righted it beneath the body. He held out his hand before it, palm up, and backed away so Lucas could do his job.

The barn seemed to shift as Lucas climbed onto the chair, but he couldn't tell if it was because the rotting piece of furniture was old and feeble or because the reenactment was making his head spin. He paused a few seconds to get his balance, and did everything he could to avoid looking directly at the body before him. Finally, he took a deep breath and turned to face Jim head-on.

With deft fingers, Lucas probed the rigid neck. It was cold and still, smooth-firm like molded plastic. No pulse, no breath, no life. Rigor had already begun to set in. Bending a little, Lucas took Jim's hands in his own and studied the stiff curve of his thick fingers. Nails bitten down to the quick, tobacco stains creating muddy rivers in the whorls of his fingerprints. He was a nail-biter, a smoker, but beyond the obvious, his hands were clean. There were no wounds, no sign of a struggle, in fact, no indicators

17

of anything beyond his bad habits. He wore no wedding ring, no watch on his wrist to mark the bittersweet passage of time.

Lucas sighed. "He's dead," he confirmed unnecessarily. "No signs of struggle as far as I can tell."

"Death by asphyxiation?"

"I'm pretty sure his neck is broken," Lucas said. "But I'm not entirely sure how. He didn't have far to fall, and it takes at least a four-foot drop to break the neck."

"Maybe he jumped," Alex guessed, pointing to the high platform of the hayloft about them.

"Then what was the chair for? More likely he just really wanted to get the job done. He threw himself with some serious force."

Alex seemed to consider something for a moment, but apparently it was too implausible to imagine that foul play was involved. "Let's just get him down," Alex said. "I think our best bet is to have two men on the ground to hold his body. I'll cut the rope." He produced a bone-handled hunting knife, originally ivory-colored but now stained tea brown and anything but police issue. "Let's do it."

Lucas and Alex switched places, and the police chief began the slow process of sawing through the thick woven rope.

Progress was slow, and made even more tedious by the utter silence that amplified the dull scratching of the knife. Each piece of rope that spun off the homemade noose made a soft snick that seemed like an echo of the sound Jim's neck must have made when it broke. Lucas saw each pop as a snapshot of Jim's sad life: his beat-up, mustard-yellow Chevy truck, the stray mutt that followed him around for a few weeks until it was mangled by a car, the bottles of Black Velvet that he bought on the first Monday of every month. The imaginary scrapbook was so sad, so rife with loneliness, that for an aching moment, Lucas's arms longed to encircle Jenna. The specters that haunted the shadowed barn drew his attention like a magnet, but Lucas gave his head a hard shake and focused his attention on Alex so that he didn't have to wrestle unseen demons.

Alex was completely engulfed in the task before him as he adjusted his weight on the chair in order to get at the rope with his other hand. His movement on the worthless piece of furniture tossed the balance to one of the shorter back legs and the flimsy chair began a teetering roll on three legs. Lucas hopped off the stall gate and made a lunge to steady Alex, but he was too far away and past the point of rescue. In an instant, Alex counterbalanced, grabbed for Jim's body, stopped himself in horror, and went flying backward off the chair. As he hit the ground with a nauseating thud, the three men maneuvered around the now swinging body of Jim Sparks and crouched down to offer help that was too late.

Alex was grimacing and clutching his right elbow, but he assured everyone he was fine, punctuated with a few choice words and "Get the hell away from me."

"Come on, Alex," Lucas coaxed, "let me take a quick look at you. Did you hit your head?"

But Alex was already getting up. "I'm fine. It's just that piece of —" He shrugged off their steadying hands and swung back to kick the toppled-over chair. As his foot made contact with the seat, a sharp crack split the air and was almost immediately joined by Alex's yelp. The chair hadn't moved.

Lucas joined Alex and bent down to see what had held the piece of furniture so tightly in place. "Foot okay?" he asked quietly.

"Shut up."

"Yup."

The chair was sticking out at a forty-five-degree angle to the ground. The back left leg had dug a deep gash in the hardpacked earthen floor of the barn and was now securely rooted in between the dirt and what looked like a thick tree branch.

"Looks like you've got quite a bit of leverage," one of the young officers quipped from over their shoulders.

Alex didn't respond to the jab, but leaned in closer to the foot of the chair and carefully dusted dry earth off the branch.

"So there're roots underneath the barn. Big deal." The other rookie cop turned away and proved himself gutsy enough to grab Jim's body and stop its dancelike sway.

"I don't think it's a tree branch," Alex mumbled. "Too far away from anything growing nearby."

"Sounds ominous," Lucas quipped.

"Mysteries R Us." Alex waved him closer. "Take a look at this."

Lucas crawled down on his hands and knees and studied the object. It was barely peeking out of the ground, a hint of grimy hardness in a parallel line with earth. Only a couple of inches were exposed, but Lucas could tell that it extended far beyond eyesight and deep underground. Dirt worn as smooth as cement banked both sides — if the chair hadn't disturbed its hard-packed

21

grave, the incongruity beneath the barn floor might have never surfaced at all.

Reaching out a tentative hand, Lucas brushed the dirt away with his fingertips, revealing a grayish white surface that was comparatively smooth despite tiny pockmarks that dug minuscule basins across the exterior. He clawed at the dust with his nails until they began to split, then he turned to Alex with a sigh.

"The knife?"

Alex handed it over without a single cynical comment.

Lucas scratched and dug, prying chunks of earth away with each vicious slash. Within minutes, he could tentatively wrap his fingers around it. He pulled gently. It didn't give an inch. Pulling harder produced the same effect: nothing.

"What do you think it is?" Alex cut in.

In the corner of his mind, a shadowy thought was beginning to materialize in smoky, elusive wisps. Lucas brushed more dust away, touched the object again, and realized with a paralyzing jolt that the doctor in him had always known what it was. His subconscious perceived it even when his mind refused to believe. "Oh, God." Lucas whispered it — a prayer, an invocation, a heartfelt, aching plea — because he knew . . . he knew what lay beneath the feet of the community's infamous outcast.

"Lucas, come on, don't get all melodramatic."

It was through a fog that Lucas managed to mumble, "I think we're looking at Angela Sparks."

A tangible quiet descended on the barn. Disbelief, thick and poisonous, choked each man as they stared at what they now knew to be a bone. A human bone. Moments trudged by before Alex found his voice. "I thought Jenna was helping her get out of town."

"Me, too."

Jenna Hudson was deep water. Mysterious, flowing, dark. She had stormed into Lucas's life late in his residency and had affixed herself indelibly, ineradicably in his mind before she ever made it to his heart. Jenna, with her baggy jeans, piled hair, bare feet. She wore her own skin as if it was an afterthought, something that she had just tossed on as she swept out the door. She claimed him without meaning to, without really seeming to care if he was hers. But he was, and from the first moment, she knew it.

Jenna was all eyes. Blue so bottomless it

was navy, almost black. And it was those eyes, in the face framed by curls that appeared to flow out of everything that was her, shadowy enough to be coal, that demanded all of Lucas. He had never been in love before, and he never bothered to question if he even knew what love truly was. He simply married her.

The first time Lucas told Jenna that he loved her, they were getting groceries. It became a Sunday ritual early in their relationship; the resident and the social worker, too busy during every other imaginable hour even to contemplate something as unnecessary as grocery shopping. And yet they found themselves spending hours as they discovered new delicacies, chased each other down aisles, and intentionally avoided every bargain. Their cart overflowed with chocolate cherry bordeaux ice cream, thin wedges of expensive cheeses, sprouted wheat bread trucked in from the organic bakery downtown.

Jenna was standing over the vine-ripened tomatoes, touching and carefully pressing and easing the chosen few into a clear plastic bag on the day it finally happened. Lucas was leaning over the grocery cart, indulging in his new favorite pastime of simply watching her.

"You know I love you."

It was a casual statement, and Jenna didn't even seem to notice. He thought about saying it again, about reaching over the tomatoes to touch her, make her feel his skin pressing against her hand, maybe even pull her close. He didn't. It wasn't until she had fastened the bag with a green twist tie and gently laid the crimson treasures in the bottom of the cart that she said, "I know."

She didn't say it back. She didn't have to.

By the time Lucas proposed to her, Jenna still hadn't managed to utter the words, but it didn't matter. He knew how she felt, or at least he was convinced enough to believe that his love was enough for them both.

He asked her to marry him the day her grandmother lost her driver's license. After her mother died, Jenna lived with her grandmother, Caroline, in a tiny flat that was closer to Milwaukee than Chicago. She drove over an hour each way just to get to work at the hospital. But her commitment to Oma dictated that she stay with her as long as she could care for the spunky eighty-five-year-old.

Lucas was with Jenna when she got the call that Caroline had been in an accident. The hospital where she had been taken was a good forty-five-minute drive, but Lucas and Jenna abandoned their date and sped to her side. The accident turned out to be a fender-bender, and Oma suffered no more than a bruised knee where her leg slid into the console inches from her seat.

When Caroline saw her granddaughter, the tears that were threatening to spill trailed one at a time down her wrinkled cheeks.

"Oma, why didn't you stop at the stop sign?" Jenna asked.

Caroline's answer solidified what they had known for some time: "I thought I stopped. I mean, I stopped in my mind."

The officer who arrived at the scene pulled Jenna aside and gave her Caroline's driver's license.

It was in the kitchen of the flat, after Caroline had bathed and relaxed enough to fall fitfully asleep, that Lucas got down on one knee. It felt strange, even to him, as the cold of the linoleum floor seeped through his jeans and into his very bones. Jenna was sitting with her legs under her in an uncomfortable wooden chair, warming her hands on a cup of black coffee and looking into its depths as if answers waited for her in the dregs.

He hadn't planned it this way. They were supposed to be bundled up beneath the lights of Navy Pier overlooking Lake Michigan. Her cheeks would be pink from the wind and a scarf would be knotted at her neck as she said something playful to him. He would have taken out the ring when she wasn't looking. She would have turned away from the water and found him there. She would have laughed and said, "Yes."

Instead, she raised tired eyes to look at him almost sadly. She asked, "What are you doing?" And he said it again, "I love you."

It was the first time he saw her cry. Jenna put out her arms and he shuffled over to her, still on his knees. She wrapped herself around him, legs and all, and held on as if she was afraid of being swept away. "Are you asking me to marry you?" He was shocked to hear the disbelief in her voice.

"Yes," he said.

She said it back. "Yes."

When they moved to Iowa to follow Caroline, Lucas left the city with no regrets. She was with him, all five foot two inches of her, and nothing else mattered. They moved into a century home on the outskirts of a town that boasted no more than one grocery store and enough gossip to last at least a hundred lifetimes.

Blackhawk was nestled against the hills that marked the border between Iowa and

South Dakota, and the muddy Big Sioux river ran a trembling line between the trees less than a stone's throw from the invisible marker of the official city limits. The cobbled main street of Blackhawk's picturesque downtown ambled past pretty houses with Dutch lace curtains and a hodgepodge collection of small-town amenities. There was a crumbling brick bank, an equally dilapidated police station, a café, a tiny library that specialized in interlibrary loans. But Blackhawk's claim to fame was a trio of antiques stores that boasted sagging shelves of what Lucas considered junk, but which people came from miles around to admire and procure for dusty corners in their own homes.

The streets were cracked, the trees ancient and gnarled, the people reserved. Blackhawk was nothing to write home about, situated in the proverbial middle of nowhere. Sioux Falls was a forty-five-minute drive away. Omaha could be reached in two and a half hours, Minneapolis in four. But the Hudsons weren't known for doing anything halfway, and they threw themselves into their new life with the same passion they directed at everything else.

Jenna started Safe House, a domestic violence aid center that specialized in helping victims of abuse begin new lives. Lucas was always stunned by the number of women who saw Jenna every week. Bustling metropolis or quiet village, violence seemed to know no boundaries.

And Lucas himself, making what he believed would be a temporary adjustment to small-town life even more easily than his wife, joined Blackhawk's medical clinic and worked alongside two other doctors diagnosing strep throat and setting broken bones.

For the first few years, Lucas felt like he was camping, on vacation from normal life. Or on an extended mission trip like the three months he had spent just outside of Tegucigalpa, giving wide-eyed orphans their first taste of medical treatment. They had hated the needles. But then two years in Blackhawk turned into four, and four into eight, until a decade had passed and then a momentous dozen years — one-third of his life — and he was officially a small-town resident.

It wasn't necessarily the life he had always dreamed of, but Jenna was the woman he had always dreamed of.

She was more than enough.

2
MEG

The first time Meg Painter met Dylan, he was crouching behind the raspberry thicket in her backyard. It was the Fourth of July, after the barbecues and the fireworks, when the night was dark and still and quiet but for the occasional chirp of an early cricket and the screams of a dozen neighborhood kids. As their parents sipped wine spritzers around the Painters' brick fire pit, the kids tiptoed through the adjoining yards of Ninth Street Circle NE, erupting in a frenzy of mock terror when they tripped over a comrade lying in ambush.

"Bloody Murder!" the shout would rise, if the discovery had not rendered the poor adolescent speechless or if the would-be murderer was too slow to seize his victim and slap a silencing hand over her gaping mouth.

Most of the time, the detection was quick, painless, and punctuated by frantic shrieks that quickly multiplied as the cry went up. "Run! Bloody Murder! Run!" And from every corner of the block they would come, tripping, stumbling, falling headlong into the warm grass in their haste to elude whatever dark shadow loomed behind them.

The front porch was sanctuary, and though the kids who gathered to play midnight games were probably too old for such frivolity, the darkness seemed prime to entertain the ghosts of their waning childhood. They sometimes ended up crawling on hands and knees after they fell in the last few yards to safety, then dragged themselves up the porch steps to slump against each other and replay the most entertaining bits of their exploits: who tripped whom, or accusations of a kiss stolen in a shadowy, secret corner.

Someone passed around a pilfered can of Bud Light that he had lifted from the cooler without detection, and they took turns sipping the half-warm beer, pretending that they liked it. Meg's older brother, Bennett, had his hand on her best friend's leg, but Sarah didn't seem to mind. And in the farthest corner of the porch, a knot of boys passed around a pack of cigarettes and lit up like they knew exactly what they were doing.

31

It was all a little perplexing to Meg. The lukewarm beer, the throaty laugh that didn't sound like Sarah at all, the innocent game that felt altogether different because a year had gone by since the last time they played it. They were older, all of them, and the knowledge of it seemed to crackle in the air around their heads like electricity.

Although it felt awkward, Meg tucked her long legs beneath her and forced a laugh of her own — a grown-up, sexy laugh that came out sounding hollow and all wrong. Some girls could pull off a sexy laugh at fourteen. Meg apparently wasn't one of them.

"Where's Dylan?" Sarah's older brother, Jess, called from across the porch. He flicked the ash of his cigarette over the railing and picked his way around the strewn bodies of his friends to sit on the steps next to Meg. "What'd you do with the new kid, Megs? Out with it."

"Dylan?" Meg repeated. Jess was grinning at her, and she could see an outline of herself reflected in lamplight of his eyes. She looked small, crouching. Sitting up a little straighter, she said, "I haven't seen him. I don't even know who he is."

That wasn't entirely true.

Meg had glimpsed the new boy — a recent

Phoenix transplant and the only unknown in the midst of a decade-old summer tradition — when everyone was walking through the outdoor buffet to fill their plates with burgers still sizzling from the grill. She bypassed the potato salad, baked beans, and greasy chips in lieu of two hamburgers, fully loaded. It was while she was squirting ketchup on the second bun that something shivered down her spine and made her look up. The yard was dotted with blankets, lawn chairs, and people, but she found him almost instantly.

Dylan was balancing on the twisted limb of a low-lying amur maple, his sun-browned legs tangled in the branches so he wouldn't tip off backward. He was staring at Meg, holding a glass of lemonade loosely in his hands as if he had forgotten he was holding it at all. There was a shock of dark hair falling across his forehead, tickling the edge of his eye, and he gave his head a little flick that could have been interpreted as a long-distance hello. When he realized that Meg was looking at him, he grinned. It was sudden and bright, a flash of brilliance that surprised her so much she almost took a step back, even though he was fifty feet away.

She glared at him, and made a point to

avoid him for the rest of the night. And she'd done a pretty good job of it until Jess started accusing her of tracking his where-abouts. As if she cared.

"Don't pretend you don't know who Dylan is," Jess smiled, leaning close. "All the girls know who Dylan is."

Meg didn't mean to tip away from her childhood friend and neighbor, but the back of her head met the porch pillar and Jess laughed.

"You're like a little sister to me, Megs. That's why I gotta keep an eye on you." He took a quick drag on his cigarette and caught Meg watching. "Not for you," he said, tossing it into the bushes. "Bad business, smoking. Bad for your health."

"But not for your health?" Meg snapped.

Jess just laughed. "Come on, we'd better find Dylan. City kid probably wandered into the cornfield and got lost."

The group of kids left the security of the porch and spread out in every direction, avoiding the warm light of the fire pit and the raucous conversation of their parents. At first Jess stayed close to Meg's side, but then one of the other guys tagged him in a run-by and they ended up careening into the darkness amid a flurry of shouts and the pounding of bare feet.

Meg wasn't much interested in finding Dylan, and didn't really care if he had tried to hide in the cornfield. She had grown up her whole life with a field in her backyard, and she knew that the horror stories weren't true. There were corn snakes in the plowed rows, but not much more, and if you were stupid enough to wander in too far, all you had to do was pick a row and follow it to the end. You'd come out eventually.

She was on her way back to the porch — to the single empty beer can and the sudden, bewildering understanding that some magic switch had been thrown and she was all at once half woman instead of all little girl — when she felt a hand snake around her ankle. It was so abrupt, so unexpected that she couldn't even gasp. The world stopped spinning in its orbit.

In the moment that she paused, Dylan grabbed her wrist and yanked her to the ground beside him. There was a patch of earth behind the raspberries where grass refused to grow, and she landed on her seat in the dust, a fine cloud of dirt mingling with the faint, tart scent of ripening berries in the air around her.

"Why aren't you screaming?" he asked.

Because I can't, she thought. She wondered if he could see her eyes, the way her stare betrayed a mixture of shock and awe.

"I'm Dylan Reid," he told her, a smile in his voice. And she knew that he was grinning at her again because she could see the moonlight shimmer off the straight row of his teeth. "It's nice to meet you, Meg Painter." He reached for her hand. When she wouldn't close her fingers, he held her hand in both of his and pumped it up and down.

"I didn't feel you," Meg finally whispered, finding her voice. "I couldn't . . . I couldn't feel you."

Dylan didn't seem at all perturbed. "What's that supposed to mean?"

She didn't say anything.

"You can feel when someone is nearby?" Dylan guessed. "A sixth sense?"

"A tickle," Meg whispered almost against her own will.

"A tickle?" he repeated, a laugh threatening in his light tone.

Without thinking, Meg punched him in the chest, hard.

But he didn't flinch. "Good arm," he commented. "What do you mean 'a tickle'?"

Meg sighed. "I just know. Okay? I know I'm not alone. I don't know how else to describe it."

"You've never been caught unawares?"

"I let myself get caught sometimes," she admitted.

They were quiet for a minute, and in the silence she tilted her head toward the bushes. Someone was getting close. Meg could hear their tentative footsteps as they gave the raspberries, and their infamously sharp thorns, wide berth. She didn't want to be discovered, curled on the ground with this unsettling stranger, so she took a deep breath to shout. Now that the mystery of Dylan's appearance was wearing off, Meg found that she was more than able to yell her little blond head off. But before she could form a word, Dylan's hand fell across her mouth.

"I caught you," he told her. "I caught you fair and square."

Furious that he would dare to restrain her, Meg wriggled and kicked and bucked until he let go. She tumbled back a little and felt a thorn tear a shallow cut along the back of her bare arm. "It won't happen again," she snapped. "It will never happen again."

She scrambled to her feet and was screaming before he could utter a single protest.

The next time Meg saw Dylan was when school started in the fall.

From first grade through eighth, Meg rode

her bike to school rain or shine. In the early years, it was a My Little Pony bike with a purple banana seat and a basket sporting faded plastic flowers. After she hit a growth spurt the summer she turned eight, Meg graduated to her brother's discarded Freestyle BMX, a rusted hunk of metal with bent handlebars and stunt pegs that led to her first broken bone — her right arm — after she tried and failed to do a double peg grind on the handrail of the library steps. Six weeks in a hard cast did much to dampen her Freestyle ambition, and when Meg was pronounced fit for regular activity, she continued to ride like the wind, but shrewdly decided to cut short her stunt career.

Meg seemed almost incomplete without the shiny black bicycle beneath her, but the pivotal jump from junior high to high school demanded a change of equal consequence. When September rolled around, Meg determined to grow up a little, not necessarily because she wanted to, but because life was plodding on with or without her. Jess, her sensible, older neighbor who had only just given up his glasses for contacts, was smoking, and Bennett, who used to aim spit wads at Sarah's hair, suddenly decided he'd rather twist his fingers through the auburn ends. The world was overbright, hard and shiny and foreign. What choice did she have but to at least try to navigate the unfamiliar territory?

With special care, Meg cleaned her beloved BMX in the frigid spray from the garden hose, and then parked it in the back of the shed for the winter. On the first day of school, she set off for Sutton High on foot. Backpack slung over one shoulder and long waves pulled away from her face in pretty tortoiseshell clips instead of multicolored rubber bands, she had to admit that she felt a bit older with every step. More mature. Ready for something that required a deep breath, maybe a little resolve.

Meg never intended to attach those feelings to Dylan. But then a car pulled up beside her when she was halfway to school.

It didn't occur to her to be startled; Sutton was small, and there had never been reason for her to be wary before. Even when she heard the car door open, Meg barely paused. Out of the corner of her eye, she registered a faded pickup truck, noted that she didn't recognize the driver, and kept on walking.

"Meg Painter!" someone called.

She looked up at the sound of her name and felt a little ripple of alarm melt across her shoulders. But on the far side of the unfamiliar pickup, she could just see Dylan leaning over to shout out of the open driver's-side window. A teenage boy was behind the wheel, and he didn't even bother to glance at Dylan as he hopped out of the passenger side and gave the creaky door a hearty slam. The truck squealed away, and Dylan was left standing in the middle of the empty street, staring at Meg with a half smile nipping at the corner of his mouth. It was a teasing look, filled with thinly veiled mirth, as if he had just remembered an inside joke and couldn't stop himself from smirking.

Unsure how to respond to his sudden presence, Meg studied him for a moment and tried to settle the irregular thrum of her heart. She didn't know if she was scared or excited, and, pulled taut between annoyance and anticipation, Meg finally settled for throwing him a haughty look and continuing on her way. But Dylan drew his backpack over both shoulders and took off after her, jogging across the street and over the curb, where he met her on the sidewalk and fell comfortably into step with her hurried pace.

"Did you feel me?" he asked conversationally. "A tickle?"

Meg frowned.

"You didn't, did you? It's Ghost in the Graveyard all over again."

"We call it Bloody Murder."

"Whatever."

She walked faster.

He lengthened his stride. "I've snuck up on you twice now."

"You did not," she told him. The moment he appeared beside her, she had promised herself she wouldn't let him know that he got to her, but it was impossible not to respond when he was so obviously egging her on.

"You can't read me." Dylan elbowed her side gently.

Meg felt sure the gesture was meant to be lighthearted, conspiratorial, but her skin prickled where his arm had glanced it.

"You said it wouldn't happen again," he pressed.

In a flash, Meg remembered. All at once she was irrational, furious, and without pausing to think, she threw down her backpack. She didn't really even know what she meant to do. Her hands were balled into fists and she wasn't afraid to use them, but Dylan grabbed her wrists and held her fast.

"If you think I'm going to let you hit me again, you're nuts," he told her. "You

41

bruised me last time."

"I did?" Meg bit back a grin in spite of herself and tried to rearrange her features to appear stern.

"And if we're going to be friends, you've gotta relax a little. I can't have you going off the deep end every time I tease you."

"Friends?" she parroted, picking out the one word in his mild reprimand that held meaning for her.

Dylan raised an eyebrow good-naturedly and gave a slow nod as if he was assessing her. "Yup, I think so," he said.

"What makes you think I want to be friends with you?" Meg jerked her wrists out of his grip and took a quick step back.

"Hey," Dylan shrugged, pulling the dangling straps of his worn backpack tight. "I'm not gonna put a gun to your head." And he breezed past her, stepping over her discarded pack and using his long legs to his advantage. He was halfway down the block by the time Meg snatched her belongings from the ground and went after him.

She didn't want to chase him, she didn't want him to look over his shoulder and see her running, hair fanned out behind her and eyes hopeful as she came. But she did. And when she drew up next to him and opened her mouth to say something, anything to smooth over her offense, he stopped her short by bumping her with his elbow again. Meg understood that it was his way of rewinding the clock, of letting her know that it didn't matter.

Dylan was forgiving. She liked that about him. And she liked it that he was perfectly comfortable to finish the last block in an easy silence. When they made it to the front steps of the high school, he simply waved good-bye and disappeared.

And though Meg didn't expect anything more than a moment on the way to school, Dylan was waiting for her after the final bell at the end of the day. He appeared to be utterly indifferent to the looks that her classmates shot him, and it felt obvious to Meg that he was above the disdain of his peers because he was a rare breed of boy. He didn't care, and in that self-security, he earned a sort of esteem that made him seem much older than his fifteen years. Meg watched him shoot her an earnest smile, and learned a lot about him in the time it took to walk the sidewalk from the doors of Sutton High to the curb.

She smiled back with a little less enthusiasm, but she didn't argue or let her steps falter when Dylan headed back the way they had come hours before. A brief inclination of his dark head was her only invitation to follow, though she realized that it was less an invitation than an expectation — he acted as if he knew that she would come. Meg stole one parting glance at Sarah, who had to stay late for band, and received a look of pure bewilderment that must have matched her own. But Meg could also tell by the expression on her friend's face that the unlikely alliance was not necessarily forbidden. So she gave in, and let herself be drawn into his wake as if Dylan emanated his own gravity.

"Did you like it?" he asked without pre-amble. They walked past the line of school buses in front of the high school, their feet falling in perfect syncopation.

"What do you mean?" Meg's voice sounded small in her ears.

"School. Sutton High. It's your first year in this place, right?"

"Yeah," she said, a little breathless from trying to match his long strides. Even though he was only a year older than her, he was a full head taller. "It's fine," Meg continued. "It's school. What grade are you?"

"Sophomore."

"Freshman," she muttered, and was in-stantly shamed by her own banality. Of course he knew what grade she was in, but she finished lamely anyway, "I'm in the same class as Sarah. You know, Jess's sister?"

Dylan caught her eye and laughed. But she could tell he wasn't laughing at her, at least, she didn't think he was. Besides, with his lips parted she could see that his bottom teeth were appealingly crooked, turned toward each other as if leaning in for a reluctant embrace. His imperfect grin was endearing somehow, and Meg found herself relaxing in spite of her misgivings. Being with Dylan wasn't the sort of awkward she had imagined. It was a certain vertigo: she felt light-headed, but with him so confident beside her, she didn't really care.

"Do you like it?" she asked abruptly.

"Like what?" He peered at her out of the corner of his eye, then checked both ways and led her across a tree-lined street.

"Sutton."

"We've been here for almost a year," he reminded her. "And yet that doesn't change the fact that I'm the perpetual new kid. You guys gotta get a life." But then he stopped himself, and it seemed to Meg that he was determined to tell the truth. Or at least a part of it. "It's not home yet," he admitted. "But it's not bad."

Meg hopped on the curb and walked it

heel to toe like a balance beam as they turned down her street. "What do you miss the most?"

"About Arizona?" Dylan paused. "I miss warm winters, geckos in the backyard . . ."

"Geckos?" Meg parroted, her curiosity piqued.

"My mom's lemon pie made with lemons from our tree, my friends, our pool, the skate park in our neighborhood . . ."

"You had a pool?" All at once Meg's inhibitions fell away. "And a skate park? My cousin would die. He thinks he's a 'pretty tight shredder.' " She framed the distinction of her cousin's self-imposed description with sarcastic quotations marks in the form of curled fingers.

"You sound ridiculous," Dylan told her cheerfully. "You sound like a poseur."

"I am," she agreed with a hearty nod. "I don't skateboard."

"Neither do I."

"Then what? Bike, rollerblades . . . ? Or did you just watch everyone else having fun at the skate park?"

"I have a Haro Freestyle FSX with skyway six spoke mags, a full chromoly fork, four bolt-on stationary pegs, and a knee-saver handlebar."

Meg blinked at him. "I have no idea what

you just said."

"I have a 'pretty tight BMX.' " He grinned. "But it doesn't do me much good around here. I can do a mean one-eighty on the half-pipe and land in a fakie, but there's no half-pipe in Sutton."

"Fakie?" Meg repeated, too startled by his admirable knowledge to worry about sounding dumb.

"Riding backward," Dylan explained.

"I have a bike," she countered weakly.

"I know."

"I broke my arm trying to do a double peg grind."

"I know."

"You do?" They were in front of her house now, and Meg stopped with her hands on her hips, considering Dylan with cool curiosity. "How do you know that?"

"Jess told me." Dylan thought for a moment then continued with a glint in his eye. "You're sorta famous, Meg."

"What's that supposed to mean?" she demanded.

"Oh, chill out," he said. Meg bristled at the familiarity with which he chastised her, but he went on before she could complain. "You're just not like other girls," he told her. "It's not a bad thing that people find you . . . interesting."

47

She wanted to be defensive, but Dylan's honesty was so candid, so ingenuous, she ended up laughing. "I'm interesting? Because I broke my arm?"

Dylan shrugged his backpack off his shoulder and held it in his hands. "I could teach you how to do it," he offered.

"Excuse me?"

"I could teach you all kinds of grinds. And some flatland tricks, but without a pipe of some sort, the air tricks are a no go."

Meg didn't even have to think about it. "Deal." She stuck out her hand with a definitive air, and when Dylan took it, she squeezed hard and shook fast, a good handshake, a man's handshake.

He shook his head at her, but his lips were curled, smiling.

3
LUCAS

The silence inside the barn was thick and viscous. Lucas could feel it pressing against his skin, a malevolent, threatening force bent on choking him. He cleared his throat loudly and fought the unexpected burn of bile in the back of his mouth. "Uh," he stammered, "it's a tibia. See? Here's the fibular notch, and here" — he dug his fingers into the earth beside the ridge of bone — "is the fibula."

"Back away," Alex commanded, grabbing him by the arm and dragging him roughly backward. "We've probably done enough damage already."

"She must be lying on her back. Legs pulled up against her chest . . ."

"You don't know that," Alex insisted. He yanked Lucas to his feet. "You don't know that that bone belongs to Angela."

"Of course it's —"

Alex's glare was enough to silence Lucas.

"I know you're not used to this," he said, "but you're a doctor. I expect a little more professionalism from you."

Lucas swallowed, nodded. He took a quick look at the two assisting cops and was reassured to see that they looked as pale and shell-shocked as he felt.

"I'm calling DCI," Alex declared, his voice steely with resolve.

"DCI?"

"The Department of Criminal Investigation. They have a Major Crime Unit that assists in death investigations, and this is way over our heads. They'll know what to do, how to exhume the body. If it is a body."

"If?"

"All we've seen is a leg bone."

Lucas didn't know if he was more disturbed to imagine that Angela's body lay crumpled beneath him or that it was just a pair of her shinbones.

"How long?" one of the younger officers asked.

"The nearest DCI office is in Sioux City, but there are a couple dozen agents statewide. I don't know who they'll call in or where they'll come from. An hour? Maybe more? But nobody is going anywhere until they've given clearance."

"I need to call my wife . . ."

Lucas watched as the three men dispersed to different corners of the barn so they could make the necessary phone calls to excuse themselves from taking kids to baseball games or for being home late for supper. He wondered what Jenna would say if he called to let her know that he would be later than expected, not to worry, everything would be okay. Would she even pick up the phone? He couldn't bring himself to dial the number and find out.

The blow of what they had found still rang and clattered inside his head as if he had been slugged. Angela Sparks was much more to him than simply a name, or now possibly a body beneath the floor of an abandoned barn. And though Alex was right to chastise him, to remind him that he was a professional and had a job to do, it wasn't easy, with her memory haunting the air above him.

Angela came back to him in bursts and impressions, remembrances of colors and feelings like a scattering of haphazard photographs in a forgotten shoe box. It was strange how the mind preserved things. He saw her as a young woman, cheeks framed by white-blond hair so fine that it blew like corn silk and was forever obstructing her mouth, her eyes. Then she was a whip of a girl sitting bare-armed and bare-legged at his kitchen table, chancing an impish grin. Now she was bruised, blinking up at him from beneath a shiner the color of ripe plums. The outfits changed, her expression, her age. But her eyes were always the same: big and sad and green as damp moss.

Jim Sparks's neglected daughter was Jenna's first client at Safe House, even though no one ever solicited her services on behalf of Angela. Jenna just happened to bump into the poor child during her very first trip to Blackhawk's only grocery store.

"You should have seen her," Jenna told Lucas afterward, as she stacked cans in neat rows on the shelves of their empty pantry. "Sweetest little thing. All by herself. She was just walking up and down the aisles, touching the boxes of cereal and bags of chips with the tips of her fingers."

"Where were her parents?"

Jenna shrugged. "It's a small town, I guess kids can go to the grocery store without their parents."

"But it doesn't sit good with you," Lucas prompted.

"No." Jenna set a can of pinto beans down with more force than necessary. "Something's not right there."

They ran into each other a few more

times, the new-in-town social worker and the little girl who Jenna learned wasn't so little after all. Angela was fourteen years old when the Hudsons moved to Blackhawk, but she was such a tiny thing, so delicate and slight that she hardly seemed a day over ten. Maybe it was her innocence that drew Jenna in. Maybe it was her undeniable beauty or her deep silences or doleful eyes. Whatever it was, it wasn't long after meeting the small, seemingly parentless, grubby Cinderella that Jenna was beyond smitten. Within weeks she had taken Angela in like a would-be adoptive mother.

"I'd take her home in a New York minute."

"That long?" Lucas teased.

Jenna rolled her eyes. "She's just . . ."

"Completely stolen your heart?"

"Give me a bit more credit than that," Jenna complained. "I feel for her, you know? No mom, worthless dad as far as I can tell . . ."

Lucas couldn't argue. Since their first encounter in the grocery store, he knew that Jenna had tried on countless occasions to meet with Angela's father, the town's notorious recluse and all-around loser. But Jim Sparks didn't want anything to do with Jenna. She tried calling, stopping by, and setting up meetings through Angela, but Jim avoided all contact. In the end, there was nothing for Jenna to do but be grateful that he tolerated her involvement in Angela's life. It was the best she could do.

It was never quite enough.

"DCI is on their way," Alex said, snapping the thin film of Lucas's memories like a soap bubble.

"Pardon me?" Lucas blinked, still dazed from the surreal slant of his unexpected afternoon.

"The state guys are coming."

Lucas nodded, checked his watch. It was going to be a long night.

"How long has it been since she disappeared?" Alex asked, honing in on Lucas's thought pattern with the effortless familiarity of friendship.

"I thought we couldn't assume that the body is Angela."

"We can't. But we do have to start asking questions. That's my first. How long?"

Those were days that Lucas didn't want to remember. They were long weeks that stretched into months of grief and loss — Jenna took Angela's disappearance as hard as if the girl had been her daughter. "I guess it's been almost eight years now," Lucas finally guessed. "She was eighteen when . . ."
But he couldn't finish that statement.

Angela was eighteen when she vanished? When she committed suicide? Or when Jim killed her?

"I questioned Jim extensively back then," Alex said. "He swore up and down that she ran away. He tried to prove it to me by pointing out missing shoes, clothes, stuff like that."

"And you believed him."

"I never said that. But there was no evidence to the contrary."

Lucas's heart felt hollow as he thought of Jenna at the computer in the first year after Angela's disappearance. His wife scoured Internet databases — the National Missing and Unidentified Persons Data System, the National Center for Missing Adults, Iowa Missing Persons Database — squinting at grainy photographs and looking for any connection, any hint of where Angela had gone and why. Later, when too much time had passed for Angela to have merely taken some extended, solitary vacation, Jenna scanned the only photograph she had of the girl and posted it on sites herself. Nothing ever came of it.

"What did you think happened?" Alex prompted.

"Back then?" Lucas was answered with a

brief nod. "Back then I thought she ran away."

"She had it in her," Alex agreed.

"Jenna didn't think so."

"I'm not sure your wife saw Angela very clearly."

"What's that supposed to mean?"

"Just that the innocent little girl she fell in love with was not the same woman who evaporated into thin air."

It was true. The young teen that Jenna took into her heart and, occasionally, into their home, changed much in the four years of their relationship. Jenna thought Angela was precocious, Lucas thought she was calculating. Angela often seemed motivated by a raw sense of self-preservation, and yet Lucas sensed a certain deliberate egotism behind her actions. Her beauty was both a bright halo and a dark shadow, something that she seemed to wield and not wear. Angela was a study in contradictions. In trouble.

"She was . . . interesting," Lucas conceded, battling his own memories, his own awkward demons when it came to Angela.

"And perfectly capable of ditching this blip on a map for bigger and better things."

Lucas shrugged.

"Are you telling me that you'd rather

forget what you know, what we assume about Angela, and just conclude we found her body?" Alex pressed Lucas, his heavy-lidded eyes narrowed in objection.

Lucas considered for a moment, hating the rippling effect of their discovery and the raw wounds it would reopen. But he couldn't deny what he believed, what he felt deep in his bones. Even if it couldn't be explained. "Yes," he said. "It's Angela. I'm sure of it."

"We'll see," Alex muttered, turning to walk away. "Make yourself comfortable. We're going to be here for a while."

They faded apart, Alex wandering back to the place where Jim's body still hung over the partially exposed column of bone. As Lucas watched, Alex pulled a pair of latex gloves from his back pocket and snapped them on. Then he bent down to study the remains with narrowed eyes. The police chief seemed to analyze every detail as if answers were contained in the dust. Maybe they were.

All at once Lucas needed to sit. To rest his head against his hands and breathe — he felt like he hadn't taken a decent breath since he arrived at Jim's farm. The red evidence tags scattered about the barn floor were relegated to a rather contained area between the door and Jim's body. Footprints were marked, as well as scrapes and unidentifiable cast-offs — bits and pieces of indecipherable clues that Lucas didn't understand or even necessarily want to understand. Alex knew what he was doing, and Lucas just wanted to stay out of the way.

He wandered deeper into the barn, almost stumbling as he avoided discarded relics from a time he couldn't claim to remember. Everything was so filthy and foreign. Suddenly Blackhawk seemed like a different world, an alien land where nothing was quite as he had imagined it to be.

A pigeon high in the rafters didn't like his unsteady progress and took to flight, casting a fine sprinkling of grime across Lucas's shoulders and hair. He ran his fingers through his short waves, fighting a shudder and mussing his hair to even scruffier proportions. Though he tried to keep it neat and trimmed, his hair was thick and unruly, adding a mischievous slant to his already boyish looks. It was why he wore glasses; he believed they made him look older. But now, with a haze of dirt on their normally immaculate lenses, Lucas wished for contacts. And a buzz cut. And that he hadn't answered the phone when he checked caller ID and realized that it was Alex on the other end of the line.

Lucas found an overturned milk crate, the sort of slotted, wooden affair that the antiques stores in town would love to get their hands on. He gave it a quick dusting with the palm of his hand then sat down, slapping his jeans to get rid of the dirt. He didn't bother to stifle the sigh that escaped his lips.

The sun was setting, sloping through the rotting roof of the barn and shedding golden particles in the musty air that looked like flung gems. He reached his fingers to touch a beam of light, splintering the cool glow into fragments on the ground.

That's when he saw it.

A rectangle of blue-lined white tucked against the blade of what he imagined to be an old-fashioned plow. A folded piece of paper too pristine to be a natural part of the dingy surroundings.

Lucas didn't think. He just grabbed.

The note was folded into a small, thick packet that obviously held something inside. His fingers fumbled with the corners, and he couldn't tell if the tremors were because of the descending cold or because of what he feared he'd find.

The note was nearly open when Lucas was torn from the paper in his hands by an

59

unexpected shout.

"Lucas! What are you doing?"

He read one word: *Angela.* Then something tumbled from the creased page and fell into the hard-packed dirt at his feet. Lucas would have reached for it, but all at once Alex was before him, ripping the paper out of his hands with a furious grunt.

"What is this?" Alex demanded, centering the page between his gloved fingers. "Where did you find it?"

Lucas didn't answer, just watched in silence as his friend scanned the paper. Beyond her name, there must not have been much else written. Alex's eyes traced and retraced the same spot.

"What is it?" Lucas echoed, for it had been nothing more than a folded piece of notebook paper when he picked it up. "Is it a suicide note?"

Alex flattened Lucas with a withering look. "I can't believe we missed this. Where did you find it?"

Lucas was shamed by the accusation in his friend's tone, but he couldn't help feeling annoyed, too. "You told me to make myself comfortable," Lucas reminded him.

"It's an expression. I didn't mean tamper with a crime scene. Where did you find this?"

Indicating the plow with a kick, Lucas said, "It was there, against that . . ."

"Plow," Alex finished impatiently. "Where exactly?"

"On the ground. The side closest to me."

Alex groaned, making no attempt to disguise his frustration. "Wait here," he said curtly. "Don't. Touch. Anything."

"What does it say?" Lucas called, watching the back of Alex's plaid shirt as the police officer retreated.

The older man paused and turned his head just enough to shoot over his shoulder, " 'Angela, I'm sorry.' "

"That's it?"

One quick nod was all he got in reply.

"No signature? Nothing?"

He was granted a terse shake of Alex's dishwater-blond head.

Lucas watched Alex leave the barn. The police chief would come back with more tags, the camera, his officers. He'd explain that Lucas had contaminated the evidence — that he'd dared to touch it. And the story would be repeated for DCI. Lucas wanted to sneak out through a back door of the barn and walk home. No, he wanted to rewind the clock and erase his involvement in this miserable tragedy. The pain of old wounds, his wife's inevitable sorrow, his best friend's contempt . . . They were like boulders pressing against the narrow frame of his shoulders.

Putting his elbows on his knees, Lucas cradled his head in his hands. The white fabric of his shoes was scuffed and dirty and the hems of his jeans were brown with dirt. As the clock ticked closer to evening, the barn got dimmer and dimmer, and outlines softened into mere hints of substance. And yet against the shadowy backdrop of the floor, Lucas could just make out a glint of something incongruous between his splayed feet.

In the midst of Alex's exasperation, Lucas had all but forgotten that in the moment he opened the letter, something had slid to the floor. He bent down, squinting at the object through clouded glasses.

It was a ring. And if his assessment was right, it was real gold, though grimy and neglected and discolored. The piece of jewelry looked sad lying there, like a dejected attempt at intimacy, an artifact of love that had long faded.

Lucas didn't even know he was reaching for the ring until it was balanced between his thumb and forefinger. A rush of horror filled him — Alex was going to be livid — but it was quickly replaced by a feeling of lament that evolved into a quiet entitlement. They wouldn't be able to get a usable print off such a delicate piece of metal, he reasoned. Not even the tiny, broken stone that still glowed with a milky opalescence was large enough to hold a clue.

Staring at it, Lucas tried to picture the ring that had graced the ring finger of Angela's right hand during her teenage years. She had claimed that it was a gift, but she had never been willing to discuss who it had come from. Was this the same ring?

It had to be. Though Lucas couldn't remember exactly what it looked like, he had to be holding Angela's ring in his hand. It all fit: Jim's three-word letter, the ring folded inside, and the body hidden beneath the sway of his lifeless feet. Sickened, Lucas palmed the ring and brought his fist to his forehead as if to pound out everything he knew.

Angela had been the beginning of the end. It was hard for Lucas to admit, but as he slumped in the dim barn, he was sure he could trace the slow unraveling of his marriage back to the little girl who had seen a loose end and began to pick it free. The distance between him and Jenna, her assertion that he just didn't "get her," their fights over Angela's growing presence in their lives . . . and now the raw, ugly truth that they were drowning in the black hole of everything that had piled up between them. It all came back to Angela Sparks.

And she had been gone for eight years, buried in the floor of a barn only a few miles from his house.

Regret made Lucas's throat ache. Regret for Angela's wasted life and the barren wasteland of his own days. It wasn't fair to link the two so intimately, and he knew it, but for a scathing moment it felt good to assign blame. It felt good to clutch the ring and hate her.

Just as quickly as his fury rose, it dissipated. How could Lucas blame a child? A hurting little girl with scars so deep Jenna claimed to have only scratched the topmost layer? Poor Angela, he thought. And then: Poor us. Poor all of us.

Lucas rose, ready to offer up the ring and face Alex's fury. His trip down memory lane had left him bleeding, and nothing Alex could say or do would trump the misery he already felt. But instead of making his way to where Alex stood half shouting into his cell phone, Lucas found that his legs were weighted to the ground. The discarded little band in the palm of his hand was tiny and hot, a circle of agony that seemed to symbolize the brokenness of everything that he held dear. It was a piece of her that no one would be able to appreciate or understand. Who had mourned her? Who sought her with the fervor of a mother searching for her child? Who had given four years of her life to nurture a girl that no one else had taken the time to love? And, who had ultimately sacrificed her marriage on the altar of that love?

They would take the ring and strip it of any remaining tendrils of her humanity, faint and fragile as the broken strands of a spider's web. It would be tossed in an evidence bag, examined, forgotten. It would languish for months or even years in a cardboard box before it would be forever lost, one last piece of Angela that could disappear off the face of the known world. He couldn't let that happen. He couldn't let this small remembrance of her slip through his fingers.

As he studied the ring, Lucas was galvanized by the belief that dental records would prove what he already knew: the body buried beneath Jim Sparks was his daughter. He didn't doubt for a second that they would have more than enough proof of her identity. The ring was inconsequential to everyone but Lucas's soon-to-be ex-wife. Alex would never know. And if he ever found out, surely after all that they had been through, there would be forgiveness enough for this one small impulse, this moment when Lucas's heart for once overrode his mind.

Closure, he thought as he slipped the band into his pocket. A reminder, a talisman, a lodestone that pointed back to the heart of all that they lost. With everything else crumbling to ashes around them, Lucas couldn't help thinking that Jenna deserved it.

And maybe, just maybe, if Jenna said good-bye to Angela, she wouldn't have to say good-bye to him.

When the bodies were gone and the farm was all but deserted, Lucas drove home in silence.

The remains DCI unearthed were no more than a bare skeleton of bones that had been crumpled and curled into a hole barely big enough to fit her small frame. The remnants of a dress, which must have once been a soft, leafy green but which time had turned the color of stone, was wrapped like hand-me-down clothes on a phantom body too desiccated to fill the crumbling folds.

The fabric turned into dust in their hands, and before they managed to unearth all of her, she had become mostly undressed, an emaciated, naked figure lying prostrate on the ground. Jim's deserted body lay zipped in a black body bag only feet from the exposed bones of her outstretched, partially mummified hand.

The DCI agents worked as if their lives depended on the fast, efficient, and gentle exhumation of the body. Lucas's heart sank further and further as they revealed the tender curve of her spine, the spaghetti straps of what he imagined to be a favorite dress, the lone sandal that lacked a mate. He thought of the ring in his pocket and was pierced by a double-edged blade of disgrace and satisfaction. Though it made him sick to imagine what Alex would think if he knew, he hoped that the stolen gift would offer his wife a measure of peace. Peace that she had been unable to attain in eight long years of trying.

It was only when her body had been placed in a black bag and delicately lifted into the back of the hearse that Alex caught Lucas's eye. "Go home, Hudson. I thought you and Jenna were going away this afternoon."

Lucas squinted at him across the dark

barn. "Maybe we'll go away tonight," he said, the slump in his shoulders indicating that they would do no such thing. Lucas and Jenna tried to date, tried to see each other beyond the walls of the house where they lived as little more than roommates, but it had become increasingly difficult to convince her that time together was worthwhile. Lucas knew that after abandoning her hours before, it would be even harder. At least Alex didn't know about their secret arrangement, about the way their marriage dangled on a thread. Not yet.

"I'm sorry that it happened this way."

Lucas arched an eyebrow. "Yeah, it's all your fault."

By the time he pulled into their detached garage and walked the thirty feet from the shed to the house, Jenna was outlined in amber through the kitchen window. Lucas could see his breath in diaphanous wisps that reminded him of ghosts. He stood in the cold for a moment and watched her, his breath haloing his face; his fingers on the ring in his pocket.

What could he say? How could he tell her?

"There's nothing for supper," she said in greeting when he finally stepped into the chilly mudroom. "Pizza? I think they still deliver this late."

Lucas nodded.

She pulled a bobby pin out of her hair and held it between her lips while she refastened a stray curl. Her ponytails were notoriously chaotic and the gesture made Lucas catch his breath. She turned away from him and yanked the phone off the wall, pressing number 6 on the speed dial. As he listened to her order the pepperoni and mushroom, he had to restrain himself from crossing the few feet between them to place a kiss on her neck.

"I'm sorry I was so late."

Jenna clicked the phone off and laid it on the kitchen counter. She looked him up and down, but she didn't ask anything. "Whatever."

Lucas felt the weight of his unspoken confession fall between them like a lie. He couldn't stand it. "We need to talk," he said. It probably wasn't the right place or the right time, but Jenna had to know.

"Not now, Lucas."

He fought the urge to take her in his arms and pull her against his chest. To press her body against his so he could absorb all the hurt she would undoubtedly feel. "You don't understand. There's something I have to tell you."

"You've already told me everything." She

sighed. "I just can't. I can't deal with it tonight."

"This isn't about us. Well, it is, but it isn't . . ."

"It always comes back to us. I told you: I can't do this tonight."

Lucas pulled a chair out from beneath the table and nodded toward it. "I think you should sit down."

"I'm not sitting down."

"Please."

But Jenna's gaze slid to the ground. She moved around him quickly, careful not to let her shoulder graze his chest, and left him standing alone in the middle of a silent kitchen.

4
MEG

Meg and Dylan were best friends long before he ever taught her to do a wheelie or ride the handrail at the public library from top to bottom. And within days of their first real interaction, Meg knew that even if she never mastered half of the tricks in his repertoire, they were linked. It was complete, irreversible.

The fact that Dylan was older than her, or the truth that Meg was a girl and Dylan a boy, didn't bother them either. Their friendship was something that they couldn't have denied, whether or not they decided to care what other people thought of their peculiar companionship. And people did find their relationship unusual.

Sarah pouted when she was suddenly and unapologetically replaced by the new boy in her friend's life, and it took months for Meg's parents to become accustomed to Dylan's frequent presence in their home. As for the rest of Sutton, everyone just assumed they were boyfriend and girlfriend.

Dylan went to great pains to rid his peers of that particular notion.

By the time the weather had cooled enough to make walking to school distinctly unpleasant, Meg had achieved some success with her aging BMX. She was thrilled with her own daring, and each new triumph ignited a fire in her belly that she couldn't quite quench. It was freezing outside, but she didn't care. After school she begged, pleaded, and finally threatened Dylan to coerce him into continuing her training regimen. Since he couldn't say no to her, and because he was almost equally as eager to see her progress, Dylan gave in.

Bundled in hats, scarves, and heavy gloves, they took to the roads for the few hours of wan sunlight that clung to the late afternoon with admirable tenacity. It hadn't snowed yet, but Meg could see her breath in the air, and each exhalation made a cold, damp cloud around her mouth so that her lips were cracked to the point of bleeding. Gone were the tortoiseshell clips and the ladylike maturity that Meg had experimented with her first day of high school. Instead, her long tresses were relegated once again to messy ponytails, and her clothes faintly resembled the cool grunge of a bona fide BMX girl. When it was really cold, she biked in a black cap pulled down past her eyebrows and a mack jacket that her dad had once used for pheasant hunting. It was red plaid, and it hung halfway down her knobby, bruised legs.

Meg was thus bedecked — knit hat tugged low, jacket dwarfing her thin limbs, jeans one good fall from fraying at both knees — when a group of guys from Jess's class happened upon her trying a new jump.

The boys who were dropped off in front of the Langbroek home were not familiar to Meg, but they acted as if they knew her anyway. As the car pulled away and turned out of the cul-de-sac, the boys aborted their path toward the house and sauntered instead to the bottom of the driveway, where they stood, arms across their chests, watching Dylan and Meg.

The unlikely duo had created a ramp of sorts at the end of the Painters' driveway. The Painters' was the highest house in the neighborhood, and the small hill it was situated on made for a short, steep driveway that ended at a sharp angle to the tar-streaked road. Dylan and Meg had taken a long piece of plywood and propped it on two plastic, sand-filled drums that they butted up to the end of the cracked cement, making an almost flawless seam. It was no half-pipe, but with sufficient momentum, it afforded Dylan enough air to pull a few tricks.

A minute before the carful of boys drove up to the Langbroeks', Meg had tried unsuccessfully to launch off the end of the ramp and spin her front tire 360 degrees before landing. She chickened out at the last minute, and spilled ungracefully off the side of the ramp, but any mild concern for her own safety was eclipsed by gratefulness that no one but Dylan had seen her wipe out. The only evidence that her ride had been less than she hoped for was Dylan's presence at her side, his hand outstretched between them as if ready to help. Or comfort.

With the boys across the cul-de-sac, Meg batted away his hand and narrowed her eyes in challenge.

"Whoa, tiger," Dylan muttered under his breath. He seemed amused. To the boys he said, "What's up?"

The shortest one of the bunch, a redhead with acne along his hairline, said, "We're just waiting for the show. We hear your girlfriend thinks she's hot stuff on two wheels."

Meg took a furious step toward them, eyes blazing and tongue smoldering with insults, but Dylan placed a stilling hand on her arm and yanked her back. When she whipped her head around to glare at him, the look on his face stopped her short. Though a smile lit up his mouth, his gaze was steel, and his jaw cut a severe line in the hazy afternoon half-light.

"Dylan," she started, and was cut off when he squeezed her arm. Hard.

"She's not my girlfriend," he told the boys, still smiling.

The redhead shrugged nonchalantly. "Could've fooled us. We wouldn't hang out with a girl that much unless we were getting some."

Meg felt Dylan bristle. His anger was so sharp, so acute it was as if she could feel his fury like hot, sizzling sparks that burst from his body. She opened her mouth to sass back, to defend Dylan, but he only tightened his grip on her forearm. It was all she could do not to gasp.

"I hang out with her because she's got more guts than most of the guys around here. I can't help it if you guys are . . . well . . ." he trailed off, lifting his hand in harmony with his eyebrows. Everything about him implied that the boys who dared

75

to oppose him knew exactly what he was trying to say.

"Spit it out, city boy." The redhead's cheeks were beginning to match his hair.

"Nah." Dylan seemed to barely contain a chuckle. "My mom says if you can't say something nice, you shouldn't say anything at all." Sarcasm dripped from his words, and he turned his back on them with a distinctly superior air. Pulling Meg with him, he bent to pick up the bike as if nothing at all had happened, and quickly checked it over to make sure that she hadn't done any permanent damage in her fall. Satisfied, he held it out for her, and when she hesitated to take it, Dylan dipped his chin in an almost imperceptible command: Take it.

She did.

Someone from behind them began to yell: "If she's so great, let's see it! Come on, Little Miss Painter, let's see you do your trick."

Dylan looked down at her and winked. His back was turned to Jess's friends, but he whispered anyway, "Go ahead, Meg. Show them what you're made of."

She began to shake her head no, but Dylan widened his eyes in what she took to be warning. The look was obvious, and Meg

76

was surprised to realize that in spite of his confident words, Dylan cared what the older boys thought of him. More accurately, he cared about what they thought of his friendship with her. Now that she was staring at him instead of the guys across the road, Meg could tell that he was desperate for her to back up his claims.

"I can't do it," she hissed. "You know I'll fall."

"No, you won't. This is just what you need — a little pressure. A reason to get it right."

"Dylan . . ." Meg implored him, but she didn't know what else to say.

"Meg . . ." he coaxed her right back, drawing such influence into the one word of her name that she wavered.

Giving him a dark look, she threw her leg over the frame of the bike. "If I kill myself, it's on your head, Dylan Reid."

"You won't," he assured her. His grin was so triumphant, she had to look away.

As Meg biked slowly up the driveway, standing on the pedals and taking her time in the hope of slowing her racing heart, she whispered an impassioned prayer: "Don't let me fall. Don't let me fall. Don't let me fall."

It was a futile endeavor, and she knew it, even though she kept uttering the words.

The God she met in Sunday school, and believed in without cause for doubt, did not worry himself with little girls and their bicycles. He had bigger problems, like famine, world peace, and orchestrating an Armageddon of alarming proportions. In comparison, her troubles seemed tiny. What was the worst that could happen to her? Humiliation? Another broken bone?

With a start, Meg understood that she could survive those things. They were temporary, insignificant. What she couldn't bear to do, what made her equilibrium on the wobbly pedals of her bike unsteady, was the thought of disappointing Dylan. She couldn't let him down.

And she wouldn't.

Meg stopped at the top of the driveway with her back to the garage door. Holding the bike between her legs, she peeled off her gloves and threw them down in the brown grass beside the cracked cement. Her hands were sweaty, and she swiped her palms against her jeans. They were watching her, she could feel their eyes boring into the top of her head, but she ignored them. She breathed through her nose once, twice, three times for good measure. Then she gripped the handlebars, positioned herself beside the bike, and started with a two-step sprint. Meg flung herself forward, straining every muscle in her body, pushing with all her might.

In one quick movement she was on the bike, feet falling to the pedals so cleanly Meg felt as if God himself had positioned them for her. Adrenaline burst through her. She stood to pedal, only three full revolutions before she hit the ramp full speed.

It was all over in a flash. Meg was flying before her front wheel cleared the edge of the plywood. Instinctively, she pulled up and thrust the handlebars away from her, anticipating with a sort of frenzied joy the moment when her hands would find the grips again.

It didn't happen.

The back tire of the BMX hit the concrete with the sudden scratch of sliding gravel and the high squeak of rubber inflicting a dark scar along the road. A split second later the front tire bounced against the ground at an awkward angle. After that, as far as Meg was concerned, the world spun out of control. She was vaguely aware of careening over the handlebars, but then everything was a blur of slow-motion pain.

Meg didn't pass out, but her brain was so jiggled in her skull that it took her nearly a full minute to realize where she was. Everything clicked back into place bit by frustrating bit. First she felt the cold of the cement beneath her back and a dull, throbbing ache in her head. Then came a singeing pain in her cheek. Flexing her muscles, she learned that her limbs felt okay, but her left hand was hot and stinging. Meg could deal with all that. What bothered her were the faces above her, the strange boys who had been sidetracked on their way to Jess's and, worst of all, Dylan.

He was on his knees beside her, one hand beneath her arm as if he was going to help her up. When she could focus on his eyes, she saw concern there, but it was immediately trumped by the uneasy laughter he forced as he told the guys, "She's all right."

Jess's friends joined him in an anxious chuckle.

"You're good, right, Meg? That was a totally righteous spill."

A totally righteous spill? Without even pausing to make sure that everything would work the way it was supposed to, Meg yanked away from Dylan's supporting grip and rolled to her knees.

"Get off me!" she yelled. And then she abused him with every obscenity she could remember, whether or not she knew what the ugly names meant.

There was a stunned silence as she stumbled to her feet and raised a bloodied hand to her equally bloody cheek. Her jaw ached, and bits of cement nestled in the broken skin along her cheekbone. Meg picked at it carefully with dirty fingernails, leveling a look so deadly at the boys surrounding her that no one ventured to say a word. Then, using her tongue, she gently explored the swell of her bottom lip, and felt a rush of blood pool behind her teeth. Without an ounce of hesitation, she spat pink at Dylan's feet.

At that, the redhead exploded with laughter and his buddies followed suit. He looked for a moment like he was going to give Meg an appreciative punch on the arm, but apparently thinking better of it, he shook his head instead and said, "Girl, you are something." He continued to mutter to himself as he walked away, but he did turn back long enough to tell Dylan, "She's a wild one, all right. You're a lucky man."

The guys laughed all the way to Jess's house, throwing the occasional awed glance back at Meg as she stood like a warrior princess over her mangled BMX.

She was so busy watching them go that she didn't realize Dylan was beside her until he put his arm around her shoulders. Shrugging him off, she whirled on him.

"How could you?"

"What do you mean?" Dylan countered, palms up in supplication.

"You knew I would fall and you let me do it! You let me do it."

Dylan took a step after her. "Are you kidding me? You're a hero, Meg. Don't you get it? You've earned more respect in thirty seconds than most guys accumulate in years of trying to impress."

She crossed her arms over her chest and tucked her aching hand beneath the familiar folds of her dad's jacket. "You're full of shit," she said grudgingly.

"No, I'm not." Dylan crossed the space between them and reached tentatively for her arms. When Meg didn't move away, he caught her by the shoulders and gave her an excited shake.

"I made a fool of myself," she complained.

"You should have seen yourself. You went for it. It was . . . wow."

Meg cocked a disbelieving eyebrow.

"You were awesome," Dylan told her. "Awesome."

"I fell on my face."

"You're not crying. Most girls would cry. Heck, most guys would cry. It only made you more cool in their eyes."

"I don't care about them," Meg blurted out. She instantly regretted it when Dylan's eyes clouded in confusion.

"Then why . . ." he began, but she didn't give him a chance to finish his thought. Wrenching away from him, she went to salvage the twisted mess of her bike. But Dylan matched her step for step and put himself between her and the BMX.

"What are you doing?" Meg demanded.

"You can't be mad at me."

"Oh, yes I can."

"You're only set for life because of me. Eternal coolness," he teased. "You can thank me now."

"I could have gotten killed."

Dylan sighed. "Don't be melodramatic." But then he pulled her hand from beneath the crease of her coat and examined it intently. The knuckles were scraped and bleeding, but the abrasions were shallow. "How's your thumb?" he asked, tracing the puffy skin that was already beginning to turn purple.

Meg waggled it, wincing.

"It's not broken," he proclaimed. "I give you a clean bill of health."

"What about my face?"

"It's lovely," he told her, dropping his gaze

so quickly she didn't have a chance to read it.

Meg swallowed. "I mean my cheek."

"So do I," Dylan said lightly. "Battle wounds look good on everyone."

It was Meg's turn to sigh. "I'm going in. I have a headache."

Dylan leaned over the bike and lifted it, straightening out the handlebars and kicking the front tire back into alignment. "It'll be fine," he reassured her. "It just needs a little TLC. I'll bring my tools tomorrow and tighten everything up."

"Whatever," Meg mumbled.

He looked lost for a moment before he shrugged and told her, "I need to call my brother for a ride. It's getting cold and I don't feel like walking."

Meg rolled her eyes. "You live less than a mile away."

"But I have at least fifty pounds of books in my backpack."

They started toward the house side by side, Dylan walking the bike and Meg gingerly fingering the raw skin of her cheek. When they made it to the garage, he stopped and studied her in profile for a moment. Then he stretched out his hand to curl it around her ponytail. He lifted the blond waves out of the collar of her coat, smoothing the strands down her back.

"You did good."

Meg felt like his dog, like she was being petted. She snatched the ponytail from his grasp and swung it over her shoulder, away from him. "If you're so determined to turn me into a boy, I'm cutting this thing off."

Dylan's gaze turned serious. "No," he said. "Don't do that. I like you just the way you are."

Meg scooted up to her room before her mother could get a good look at the damage inflicted by the jagged concrete of the cul-de-sac. "Dylan's gonna use the phone!" she yelled, taking the stairs two at a time and avoiding the hallway that led to the kitchen.

From the back of the house, Linda Painter called, "He can stay for supper! We're having roast and mashed potatoes."

It was Dylan's favorite, and Meg paused on the landing to see if her mother's invitation was too tempting for him to resist. But though his smile sagged visibly when the warm aroma hit him, Dylan was already shaking his head no.

"Sorry, Mrs. Painter," he started, heading off toward the kitchen. "My mom's expecting me home."

Relieved, Meg left him to make the phone call and sprinted the last of the steps. Steering clear of her brother's closed bedroom door and the throbbing bass that made the hinges squeak, she locked herself in the bathroom, where she tried to evaluate her injuries. Nothing too serious, but the scrapes on her cheek would soon be accented by a long, purple bruise. Her cheekbone was already beginning to discolor.

After she had washed her face and held her burning hand beneath a stream of ice-cold water long enough to make it numb, Meg found herself staring at her reflection in the mirror. The girl before her was perhaps a little too thin, with angular features that echoed her slight frame. Her nose was narrow, her eyes wide, her mouth shapely but a bit too big for the rest of her face. Meg's mother always told her that Painter girls grew into their beauty, and looking at herself now, Meg knew what she meant. In her own face she saw the potential for loveliness, but it was not a present reality. It didn't make her sad; it made her anxious.

Raising her hands to her hair, Meg loosed the ponytail that Dylan had clutched only minutes before. Blond locks the color of harvest spread across her shoulders and down the camouflage arms of her heavy jacket. The waves were twisted and tangled, half curly and half kinked. They looked messy and unkempt, too long by a good six inches.

Meg stepped back from the counter, put her hands on her hips, and sighed. "I need a haircut," she told the girl in the mirror. "And maybe . . ." She crossed to the top drawer beside the sink and rifled through the flower-print bag containing her mother's makeup. "This."

The sticker on the bottom of the tube of lip gloss told Meg the color was Summer Sunset, but she thought it looked like blood on her mouth. She grimaced at her reflection for a moment, then swiped at the offensive makeup with a tissue. When she found that her lips were still stained with the tint, she washed her face again.

Dylan had said that he liked her the way she was. She hoped he meant it.

"What happened to you?" Greg Painter asked Meg when she finally made her way downstairs for dinner.

"I fell, Dad."

His hand found her cheek and grazed the broken skin with a gentle thumb. "How did you fall?"

Of course, he knew exactly how she fell

and who she was with when it happened. The seemingly never-ending parade of cuts, bruises, sprains, and strains she regularly sported didn't sit well with her father, and Meg had learned early on that he couldn't stop himself from pointing out the obvious where Dylan was concerned. It was as if he didn't quite dare forbid her to see her new friend, but hoped that by reminding her of the trouble she got herself into when Dylan was around, she'd change her mind about the relationship entirely.

"How?" he pressed.

Meg pursed her lips and tolerated her dad's ministrations in silence. She only admitted the truth about what happened when her mother slipped into the dining room carrying the final serving bowl.

"I fell off my bike," she said then, extracting herself from beneath her dad's hand and going to take her place beside Linda at the table.

Greg rolled his eyes. "I'm giving that bike away," he snapped, dropping into his own chair.

"Don't be ridiculous," Linda told her husband. "She loves that bike."

"Look at what it does to her!"

Linda turned to Meg and cupped her daughter's face in her hands. "It'll heal," she said. "Not even a hint of a scar." She smiled a secret smile at Meg, a mother-daughter vow of understanding contained in the private lift of her lips.

Meg wasn't completely clueless. She fully understood that her dad bristled at the thought of Dylan because he was older, virtually unknown, and a boy. And she knew that her mom had a soft spot for Dylan because of those very same things. Linda treated her only son with the same mix of adoration and resolve, her affection tempered with an even hand that seemed to say, "I know you need tough love."

As if she could read Meg's mind, Linda looked up from the table and asked, "Where's Bennett? Did you tell him it was suppertime?"

"Five times at least," Meg assured her.

"Knocking on the door doesn't count."

Meg shrugged. "Then no. I didn't tell him it was suppertime."

"I'm on it," Greg said with a sigh. He pushed himself away from the table and took the steps two at a time on his way to claim his son from the smelly dungeon that was his room.

"I want details," Linda whispered when he was gone.

"We were doing jumps off the ramp," Meg

started, editing ruthlessly. "I tried to spin the handlebars and fell."

Linda bit the inside of her cheek and gave her daughter a stern look.

"What?"

"Spill it."

Meg picked up her fork and spun it between her fingers like a baton. "Jess had some friends over," she confessed. "They saw me and Dylan, and . . . it was no big deal."

"You were showing off?"

"Mom." Meg glared. "I was not showing off."

"Proving yourself."

"Something like that."

Linda looked hard at her daughter for a long moment. Then, sitting back in her chair, she crossed her arms over her chest and muttered, "Mm-hmm."

"What?"

"Nothing," Linda said, but she leaned over and gave Meg a quick, smacking kiss on the forehead.

"What?"

"What, what?" Greg asked walking back into the dining room with sixteen-year-old Bennett in tow.

"Nothing," Linda said again. "Sit down, both of you. Supper's getting cold."

Meg watched as Bennett slumped down opposite her. He studied the table with all the disinterest of a stereotypical angst-ridden teen. His half-closed eyes and the way he swiped his hand beneath his nose as if he hardly realized the appendage was attached to his body made Meg giggle. It was all an act. She knew that when the music blared in his bedroom and he was supposed to be staring blankly at the ceiling daydreaming about girls — maybe even her own best friend — he was actually penning advanced calculus homework in his careful hand. More than once she had caught him in the act, and by the way he reacted, Meg was convinced that he couldn't have been more embarrassed if she had caught him smoking a joint. The thought only made her giggle harder.

Bennett looked up at her for the first time since walking into the room. "What's your problem?" he challenged. Then, seeing her cheek, he added, "Another fall, Little Miss Tony Hawk?"

"He's a skater," Meg said, rolling her eyes.

"Oh, I forgot. You're a biker." The way Bennett said the word made it sound as if nothing could be more distasteful. "So lame, Megs. So completely pathetic."

Meg was about to bite back when her

parents both cut in.

"It was an accident," Linda said.

"Dylan talked her into it," Greg accused.

Bennett looked from parent to parent, apparently measuring their words before he turned his gaze to his sister. "This Dylan boy sounds like trouble to me."

Meg was incensed. Bennett took no interest in her life whatsoever except to screw it up when given the chance. She longed to leap across the table and yank at his longish curls. She'd call him a wannabe, a poseur. It was common knowledge that she had more nerve, spunk, and spirit than her quiet, straight-A brother. He was a closet nerd.

But Meg never got the chance.

Linda grabbed her daughter's hand forcefully and gave her husband a pointed look. "Pray," she said, her request a thinly veiled command.

And though Meg could tell that her dad wanted to follow up Bennett's commentary with more Dylan abuse, he obeyed his wife and bowed his head.

Meg followed suit, but after her father had said a few lines, she dared to sneak a peek across the table at her brother. He was looking at her, and when she caught his eye, he thrust his chin at her in an unspoken challenge. She grinned, and knowing that he wouldn't make a sound, kicked his shin beneath the table with all the strength she could muster.

Bennett's gaze flickered, but he didn't even wince. Instead, he winked, and mouthed something that looked an awful lot like "He's using you."

Or maybe Meg only saw what she had already started to believe.

5
LUCAS

Lucas woke up with light behind his eyes. The sun was streaming in the window beside the bed he used to share with Jenna, and without looking, Lucas knew that a glowing sliver of gold was pouring itself across the pillow. His mouth was dry. His bones hummed with the ache of a deep, dreamless sleep, the kind of twinge that invited his body to stretch and unfold itself in a morning jog. But instead of rolling out of bed, he rolled over. His years-old routine was becoming more of a memory than a daily habit.

The house was silent. So far this fall, Lucas hadn't turned on the furnace, but it was just about time to do so. The air around his face was cool, but underneath the down comforter, Lucas was bathed in humid heat. Too hot inside but too cool outside — he could feel the frostiness of the air nip at his face even as his body radiated an almost sticky warmth. Not time to get up just yet.

Lucas could almost imagine that Jenna was breathing beside him. She moaned in her sleep — a soft, unconscious sigh that he had fallen in love with long ago. He missed listening to the gentle protest in each exhale, the sweet familiarity of her night sounds, and even the way she curled away from him, her backbone pressing lightly against his arm as he lay facing the ceiling.

But his bed was cold and empty. Silent as a tomb.

When Jenna had told him that she was moving out, he begged her to stay. She said she needed time and space, a place where she could untangle the mess that her life had become.

"We can do that together," Lucas said, his voice low and husky, desperate.

"No, Lucas, we can't. I think the last several years have proven that."

"Why don't we try counseling again?"

Jenna suppressed a little shudder.

"It wasn't that bad."

"Look, I don't want to go there. I don't want to dredge up everything that happened and try to come to terms with it all. I just want to move on."

Without me, Lucas thought. But he said, "Stay. Please. I'll move into the attic room.

You'll hardly know I'm here. Just please don't go."

Jenna had shrugged, and the conversation was over. For an entire week Lucas hoped that she had abandoned her plan entirely, that somehow in a stunted, brittle conversation he had managed to convince her that their marriage was worth fighting for. But when he replayed their dialogue again and again, he realized that there were no fighting words contained in their exchange at all. He hadn't shouted a battle cry, a bold declaration of the war he was willing to wage in the campaign for his wife. He had whimpered a plea.

It had unnerved Lucas not to know what to do. He was the sensible one, strong and levelheaded and dependable. At work and at home, he specialized in doling out solutions, answers to problems both simple and sophisticated. But losing Jenna had crept up on him in the night. Her gradual disentanglement from their relationship, from their life together, had come on so slowly and stealthily, he didn't realize it was happening until the day she walked into the attic and became little more than the woman who shared a house with him.

One night almost exactly a week after she told him she was going to move out, Jenna brushed her teeth in the bathroom like normal, but instead of crossing the hall into the bedroom they shared, she mounted the steps to the attic. Lucas hadn't even noticed that she had moved her clothes out of the closet and taken her favorite pillow. Or that the wall between them had been mortared with an extra layer of bricks. He couldn't even form a single coherent thought as he watched her walk straight-backed up the stairs and out of sight, and when the slim curve of her ankle finally disappeared, he stood in the hallway, watching the spot where it had been, heartbroken and longing. He was bereft, holding all the frayed edges of the ties that bound them to the house, to each other, to all that they had shared and known, and hoping he could somehow weave them back together. He didn't know how to begin.

Lucas knew that he should have called after her. He should have at least tried to make her take the master bedroom. Better yet, he should have marched up those stairs and carried her back down like a child. Laid her on their bed. Made love to her.

Or just held her.

He did none of those things.

And in the murky light of a fall morning, he wished for nothing more than that he had done something. Anything.

I took the ring, Lucas thought. It was too little, too late, and maybe not the right gesture at all. But he had done it, and now he had to live with the ramifications.

Lucas both wanted and didn't want to give Jenna the ring. He leaned over the side of the bed and took it from the nightstand where he had placed it the night before. It felt warm in the palm of his hand, the coil of gold an obvious and almost painful sphere pressing against his skin. Tell her, he thought. Go upstairs, lift her from sleep, and look into her eyes. Tell her what you saw. But now that he was home, away from the crime scene, the bustle of DCI agents, and all the questions, he was speechless. Maybe Jenna wouldn't understand his gift. Maybe it would hurt her more than it helped. And although he believed with all his heart that the body beneath the floor of the barn was Angela Sparks — and that DCI would quickly and easily determine that fact — it didn't erase what he had done.

Sane, trustworthy, respectable men didn't steal evidence from a crime scene. And straitlaced, idealistic, reliable Lucas Hudson didn't either. At least, not until he saw the glint of the ring.

The telephone was far enough away that

when it rang, it was more a dream than reality. Lucas finally turned his head so that his ear was angled at the door, and after a moment of lying perfectly still, he heard it. Quickly, he swung his feet to the floor and slithered out, grabbing his robe off the chair and gliding to the bedroom door on the balls of his feet. The door made the tiniest creak at his touch, but when he looked back to see if he had disturbed Jenna, he remembered that he slept alone. He flung the door open.

Taking the stairs two at a time, Lucas reasoned that he had probably already missed the call. The answering machine would get it. He should have stayed in bed. But it was too late to turn back. He had committed himself to the chore and now he wanted to make it worth his while — no lousy hang-up. The kitchen tile bit his bare feet as he sprinted across the floor, but Lucas did reach the phone in time. The answering machine clicked on just as he swept the phone out of its cradle.

"Hello?" His voice was groggy with sleep and accompanied by a tinny, mechanical voice insisting that the Hudsons were not able to take the call. "Hang on a second, let me turn that off."

"Lucas? You're such a slacker — were you

still in bed?" Alex was loud enough that Lucas had to yank the phone away from his ear.

"No," Lucas lied. "Jenna and I were just having a lazy morning." He spun around to look at the clock on the stove, which read 8:30. Surprised, he used his free hand to massage his face and ended up hiding a wide yawn, even though he knew Alex couldn't see him through the telephone.

"You're a bad liar, Lucas. Always have been," Alex ribbed.

"Okay, caught me." Lucas yawned again. "I can't remember the last time I've done that — slept so late, I mean." He lowered himself into one of the kitchen chairs.

"Hey, I'm glad you did. Kids wouldn't let me — Lily jumped into our bed at five freakin' thirty this morning, ungodly — but I envy you. Do it every day if I could."

Lucas held his tongue. People often didn't realize how seemingly benign comments like that cut Jenna to the quick. Him, too. Five freakin' thirty sounded pretty fantastic if it meant that a child had been the alarm clock. Lucas couldn't help wondering how different his whole life would be if he could laugh with Alex about the so-called chore of children.

"We're starting with interviews this morning," Alex went on. "We've been calling since seven o'clock, and have a few appointments lined up already."

"On Sunday? I'm surprised the fine residents of Blackhawk are willing to part with their Sunday-morning routine."

"Oh, everything has to be before or after church, but not during dinner with Grandma or anytime in the three-hour afternoon nap slot."

Lucas laughed in spite of himself.

"When can I count on you?"

"Me?"

"You need to give an official statement, Lucas."

"With you?"

"DCI will interview you."

Massaging his face with his free hand, Lucas thought about the ring that he'd left on the nightstand when he ran to catch the phone. Did they suspect that he'd taken something? Were there imprints of the ring on the paper of Jim's suicide note? Could the naked eye determine that sort of thing?

"You there?"

"Nine o' clock," Lucas said. "I can be there at nine."

"We're set up at the station. Just park around back and let yourself in the back door." Alex hung up without saying good-bye.

Upstairs, Lucas plucked his jeans from the floor where he had discarded them and pulled a fresh T-shirt from the dresser drawer. He tucked the ring in his pocket, stabbed with a moment of guilt so intense that he almost convinced himself he would turn the ring over to DCI as soon as he saw them. But then he heard the creak of Jenna's feet on the floor above him. She was probably pulling the curtains tight, trying to eliminate any gaps where the light creeped in. Jenna wasn't a morning person, and she liked to be gentled into her day. It killed him to think of her up there. Without him.

Grabbing his keys from the kitchen counter, Lucas consoled himself with plans for their afternoon. When he got back he'd talk Jenna into going for a drive; they'd get out of Blackhawk and maybe even go to Intermission, her favorite restaurant. Sioux Falls was a good forty-five minutes away, but nothing was open in Blackhawk on Sunday. Besides, it would be good for them to get out of town for a few hours at least. He just couldn't bring himself to give her the ring so close to the crime scene.

The interview was brief and to the point.

Though Lucas had worried about being faced with questions that he didn't know how to answer, the DCI team appeared almost disinterested in his testimony beyond the specifics of his short-lived role as coroner. It seemed his profession placed him above suspicion in their book. The thought both comforted him and compounded his guilt as they rehashed his discovery of the note. But that, too, seemed perfunctory. He was in and out in half an hour.

Standing in the gravel lot behind the police station, Lucas took out his cell phone and dialed home.

"Where are you?" Jenna answered, relying on caller ID to negate the need for a proper hello.

"Good morning," Lucas countered. He could imagine the sleep-tousled explosion of her dark hair, the pillow creases in her cheek. "Are you dressed?"

"I asked you a question."

"Sorry. I'm at the police station." He sucked in a quick breath. "It's a long story, and I'd like to tell you about it over breakfast. Are you dressed?"

"Yes."

"Can I pick you up?"

"I don't think so, Lucas."

"Please. I promise, I won't say a word

103

about you moving out. I just want to talk."

Lucas could tell that Jenna wasn't happy about it, but she consented to breakfast all the same. He was quietly hopeful.

When he pulled into their long driveway, Jenna was already letting herself out of the house. She let the screen door slam behind her and made her way across the grass, stepping high to avoid soaking the hem of her khakis in the icy morning dew. He smiled at her as she came, but her eyes were downcast, and when she dropped into the car beside him, she fiddled with the heater controls instead of looking at him.

"It's chilly," she said, turning on the heat.

"Good morning," Lucas said for a second time, determined to coax even a little cheer out of his wife. He leaned over the console and dared to give her a kiss on the cheek. Her eyes fluttered closed, but Lucas couldn't tell if it was because she secretly relished the brief contact, or if she was merely allowing it for his sake. He hoped for the former.

"Good morning," Jenna finally said back. "Where are we going?"

"Fairfield? I think that little family restaurant is open on Sundays. Or we could go to Sioux Falls. Do a little shopping . . . ?"

She shook her head. "Pancakes. Coffee.

104

No shopping."

"Fairfield it is."

The drive was quiet, the roads all but deserted. Partway there, Jenna turned off the heater and cracked her window an inch. She stuck her fingers out above the glass and tasted the wind with her fingertips. When she pulled them back in, the ivory tone of her pale skin had faded to wool white. She laid her hand against her neck as if to absorb the cold and shivered.

The air between them was thick with things unsaid, and Lucas considered jumping into the deep end and bringing up just one of the roadblocks between them. But what good would it do? He had learned long ago that Jenna's grief was something she liked to shoulder alone. It seemed like every time he tried to enter the dark hall of her private sorrow, he ended up pushing her further away. He wanted to fix things, to rationalize the hurt away, to help her see that there was always a glimmer of light at the end — even if it was faint and flickering. But she didn't want to hear it.

Within twenty minutes they were parked outside Miss Penny's, a greasy spoon on the outskirts of Fairfield. It was exactly the sort of unattractive building that Lucas scorned when they first moved to northwest Iowa.

105

But in the years of his slow conversion from city boy to country lover, he grew in appreciation for the no-frills attitude that shaped small-town, Midwestern culture. Everything was about function and frugality, and even if he didn't always agree, he couldn't help but respect the understated aversion to affluence.

A sign invited them to seat themselves, and Lucas obliged, taking a clean-looking booth next to a window. The benches were covered in an outdated paisley print that sported cigarette burns from the days before Iowa enforced the smoking ban. Now, even years after the last Marlboro was lit in Miss Penny's, the faint scent of tobacco still clung to the stained fabric covering the bench where Lucas sat.

Jenna slid in opposite him and ordered coffee with a raised eyebrow and a flick of her wrist. Tipping an imaginary pot, she held up two fingers and nodded, giving a quick smile to the waitress who was all the way across the room.

"Want a menu?" Lucas asked, even though he knew the answer. He pulled only one paper bifold from behind the salt and pepper shakers.

"Nope."

"Two buttermilk pancakes, butter and

syrup on the side. One egg, over easy. One slice of bacon, crispy." Lucas didn't have to guess to know her order.

"Does that mean you pay attention or that we've been married too long?"

"It means I know you." Lucas stared at the menu in front of him, trying to ignore Jenna's attempt to pick a fight. "Would you rather have a loaded omelette or French toast with apple compote?"

"The omelette," Jenna said. She metabolized food at the rate of a teenage boy and would happily finish whatever her husband didn't eat.

"The omelette it is."

They ordered when the waitress brought them their coffee in two mismatched mugs. Lucas ignored the oily reflection of the surface and took a few long sips, grateful for the bitter burn as it went down.

"So," Jenna said, just like he knew she would, "why don't you tell me where you were last night."

"Alex called me to the old Timmer farm," Lucas murmured, still looking into the dark depths of his coffee.

"Jim's place?"

"Yeah."

"But why . . . ?"

Lucas could hear the uncertainty in her

voice, the hope even after all these years. It killed him. "I was called in as coroner." He looked up in time to see her eyes widen.

"Jim?"

"He hung himself," Lucas said, feeling the oppressive weight of those words.

Jenna gasped a little. "You're kidding me."

"I'm afraid not."

The only sound for a few moments was the clink of Jenna's spoon as she stirred her coffee, a faraway look in her eye. She liked her caffeine straight — no cream or sugar — but she always stirred it anyway. Lucas figured it was just another manifestation of her constant need to keep moving. She fidgeted, she tapped, she squirmed. She stirred.

"Jenna?" Lucas said her name softly, wondering what she was thinking. Wondering if he could tell her the rest.

"I guess I'm not completely shocked," she muttered.

"Neither were we."

"I wonder what . . ." but Jenna didn't finish her thought. She didn't have to. They both knew that her mind was on Angela.

Lucas felt the pressure of what he had seen settle like deadweight on his chest. He struggled to breathe beneath the crush of it. This will destroy her, he thought. But the words had to be said. They had to come from him.

"There's something else," he croaked.

"What?" She seemed hesitant, but she caught his gaze and held it.

"We found . . . a second body."

"Another body?"

He wanted to jump in and reassure her, to tell her that it was most likely not Angela, even if he was sure that it was. Anything to prolong the inevitable. But it was too late. Jenna's cheeks had been blushed by the wind as they crossed the parking lot at Miss Penny's, but as he watched, the color drained from her face. Her lips parted, just a little, enough for him to hear the tiny moan that escaped before she could stop it.

"Honey," he said, reaching across the table for her. He tried to take her hands in his own, but she slipped them from the table and dropped them in her lap. "I'm so sorry. I'm so, so sorry . . ."

Jenna lowered her head, her gaze turned toward her hands where he couldn't see what was happening in her eyes. Was she crying? Suddenly Lucas regretted telling her. He should have waited, he should have found another way. He fumbled in his pocket for the ring, anxious to do something to ease her pain.

"Where did you find her?" Jenna asked before he could say anything more. Her voice was quiet but steady.

"Uh," he cleared his throat, "in the barn."

"Where?"

"Buried beneath the floor."

Jenna looked up, her eyes bright and clear and hard. He wasn't expecting that. "Recently?" she demanded. "Was she buried recently?"

"No," Lucas said. "Alex called in DCI and they think that the body was buried several years ago."

"Eight?"

He shrugged. "If she was buried eight years ago, they seem to think she was unusually well preserved. But it's not impossible. The ground there is mostly clay. And . . ." He struggled with how much to tell her, but the set of her face made him go on. "And she seems almost mummified. They're not sure why, but likely because of where she was buried and how protected she was."

"How do you know the body was a woman?"

"Bone structure. Clothing. She was wearing a dress. Or, what was left of a dress."

Jenna nodded then took a swig of her coffee and set the mug down hard. "It's not

Angela," she said, leaving no room for argument.

Lucas was stunned. "Jenna," he coaxed, "of course it's —"

"It's not Angela," she repeated, louder this time. "I don't know who you found, and I feel very sorry for her, but it's not Angela."

"Honey, be reasonable."

"Reasonable?" Jenna looked as if she wanted to spit at him. "You think I'm being unreasonable? Nobody knew Angela better than me. Nobody. I'm telling you — it's not her."

"But the evidence —"

"There is no evidence! Not yet. Does Alex think it's Angela? Do the DC guys?"

"DCI."

"Whatever. Do they?"

Lucas rubbed his jaw and studied the multicolored flecks in the Formica tabletop. This wasn't exactly going as he had expected. "No," he said eventually. "They can't draw conclusions based on conjecture."

"Exactly." Jenna sat back against the plush bench as if relieved. "It's not Angela."

"Just because they can't say so doesn't mean it's not her," Lucas argued. "I think it would be good for us to deal with this. To accept what's happened and put it behind us."

"Put it behind us?" Jenna scoffed, like nothing could be more ludicrous. "You want me to just put Angela behind me? What does that even mean?"

"It means that maybe we can finally get some closure from all of this. Maybe we can finally move on."

"Closure? Do you want it to be Angela?"

"Of course not. But I think we need to accept that there is a very real possibility that it's her."

"Lucas, when are you going to learn that everything doesn't come neatly packaged?"

"What's that supposed to mean?"

She split him with a glare so pointed, he nearly recoiled. "That life doesn't follow your rules. It's not half as neat and tidy as you'd like it to be."

Lucas was so hurt and confused, he was almost speechless. "What are you talking about?"

But Jenna answered him with another question. "Why do you always do this?" she asked, the exasperation in her voice bubbling just beneath the surface.

He waited, carefully measuring his next words. "Do what?" It was the best he could come up with.

She gave him an as-if-you-don't-already-know look, but wasted no time in telling him, "You have everything all figured out, including my reaction. You can't tell me how to feel, how to respond to this" — she fumbled — "this news you've just dumped into my lap."

"I'm not," he cut in.

"Yes, you are," she shot back. "This doesn't feel right. Nothing between us feels right anymore."

In his mind he replied, That's because you've shut me out, you hold me at arm's length. You've moved out of our bedroom. Out loud he said, "We're bringing other things to the table now. This isn't about Angela anymore, is it?"

"Stop psychoanalyzing me, Lucas Hudson," she responded lethally.

"Jenna —"

"Something has been happening to us for a long time, Lucas. Until you're ready to start being honest with me and with yourself . . ." She trailed off. "Until" was one step away from "unless," an ultimatum. But she didn't finish. He was thankful that she didn't.

They looked at each other for a moment, his eyes sad, hers angry. When she finally broke contact, it was as if she couldn't get out of the café fast enough. "I'm not hungry. I need some fresh air." It was hardly an excuse, but Lucas let her go. In one abrupt movement she was out the door, hurrying across the parking lot. He watched her through the window, cringing when she zipped up her jacket against the autumn chill and hit the sidewalk at a restless jog. She turned a corner and was out of sight in less than a minute.

Alone in the booth, Lucas stared at her half-empty coffee cup, the napkin that lay perfectly parallel to the chipped, porcelain handle.

He realized he loved her so much, it hurt.

6
MEG

Meg forgave Dylan in record time. Though she loved to hold a grudge, she found it difficult to remain angry with him. All those cold stares, intentional snubs, and mildly caustic remarks that stung like salt in an open wound were abruptly abandoned when she realized that what he had told her in the cul-de-sac turned out to be true: she was instantly cool. Her epic wipeout was broadcast among Jess's friends and beyond, and since Sutton was small and well connected, the entire incident contributed much to her popularity.

Unconcerned with her social status for all the years prior to her relationship with Dylan, Meg suddenly found herself the unwitting recipient of obvious respect and admiration. True, she wasn't an It Girl — a perfectly coiffed and giggly confection of teenage fluff who garnered the sort of attention that would undoubtedly make her dad start propping a shotgun by the front door — but it wasn't like she wanted that sort of popularity anyway.

Instead, Meg was definitely a girl, but acknowledged as one of the guys, an accepted entity in both worlds. The girls in her school envied her familiarity with the cute, inaccessible boys they had crushes on. And the guys treated her as a loyal sidekick, not quite on par with the rest of the Y-chromosome clan, but a different and wonderful breed altogether. They actually asked for her advice, enjoyed her sharp-tongued company, and told off-color jokes in her presence. Once, when the boys in her class had a big weekend sleepover, they told her that they wished she could come, but their mothers would never permit it.

Meg laughed. "Like I'd want to hang out with you guys anyway. You'll probably just sit around all night picking your own toe lint and laughing at your farts."

Somebody lunged at her, but Meg was already gone, ponytail swinging behind her as she ran.

In spite of her newfound star status, her generic brand of small-town fame, one constant remained unchanged in Meg's satisfying life: Dylan. While her parents struggled to keep tabs on the flood of phone calls, on the unexpected comings and go-ings of their daughter, and while her friends fell headlong into the excitement of adoles-cence and Meg's coveted place in it, Dylan offered the sort of steadfast stability that engendered absolute adoration.

Meg fell for him. Hard.

Though it was impossible to pinpoint exactly when Dylan became more than a friend in Meg's untried soul, she attributed the physical ache of a heart cleft in two to the closing night of the Sutton High spring play.

Since Dylan was practically a member of the Painter family by the time he secured the role of Orlando in *As You Like It,* Meg went to the outdoor performance with both of her parents. Linda had managed to wrestle her contractor husband into a tie, and though it was a plaid-patterned relic from Meg's toddler years, she was proud to be sitting on the flimsy folding chairs with her mom and dad beside her. The entire event left Meg feeling a little pink-cheeked and breathless, and not just because Dylan had to kiss the raven-haired beauty who played Rosalind.

"It's weird," Greg Painter said halfway through the play. He had leaned over to whisper in his wife's ear, but Meg could hear him plainly from her place on the opposite side of her mother.

"Shhhh," she hissed at the same time that her mom whispered, "What's weird?"

"That pretty girl is dressed up like a boy, and Dylan's pinning love poems to trees." He arched an eyebrow. "It's weird."

"It's Shakespeare." Linda smiled indulgently. "And Dylan is doing an amazing job. Orlando can come off as a bit of a wimp, but Dylan's playing him ironic. Satire from a sixteen-year-old. I find that impressive."

"Shhhh." Meg knocked knees with her mom in warning. "If you two don't shut up, I'm quitting."

"Quitting what?"

"This family. I'm done. Seriously. I'll run away or something."

"We could put a hot tub in her room," Greg muttered under his breath. Linda had to press her fist to her mouth, apparently to keep herself from laughing out loud.

Meg thought about leaving, but whether or not her dad appreciated Dylan's obvious talents, she did. And she couldn't have moved from her seat even if she wanted to. They had been friends for nearly a year, and in all that time she had learned that Dylan was a man of many talents — and almost as many secrets. When he announced that he was trying out for the play, and then when he was chosen for the lead over a dozen boys who were older and more experienced, Meg didn't know whether to be proud or embarrassed. Dylan, an actor? But somehow, it worked for him.

Watching him onstage, that famous half smile toying with the corner of his mouth, Meg felt like she was catching a glimpse of a familiar stranger — a face she knew, or thought she knew, across a crowded room. And all she wanted to do was soak in each shift and nuance of his every expression.

Afterward, when everyone was waiting in a line to congratulate the actors, Meg was surprised to feel her palms begin to sweat. She wiped them on the silky fabric of her vintage skirt, a flowing, bohemian-looking design that would have made a beautiful sari. Though she had loved it when she found it hanging dejected on a rack at Goodwill, all at once she regretted her careless choice. The woven flip-flops, hemp bracelets, and simple T-shirt the exact color of cornmeal seemed insufficient somehow. Her hair was soft and long, fresh from the shower, and her face was unadorned but for a dab of lip gloss that her mother had bought specifically for her. Staring at her feet, Meg realized that even her toes were bare. No polish, no tiny rings, nothing to make her feel feminine or attractive. She wished she had done something more. Didn't Dylan deserve more? The thought startled her.

When the reception line finally wound to the end of the queue where Orlando stood with Rosalind, Celia, and Oliver, Meg found that the boy she knew as Dylan was nowhere to be seen. Up close, his skin shimmered orange underneath the stage makeup, and he had one arm draped casually around the girl who played Celia, even though he was supposed to be posing with Rosalind. There was something cavalier and flirty about the way he leaned into the smaller, sweet-faced Celia, and Meg felt a rush of possessiveness surge through her. But before the feeling could translate to hurt on her face, Dylan glimpsed her out of the corner of his eye.

Everything about him lit up, and with no regard for the fact that her rather imposing father had his arm linked through hers, Dylan hopped off the curb where he was standing and slid his arms around Meg's waist. He squeezed her tight, lifted off her feet for a second, and then dropped her as quickly as he had caught her up. In all their hours and days and weeks together, he had never hugged her. The unexpected contact made Meg tingle from head to toe. She wanted to reach for him, to lay just her finger against the stiff leather of his jacket and make the feeling linger.

"Isn't it awesome?" he asked.

She had no idea what he was referring to. The play? The fact that he had three girls like the points of a triangle around him? Or had he felt what she had in the moment he held her fast? That they fit like the pieces of a puzzle, like a bolt sliding home. Her chin belonged in the spot where his shoulder met his neck. And Dylan's arms were made for the narrow line of her waist. For one of the first times in her life, Meg felt a blush thaw like snow across her hot cheeks. She wanted to put her hands to her face, to feel the dampness there. Was it obvious? Did everyone else know that they were meant for each other?

"Isn't it awesome?" Dylan asked again.

This time she forced herself to nod. "Yes, it is."

Her father probed her along, and as she walked away from Dylan, Meg suffered the weight of what she knew to be true press so heavy against her chest, she struggled to breathe. It was suffocating, and she fought the realization of her feelings for him in futile frustration until the moment her heart finally gave way and split open along the seam, an overripe peach rending its flesh. She hadn't known that it could burst like that. Or that the fissure wouldn't mend with time — that it would continue to leak.

That death by devotion is a slow, aching bleed.

"I know where the cast party is," Sarah whispered, catching Meg's arm and pulling her away from the group of people that had congregated in the parking lot after the final curtain call. "Everyone is going to Lisbeth's house first. You know, Rosalind? Anyway, her parents are hosting a little celebration, but everyone is going to duck out early and head to Ethan's farm."

"Ethan?" Meg crossed her bare arms to ward off the light breeze that was raising goose bumps across her skin. "The sound guy?" He was slight and quiet, the last person anyone would suspect of throwing what would undoubtedly be a wild house party.

"Yeah." Sarah's eyes glinted. "His parents took off for Florida this morning and he's staying home alone with his older sister."

Meg considered this for a second. "How are we going to get there?"

"Jess'll drive us. All we have to do is sneak

out. He told my parents he's crashing at a friend's house tonight, but he said he'd meet us at the park if we want to go."

"Why would he do that?" Meg was instantly suspicious. Jess was a junior, and chauffeuring around his freshman sister and her lame best friend of his own free will smacked of ulterior motives.

Sarah laughed. "Because I promised him I'd do his chores for a month."

A slow smile spilled across Meg's face. "How generous of you. Thanks for including me in your little intrigue."

"As if I'd go alone." Sarah stifled a little shiver, but Meg couldn't tell if it was because she was cold or because she was excited about the possibilities of the night spread out before them.

At home, Meg changed quickly out of her boho skirt and slipped into a pair of jeans and a fitted T-shirt. It was V-necked and a rather plain chocolate brown, but there was a tiny bird silhouetted in blue just above her heart. Meg hoped it struck the right note between casual and sexy, and teased her hair with a bit of spray gel to complete her offhand look. Then she threw a pair of pajamas into her backpack as well as her toothbrush and a tube of travel toothpaste.

"I'm spending the night at Sarah's," Meg

123

called as she tripped down the stairs two at a time.

Linda Painter looked up from the ten-o'clock news and surveyed her daughter. "At this time of night? Sweetie, what's the point?"

"The night is just beginning," Meg teased.

"That's what I'm worried about." Linda motioned Meg over and pulled her daughter's head down for a quick kiss. "Don't stay up too late. I need you to help me with the garden tomorrow."

" 'Kay."

"And keep it down. The last thing the Langbroeks need is a bunch of teenage girls making a racket all night long."

"There's only two of us," Meg said, swinging her backpack over her shoulder and heading for the entryway. "And we aren't exactly the racket-making type. Say good night to Dad for me."

"He's already asleep."

"Then tell him good morning." Meg laughed, and shut the door behind her.

Meg and Sarah waited until after eleven, when the Langbroek house was still and silent except for the faint hum of the refrigerator. "My dad sleeps like the dead," Sarah whispered, even though they were still in her bedroom with the desk lamp on and a

CD playing softly in the background. "He won't hear a thing."

They had decided to leave everything as is, lock the bedroom door, and sneak out the window instead of creeping through the house. Sarah's room was on the second floor, but the flat roof of the garage was directly below her window and the jump was less than ten feet. They reasoned that the slight slant of the roof and the spongy floor of old shingles would cushion their fall.

"What time are we supposed to meet Jess again?" Meg asked, easing the screen out of the window and setting it against the wall.

"Eleven thirty."

"He's not going to show." Meg gripped Sarah beneath the elbow and helped her shimmy up to the window ledge.

Sarah giggled. "He will. He hates laundry duty and it's his month. If he doesn't come for us, I'll sneak my red scarf in when he's washing his whites." And then she pressed her hand to her mouth, wiggled her eyebrows at Meg, and slid off the edge into the darkness below. There was a muted squeal, a thud as she hit the roof, and then a scramble that sounded like pebbles on pavement.

"You okay?" Meg hissed into the darkness.

"Fine," Sarah called back, and her voice was so light, it floated right past the window and headed for the stars. "So, so fine . . . I love sneaking out. Let's do it every night."

Meg didn't answer but lifted herself off the windowsill and flipped around, grabbing the edge. Then she slowly lowered her arms until she dangled a few feet from the roof. She let go and landed lightly.

"I'm doing that next time," Sarah said. She was rubbing the seat of her jeans. "Did I rip a hole in my butt?"

Swatting her friend's behind, Meg laughed. "Nah. And if you did, no one would notice anyway."

"I'm offended by that," Sarah pouted. "Are you saying my butt isn't worth noticing?"

"Never. It's a very attention-worthy derriere."

"Derriere? I think the play got to you. Or, at least, someone in it."

Meg chose to ignore that comment as she walked along the edge of the garage roof, looking for the best place to jump down. But Sarah wasn't so easily deterred.

"Come on," Sarah said. "Admit it. You are so in love with him. You want to marry him and have little Dylan babies."

"Hardly."

"Hardly? That's the best you can come up with? You are in love with him. I thought it was just a crush."

"We're friends," Meg said in the moment before she disappeared over the edge of the roof and clambered off the little lean-to that housed the garbage can onto the damp grass below.

Sarah was a second behind her. "Some friend," she muttered. "I wish I had a friend like that."

"What's that supposed to mean?"

"Are you friends with benefits?"

"Oh," Meg said with a groan. "Don't be disgusting."

They took off in the direction of the park, keeping to the fenceless backyards and avoiding the warm circles of light cast by streetlamps. Meg tried to check the time on her watch, but it was too dark. In spite of Sarah's assurances otherwise, Meg seriously doubted that Jess would come for them, and she wasn't even sure that she wanted him to. There was something sparkling and illicit about sneaking out, the whole world seemed sharp-edged and shiny, but she couldn't help wondering what the party would hold. Surely Dylan would be there, but Meg didn't know if he would greet her as a friend or an intruder. She could picture him with his arm around the girl who played Celia, but her skin still tingled at the thought of his embrace. He could have one or the other, not both. Meg tried to stifle the hope that beat powerful wings against her chest.

"Told you he'd be here!" Sarah suddenly squealed, sprinting as they neared the park. Sure enough, Jess's car was pulled over on the side of the road, engine on but headlights off. Someone was in the driver's seat, but it looked like the rest of the car was full, too.

"You'll have to sit on laps," Jess said rolling down his window and indicating that the girls should hop in the back. "And the taxi fare has just been raised. Two girls equals two months."

"Two months?" Sarah choked. "That's so not fair."

Jess grimaced in a parody of concern. "Life's not fair. You coming or not?"

"Nah." Meg sounded nonchalant, but her heart was beating so hard it matched the bass line of whatever song Jess had cranked up on the pathetic radio in his clunker car. She desperately wanted to go to the party, but standing in the strange aura created by the unfamiliar music, the hot, sticky huddle of guys in Jess's car, and the uncertainty of the night before her, she had to admit that she was also very afraid. Meg didn't do afraid. At least, she pretended not to. All at once she wondered if courage was nothing more than a clever disguise for fear. If so, she definitely considered herself brave.

"What do you mean, nah?" Jess seemed to be glaring at her.

"I mean we're not coming."

"We're not?" Sarah squeaked.

"No. It's not worth it."

Meg started to walk away, and after a moment's hesitation Sarah followed. "Meg, I —"

But she didn't have time to finish before Jess called across the pavement. "Get in." The back door creaked open and even from halfway across the street Meg could catch a cloying whiff of cigarette smoke and cologne.

Jess didn't have to say it twice. Sarah was already jostling her way into the backseat by the time Meg turned around, and though Meg had to stifle a twitch at the thought of climbing onto the lap of the boy who held the door open for her, she gave him a tight-lipped smile and did it all the same. He had red hair and a knowing smirk, but Meg pretended that she didn't remember him.

"No seat belts," he said apologetically. And then he slipped both his arms around her waist and held on tight.

Meg suffered the ride in silence, mostly because Sarah was chattering so happily, she couldn't have gotten a word in edgewise if she wanted to. But she was also acutely aware of the stranger's hands around her, and the heavy burden of doubt that made it hard for her to breathe. Meg knew what happened at these sorts of parties. She was prepared for the drinking, and maybe even for things to get a bit out of control. But she couldn't shake the Hollywood-inspired image that seemed imprinted on the back of her eyelids whenever she squeezed her eyes shut. It featured a couple in a darkened corner, maybe even a quiet room, wrapped so tightly together it was impossible to unravel one from the other.

Would she find Dylan like that? Curled around some other girl? Or would it be her? Meg wasn't sure that she liked any of her imagined scenarios.

When Jess pulled up to Ethan's farm nearly ten minutes later, the party was in full swing. The yard was overflowing with cars, and someone had started a pallet fire on a concrete slab in front of one of the barns. At first glance, it was more laid-back than Meg had thought it would be. There were groups of teenagers standing in loose knots around the fire and beyond, and the sound of their laughter seeped through cracks in Jess's car the instant he killed the engine. Nobody seemed drunk or out of control. And as far as Meg could tell, no couples were sneaking off to secluded corners to explore each other in secret. Very un-Hollywood. And very comforting.

"Thanks." The redhead grinned, squeezing Meg one last time as everyone piled out of the car.

"For what?" Meg said, bristling.

He shrugged, but his gaze was taut and full of meaning. He tapped a finger beneath her chin and then turned to join Jess and the other guys as they strode down the hill. Meg watched him pause, whip around, and call back smugly, "He's not here, you know. Dylan."

She couldn't help herself. "He's not?"

"I think Orlando decided he liked Celia better than Rosalind. And apparently better than his little protégée, too. They wanted some time alone." He winked at Meg suggestively, and took off toward the fire without a backward glance. He accepted the beer that someone passed him and threw back his head to laugh at some joke Meg couldn't hear. Or maybe he was laughing at her.

"He's an ass," Sarah said, putting her arm around Meg's shoulders. Meg couldn't decide if her best friend was talking about the redhead or about Dylan.

Both, she thought, but it didn't make her feel any better.

7
LUCAS

Lucas wanted to run after Jenna, but he knew from past experience that chasing her would only make things worse. She needed time alone, time to process. It killed him to sit still, so he tapped his foot and fingered the ring on the sticky tabletop of the restaurant booth. The waitress came seconds after Jenna disappeared from view, and though the food she set before him was steaming and fragrant, Lucas felt like his appetite had left with his wife. He ignored the omelette.

Instead of eating, he twisted the ring, studying the etched leaves that adorned the band and wondering what had cracked the tiny stone. He had hoped to offer the ring as proof, as consolation. As a sort of final period, a tangible resolution to a story without end. Their history with Angela was a meandering tale that faded like a watercolor left out in the rain — it seemed as thin and endless as fog over water.

Lucas had hoped to clear the air. To offer Jenna a priceless gift — something that both acknowledged their loss and allowed them to move on. But he knew now that his evidence would only make Jenna angry. He wished he had left the pathetic piece of jewelry on the ground of Jim's barn. Especially when he found an engraving on the inside of the band.

There was a manufacturer's imprint, a signature of sorts that stamped the gold with the initials *MKD.* He didn't know what MKD stood for, but that didn't bother him. It was a postmarket inscription that caught his eye — MINE — in a sweeping arch of letters too bold to be mistaken.

Lucas ran the tip of his forefinger over the spot, feeling the brush where the laser had cut the gold. It was a bit of a creepy inscription no matter what the intention had been. Who had given Angela such a backhanded gift? Who dared to assert possession of a girl who barely possessed herself? Jim? The thought infuriated him. Jim had forfeited any claim to his daughter years ago. Some boyfriend? If there was anyone special among Angela's numerous beaus, Jenna hadn't known about it.

Maybe the ring, and the person who gave it to her, held the key to why Angela found herself crumpled in a shallow grave.

Lucas felt a jolt of white-hot rage.

Thankfully, Jenna was only gone for half an hour or so, and when she returned, Lucas saw her coming in time to pocket the ring and drop a twenty on the table. He met her at the car, ready to try to work things out, to smooth over the altercation with an apology, but Jenna was as chilly as the autumn air. They drove home without exchanging a word.

By Wednesday, Lucas and Jenna were still avoiding each other, breezing past each other in a house that seemed cavernous because of the distance between them. Lucas threw himself into work and spent his free time hassling Alex for information on the ongoing case. He called Alex, texted him, shot him the occasional e-mail. And when Alex became taciturn and claimed confidentiality, Lucas obsessed about the ring. He even scoured old photographs in search of Angela's hands, hoping he could match the piece of jewelry he held with the ring that he was almost certain she had worn.

But Lucas didn't find many pictures of Angela, and her hands were hidden in all of them. As for pestering Alex, Lucas did learn that Jim's death was ruled a suicide, and that the bones beneath him had belonged to a young woman in her late teens or early twenties. Another piece of the puzzle fit. But he didn't tell Jenna that.

Because Lucas didn't seem to have the tools to fix what was wrong at home, he worked overtime to make things right at the clinic. But as the week wore on, he found himself fatigued, distracted. The ring was heavy in his pocket, and Jenna's distance weighed heavy on his heart. He felt anchored and useless.

On Wednesday afternoon he struggled to pay attention to a boil, a common cold, and a routine physical, in that order. But his mind was elsewhere. When he finished up the physical, Lucas made his way to the reception desk at the clinic and stared over his nurse's shoulder, trying to gauge what the damage would be if he sneaked out for the rest of the afternoon.

"Impossible," Mandy muttered, ascertaining Lucas's business at the front of the clinic before he even said a word.

"You could get me out of this," he coaxed, glancing up quickly to survey the waiting room full of ailing patients. He smiled benignly and moved his mouth closer to Mandy's ear. "They can't hear me, can they?"

"They're sick, not deaf." Mandy rolled her eyes. "But at least you're whispering. There is a reason we put twenty feet between the reception desk and the first of the chairs." She elbowed him out of the way and, pushing off the floor, slid across the enclave on the castor wheels of her chair. Pulling two charts from the wall of files, she handed them to Lucas. "You've got a broken arm follow-up in room one and a potential bladder infection in two. I've already run a urine sample. I'll pop in with the results in a minute."

"And these?" Lucas sighed, waving the charts.

"They're your next two patients. I thought since you walked all the way up here, you could save me a trip back. Helen is on her break, so I'm pulling double duty."

"Sure, glad I could help out." Lucas turned to leave, but Mandy caught the end of his white coat and gave it a tug.

"Hang in there." She winked and plastered a smile on her face to greet the next patient, who was already standing at the counter.

The rest of the afternoon passed in a blur of symptoms and sympathy, except for one appointment when both of Lucas's hands were busy with the Doppler, trying to find a fetal heartbeat in a woman sixteen weeks along. Pressing the handheld device to the young woman's stomach, Lucas circled slowly beneath her belly button, finding first her own heartbeat resonating through the placenta and then, incredibly, the race of the tiny heart inside her. His hand flinched imperceptibly upon finding the body that was only inches away from his touch.

"Is that it?" the woman asked breathlessly. "I've never heard it before — they couldn't find the heartbeat at my last visit."

Lucas nodded but didn't make eye contact with her. The baby was moving and he had to concentrate on the rotation of the Doppler as he tried to follow the sound of her little heart. "One hundred and fifty-two beats per minute," he finally managed. "Well, more or less."

The woman was still trying to hold her breath, her eyes riveted to the ceiling and a smile playing at the corners of her mouth. "That's high, isn't it? Am I having a baby girl?"

The sound of sharp static interrupted the steady pulse that filled the room. "The baby's kicking," Lucas commented, a smile beginning at the corners of his own lips. "And no, heart-rate doesn't really mean anything at this stage. Closer to your due date there's some truth to that old wives' tale, but I wouldn't put any money on it."

For a moment, the sound was lost and Lucas had to struggle to find it again. When he did, the room was hushed except for the even whisper of blood being pumped. It was more beautiful than any music he had ever heard. It was the throb of something so real, so profound that Lucas's heart ached for the life that held so much promise at such a young age. All the years and love and life; every smile and tear and breath contained in someone so amazingly small no one would ever know she existed unless her mother chose to share her secret. It was nothing short of miraculous.

Finally, hesitantly, Lucas pulled the Doppler away and handed the woman a towel to wipe the gel off her belly. "Everything looks good," he said with his back to her. "You seem to be healthy, the baby seems fine."

But even as he offered those encouraging words, he fought the almost overwhelming desire to run a set of labs. HCG levels, progesterone, maybe a thyroid scan. Had anyone ever talked to her about Factor V Leiden? Sixteen weeks was early for an ultrasound in a low-risk pregnancy, but you could never be too careful . . .

"I guess your next appointment will be a scheduled, routine ultrasound — if your insurance will cover it. You'll get to see the baby." Lucas forced himself to stop projecting and offered her a thin smile. She was just finishing the top button on her jeans, looping it through with a hair tie because her protruding belly was just large enough that she could no longer do up the button.

"Good." She grinned at him.

"You can make the appointment at the front desk." Lucas passed her a piece of paper and rested his hand for a moment on her arm. "Good luck," he said sincerely, wishing her the best since he wouldn't see her again; she was Elliot Townsend's patient. He opened the door for her like a gentleman and she was gone.

Lucas stood for a moment in the silence of examination room number three, listening to his own heartbeat pound in his ears. With one hand he reached into his pocket and handled the ring concealed there. When his finger made contact with the cold metal, the absurdity of everything that had happened in the past few days suddenly became alarmingly clear. Dead bodies, stolen rings . . . and worst of all, another fight with Jenna. It didn't matter. None of it mattered except Jenna, and upon realizing it, Lucas felt almost triumphant in his resolve.

He hadn't even had a chance to show her

the ring. And maybe it was better that way. She had had a little time to warm up to the idea, to absorb the shock of what had really happened. When he showed her the ring, she'd accept it, and they could say good-bye together. Start over.

Tonight he'd go home, apologize to Jenna, and try to put all of this insanity behind him. He'd fire up the grill one last time and make his famous grilled chicken and baby red potatoes and uncork a bottle of their favorite ten-dollar wine. They'd drink the entire bottle before they realized it was gone and then finish with ice cream eaten directly from the carton. Lucas made a mental note to stop by the grocery store on his way home and try to find the same chocolate cherry bordeaux ice cream they used to love in Chicago.

And over ice cream, he'd give her the ring. A gift. A peace offering. And maybe, just maybe, he would bring up the issue of adoption. His heart caught at the thought; he didn't even know himself if it was from fear or anticipation. But he did know that it was time to at least let Jenna know that he was thinking about it. That maybe they could find their way back to each other if they cradled a baby between them.

Swinging out of the room, Lucas met

Mandy in the hall and handed her the young woman's file. "Next?" he asked quizzically, but there was still a light in his eyes from the heartbeat that continued to echo softly in his ears and the thought of ice cream on the floor of the living room with his wife.

"Oh, you'll like your next patient." Mandy pursed her lips so that he couldn't tell if she was serious or not. Nodding her head at one of the doors, she handed him a chart.

"How 'bout a break first?" Lucas tested her, feigning exhaustion as he slumped against the hallway wall. "It's not fair that Elliot and Scott get to take their holidays at the same time. How do you expect me to keep up with all of it?"

"You're superhuman. It's what heroes of your caliber do."

"What can I say?" Lucas struck a Superman pose, right fist lifted in the air, and breezed past Mandy, knocking briskly on the door of examination room one before he entered. He flashed Mandy a sly look and closed the door, turning his attention to his patient.

"You're certainly in a good mood."

Lucas looked up from the chart he was holding to find Alex sitting on the examination table. His legs were dangling off the side, and his hand was poised on his right leg, fingers balanced so that it looked like he was holding a cigarette between his first two fingers. It made Lucas laugh out loud.

"What's funny?" Alex grunted.

"I hope you know you're not allowed to smoke in here." Lucas indicated his friend's hand with a tip of his head.

Alex grunted and put his hands palm down on his knees. "I haven't smoked in over ten years, but I still crave one when I'm stressed."

"You stressed?"

"Always."

"Join the club." Lucas sighed and fell into the swivel chair opposite his friend. "So, are you here for personal reasons? Or professional?"

"Little of both. I came in to see if I could talk to you for a minute, but Mandy said you were too busy. As I was leaving, though, she asked me how my cold was doing."

"She's a shifty one, that Mandy," Lucas said, silently thanking his angel of a nurse for finding at least a tiny break for him. "My appointments usually take fifteen minutes, so I guess that's all we've got."

"I don't even need that much."

As Lucas studied his friend's face he realized for the first time since entering that

Alex was not his usual jocular, sarcastic self. "Hey, you really are sick," Lucas teased. "Where's the witty comment, the mile-a-minute banter, the —"

"Stuff it."

"Fair enough. What can I do for you?"

Alex cradled his forehead in one beefy hand. "Nothing, really. It just weighs on me, you know?"

"The case?" Lucas questioned, though he knew that the police chief thought of nothing else.

"Our chances of identifying this woman are slim to none. Rather, their chances. It's not my case anymore, you know."

"Unless it's Angela," Lucas said, ignoring the bitterness in Alex's voice.

"The only dental records we have for her are fifteen years old. Jim took her to the dentist once. She was eleven."

"So she had some permanent teeth. Enough for a match?"

"We'll see. But the earrings were a definite dead end."

"Earrings?"

"We found a handful of studs in the dirt of her grave. She must have had her ears pierced. Do you remember if Angela had pierced ears?"

"Double-pierced. Two on each side," Lucas recounted.

Alex shrugged. "Doesn't matter anyway. They're department store cheapies. A dime a dozen. Millions of women across the United States must wear them."

"What about interviews?" Lucas didn't feel like having another argument over whether or not the body was Angela.

"Day and night," Alex muttered. "We've talked to everyone who knew Jim, worked with Jim, lived near Jim, served in the Guard with Jim . . . liked him, hated him, and everything in between."

"And?"

"People can hardly remember what they had for breakfast, much less what happened five years ago."

"Five years?" Lucas repeated, surprised by the number. "They think the body has been in the ground for five years?"

"It's not an exact science, but yeah. Give or take."

Lucas tried to keep his face neutral as he took in the news. Angela had disappeared from Blackhawk eight years ago. What had happened in the three years between?

"I know what you're thinking," Alex said. "I've done the math, too. Either he had her hidden away in some yet-to-be-discovered den of horror, or it's not her."

"You know what I think."

"Masochist. You'd go with den of horror every time." But then Alex sighed, giving in. "Five to ten, Lucas. That's the guess right now. The ground was so hard. And it was more clay than dirt. It was like she was preserved in concrete. We'll know more in a couple weeks."

Lucas managed a wry laugh, but his mind was on the ring. MINE. Was it some twisted token of ownership? He hated to imagine worst-case scenarios, but it was hard to stop his mind from tripping down frightening paths of terror and dread.

Suddenly, the innocent ring seemed crucial somehow. He almost took it out of his pocket. Offered it to Alex. Almost.

But a surge of defiance stopped him. The ring was Jenna's. His. Theirs.

The rest of the day passed like an unstable weather front. Lucas tried to cheer himself with the thought of taking a few steps toward reconciliation with Jenna — supper and wine and honesty would go a long way, wouldn't they? But the dejected slump of Alex's shoulders as he walked out of the examination room left a lingering sense of turmoil that Lucas couldn't escape.

By the time he left the clinic and slouched into his car, Lucas was short-tempered and mutinous. He wasn't used to playing the part of the rebel. But it was intoxicating somehow, and as he started the car he reassured himself: They'll know it's Angela soon enough. And don't forget the ice cream.

Thankfully, the supermarket was virtually empty and Lucas was in and out in less than five minutes: no cash register lineups, no awkward conversations that ended with "So do you think I should get this checked out?" And, sadly, no chocolate cherry bordeaux. The ice cream section changed seasonally, and though they had lived in Blackhawk long enough for it to be more home than any other place he'd ever lived, Lucas could never quite give up hope that their favorite flavor would one day magically appear. It never did, although praline ricotta gelato had once made a brief, extraordinary debut. It didn't last long. He settled for Peppermint Stick and a bag of Double Stuf Oreos. Disappointing, but Lucas tried to cheer himself with the notion that at least they wouldn't need to use spoons. The Oreos could do the scooping. That was romantic, right?

The drive down Blackhawk's main drag, Highway 10, and through the tree-lined residential districts was reflex for Lucas. He didn't notice the riding lawn mower that was taking up half the street except to swerve around it. He didn't notice the ancient shade cast by oaks so old and enormous that their canopies intertwined across the street and created pools of sunlight on the concrete like a thousand golden coins. He didn't pay attention to anything until he was cocooned in his kitchen, staring at the blinking red light of his answering machine. Past experience told him not to press Play, but he did all the same.

"Lucas, it's Jenna. I've got a relocation tonight. I'll probably sleep at the office."

The house was static with Jenna gone, filled with questions and uncertainties. Lucas wandered from room to room, straightening up as he went because it was the only way he knew to clear his head. As he hung up one of Jenna's shirts, put out fresh towels in the bathroom, and emptied the recycled paper bin in the den, Lucas found himself starting down a road that he wasn't sure he wanted to be on.

Lucas hated himself with every ounce of his being, but it was as if an unfamiliar man held sway over his body as he stood before Jenna's laptop. When he had swept through the den in his tidying frenzy, the matte black case of her Lenovo ThinkPad peeking out from behind the overstuffed chair where she did her writing had caught his eye. From that second on, the idea slowly took form, and although he tried to ignore its insistence, the next step on his self-appointed road to insanity would not be disregarded. The outrage of Angela's shallow grave and the three unaccounted-for years made him almost irrationally furious.

"I'm sorry," he muttered to no one in particular. But he didn't mean it.

The metallic snitch of the case unzipping ripped through the house. Lucas twitched his head around, waiting for Jenna to step into the room and demand to know what he was doing. But all was silent, and now that he had committed the first violation, it was easier to continue. When the computer was plugged in and Microsoft Windows blinked colorfully on the screen, Lucas felt his stomach turn over with a kind of excitement that made him feel somehow wild. Alive. He was taking control.

An icon labeled Case Files hung inconsequentially in the lower left-hand corner of Jenna's desktop, and with his forefinger on the mouse pad, he carefully clicked it. A blue box labeled Password Required and a blank for typing it appeared.

Of course it would be locked with a password.

Lucas felt his conscience shudder. To strengthen his resolve, he reached into his pocket for Angela's ring and slipped it on his pinky. It pinched his finger, a dirty, dejected reminder of why he was doing something that Jenna might never forgive if she ever found out.

The cursor flickered at him in the blank, demanding a password. Not quite knowing how or where to begin, he started with the most obvious: Jenna's maiden name. Pecking at the keyboard, he typed RIVERS.

Incorrect Password.

It couldn't be that easy. Racking his brain for anything and everything that might be important to Jenna, he tried again.

PEONY, her favorite flower.

Their first telephone number, 729-0098.

BEOWULF, the name of their chocolate lab who had been hit by a car last summer. And then BEOWOLF because he wasn't sure if he had the spelling right.

GALAPAGOS, Jenna's dream vacation destination.

Incorrect Password mocked him over and over.

Lucas continued to type, allowing his

fingers to stumble in whatever direction they saw fit, though his options became slim and his determination wavered.

It was somewhere around the fifteenth try that Lucas realized with a start that he knew her password. It was a bit of a shocking thought — one that he pushed down and tried to ignore while he keyed in her mother's maiden name and the make and model of their first car. But the word that crept from the back of his mind now crouched in plain view and waited to be acknowledged. The more he tried to ignore it, the more it made itself known. It was on his lips.

Staring at the computer screen, Lucas gulped back a feeling that ached more than guilt. It was a rawness, a vulnerability that made him both ashamed of himself and angry at Jenna. What right had she to keep that name so close to her when they had agreed that it was best left unsaid?

His eyes clouded as he mouthed it, and when the blue box once again appeared, he tenderly, slowly typed it in: AUDREY.

Access Granted.

Lucas couldn't stand to read the documents in the house he shared with his wife. It seemed wrong somehow, as if the walls had ears, the lamps eyes, and they would whisper his transgression in an endless round of old-house creaks and sighs. But he printed off every page of his wife's files on Angela, and when the printer ran out of paper, he used the backs. Then he gathered the thick bundle and crammed it loose-leaf into an unused binder so that he could transport it to his office undetected.

The streets were painted ocher and gray when Lucas pulled into the parking lot of the medical clinic. Another evening spent at work, and Lucas sighed as he made his way through the darkening building. The place was beginning to feel like home, but not in a good way. Behind the four walls of his meticulously clean and organized personal office, Lucas felt trapped and claustrophobic. He didn't spend so much time at work by choice, but lately he practically lived in the medical clinic because his house with Jenna became less of a home with every passing week. When had everything begun to show cracks?

The binder hit his desk with a thud and Lucas slumped into his chair with the same discarded air. He put his forearms on the smooth cherrywood surface and leaned over with a sharp exhalation that betrayed just how hard his own transgression had hit him. This was just another sin to add to his steadily growing list. A wry smile teased the corner of his mouth. The perfect, dependable, stable Lucas Hudson was about to fall a little further from grace.

To get his bearings amid Jenna's lengthy notes, Lucas first did a quick survey from the beginning of the stack of papers to the end. He found that his wife had documented every meeting with Angela, from informal coffees to long sessions at her office. The initial report was the longest and most official-looking, complete with sections for Background, Assessment, Intervention, and Referrals. After that, things became a bit more sporadic, and her pages featured bulleted lists and single-paragraph summaries of conversations and interactions.

When the last of the pages had been riffled through, Lucas closed his eyes and pressed his knuckles against the blue-veined lids. As a doctor who took his own Hippocratic Oath very seriously, he wrestled with a sinking feeling of ethical suicide. But the ring still nipped above the knuckle of his pinky, and the pressure against his skin was enough to make him continue.

"Jim," he reminded himself. "Only references to Jim."

It helped a little that when Lucas started

to read the documents in earnest, his eyes automatically glossed over any personal information about the teenage Angela and lighted instead on every reference to her disreputable father. Lucas had no desire to dirty his hands in the mire that was Angela's private life; he just wanted to know more about Jim. Who was Jim Sparks? Who did he have ties to? Did he have a violent past? Was he capable of killing his daughter in cold blood and burying her beneath the hard floor of his dilapidated barn?

Before long, Lucas had used the erratic notations and occasional references about Angela's family situation to piece together a pretty grim picture of life in the Sparks home. He grabbed a new legal pad from the bottom drawer of his desk and began to scratch out random, hurried notes.

Some of the things that Lucas learned merely reinforced the rumors that he had heard ever since moving to Blackhawk. He wasn't surprised to discover that Angela's mother had died of breast cancer when her daughter was only four — Dee Sparks's brief but courageous battle with the disease was common knowledge. Nor was it shocking to read that Jim never remarried or fathered any children he would admit to besides Angela. But there were other insights that made Lucas's stomach clench.

A need for order in the crumbling chaos of his life caused Lucas to tear the top sheet off his notebook and crush it into a ball that he aimed nowhere in particular. Then, on a fresh sheet of paper, he created a column simply titled "Jim," and putting aside his emotions, began to jot down anything he considered important.

Single father.

Employed at a chicken processing plant — night shift.

Corporal in the Air National Guard.

Lucas shook his head at the last bit of information. Though he saw Jim in his uniform from time to time, it was always a little unbelievable that the same man who couldn't muster the energy to pull his trash can to the road on garbage day had maintained the rank of corporal in the Air National Guard. And it was even more implausible that he actually showed up at the 114th Fighter Wing in Sioux Falls, South Dakota, sober, on time, and in a clean and neatly pressed uniform every weekend he was scheduled for duty.

It didn't seem right that someone with Jim's position of responsibility and respect could also earn the final notation that Lucas wrote in his careful column.

Abusive.

True, Jenna's notes didn't specifically say that Jim abused his daughter, but it all came down to semantics as far as Lucas was concerned. The neglect that Jenna chronicled was more than enough evidence of the dead man's crime.

According to the pages fanned out across Lucas's desk, Jim had severely physically neglected Angela when she was a child. Inadequate food, clothing, and sanitation, as well as lack of supervision contributed much to the problems that Angela experienced in high school and beyond.

"Mr. Sparks cannot determine his daughter's needs because he lacks the knowledge and empathy for child rearing," Jenna wrote. "The home is unsanitary, Angela's personal hygiene has been neglected, and empty bottles of Black Velvet litter the kitchen and living room."

It was no secret that the cheap Canadian whiskey was Jim's drink of choice. Lucas could almost smell the sickly sweet scent that oozed from Jim's pores, and he added another bit of information to his list.

Alcoholic.

Staring at the word for a moment, he gave in to his own cautious prudence and reached to carefully pen a question mark behind the written accusation. As far as he knew, no one had ever proved that Jim was an alcoholic. Proof? The thought made Lucas grunt. What did he want to see? A test with a big, red *F*? He scribbled over the question mark with a heavy hand.

"Mr. Sparks's expectations are unrealistic," Jenna continued on another page. "He refuses to access local support systems, even on behalf of his daughter. Offers from neighbors to help him with Angela are ignored, and though I've tried on several occasions to convince him to apply for state-funded medical insurance, he refuses. Therefore, Angela does not get proper medical or dental care."

Lucas discovered that Jim had left his daughter alone for hours. Sometimes days. Angela recalled fending for herself as she lived off boxes of dry cereal and cans of generic pop with names like Yee-Haw and Dr. Thunder. And Angela admitted that things were only worse when Jim was around. Her father was harsh and denigrating, and he used every opportunity to reject both his daughter's presence and her needs. She was blamed for everything from bad weather to empty cupboards.

"Mr. Sparks uses Angela as a perpetual scapegoat. And because she attracts his blame, she is inattentive, uninvolved, and withdrawn. Her passivity at school and difficulty comprehending day-to-day work sometimes translate into feelings of anger and, according to her teachers, a desire to act out. She feels defenseless. She feels helpless and alone."

Beneath the typed paragraph, there was a single line, a late notation that Jenna had chosen to highlight in a band of bright yellow. Lucas read and reread her private speculation, wishing he could talk to her about her years-old assessment.

"Is Angela telling me everything?" Jenna wondered in writing. Lucas felt like he could hear the quiet rise and fall of her voice in the cryptic words. Then, "Is Jim more violent than his daughter is willing to let on?"

"Yes," Lucas wanted to say. "And in a matter of days, everyone will know."

It was little comfort.

8
MEG

Meg Painter didn't believe in gray. In her world, everything was either black or white, right or wrong, hot or cold. She was unapologetically all or none, and when Dylan walked away from her after his transformation in the Sutton High spring production, she turned her back on him and did everything in her power not to look over her shoulder. Brave intentions aside, her self-imposed exile proved weak and ineffective.

Although she struggled to leave her former best friend behind, Meg couldn't cure herself of him. She couldn't stop herself from falling all over again every time he entered a room. She couldn't stop herself from thinking about him in the quiet moment before she drifted into sleep, when her mind was still and soft, submissive to thoughts that she tried to repress all day long. And though it was tacitly understood that they were no longer what they had been

— contentedly inseparable, two halves of the same — Meg and Dylan continued to see each other all the time, especially when school started again in the fall and she had to pass him in the halls every day. If Meg could have excised the corner of her heart that seemed to beat for Dylan alone, she would have done it without pause. But ridding herself of the ache of his loss wasn't as simple as a sudden amputation.

The one small blessing that Meg could ascertain in the slow decay of her life as she knew it was that no one else seemed to notice that everything was not as it should be. Her days were more or less normal, though the space that Dylan had occupied felt dry and barren, cracked in the places where Meg had planted daydreams like a hopeful gardener. No one heard the echo of her loneliness against the walls of the chasm that marked what might have been. Least of all Dylan, who gave up on the girl who had played Celia soon enough and turned to Lisbeth, his beloved Rosalind. And then to some girl almost farcically named Candi. More specifically — as she liked to point out — Candi with an *i*.

In early September, when Jess started a band in his garage and asked Dylan to play bass, for some unfathomable reason he made sure that Meg was invited, too. Her place in the revels was ingenuous, but it felt cruel to Meg all the same.

"Do you play?" Jess had asked her one afternoon as they shot hoops in the cul-de-sac. The Painters had put up a basketball hoop on their side of the circle when Bennett turned ten and his father still had high hopes for his physical prowess. Not to be outdone, Jess's parents soon followed suit and erected an identical hoop on the opposite corner. The improvised basketball court was enormous, but it allowed for teams as big as the growing neighborhood could devise. Meg spent hours pounding a ball against the pavement, but Bennett never really used it. Conversely, Sarah never touched a basketball, but her brother, Jess, could be found most afternoons taking shot after shot. Meg learned to do the perfect layup from watching Jess.

"Basketball, BMX, Bloody Murder . . ." Jess continued, teasing. "I know you're athletic, Meg, but do you have an artistic side, too?"

"I played the recorder in third grade," she told him, straight-faced. "You should hear my rendition of 'Mary Had a Little Lamb.' "

Jess laughed and tossed her the ball.

Meg lined up behind a crooked, spray-painted free throw line and took her time measuring the angle. Dribbling a few times, she straightened and let the careful shot arc from the quick flow of her arms. Nothing but net.

"Though I'm sure your recorder skills are impressive, I don't think that's quite the sound we're going for."

"Too bad." Meg caught the rebound and bounced it back to Jess. "What are you going for?"

He grinned a lopsided smile that pulled one corner of his mouth into an attractive dimple. It caught Meg by surprise, but before she could marvel at the realization that Jess Langbroek was more man than child, he told her: "We're the original Sutton grunge band."

It was Meg's turn to laugh. "Cover tunes?" she asked. "Or will you write your own stuff?"

"All original, of course." He shot and the basketball slammed off the backboard and careened across the cement.

Meg chased it down, then spun on her heel and threw it back toward the hoop in a hard, fast curve. The ball rode the rim for a spin or two and tipped through the net. "We should be playing for money," she grumbled.

"You'd clean me out, Meglet," Jess joked, using a nickname that she hadn't heard in years. She was about to bite off some witty retort, but before she could, Jess snagged the rebound and threw the ball at her with more force than necessary. Even though she caught it, it thumped against her chest.

"Oh," she moaned, not bothering to disguise her good-natured sarcasm. "You're too tough for me, Jess, too manly. Where's Sarah?"

He seemed taken aback, but shrugged it off. "Dunno."

"Maybe I'll go see if she's around," Meg said, lobbing the ball back at him granny-style.

Jess watched her go, but as she neared the garage door, he called, "Where's Dylan?"

Meg lifted her hands, admitting she didn't know without uttering a word. Her gesture seemed casual, but the truth was that she didn't trust her voice not to betray how she felt about Dylan's growing absence.

"I thought you . . ." he cocked his head at her for a moment, and Meg was convinced she could see wheels spinning behind the cool watery blue of his eyes. "Nothing."

"Nothing?"

"Nah. Just come to practice tomorrow night. If you can't play an instrument, we'll try you on vocals." Jess began dribbling the ball, concentrating on the basketball hoop instead of Meg. "Do you smoke?"

"No."

"I'll get you a pack tomorrow. I like the husky smoker sound."

Meg flipped him the bird, and though he was watching his ball as it collided against the rim and recoiled from the net, he gestured right back at her. She opened her mouth to yell at him, but even at a distance, she could tell that he was smiling.

The next night, Meg didn't head over to the Langbroeks' garage until nearly an hour after the so-called music started. Mostly the sounds bleeding from beneath the far-from-airtight doors were comparable to some form of primitive torture — Meg could easily imagine giving up all her secrets if subjected to such tuneless nonsense for any amount of time. But she had told Jess that she would come. Sort of.

Whether or not she cared to admit it, Jess had nothing to do with Meg's decision to partake in the inaugural festivities of his little wannabe band. She knew that Dylan was there. She had heard the throaty rumble of his brother's pickup when Dylan was dropped off. His presence was more than enough reason for her to endure any off-key attempts at music, but not convincing enough to make her run across the cul-de-sac the moment the first withering note pierced the night.

When Meg did finally decide to grace the guys with her presence, she slipped into the garage unnoticed and stood for a few minutes with her back to the door, taking it all in. The group didn't have microphones, but a few of them had shoddy-looking amps that boasted long cables like the curling tails of fantastical creatures from some Dr. Seuss book. Dylan was one of the boys with an amp, and he sat straddling a short stepladder, one foot resting on the piece of equipment with a possessive air. His bass sported a crack in the side and a hand-me-down veneer, but he had the instrument spread across his knees almost lovingly. Every once in a while he plucked a single string, and the resonant hum of a low, deep note would pool like water beneath the cacophony of other instruments. Meg could feel the reverberation of it in her heart.

Tearing her eyes from him, Meg found Jess at the center of the space the guys had cleared between a tarp-covered car and the tangled row of Langbroek family bikes. He seemed to be tuning his acoustic guitar, the pick between his teeth as he tried to get each note just right. Meg doubted he had the faintest clue what he was doing.

The rest of the band seemed equally unqualified for the task before them. There was a drummer who appeared to be more interested in twirling his drumsticks than using them to encourage a steady beat into the din, and a guy with an electric guitar whose tongue peeked from between his clenched teeth as he struggled with chord after chord. A fifth member looked instrumentless, directionless, and completely clueless. All in all, Jess's band painted a very sorry picture in the musty garage, and Meg groped behind her back for the door handle and escape. It was just too much: too much noise and testosterone and striving. Too much uncertainty. She felt distinctly out of place.

But just as she was about to leave, Jess looked up and noticed her. The line etched across his forehead cleared and he said something, but Meg couldn't hear him over the ruckus. Reluctantly, she let go of the door and cupped an ear.

Jess turned to his band, using his arms to hush them. It took a few moments, but they eventually caught on, and in the ensuing silence Meg could feel the ripples of phantom sound waves like static in the air.

"You came," Jess said, breaking the blessed peace.

Meg pursed her lips and nodded once. "But I can't stay," she began, tipping her thumb over her shoulder as if the reason for her leave-taking stood just out of sight. "I've got . . . uh . . ."

"You can't go," Jess broke in. He glanced quickly at Dylan and said in a stage whisper, "Dylan needs you to focus, he's really screwing things up here."

"Uh-huh." Meg rolled her eyes and was momentarily thrilled to see Dylan do the same. His lips pulled into a desultory smile, but he didn't wink at her like he once would have.

"Come on," Jess urged. "Stay. I bought you smokes, just like I promised." He reached into the breast pocket of his button-down shirt and threw a pink-and-white pack of Virginia Slims at her.

Meg caught the little box in one hand but dropped it to the floor the moment it made contact with her palm. "I don't smoke girly cigarettes."

Jess tried to hide a smile, but Dylan grinned outright, only bothering to bring a concealing fist to his mouth when Meg glared at him.

"What?" Dylan said defensively when she didn't avert the icy insistence of her gaze.

"Don't laugh at me." She made each word hard and cold, a tiny pebble of anger that she aimed with lethal accuracy.

"I'm not . . ." but Dylan trailed off, incapable of defending himself.

"Oh, yes you are."

Jess split the taut moment by slipping his guitar strap over his head and crossing the cement floor to take Meg by the arm. One hand held his guitar by the neck, and the other hand cupped Meg's elbow. "Nobody's laughing at you," he said, steering her toward the center of the room. "You're . . ." he fumbled, "you're perfect, Meg. Always have been, always will be. There's a reason Dylan prefers your company to ours."

There was something left unsaid in the room, and Meg could feel the small bubble of shared tension tight against her chest. But just as quickly as she perceived it, the feeling dissipated, and she was left standing in the middle of the group with empty hands and a sour look on her face.

All at once she realized that the boys stood over her, taller, bigger, and older, and a prickle of unease raced across the surface of her skin. Out of habit, she looked to Dylan and was happy to see that he was already coming off the stepladder, swinging his leg down in a theatrical dismount that made it seem as if he straddled a horse instead of a paint-splattered tower of aluminum. To Meg, it seemed as if he was coming to her rescue.

"Don't tease her," Dylan said, reaching for Meg's other arm and holding on tight. "She bites. I know from experience."

The friction Meg felt burst and scattered, and within a few seconds she became aware that the guitarist was strumming the first three chords of "Free Fallin'."

"Can you play anything other than Tom Petty?" Jess bellowed, letting go of Meg so he could cuff the boy on the side of the head. But though his attention seemed immediately diverted, Meg felt the slow release of his fingers and understood in a moment of unanticipated clarity that he was reluctant to let go.

"You're pretty young for this crowd." Dylan's hot breath tickled Meg's ear as he led her to the corner where his amp crouched in wait. He didn't push her down, but she sank anyway, and sat looking up at Dylan with an uneven fringe of bangs falling in her eyes.

"Jess invited me," she said.

He glanced over at the older boy and

chewed his bottom lip in an uncharacteristic display of . . . concern? worry? thoughtfulness? Meg couldn't quite tell.

"Why?"

"I don't know," she spat. "He thought you wanted me around, I guess."

Dylan turned his gaze toward her and didn't say anything for a moment. "I do want you around," he managed eventually, but Meg could tell that he didn't mean it. Or, at least, he didn't mean it completely. She couldn't read his expression, but he stayed close to her, almost hovering, his stance bordering on protective.

"What happened?" Meg asked, surprising herself. The room was filling with noise again and she hoped that Dylan hadn't heard her, but he squatted down and began to fiddle with the dials on the amp where she sat. She shifted her legs to the side.

"What do you mean?" Dylan sounded nonchalant.

"Nothing."

"You asked what happened. With Jess?"

With us, Meg wanted to say, but she held her tongue and motioned instead to the bass that he had propped against the stepladder.

"Oh," the word seemed laced with disappointment. "It was my brother's. It cracked."

"Obviously."

"The strap peg pulled out and he dropped it on the kitchen floor," Dylan clarified. "He was never very good at playing it anyway."

"Are you?"

"No."

"Figure this will go anywhere?" Meg was asking about the band, but for some reason the question came out unnaturally high.

Dylan didn't seem to notice. "Of course not. It's just something to do." Then, out of the blue he said, "Do you remember when we met?"

"Last year. Fourth of July. Behind the raspberry bushes." Meg could still smell the candied-tartness of the berries and the sharp, warm tang of her own summer sweat. It was a sweet and sudden memory. She flushed.

Dylan completed the scene for her. "We were playing Ghost in the Graveyard." He had abandoned the dials and now crouched with his forearms on his legs, meeting Meg's eyes with a look so serious he demanded her full attention.

"We call it Bloody Murder," she said slowly. "What about it?"

"Remember how you were the best player? How you always knew where everyone was?"

Meg's brow darkened in warning. "Don't

you dare make fun of me —"

"I'm not," he insisted. "You were the best player. You did always know where everyone was. And I think it means you understand people."

She grunted.

"Come on. You knew that Sarah avoided the shadows because she was afraid of the dark, and that some kids wouldn't go near the trees or back by the fence where your dad cleans his pheasants after hunting."

She inched her knees imperceptibly closer to his.

"You're observant," Dylan admitted. "I don't think you have some sixth sense or anything, I just think that you have a good head on your shoulders and an ability to see things in people that others are too preoccupied to notice."

When a smile splintered the granite of her gaze, he smiled back.

"I'm right, aren't I?" he asked.

"I don't know. Can't say I've ever thought about it."

"Okay, I'll tell you then: I'm right."

"Fine. So what?"

The smile faded from Dylan's mouth. "Do you still have it?"

"What?"

"Your good sense? Your ability to see

things in people that others can't?"

Meg shrugged. "I don't know. Does it matter?"

"It might." Dylan looked over his shoulder, then stood up quickly, placing his hand on the amp beside Meg and brushing past her cheek as he moved. "Be careful around Jess," he whispered.

When Dylan strode off across the garage, Meg was left to ponder if she had heard him correctly. Maybe he had said: Be careful with Jess? Or: Be careful about Jess? But try as she might to ascertain why Dylan would say such an incomprehensible thing, by the time practice was officially over, nearly an hour later, she was no closer to determining his intent than she had been in the split second after he gave his cryptic warning.

It was a senseless caution, an utterly useless admonition, when Meg had known Jess practically her entire life. Jess was a year younger than Bennett, and just as much a brother to her as her own snarling excuse for a sibling. In fact, Jess was probably more of a brother to her. After all, before he outgrew such childish nonsense, he had spent many long evenings with her playing Kick the Can, Bloody Murder, and Capture the Flag. He had taught her to balance, align her elbow beneath the ball, focus on

173

the rim, and follow through for the perfect shot. Every once in a while, he even went so far as to throw a bag of microwave popcorn in for her and Sarah when she was spending the night. And, of course, there was the night he escorted Meg and Sarah to the secret cast party. Why did she need to be careful around Jess?

Meg decided to corner Dylan before he left and demand to know why he would say something so ridiculous. The cloak-and-dagger menace of his dark advice scared her a little — she didn't mean to draw parallels between her favorite childhood game and her trusted neighbor, but for the first time, the name Bloody Murder seemed unnecessarily gory, even obscene.

But she never got the chance to press Dylan for more information.

When everyone started packing up, Jess unplugged his acoustic guitar and went to sit on a lawn chair that he snagged from a nail in the garage wall. With the chaotic shriek of instruments stilled, he began to pluck out a tune so lovely and soulful that Meg found herself completely transfixed. The steel strings cried a little as Jess's fingers rose and fell in a quiet, unhurried step that reminded Meg of slow dancing. The melody was all stops and starts, back

174

and forth, cheek-to-cheek. In the moments between notes, Meg's heart ached with the agony of waiting.

No one else seemed to notice that Jess could play. That he could really play. It was unplugged, it wasn't rock and roll, and Meg was convinced that what she was listening to was a language that the other boys didn't understand and therefore didn't hear. She felt sorry for them.

After a long while, Jess's fingers stilled, and Meg came to so suddenly she felt a jolt of surprise. Blinking, she looked around and discovered that she was alone with Jess in the garage. He was staring at her. She remembered Dylan's words, but she wasn't afraid.

"I didn't know you could play like that," she said when the silence in the room demanded that she break it.

Jess ducked his head to hide the smile that bloomed there. "It's not that hard," he demurred. "I could teach you."

Meg laughed. "No thanks. I'd somehow manage to get my fingers twisted in the strings and end up losing a few tips. I hear you don't need them, but I kinda like them all the same." She tapped her fingertips together in proof of her affection for them.

Drumming his own fingers on the wooden

body of his guitar, Jess created a cascade like falling water drops. "Understandable," he said. Then he gently lowered the guitar to the floor of the garage and took a few hesitant steps toward Meg.

She didn't even realize that she was backing up until her bare calves skimmed the edge of a Rubbermaid storage box. It wasn't fear that made her retreat, but there was something in his approach, something in the intent of his eyes on hers that she couldn't begin to discern.

"I could walk you home," Jess offered.

That caught Meg off guard. "I live across the street."

"I know," he said quickly, shaking his head a little as if he hadn't really meant it at all. "I just . . ."

And in a rush of understanding, Meg knew. She was barely fifteen years old, inexperienced and naive in the ways of love, but looking at Jess's face was like peering into a mirror. The way she felt for Dylan was the way Jess Langbroek felt for her. It was all she could do to breathe around the furious storm of that thought. She wanted to say, You're almost eighteen. But she could tell that as far as he was concerned, that small truth was irrelevant.

Jess must have interpreted her silence as

an invitation because he edged close enough for Meg to see the sun-washed tips of his russet hair. His smile was shy when he reached for her hand, but timidity didn't stop him from holding her fingers lightly and lifting them as if to study each curve and line.

"I could walk you home," he said again.

Meg tipped her head because she couldn't bring herself to look at him anymore. On the floor their toes were almost touching; Jess's sandals looked enormous and impossibly grown-up next to the dirty gray canvas of her tattered sneakers. She wanted to cover the dingy arc of her tennis shoes, to take her fingers back from his grip, to hide.

But Jess wanted to find her. Before she could contemplate moving, she felt the touch of his forehead against hers. It was light, he barely brushed the surface of her skin, but it made her lift her face almost imperceptibly. When she did, he was there, his mouth against hers giving the faintest impression of warmth and nothing more. It was so soft, so subtle, it was almost as if he hadn't kissed her at all.

Later, Meg would wonder why she did it. Why she encouraged him when, before the moment his lips touched hers, it had never once occurred to her to think of Jess as anything other than her neighbor, her childhood friend's older brother. But no amount of future regret could erase the fact that when Jess pulled away Meg leaned into him, finding his mouth so that she could feel, really feel, what it was like to be kissed.

It was a spinning, tumbling, excruciatingly changing experience. It was like flying and falling all at once. It was gentle and perfect and sweet. She never wanted it to end and she couldn't wait for it to stop.

And it wasn't until she pulled away that Meg realized she had imagined it was Dylan she kissed.

9
LUCAS

Jenna didn't come home that night.

Or, if she did, Lucas wasn't aware of it. He slid between the cold sheets with a sickening sense of remorse, a knot of regret in his stomach that suspended him between relief at her absence and longing to hold her close, to know that his act of betrayal hadn't put the final nail in the coffin of their marriage. But she couldn't know, could she? Her computer was right where she had left it, and Lucas had shredded the printed sheets before he left his office. Somehow, knowing that he would get away with it didn't make him feel any better.

Sleep proved elusive. As he tossed and turned, he continued to slip over the invisible divide in the middle of their mattress where he was supposed to meet the soft resistance of Jenna's prostrate form, and he missed her even more than he had the first night that she was gone from his bed.

Gone. It was a hollow, echoless word that sank into the marrow of his bones with a heavy finality that made him feel achingly alone. She'll come back, he told himself. She's spending the night at Safe House. But the reminder, no matter how calm and logical, did not offer him any comfort.

Lucas stirred early in the morning, surprised that he had slept at all, and sat up straight in bed as if he had failed to keep vigil. Rubbing his face with his hands, he glanced into the hallway and found evidence of her early-morning return. Her clothes were abandoned in a tangled pile just outside the bathroom door, and the carpet was sprinkled with damp where she had walked to the attic stairs after her shower. He hadn't heard her?

Still shrugging off the final webs of a grasping sleep, Lucas made his way to the bathroom on unsteady legs. Though he was in a hurry, he went out of his way to step on the dark spots scattered across the floor where Jenna's feet had been. It was a ritual of sorts, a habit that Lucas had started weeks ago and couldn't shake no matter how ridiculous he felt as he touched his toes to the places where Jenna had walked. Sometimes, brushing against the water that had slid from her body was his only contact with her in a day that seemed longer for her absence.

He showered quickly and dressed without giving a moment's thought to the shirt and pants that he yanked off their respective hangers. Years of living with Jenna had taught him that if he hoped to see her at all during the week, his best bet was a few minutes over coffee before she left for work. The gurgle and hiss of the coffeemaker dripping a final cup into the pot whispered up the stairs, and Lucas knew that if he didn't get a move on, she'd leave without saying good-bye.

Taking the steps two at a time, he launched himself onto the main floor of their sprawling house and trotted noisily into the kitchen. Jenna was pouring coffee into a pink breast cancer awareness travel mug, her bag already slung over her shoulder and her shoes on.

"I didn't hear you come in last night," Lucas said. He sounded a little too cheerful, even to his own ears.

Jenna spun to greet him, her eyes brilliant with something he hadn't expected: joy. She was radiant, emanating a sort of tangible happiness that made Lucas want to hold her at arm's length and study every nuance of her shining face. He was startled into laughter, but Jenna put a finger to her smiling lips and shushed him.

"What?" he asked, crossing the room to embrace her.

"Shhhh . . ." She wiggled out of his grip and took him by the hand, leading him in the direction of the living room.

"What's going on?" Lucas whispered.

But she just shook her head.

When his cell phone vibrated at his hip, Lucas yanked it out of the holder with his free hand and studied the screen. Had it been anyone other than Alex, he would have ignored it altogether, but Jenna saw the screen, too, and nodded briefly.

"Take it," she whispered.

"Hey," Lucas said into the phone, wrinkling his forehead in the direction of his still-grinning wife. "What's up with you?" he mouthed to her.

"Lucas, we gotta talk," Alex barked.

But Lucas was barely listening.

Jenna winked at him as they stopped just behind the sagging plaid couch that sat smack-dab in the middle of their spacious front room. She put a finger to her lips again, then pointed over the back of the couch, indicating a pile of blankets and pillows that rose and fell in a silent, steady rhythm.

"Lucas? You there?" Alex questioned, his voice small and faraway as the phone slipped a little from Lucas's hand.

There was a woman on the couch.

She was buried beneath a heap of afghans that had been pulled all the way up to her chin. One hand had escaped the press of blankets and rested on the pillow beside her face. The white-blond sweep of her long hair half covered her cheek and the splay of her fingers with a smooth wave of soft curls. Her skin was tan, her lips still stained with yesterday's lipstick and parted slightly as she breathed.

Lucas took a step back.

"Are you listening to me?" Alex asked, raising his voice as if the connection was bad.

"Yeah," Lucas finally muttered.

"It's not her." The words came out in a rush, a sprint of excitement at sharing the news they had all waited for. "The dental records are not a match. The body isn't Angela."

"I know."

"What?"

"I know," Lucas repeated, forcing himself to speak around the numbness. His eyes flashed to his beaming wife, back to the still figure on the couch. "I know it's not Angela.

She's in my living room."

"What is she doing here?" Lucas demanded when Jenna dragged him back to the kitchen. He had all but hung up on Alex, insisting that the police chief keep his distance until Lucas could at least make a little sense of the situation. If Alex had his way, he would have jumped in the car in his boxers and driven to the Hudsons' house for an on-the-spot interrogation. But Lucas was insistent, and in the end, he won. Though he seriously doubted that Angela managed to sleep through the hushed ruckus of their discovery. It unsettled him, the thought of her lying on his couch, awake and listening. "What is Angela doing here?" he repeated, his voice tripping over the syllables of her name.

"Where else would she be?" Jenna seemed to think the question was ridiculous.

He stumbled. "I thought . . ."

"I know what you thought. You were wrong. If I were the type to say 'I told you so,' this would be the perfect time to break out a little victory dance." Jenna did an off-balance pirouette and grabbed her coffee off the counter with a triumphant sweep of her hand. Taking a sip, she sucked in her breath as if scalded. Lucas interpreted the

184

sound as reprimand.

"Where has she been? Why did she come back? How long is she going to stay?"

Jenna shrugged. "We've got lots of time to deal with the specifics. For now, all you need to know is that she showed up at my office last night. She heard about Jim and flew in from the West Coast."

"The West Coast?"

"Yup."

"But . . ."

"Tonight, okay? We'll talk about it tonight. I've got to go."

Lucas glanced back at the living room and shot his wife a desperate look. His mind was a snarl of shock and confusion, but there was one thing that he knew without a doubt. He did not want Angela Sparks staying under his roof. "Do you think it's a good idea for her to be here?" he asked. "I mean, in our house . . . She's a former client, after all."

"I want her here," Jenna whispered. She grabbed his arm and dragged him toward the mudroom attached to the kitchen. It was cool, and she pulled her coat off the hook beside the window and tugged it over her sweater and the strap of the bag she had crisscrossing her chest. "Look, she's going to be here awhile and that's just the way it has to be. Don't make her feel uncomfortable. You two haven't always had the best relationship."

You don't know the half of it, he thought. He wanted to say something in response, something keen and intelligent that would make her realize that having Angela in their house was not a good idea. Instead, one look at the fierce edge in Jenna's eye and he deflated as if her words were pinpricks; they pierced the core of his intention and all his careful plans leaked out. The only remnant of his former conviction was a stone of tepid resignation, a hard and bitter fragment that reminded him of the distance between them. It was still there in spite of her irrepressible delight at seeing Angela again after all these years.

"Okay," he said. "Fine."

"Just fine?" She groaned and reached over his shoulder for her car keys. "You're impossible. I can't figure you out."

"What do you mean?"

Rather than turning to leave, Jenna paused for an instant and looked at her husband. Really looked at him. Her eyes were clouded somehow, dark and unreadable beneath the fleeting thrill of having Angela in their home. Surprise rooted Lucas to the ground when she stood on tiptoe to kiss him full on the mouth. It was a fierce, selfish moment of contact, an intimate act that somehow felt analytical and detached. But Lucas leaned down anyway and tried to kiss her back even as she broke away from him and reached for the door.

"Jenna?" he called.

She glanced at him. "This is more than fine, Lucas. This is great. I've waited eight years for her to come back. Do you understand that? Eight years."

The door was half open when Lucas caught her from behind. She spun easily in his hands, her waist small and familiar and lovely beneath his fingers. Something inside Lucas had fractured — the fine, strong vein of his self-control — and he lifted her off the ground. Kissed her again. Soft and sweet. Long. A kiss on his terms.

Jenna swayed a little when he set her down, but Lucas kept his hand on the small of her back. She wouldn't meet his eyes, and she groped for the door handle with her head tilted toward their feet. Lucas kissed the top of her head once and let her go.

When Jenna pulled out of the driveway and disappeared from sight, Lucas realized that his face was all but pressed to the glass in the back door, his nose an inch from the pane, the cold outside radiating through the thin window and nipping his skin with the hint of winter to come. A wry smile teased his mouth, and he took a deep breath, blowing it all out against the window so that a circle of condensation formed on the glass. He fanned his fingers and touched them to the spot, crowning the memory of where Jenna had been with the five-point blessing of his hand.

"Jim hated it when I did that."

Lucas jerked around and saw Angela leaning against the doorframe between the kitchen and living room. There was a careless, almost condescending smirk on her face, and from the casual way she propped one foot against the thick molding, it was easy to imagine that she had been standing there for ages. With her rumpled hair, bare legs, and sleepy eyes, she was an impression of beauty wrought by reckless hands.

"Excuse me?" Lucas sputtered.

"The glass thing," she said, moving to stand in front of the sink. Her stride was graceful, unhurried; she seemed to move on tiptoe like a ballerina posing as an unexpected houseguest. "Where're your cups? Same place they always were?"

"Yeah, the cupboard to your right," Lucas responded automatically. "How long have you been standing there?"

Angela ignored the question and focused on filling a plastic cup with tap water. "Thanks for letting me crash on your couch last night," she said between gulps. When the glass was drained, she passed the back of her hand over her mouth and looked Lucas over from head to toe and back again.

"Sure," Lucas muttered belatedly. What did one say to a woman who melted into thin air, leaving nothing but broken hearts and questions in her path? "Uh, welcome home."

"This isn't home."

Angela hadn't changed much in the years of her absence. True, she was older. She had softened, filled out. At twenty-six she still could still pass for eighteen, but to Lucas's eyes she bore a lifetime of scars that seemed to hide just beneath the surface. Her arms were crossed in a stance of defensive aggression, the sort of passive position that betrayed her desire to both protect herself and also lash out if necessary. He remembered the posture well. It made Lucas tired just to look at her clinging to the balance as if her very life depended on making him believe she was tough.

With a sigh, he stepped up the two stairs that led back into the kitchen. Giving her wide berth, he opened the refrigerator and pretended to study its contents. But instead of respecting the tangible discomfort filling the space between them, Angela swept across the floor and came to stand beside him in the wan light of the refrigerator bulb.

"Got any soy milk?"

"No."

The quick exhale of her breath warmed Lucas's neck. He straightened up and tried to back away, bumping into her as he made a clumsy exit.

"Tofu? I like it scrambled with green peppers and soy sauce."

"Pardon me?"

Angela turned to wink at him. "I'll take that as a no. No soy milk, no tofu . . ." She bent to pull open the produce drawer and emerged triumphant with a slightly bruised apple. "I can make do with this. I won't even ask if it's organic."

"It's not."

"I said I wouldn't ask."

"It was implied."

Angela shut the refrigerator door with her hip and stood tall and willowy in the center of the kitchen, stately and imperious, and looking for all the world like she owned the place. She locked Lucas in a calculating gaze, her bottom lip tucked between her teeth so that a thin sliver of white shone between the curve of her lips with a sort of feline restraint. It wasn't until she started shining the apple on the fabric of her nightshirt that Lucas realized that she was wearing one of his shirts. One of his favorites. It had been hanging in the laundry room, freshly washed and waiting to be ironed. He wondered if he would have to burn it now.

"So," she said, taking her time to draw out the word. And then she didn't say anything more.

"So what?"

Her laughter was sudden and bright, like a burst of something cool and sweet on Lucas's tongue. Angela was utterly disarming. There was no way around it, and Lucas finally gave in to discomfort, embracing the awkwardness as a way to hold her at a distance. He wouldn't try for her. He wouldn't let himself be cowed. Shrugging a little as if to dislodge the clinging hazard of her presence, Lucas grabbed a fat loaf wrapped in wax paper from the counter behind him and cut a thick slab of banana bread. Life as normal, he told himself. Just act normal and maybe she'll buy it.

The polite thing to do was invite her to share the bread, but the first bite got lodged

191

in his throat. So, instead of speaking, Lucas held up the crumbly loaf in a halfhearted offering and hoped with all his might that his eyes wouldn't water in front of Angela.

Still smiling a secret smile, she shook her head, declining with a capricious flick of her attractively pointed chin. But instead of leaving the kitchen, as Lucas silently wished she would, Angela grabbed a chair from the table and poured herself into it in one fluid, elegant motion. She curled her legs beneath her and Lucas had to look at the ceiling to stop himself from noticing the long lines of her uncovered legs.

"I didn't know Jenna baked," Angela said.

"She doesn't," Lucas informed her. "This is from Minnie Van Egdom. She thinks that baked goods are better collateral than Medicare checks for her regular doctor's visits."

"And?"

Lucas chewed. "I'd take one of Minnie's breads over cash any day of the week. Would you like some?"

"Do you know what's in it?"

"I'm no professional, but I'm guessing bananas, eggs, flour . . ."

"Sugar, butter . . ." The tone of her voice made the ingredients sound downright poisonous.

"I hope so."

"I'll pass."

"Your loss."

They were quiet for a few moments as Lucas munched his breakfast and Angela turned the apple over and over in her hands. She studied it intently, appearing as if she was looking for just the perfect spot to taste the blushed, golden flesh. But from time to time she also glanced up at Lucas, and more than once she caught him looking at her. His eyes spun away, hers held firm.

"Ask me," she demanded after Lucas finished his hasty breakfast and rinsed his fingers beneath the kitchen faucet.

"Ask you what?"

Angela rolled her eyes and finally took a bite from the apple that she had been spinning through her hands. It split beneath the pearl line of her teeth and sprayed a fine drop of fruit juice against the corner of her mouth, where it hung like a jewel. She wiped it with the tip of her pinky. "Ask me why I'm here," she said, her mouth full.

Lucas sighed. "Why are you here?"

She swallowed, stood up.

His back stiffened, his fingers went numb. In the instant her feet found the floor, the clock wound back eight long years and an old but familiar sinking sensation burrowed

193

deep through his heart and beyond. Angela hadn't changed much at all in the time she was gone; her eyes were maybe a little harder, cold and shiny as they reflected his own torn face back to him. But she was still the same Angela; that much was apparent. And he thought she would do it again. That she would extend the double-edged gift of her so-called friendship.

Back then, Angela was a constant presence in their lives, an honorary Hudson. Jenna had been working with her for nearly four years running, and the young woman had impressed herself upon Jenna's heart and mind so completely that she broke all her own rules and let Angela in on a personal level. It was risky and draped with potential problems. But he'd let it go on, because Jenna's desire to help was so tangled in every bit of who she was that he feared tampering with any frayed edge of her motivation would unravel her from the inside out.

None of that changed the fact that he was acutely uncomfortable around Angela. As she got older, she radiated a kind of latent lust, an almost predatory sensuality that wafted off her like a heady perfume. Lucas was grateful every day that she never acted on the impulses that seemed as natural to her as breathing. At least, she never acted on them until a month before she disappeared.

Angela had been spending the odd night on their couch, crashing there when her father's drinking or some other unspeakable, and unspoken, reason drove her from home and into the only place in Blackhawk that she claimed she felt comfortable. When she arrived that night, Jenna and Lucas were on their way out the door for a bike ride. It was late to be out, but a vicious storm had raged for hours, and as the last remaining clouds scurried across the sky, they left stars like diamonds sparkling wet and lovely in their wake. It was breathtaking, and Lucas was just lacing up his tennis shoes when a frantic fall of knuckles against their back door split the night.

"We can't leave her alone," Jenna sighed after Angela was safe and settled in the living room.

"Why not?"

Jenna sighed. "Go ahead without me." She began to unzip her windbreaker, but Lucas put his hand on the pull and tugged it back up. He traced his wife's face with his fingertips and absorbed the weary downturn of her mouth. He tried to erase the frown with his thumbs, and when that didn't work, he sprinkled her lips with gentle kisses until she gave in and kissed him with equal relish. She pulled away and smiled at him for real.

"You'll stay with her?" Jenna asked. "Just this once? I know you've never been alone with her before, but hasn't she been a part of our lives for long enough? She's practically our daughter."

Jenna had never even hinted at that sort of sentiment before, and it caught Lucas off guard. He wanted to argue, but Jenna looked so happy and hopeful he said instead, "Fine, but promise me you'll be careful."

Jenna crossed her heart with a slender finger and slipped out the door before he could change his mind.

In the living room, Angela was watching a show on HGTV. A boyish-looking man with tousled hair held his pretty wife's hand and pointed out the arching soffits around the windows in a house that looked too expensive for a couple who couldn't be a day over twenty-five. But Lucas didn't watch the television. His eyes were riveted to Angela as she stared at the screen, her jaw soft and open in the sort of wistful admiration that made Lucas believe she had sighed in the moment before he stepped into the room.

She looked so fragile sitting there, with hope so naked and desperate in her beautiful face that Lucas almost put his hand to her shoulder in a show of solidarity. Almost.

He was glad that he didn't.

As soon as Angela caught sight of him in the room, her demeanor underwent a change so quick and complete, it was as if a switch was flipped in her psyche. A different person emerged and peered at him from beneath seductively lowered lashes.

She was eighteen years old, but she didn't seem like a high school senior. There was a wisdom in her eyes that made Lucas feel inept, as if this girl had experienced more in her short, sheltered lifetime than he could ever hope to know. And her maturity didn't end there. When she smiled at him, Lucas felt the full impact of her intentions as if she had whispered her desires in his ear. But with Angela, you never could tell. Was she teasing him? Or did she really want him in the way her eyes confessed?

Lucas was afraid of Angela. The realization overtook him as he sat opposite her in a rocking chair that creaked his fears in an uneven staccato of high-pitched cries. She was dangerous. She stood poised to topple his world with one flick of her perfectly shaped wrist. Nothing good could come from being alone with her, even for a half hour.

So he tried to make small talk. He tried to hold her at bay by talking about every inconsequential thing that popped uncensored into his mind. It worked until he asked the wrong question.

"So, who do you hang out with on weekends?"

"I don't really have friends," she murmured, somehow making the admission seem mysterious, desirable. Friends? Beauty queens fit for the pages of magazines don't trifle with such trivialities.

"Come on," Lucas pressed. "A girl like you? No friends? Boyfriends?"

Angela glanced at her lap, and when she looked up he couldn't tell if her gaze was teasing or insistent. She licked her lips. "It's complicated," she told him.

"Complicated?"

"I like things complicated," she admitted, trying out a slow smile and watching its effect on him. "Want to make it more interesting?"

It wasn't an invitation, not exactly, but there was no doubt in Lucas's mind that his wife's far-from-innocent protégée had just offered the unthinkable. But before he could unknot his tongue and react, Angela uncurled herself from the couch and crossed the room. She put her hands on the armrests of his rocking chair, over his forearms, trapping him. He could have flung her off in a second, tiny thing that she was, but he was shocked. Stunned. Immobile. And maybe, just maybe, a little bit curious.

For a second, Lucas didn't react at all. It was more than enough. She bent down, her hair falling over her shoulders, brushing his face while she studied his lips and avoided his eyes. Then her mouth was on his, hard and demanding, tasting of something unrecognizable but sweet.

If he kissed her back, it was only for a moment. And only because he was too astonished to stop it. Not, he tried to convince himself, because she was enticing.

When Lucas jerked away and stood up, Angela fell back with a laugh. He didn't know if she was laughing at him or at the situation. And he didn't know if the kiss was a game or if she meant it. He didn't want to know.

"Jenna will be home in a minute," he muttered.

Though he intended for his blatant reminder to snap Angela back to reality, to awaken the guilt that should be grinding away at her conscience, the girl was unfazed. She merely flopped back down on the couch, picked up the TV remote, and cranked up the volume. No word of explanation. The superior tilt of her profile made it seem to Lucas as if she had dismissed him.

Now, the same woman was in his kitchen, approaching him with the same half smile that was burned forever in his memory. And Lucas panicked. It wasn't that he found her irresistible, he had resisted her before. Sort of. But that night was ancient history, and much had happened in the time between. Lucas's mind flashed to Jenna and the startling kiss in the mudroom only minutes before Angela sauntered back into his life. It was worlds away from the tenderness of the encounter that had made a younger Angela's implicit offer easy to disregard. Much had changed.

Lucas was sure that Angela could sense that. That she could take one look at his face and see the hurt there, read the long, sad poem of their brokenness in the lines around his eyes and mouth. He knew what she was going to say, what she was going to do. And he didn't know how he would respond.

"Why am I here?" Angela repeated, stopping inches from his rigid chest.

He waited for her touch, for her hand

against him in an act of desire, maybe even longing. Something he hadn't felt from a woman in a very long time. But it didn't come. She cupped the apple below the curve of her neck, pulled it tight against the striking line of her collarbone as a talisman of sorts.

"I'm here because I'm going to clear my father's name," she whispered. She reached around him and dropped the uneaten apple in the trash can beneath the sink.

Then Angela walked out of the kitchen, hips swaying against Lucas's shirt, pulling the fabric tight, and he couldn't form a single coherent thought.

It was the last thing he'd ever expected her to say.

10
MEG

The day after the garage kiss, Jess drove up to the Painter house at a quarter to eight and gave the horn of his hand-me-down Citation a cheerful honk.

"What is Jess Langbroek doing in our driveway?" Meg's mother asked, peering between the slats of the Venetian blinds. One hand was on her hip and the other still clutched the spatula that she had used only a moment before to flip a neat row of pancakes on the long, flat griddle that straddled two elements of her expansive stove.

Meg's head jerked up in shock. She was at the counter, pretending to eat a bowl of Cheerios even though her mother was happily pouring rounds of sweet, fragrant batter for her dad and brother. Linda's from-scratch pancakes were world-famous, or at least Sutton-famous, but Meg wasn't in the mood. Her cereal was untouched, sparkling with a fine dusting of sugar and dotted with fat slices of banana that were slowly turning brown.

"Honey?" Linda prompted, and though her endearment could have been intended for any one of the members of her family, she looked directly at Meg. "Do you know why Jess is here?"

Meg cleared her throat and stirred the soggy Cheerios with her spoon. "I don't know, Mom. Maybe he's here for Bennett."

Bennett was only a year older than Jess, but the two hadn't been close since preschool, and he was already shaking his head no. Swallowing a mouthful of pancake, he shot Meg a meaningful glance. "Jess's not here for me," he said.

She shrank. How could he know? But he didn't know, he couldn't. Meg tried to glare at him, but mustering the appropriate disdain was beyond her. She had barely slept at all the night before, and the evidence of her insomnia was apparent beneath her eyes in pale blue smudges that shone like the memory of a faded bruise. No one had warned her that first kisses caused sleeplessness.

If her mother had noticed the dark lines, she hadn't pressed her, and was even gracious enough not to fuss when Meg turned down pancakes and opted for cold cereal instead. Though it wasn't like her daughter to turn down warm food, Linda's only interference was to lean over Meg's shoulder and slice half of a ripe banana onto the little O's.

But Jess's appearance in their driveway made Linda look at Meg again, her eyes flicking between the girl and the window as if the answer resided in the strained air between the two.

"Well, he's coming to the door," Linda said. She quickly tested a pancake, then flipped all four of them with a practiced twist of her wrist. Depositing the stack on a serving plate in front of her husband, she set the spatula on the counter. "Don't anyone get up now," she teased. "I'm not doing anything anyway. I'll get it."

Meg was grateful that her mother answered the door, because there was no way she could have trusted her legs if Linda had told her to go. The truth was, as ordinary, as commonplace as Jess's kiss had been, she had spent every minute of the night reliving it. Face turned into the pillow, she thrilled at the thought of her first kiss, remembering the scent of his cologne, the lay of his hand, the way her hair fell against their cheeks side by side. And then, as quickly as her chest danced with butterflies at the memory, her stomach filled with dread.

It should have been Dylan.

But there was no time to contemplate the back-and-forth of her excitement — the almost bittersweet sense of both joy and loss — because suddenly Linda walked into the kitchen, trailing Jess behind her like a puppy on a string.

"Look who's here for Meg," Linda said, her voice blithe and her eyebrows raised just a touch higher than their normal, attractive arch.

Meg's dad put down his fork and pushed away his empty plate. Sliding off the stool where he had been sitting, he said, "I don't know why you're here, Jess, but Linda will be insulted if you don't stay for a pancake."

"Thanks, Mr. Painter." Jess grinned, taking the stool without a moment's hesitation. "I won't stay long. I'm actually here to pick up Meg for school."

Meg was grateful that Bennett was between her and Jess so that she didn't have to watch him as he spread butter on a pair of pancakes and drizzled warm syrup all over them. But though she didn't have to look at Jess, she couldn't miss the fleeting glance that her dad darted at her mom. Something instant and wordless passed between them. Meg closed her eyes. She didn't want to know.

"School is only a few blocks away," Greg said. "Meg's been okay walking so far."

"Just under a mile," Jess corrected without malice. "And it's getting cold." He peered around Bennett and gave Meg a hopeful, conspiratorial smile.

Her lips pulled up faintly in reply, but she was too shy to meet his gaze for more than a second.

"Meg?" her father asked, giving her permission to answer for herself.

She gulped. "Okay."

The entire exchange was light, insignificant. But when Meg accepted Jess's offer, the room seemed to exhale, to acknowledge that Jess wasn't asking out of neighborly benevolence. Greg sighed a little, and Linda took Meg's bowl and emptied the sloppy contents into the sink, pushing the cereal into the garbage disposal with her spoon, each swipe deliberate but calm. Bennett was the only one who seemed unfazed, and he downed the last inch of his orange juice and left, his brooding shoulders hunched no more or less than they usually were.

"Well," Linda said, taking charge of her kitchen with the one drawn-out word. "Better hurry up. You two don't want to be late."

Half of a syrup-drenched pancake was already gone, but Jess grinned between bites and assured her that he would get Meg to school on time.

"It's not you I'm worried about," Linda told him. She wiped her hands on a dishcloth and wiggled her finger at Meg in summons. "Come on, hon. I have that note ready for you."

Meg had no idea what she was talking about, but she was happy to follow her mother to the front door where Linda dropped the subterfuge with a knowing chuckle. "Meg, Meg," she sighed, untangling a scarf from the collar of her favorite coat. It was a shapely tweed woven in browns and creams, and as Meg watched the pretty, matching scarf unravel in Linda's hands, she focused on the wide collar of the coat, the cut of the straight hem.

"You know," Linda said turning to wind the scarf around Meg's neck, "you're not allowed to date until you're sixteen."

Horrified, Meg sputtered mutely. "I — I'm not —"

Linda buttoned the corner of her mouth in a wry pucker. "I saw the way Jess looked at you. He's been looking at you like that for a long time, but I think you may have finally noticed it."

"For a long time?" Meg repeated.

"A year at least. Maybe years." Linda tilted her head thoughtfully. "He's a nice boy, Meg, but he's older than you."

"He doesn't feel older than me."

"He is."

"Two? Three years? That's not so much."

Linda pushed her breath out with a decisive nod. "It's irrelevant, really. What's done is done. If I told him to leave you alone he'd only want you more."

"Mom," Meg whispered, peeking over her shoulder to make sure that Jess hadn't finished his pancakes and wasn't standing behind her listening to every mortifying word. He was nowhere to be seen.

"Just a few rules," Linda continued, ignoring her daughter's obvious embarrassment. "You can't be alone with him. Group dates only. And no kissing."

Meg's heart sank so fast and so visibly that her mother laughed a soft laugh and pulled her close. "I'm teasing," she whispered. "Well, not about the date part. But now I know you kissed him."

"He kissed me," Meg amended, but then, remembering how she had leaned into Jess, she immediately felt guilty.

"It's okay," Linda assured her. "But promise me you'll be careful."

It was the second time that somebody had warned her to be careful with Jess Langbroek, and Meg resented the intrusion. "I can take care of myself," she told her mom.

"Oh, I know. Maybe I should be cautioning Jess."

"Leave Jess to me," Greg said, sneaking up behind his wife and daughter and enfolding the both of them in his ample arms.

"Dad," Meg complained, pushing away. "You guys are ridiculous. This is insane. I'm not a baby."

Greg pulled his wife close and rested his chin on the top of her head. She fit so perfectly against his chest that it seemed to Meg as if her mother's every contour was made for that spot alone. Closing his eyes to enjoy the feel of his wife against him, Greg mused as if Meg wasn't even in the room, "You know, I always thought Dylan would be the first in line. I have to admit this comes as a bit of a surprise. We were worried about the wrong boy."

At the mention of Dylan's name, Meg's skin bristled. All at once she felt hot and cold, restless and tired, as if the mere thought of him was enough to whip her into a discouraging frenzy of contradictions. She wondered if she would be feeling this way if Dylan had been the one to kiss her in the garage. If she would be standing here, stunned with the understanding that something had been lost, had slipped between her fingers before she had a chance to realize it was gone. But she couldn't stand to think like that, so she muttered, "Dad, please."

"Okay, okay," he relented. "I won't make fun of you anymore." Greg unwrapped himself from his wife and grabbed Meg by the shoulders to plant an earnest kiss on her forehead. "But whether you like it or not, you're still my baby."

It felt different to Meg, her dad's heartfelt blessing, and something inside her loosened and floated away as if she had come undone. She pulled the edges of her innocence tight around her and tried to tuck in the flapping corners, the places where Jess's kiss had begun to unfurl the bud of her youth like a flower forced to bloom in December. But it was no use.

When Jess bounded into the entryway and said it was time to go, she followed him resolutely, stepping out of her expectations with an air of determined acceptance. Life's not fair, her dad had once told her. She hadn't known what he meant until she saw Jess almost reach for her hand, almost, and then stop himself because her parents were watching. She realized that it wasn't fair because this could only end badly. It wasn't fair because she didn't want Jess; she wanted Dylan. It wasn't fair because she had grown up without warning, overnight.

It wasn't fair because nobody ever got what they wanted, no strings attached.

Since Meg was taking an accelerated humanities track, she had second-period English with Dylan, even though he was a junior and she a lowly sophomore. She usually looked forward to seeing him for at least a portion of her day, but after Jess gave her hand a little squeeze in the hallway and strode away after the first bell, she dreaded seeing Dylan with a sober shame that seemed ridiculously out of proportion to the harmless incident that had caused it. Though it had taken a combination of Jess's inexplicable, early-morning appearance on their doorstep and Meg's own thinly disguised discomfort for her parents to connect the dots between their daughter and her brand-new boyfriend, Meg knew that Dylan wouldn't need any such numbered puzzle to put the pieces together. He knew her. That was all there was to it.

She was right.

When she walked in to English a few

seconds before the bell, Meg couldn't stop herself from glancing across the row at Dylan. His desk was one seat behind hers and to the left, and while she hated herself for casting a furtive look in his direction, catching his eye was as much a part of her daily routine as brushing her teeth. It had to be done. She tried to be discreet, but Dylan was waiting for her silent hello, and the cool discretion she had practiced melted away under the force of his eyes. Her face was a study in regret; she could feel it.

I wanted it to be you, she thought, her words fine and insubstantial, evaporating even as she dared to think them.

Dylan blinked. Looked away.

It was the lack of expression that told Meg his cryptic caution in the garage had been about the very thing she had let happen.

She sat through English in a thickening fog of discontent. As her teacher droned on about pathetic fallacy in Shakespeare's tragedies, Meg's misplaced disgrace at kissing a boy she had never hoped to kiss slowly transformed into a tough knot of anger. She directed her fury at Dylan, and the list of his transgressions unwound to become long and multifaceted. From yanking her down behind the raspberry bush that summer to shooting her a pat glance that she was now convinced bordered on disdainful, Meg built a case against Dylan that was so solid, she determined to confront him the moment the bell rang.

Nearly an hour later it did, and she all but flew out of her seat, ready to race after him if he cut a hasty retreat. But Dylan was standing beside his desk, backpack clutched loosely in one hand and an indecipherable half smile on his face. The fact that he was waiting for her, that he was capable of pretending everything was okay, only made Meg more upset.

"Did you have a good time last night?" Dylan asked as their classmates filed out around them. His smile could only be interpreted as a smirk.

Meg glowered. "You left me there alone."

"Well, you seemed . . . entranced."

The tone of his voice was enough to make Meg long to hit him, but someone pushed past her just then and she stumbled a little. It was a small thing, but it jostled her willpower. "That's not fair," she managed.

"It's a free world, Meg." He started walking toward the back of the emptying classroom and she followed him as if they were connected, as if she had no choice but to fall in step.

"You were my friend," she whispered

through clenched teeth, her breath hissing over his shoulder.

Dylan stopped just outside the classroom door and tucked in close to the wall. The hallway pulsed with teenagers rushing to their next class, and though Meg should have felt conspicuous about their public tête-à-tête, it seemed as if they were utterly alone. No one existed for her but Dylan, and she pulled her bag against her chest to shield the place where he could inflict the most damage.

"What do you mean I *was* your friend?" Dylan asked.

Meg was surprised to see something real in his eyes, but it only fueled her fury. "Come on," she snorted. "Don't act all wounded. We fell apart and you know it."

The door that he had momentarily left open for her slammed closed; his look turned glassy, cool. "Meg, you're overreacting. I didn't take you for the soap opera sort, but this is downright *Days of Our Light. Guiding Lives*? Whatever."

She stared at him for a long moment, realizing for the first time that she had never stopped to imagine life without him. Dylan was family. He was friend, constant, brother. Any distance between them had felt like only that — a little space, amendable by a few steps, a bit of give and take. Until now. "You're overreacting," he said as if all that had transpired between them was only the variable relationship of the young, those who claimed a different friend every week, sometimes every day.

We're more than that, Meg wanted to say. But if he didn't already know that, it wouldn't do any good at all to tell him so.

"Okay," she said instead. Just okay, as if he had made good sense and she accepted it at face value. Okay, I understand your easy answer, your casual dismissal of me. Of us.

Though she believed it was what he wanted to hear, Dylan seemed taken aback by her compliance. Meg couldn't stand it; she couldn't take the dumb look on his face. Don't cheapen it, she thought. Don't cheapen everything.

"Okay what?" he asked hesitantly. "I don't know what okay means."

Suddenly she realized that for once she held the cards. This was going to end, and it was going to end on her terms. No matter how bad it hurt. Meg fit a tight smile on her face and dropped her backpack. She wasn't completely naive, and she knew that there was something in her, about her, that most guys found attractive. Might as well make use of it.

Meg took a deliberate step toward Dylan and put her arms around his neck, tucking herself against him. He went rigid for a second, then seemed to remember how it was done and slipped his arms around her, too.

She had hugged him before, but this felt different. He was a stranger, and she thrilled to the lingering hint of soap and the delicate trace of fabric softener woven through the cotton of his T-shirt. But this wasn't about falling for him all over again. It was about saying good-bye. When she couldn't hold him a second longer, she turned her face into his neck, brushing the tip of her nose against the hollow beneath his chin for a brief instant. Then she backed away, feeling his arms slide off her with what she hoped was reluctance, and picked up her bag.

"I'm going to be late for class," she said, trying to be flippant, light. "See you around, Dylan."

It was as good as good-bye.

11
LUCAS

"She did what?" Alex gave a long, low whistle that let Lucas know exactly what he thought of Angela's masked flirtations. "You're a stronger man than me."

"Give me a break," Lucas complained, trying to drive with his knee as he flicked on the blinker with his free hand. He swerved a little and reconsidered his stance on cell phones and driving. "You're crazy about your wife," he said, coming back to the conversation. "You'd never cheat on her."

Alex's laughter made Lucas pull the phone away from his ear. "You thought I was talking about cheating? I meant, I would have thrown her out of the house. Wearing my shirt like some B-movie seductress . . . Snuggling up to me when my wife is gone . . ."

Lucas recoiled at the exchange. Though no one knew about Angela's kiss all those years ago, he felt like his momentary lapse was written across his forehead. "She's . . . not well," Lucas said quietly. He hated talking to Alex on the phone; it was impossible to know if his friend was joking or serious. "And I wouldn't cheat either."

"I know," Alex assured him. "Wasn't insinuating that."

"You heading over to the house?"

"Yeah, Miss Sparks and I have a lot of catching up to do. One of the DCI guys is coming with me. I'd like an outsider's perspective on our little Lolita."

"She's not so little anymore," Lucas muttered.

Alex laughed. "All the same, I'm hoping to catch her a bit off guard."

"It's not like you to use intimidation techniques."

"I've never investigated a homicide before."

And there it was. The undeniable truth. The body in the barn wasn't Angela Sparks. Lucas thought about his scrawled list, his carefully documented allegations against Jim. He mentally added one word: murderer. The only question now was, who? Who? Lucas's heart banged an extra beat against his chest at the implications of Angela's reappearance. He touched his palm to the outside of his pocket and felt the loop of the ring hiding there. Maybe it wasn't Angela's. Maybe it was *hers.* But he couldn't think about that right now.

"Look, I gotta go. I'm sitting in the parking lot and if I don't get moving I'm going to be late."

"Don't let Mandy catch you doing that now."

"Nope."

"Keep me updated."

"Will do."

Alex had never held with formal greetings or farewells, and Lucas clicked his phone shut without saying good-bye. He slid it into the leather case at his waist, wrestling with the wish that he had never called Alex at all. Instead of making him feel better, his friend had only compounded his confusion.

Once in the office, a quick glance at Mandy told Lucas that she was in one of her effervescent moods. More than that, she was poised to kid around, to rib him about walking in the door late again, even if it was only by a minute or two. Her smile was impish and dimpled on one side, and though it was a source of no-strings-attached joy in Lucas's life, he didn't hesitate this morning to wipe it off her face with a gruff hello that left no room for cheerful banter.

"Uh, hi, Dr. Hudson," Mandy said, a

blank look quickly replacing the lively sparkle that had greeted him. "Your first appointment is already here. Mrs. Van Egdom. I put her in room four."

Lucas took the proffered file but didn't even stop to glance at it. "More banana bread?" he quipped, feeling guilty for dampening her sunny humor. But instead of sounding lighthearted and funny, his comment came off just plain mean. Mandy seemed shocked, but Lucas was too weary to defend himself, so he slunk away to his office without another word.

Shrugging off his jacket, he tossed it over the back of his desk chair. His lab coat was hanging dejectedly from a hook on the back of his office door, and Lucas animated the crisp, white fabric by thrusting his arms into the sleeves. His stethoscope coiled around his neck like an aged pet settling into a beloved position close to his heart, and the digital watch in the pocket of his coat fit snug and perfect around his left wrist. The transformation was quick and complete. Suddenly Lucas felt ancient, as if he had been doing this for centuries instead of a mere decade.

The body in the barn wasn't Angela.

The truth was a hot stone in the pit of Lucas's stomach.

There were patients waiting for him, but Lucas didn't care. He bent over his desk and flicked the computer mouse so that his monitor sprang to life. Clicking on the Internet icon, he quickly found a search engine and typed: missing women in Iowa. More than 43 million results. His chest seized. What had Alex said? The time range could be anywhere between five and ten years? Lucas created a custom range for his search, and the results dropped to about 900,000. The first hit was a forum. Melissa Anne. Crystal. Andrea. Regina Sue. Missy. Their names went on and on.

Woman reported missing. Described as white, 5 foot 3, 120 pounds, with brown eyes and light brown hair. Last seen wearing blue jeans, a white tank top, and leather sandals.

Missing woman. Blond hair, blue eyes. Approximately five and a half feet tall. Last seen exiting Dahl's Foods on Ingersoll Avenue.

It has been one year since a Bettendorf, Iowa, woman went missing, and her family is still searching for answers about her disappearance.

Lucas pressed his fists against his closed eyes until fireworks sparked behind his eyelids. There were so many of them. So very many missing women. And if the woman buried beneath Jim's body wasn't Angela, who was she?

The morning dragged for Lucas, and though he longed for a reprieve, for a call from Jenna, Alex, anyone, to lighten the heaviness of his day, none came. People circled in and out of his office, and yet he descended into a loneliness that stretched as long and far and empty as a world without end. Even his moment with Jenna — her stolen kiss, and his — wasn't enough to make him forget the long lists of women. The way their stories ended mid-sentence with nothing more than a smudge of ink and a hundred questions.

By the time lunch rolled around, Lucas was so agitated, he decided to make a meal out of leftovers from the refrigerator in the lab. He was too shaken up to tiptoe around conversation at Blackhawk's only café, and too rattled to go home, in case Angela was still lounging on the couch looking all sexy and disheveled in his favorite shirt. Thankfully, behind a half-empty box of influenza immunizations, he unearthed an everything bagel and a tub of I Can't Believe It's Not Butter!. Better than nothing, even if the bagel was stale.

Mandy met him on the way back to his office. She was wearing a red, belted jacket that seemed incongruously stylish paired with her baby-blue scrubs and sturdy, white vinyl shoes. Fashionable or not, Lucas couldn't help but love her, because her lips were upturned in a hesitant smirk that told him she had already forgiven his earlier snappishness. Though she didn't say the words, everything about her demeanor asked, Are we okay? His smile in response was dim but unmistakable.

"Staying for lunch?" Mandy indicated the bagel with a tip of her head.

"I've got lots of paperwork," he lied. "Just lock the door behind you."

"Want me to pick something up?"

"When I have this delectable thing?" He tapped the edge of the bagel on the tub of margarine. It made a hollow, bopping sound that proved just how old it was.

"Yum." Mandy arched her eyebrows. "Too bad there's not two."

"I'd share."

"No thanks."

"Your loss."

"Mm-hmm." Mandy slipped the strap of her purse over her shoulder and turned to go. "I'll be quick."

"You've got an hour; don't rush."

She laughed a little. "If I didn't know better I'd think you want a little alone time, Dr. Hudson."

He waved her out the door with a sweep of his hand and lumbered to his office like the old man he was convinced he was. The front door bumped closed and then he heard the dull click of Mandy's key turning the dead bolt. Silence. Peace. Solitude. Lucas sank into his chair and dropped his forehead against his desk. It was hard and cool. Somehow the clean line of the wood against his brow was soothing. But in the quiet, his mind began a frantic race in a dozen different directions.

Before he could sort out a single trail of thought and follow it, Lucas was startled by the sound of a key in the lock and the front door being opened. He sat up quickly, took a steadying breath and called, "Forget something?"

Mandy didn't answer.

"In case you've changed your mind, I decided not to share my bagel," he said a little louder.

The carpet in the reception room muffled the sound of footsteps, but Lucas could tell that Mandy was still on her way to his office. He resisted the urge to roll his eyes and pushed back from his desk to meet her at the door. It had to be her car. Dead battery? Flat tire? He wasn't in the mood to play mechanic, but the rules of chivalry required his compliance.

"FYI, I haven't changed a tire since college," Lucas threw over his shoulder, snatching his coat from the back of his chair.

"I don't want your bagel, and if I'm supposed to be impressed by your lack of tire-changing skills, I'm not." Angela materialized in his doorframe with all the audacity of a guest who knew she was unwanted but decided to come anyway.

All Lucas could do was stare.

"Nice office," she commented, raking her eyes over the bare walls of his dungeonlike space. The insincerity in her tone was completely unmasked.

"What are you doing here?" Lucas demanded, finding his voice.

"Oh" — Angela fanned her fingers in the direction of the front door — "the nurse in the red coat let me in. She remembered me. Probably figured we have a lot of catching up to do."

"That's not what I asked."

For the first time since she appeared outside his office, Angela looked directly at Lucas. "You don't have to be so defensive. I brought you lunch."

All at once he noticed the greasy paper bag in her hand and caught a whiff of what could only be kung pao chicken. It's probably poisoned, he thought. But his mouth watered all the same.

Angela must have interpreted his silence as permission to enter, because she suddenly swept into the room, carrying with her an air of entitlement that mingled with the cloying scent of her perfume and the spicy tang of takeout Chinese. "Don't worry about me," she said, dropping the paper bag on his neat desk. "I'll find myself a place to sit."

Lucas felt a twinge of guilt as he watched her lift a stack of medical journals off the only other chair in the room. His own padded, ergonomically correct chair was a throne compared to the rusted, folding contraption that housed his extra junk, and he knew that he should offer it to her. It would be the gentlemanly thing to do. But he couldn't move. Her startling presence in his office rooted him to the ground. What had Mandy been thinking? Why on earth had she let Angela in? Not even a word of warning . . . Angela could be very convincing, but Lucas made a mental note to have a serious talk with his reckless nurse.

The metallic screech of the folding chair

brought Lucas back to the moment. Angela pulled up across from him and reached for the bag as if she intended to serve a fast-food picnic right there on his paper-littered desk. Lucas was too stunned to protest, and accepted a carton of something hot and aromatic when she offered it to him.

"I got kung pao chicken and moo goo gai pan," she said. "I was going to let you pick, but I want the moo goo."

"Moo goo? I thought you only ate healthy food."

"It's vegetarian."

"It's from the Golden Dragon." His grimace betrayed the questionable reputation of the greasy dive.

Angela's eyes flashed to his. "You're not complaining, are you? Because I could always leave you with your bagel if you prefer."

Lucas blinked at her. Then he shifted his attention to the bagel and scraped it into the garbage can with one fluid motion. He added the tub of margarine for good measure.

"A thank-you would be nice."

He rolled his eyes. "Thank you."

"I only want your gratitude if it's sincere," Angela told him icily. One eyebrow was arched in threat, and Lucas imagined she could loose arrows from her steely green gaze. It was a good thing she couldn't; he would have been six feet under in seconds.

It couldn't be helped. The laughter he tried to contain erupted in a sudden, unattractive snort. At first he tried to quell it, but when he saw the corner of Angela's hard-set mouth tremble a little, he burst out laughing. Lucas watched as she covered her lips with a shapely, manicured hand, hiding the grin that she didn't want him to see. But though she didn't join in, her eyes danced above the white-tipped points of her square-cut nails.

"I'm sorry," Lucas sighed when the strange fit passed. "This is just . . ."

"Weird?" Angela offered. "Awkward? Unexpected?"

"All of the above and more," Lucas admitted. "And it's completely unprecedented. I don't know what to do with you, Angela Sparks."

"I go by my mother's maiden name now," she said. "I'm Angela Webb."

"That would explain why we never found you."

She stared at him. "I didn't realize you looked."

It seemed like an innocent comment, but it inverted Lucas's mood in an instant. He glared at her. "Are you kidding me? No letter, no call, no explanation? We thought you were dead."

"As you can see, I wasn't. I'm not."

Lucas leveled a finger of accusation at her. "It nearly killed Jenna when you left. You were like a daughter to her."

"She's not old enough to be my mother," Angela whispered into her lap.

"It doesn't matter. She loved you like a daughter, and you just disappeared into thin air."

"I'm sorry."

The apology sounded sincere, but once it was voiced, Lucas knew that it was not enough. It would never be enough. He doubted that Angela could ever make up for the agony that she had caused. All the sleepless nights, misplaced blame, tormenting questions that always ended in what if? Lucas couldn't begin to imagine how different his life would be if Angela had not run away and broken his wife's heart.

"You should apologize to Jenna, not to me."

He pushed a heavy breath between his teeth. It would be cathartic to skewer her here and now, without Jenna's steadying presence to remind him that Angela was a scarred woman, fragile. She didn't seem

229

fragile, she rarely had, but as much as he wanted to accuse her of all the things that had gone wrong after she left, he wouldn't let himself. He still had some self-control. So, instead of laying into Angela, Lucas laid his hand palm up on the desk. "Got a fork?" he asked, forcing himself to change the subject.

"Just chopsticks." Angela produced a pair wrapped in white paper and attempted a crooked, placatory smirk. "You still know how to use chopsticks, right?"

Lucas couldn't stop the sad smile that sprang to his lips. The truth was, he had taught her to use chopsticks, and the bittersweet reminder unearthed a vault of buried memories. Thankfully, it was a fond recollection, one of the only pure, unadulterated moments between the three of them. Before Angela grew up too quickly and began to use her God-given assets to manipulate, there had been times worth remembering. They had been like a family. An unconventional family, for sure. But weren't they all?

Looking at her as she sat with her face downturned, Lucas had to remind himself that Angela was a victim. As much as he wanted to vilify her, he had to admit that her life overflowed with a sort of sorrow that he couldn't begin to comprehend. The young woman who had giggled at his kitchen table as she struggled with a pair of cheap, unwieldy chopsticks that left miniature splinters in her soft hands was the same woman who was across from him now. Flaws, faults, foibles, and all.

He steadied himself and reached for the chopsticks. "I think I still remember how to do it."

But the last time Lucas and Jenna had made the trek to the Golden Dragon — the nearest Chinese restaurant to cloistered little Blackhawk — was a few months before Jenna decided they needed a separation. In the time since then, Lucas's right hand had all but forgotten how to loosely hold the willowy sticks, and in the end he had to forage around the reception desk until he found a plastic spork to eat his kung pao chicken.

Angela, brandishing the chopsticks like a pro, was gracious enough not to say a word.

It was only after they'd eaten in silence for a few minutes that Lucas broke the stillness. "I have a few questions for you," he began. Angela tensed visibly, but before she could argue, he continued, "I'm sorry, but you owe me that at least. I'm not taking no for an answer."

She swallowed and reached for the bottle

of water that she had taken out of her purse. Gulping half of the liquid, she was finally able to look him in the eye. "Three," she said without explanation.

"Excuse me?"

"Like three wishes. I'll grant you three questions. Freebies."

Lucas smiled. "And then what? I have to pay?"

Angela lifted a shoulder in coy nonchalance.

"Okay, I can deal with that." Lucas took another bite and chewed thoughtfully as he formulated his queries. If she was going to play games, he'd have to be careful what he asked. "I know why you left," he mused. "Or at least, I think I do. So I guess my first question is, Where have you been?"

"California."

When she didn't elaborate, he tilted his head in annoyance.

"Okay, okay. Sob story. Here it comes."

Lucas nodded in encouragement.

"I left when Jim got drunk one night and threw a bottle of whiskey at my head. At the last second I moved and the glass smashed into the wall behind me. I found a shard in my cheek." Her eyes went blank for a minute. "The blood ran down my jawbone and dripped on my T-shirt. I had blood on my shirt like splotches of paint."

He didn't dare to push her, even when she paused so long that he wondered if she'd be able to finish her story.

"You know, I could feel that bottle brush past my head."

Lucas could tell that the memory was hard to relive, and he was tempted to give her an out, to let her know she could stop. But he had to know.

When she'd gathered herself enough to go on, Angela said, "That was the last straw for me. I packed a duffel bag that night and hitched a ride across the country."

"You hitched? You were eighteen years old!"

She flattened him with a scathing look. "What are you, my dad?"

The barbed irony of her disguised accusation wasn't lost on Lucas, and he shook his head mutely.

"If you want me to answer your questions, you'd better learn to shut up."

He glared at her, but ducked his head and filled his mouth with more rice, hoping it would help him to stop adding commentary to her story.

"So I got a ride with some trucker who was on his way to Coeur d'Alene. Don't worry," she assured him with a patronizing shake of her head. "He was a new grandpa who said I reminded him of his daughter before she got married. The guy was a saint. Drove me as far as Idaho and then hooked me up with a friend of his who was doing a leg to L.A."

Lucas didn't realize his spoon was suspended in midair until a chunk of saucy brown chicken plopped on his desk.

"I didn't want to go to Hollywood," Angela said. "So he dropped me off near this fantastic little town north of the So Cal madness. San Luis Obispo? Ever heard of it?"

Her voice was flecked with pride and Lucas could tell that she was besotted with her newfound home. There was a certain satisfaction in her demeanor, an obvious pleasure that bordered on delight. "No," he said, wishing he could say yes. "But it sounds great. I'd like to ask you what you do there and how you like it, but those questions don't factor into my allotted three."

Angela grinned. "I was going to tell you those things anyway. I'm a manager of a coffee shop on the boardwalk. And I love it."

"Sounds like a good job." Lucas smiled.

"It is."

"And . . ."

"Do I like it there?"

He nodded, even though the answer was obvious.

"I love it." Her joy was bright and sudden, so palpable in the dreary enclosure of his dark office that Lucas felt a quick and unexpected rush of happiness for her. "It's home," she mused. "More home than Blackhawk has ever been to me."

Lucas nodded as if he understood.

Angela twirled her chopsticks in the remnants of her meal. "You have two more questions," she prompted.

"I asked you in the kitchen why you were here, but now I want to know why you said what you did. Why do you want to clear your father's name after everything he did to you?"

Angela sighed. "I knew you were going to ask that. It's complicated, Lucas. Things change. People change. You know that. You've got to know that."

I do, he thought. Better than you realize.

"I called Jim after I had been gone a couple years. I was so angry at him when I left, but in San Luis I found a good community . . . I got some counseling . . . My counselor suggested I make contact, so I did."

"That was . . ."

"Dumb."

"I was going to say brave."

"Maybe it was a bit of both."

Lucas gave up on his rice and crammed down the top of the wax-coated container. Shoving it away, he leaned his forearms on the desk and asked with some trepidation: "How did he respond?"

"He didn't at first." Angela looked at the bite she had poised in the air, and then dropped it as if she had suddenly lost her appetite and abandoned her meal, too. "He didn't say anything for so long that I almost hung up. But then I heard him whisper, 'Where are you?' I thought at first that he wanted to know because he was going to hop on the next plane to come and kill me. But his voice didn't sound like that."

Lucas didn't even need to articulate the question that was on the tip of his tongue.

"He sounded . . . desperate?" Angela searched for the right word. "I don't know, I have never really heard Jim sound like that before."

"So you . . ."

"Hung up."

"Of course."

"I called back a few days later. I didn't tell him where I was, but I let him know that I was okay." Angela paused, remembering. "The thing that really blew me away was that he actually seemed to care. He was concerned, in his own way."

Lucas hadn't expected to hear that about Jim, and it rattled the seedy bio that he was carefully constructing around his would-be cold-blooded killer. But before he could contemplate the implications, Angela continued.

"About a year after I first called him, I trusted him enough to tell him where I was."

"You do realize that he probably had caller ID and knew where you were all along."

Angela shrugged. "That's why I trusted him. I'm sure he knew, but he let me call all the shots. He never phoned me or tried to contact me in any way until I invited him to."

"So, what? You two just patched things up and had a peachy long-distance relationship?"

She narrowed her eyes. "Hardly. Sometimes I'd call and he'd be so drunk I could barely make out a word. But other times he'd be a few drinks from the edge and he'd talk to me. Really talk. He'd tell me about my mother or his time overseas . . . He had a hard life. That doesn't excuse his actions, but it does explain them."

Leaning back in his seat, Lucas scoffed, "I don't want excuses or explanations. I want to know who he buried under the floor of his barn. I want to know who he killed."

"No one," Angela growled. Lucas was shocked by the vehemence behind her defense. "Jim didn't kill anyone. The only person he wanted to hurt was himself. I just happened to be underfoot. My pain was peripheral."

"I can't believe you're saying this."

"Don't judge me, Lucas Hudson. You didn't know him."

"Angela, I —"

"You didn't know him. Do you know that he sent me most of his paycheck every month after we started talking again? That it was one small way he could see to make amends? Do you realize that he had no one? That he was completely alone in the world except for a daughter who would only allow him a weekly, ten-minute phone call? Do you know that he called me the night he killed himself to say good-bye?" She was starting to breathe heavily, and she swiped the heels of her hands against the wetness that dampened her cheekbones. "Can you imagine what it felt like to answer the phone and hear him say that? To know that I was two thousand miles away and there was nothing I could do to stop it?"

"You could have —"

"What? Called you? I'm sure you would have been a big help."

"But what about —"

"The body? I don't know who she is, but I do know that Jim had nothing to do with her death. I'm going to prove it."

And before Lucas could lift a hand to stop her, Angela surged out her chair and all but ran out his office door. He sat dumbfounded, watching the spot where she had disappeared and fighting back a deep and inexplicable longing to follow.

It wasn't until she was long gone that he realized he had only asked her two questions.

12
MEG

Meg learned in physics class that an object in motion will remain in motion until an external force is applied to it. Though Newton's indisputable law was hardly rocket science, copying down those words in her spiral-bound notebook was a moment of sudden clarity for Meg, a moment of understanding that thrust the beginning of her high school experience into the spotlight, where she could probe and dissect it. After only a few moments of self-evaluation, she was convinced that her life was all the proof Newton could ever need.

When it came to Jess Langbroek, she was a girl in motion, and no external force dared to apply itself to her relationship with the respected, older, and infinitely more mature young man. It was out of character, but Meg felt like a leaf in the wake of his charming esteem, for everywhere she went, she was swept along in whatever tide of admiration carried him from day to day and week to week.

It wasn't entirely unwelcome. Being with Jess had its share of perks, and when Meg was willing to be honest with herself, she could admit that loving him in her own platonic way held a certain undeniable joy, like waking to the soft sunshine of a new day. It was constant, expected, maybe even easy to overlook, but when she took the time to turn her face toward his light, it was comforting and warm. He adored her. Who wouldn't want to bask in such devotion?

But none of that stopped her from yearning for Dylan.

Unbelievably, as the year went on, Meg's feelings for Dylan didn't lessen. Those deep-rooted, tall-standing oaks of emotion that were planted when she was nothing but a little girl only flourished in the darkness where she hid them beneath reckless inattention. She ignored them and they grew to alarming proportions. There was nothing for her to do but live with a soul divided: agonized that Jess held her hand but not her heart, and equally unsettled that the man who could own her with a touch never lifted so much as a finger in her direction.

As Jess prepped for graduation at the end of Meg's sophomore year, she anticipated his eventual departure for college with a sort of mixed excitement. He was an indelible part of her life, and she knew that she would miss him with an ache that would not be easily relieved. But freedom was like a cool breeze on her cheek, the softest whisper of a storm to come, and she welcomed it. She knew that after the rain everything was fresh, new. What she didn't know was that Jess's plans were not her own.

"You'll miss me when I'm gone," he told her one night when they were studying together. He was sprawled out on the couch in the Painters' living room and Meg sat on the floor beside him, surrounded by books and pillows.

"Oh, I know," she admitted, flipping a few pages in *The Scarlet Letter* and deciding she'd better read, not just skim. Her attention was elsewhere, and she didn't realize that his statement was anything more than the subtlest of teasing.

"I mean it," Jess said, sitting up straighter. "I'm going to miss you. You'll miss me, too, right?"

It was the hint of unease in his voice that made her look up, and when she did, he caught her face in his hands.

"Right?" he persisted.

"Of course." Meg peeked out of the

corner of her eye to make sure that her parents weren't coming out of the kitchen. Though the "no dating until sixteen" ban had expired, Meg felt awkward flaunting her relationship in front of her mom and dad.

"Are you going to miss me or not? You were slow to answer," Jess taunted her.

"No, I wasn't." She tried to pull away, but Jess wouldn't let go. Still cradling her face, he ignored her frantic glances toward the kitchen and laid a tender kiss on her forehead. Then he brushed the tip of her nose, each cheek in turn, her mouth.

Meg sprung back as if stung. "My parents are in the other room," she hissed. "Knock it off."

Jess grinned, but he let go of her and slumped back against the cushions. "They love me," he cooed. "I could take you upstairs right now and they'd let me go."

"Whatever." Hoping to turn his attention to other things, Meg reached out and pinched the soft spot behind his knee, twisting her fingers a bit as she did so.

"Ah-h-h!" Jess bent at the waist and pried her hand away. "You little minx. You troublemaker. You tease. I can't believe you just did that to me."

"I'll do it again if I need to," she said, flipping her hair over her shoulder with a haughty flick of her wrist. But she had to tuck the inside of her lip between her teeth to stop herself from smiling at him.

"What am I going to do with you?"

"You won't have to worry about it for much longer," she assured him. "School will be out in a few weeks and then summer will fly by. You'll be college bound in no time."

"That's what I'm afraid of."

"Big school, big scholarship . . . Everyone has big plans for you."

"Big deal," he murmured, sounding sad.

She yielded then, and laid her head in his lap to let him know that she was still his. At least for now. If college life for Jess proved to be anything like it was for Bennett, Meg would be little more than a fond memory in no time at all. The thought both dismayed and excited her. But Jess's leaving wasn't something that she could contemplate while he was still in the room; she feared he'd misunderstand the spark in her eye. So Meg turned her face into the stiff fabric of his jeans and hid from her uncertain future in the fleeting consolation of the present.

Jess spread his fingers and combed them through her loose hair. She still wore it long, partly because he loved it and partly because it held a certain easy security for her. It was a curtain, but there was something soothing in the way that Jess parted it, and she sighed a little when he stopped brushing at the nape of her neck and bunched her waves in the palm of his hand. Tugging back gently, he coaxed her to look at him.

"What?" she asked, refusing to lift her head.

"What if your parents walk in?"

Meg sat up reluctantly and wrinkled her nose at him. "I was comfortable. Bad time to switch roles on me."

"I wasn't done talking."

"About college?"

"About leaving you."

Meg dropped her gaze, because she couldn't stand to look at him when she knew their thoughts ran different tracks. That though they met, they also diverged.

"Hey," he whispered. "Hey."

She couldn't ignore him, so she took a deep breath and tried to settle a faint smile on her lips. Hurting him was something she swore she'd never do. But she never got to see if her ruse worked or not, because her eyes never made it past his hands.

Meg loved Jess's hands. They were strong, generous somehow, and marked with small scars and lines that bespoke a depth that seemed beyond his years. And when she lifted her eyes, those storied hands were cupped in his lap, and between the thumb and forefinger of his right hand, he held a ring.

Panic seized her. "Jess, I —"

"It's not an engagement ring," he laughed, obviously enjoying her discomfort. "It's not even a promise ring."

"What then?" She didn't mean to be so harsh, so blunt, but the words were out of her mouth before she had a chance to gentle her response.

Jess didn't seem to mind. He reached for her left hand and held it in his. Without asking permission or waiting to see how she would react, he singled out her index finger and carefully slid the ring all the way down. It didn't get stuck once. It fit perfectly.

"There," he said, satisfied. "You're not really the jewelry type, but I think this suits you."

"What's that supposed to mean?" Meg was momentarily distracted.

"I like it that you're not the jewelry type," Jess clarified.

"Good."

"But I do think this works for you."

Meg gazed at the ring for a few seconds, startled to find that she actually did think it was pretty. It was earthy somehow, natural, but there was a small stone that glowed at the center. She liked the muted sparkle on her hand. Trying to be discreet, she swiveled her wrist a little, letting the smooth band catch the light. But when Jess covered it with the protection of his palms, she didn't complain.

"So . . ." she started, waiting for him to fill in the blanks.

"So it's just a little present. A thank-you of sorts."

"Most people send a card when they want to say thank you."

Jess shrugged. "I'm not most people, I guess. Besides, I couldn't decide between the card with the ape and the one with the flowers."

"Definitely the ape."

"I thought so. But I went with the ring instead." He offered her a shy smile and leaned in close. "It means thank you. It means you're amazing and I'll miss you and don't forget about me."

Meg thought he looked unbearably sweet with his face only inches from hers, so sweet and earnest and hopeful that she laid a breath of a kiss on the corner of his mouth. It was her own thank-you. She expected him to kiss her back, and she was prepared to say something light and funny before pulling away. But instead, Jess squeezed his eyes shut and let his forehead fall against hers.

"It means I love you," he said. Then he wrapped his arms around her and held her so tightly her chest was pinched and aching.

Her arms went around him automatically, but Meg was numb. She buried her face in the warm crook of his neck where it didn't matter that her cheeks were drained and white.

Jess left in the fall amid quiet fanfare and choked good-byes. He was the oldest child of the Langbroeks, whom the Painters had called neighbors for well over a decade, and the pride of his parents rested on his shoulders like polished armor. In fact, the whole neighborhood participated in the advent of his new adventure by loading his car down with baked goodies, handmade patchwork blankets, and good wishes as thick as the harvest of apples on the tree in the Langbroeks' front yard. The evening of his sendoff, Meg stood beneath the tree — so heavyladen with ripening fruit that Mr. Langbroek had propped up sagging branches with lengths of cut two-by-fours — and thought that Jess must feel just like that. Like he was hung with a hundred burdens of hope. They were sweet but heavy, and Meg both envied and felt sorry for him in turn.

"You doing okay?" Mrs. Langbroek asked, coming up to Meg and putting a consoling arm around her shoulders.

Meg smiled. "Yeah, doing fine."

"He's going to miss you, you know."

"He's going to have a wonderful new life at college," Meg countered.

Mrs. Langbroek gave her a strange look. "That may be, Meg, but if you ask me, that boy is going to marry you someday."

The comment was startling, unexpected, and Meg was stunned speechless. Thankfully, Mrs. Langbroek didn't wait around for her to respond, but spun away to give her famous broccoli salad one last stir. The bowl was displayed in the center of a long strand of picnic tables, and Jess's mom had to give her back to Meg in order to tend her potluck offering. Indebted to Mrs. Langbroek's short attention span, Meg avoided any further conversation and simply walked away.

The evening was gently warm, as if summer had released its suffocating stranglehold just so that Jess could enjoy one last perfect night at home. Though the weather alone would coax people out of their houses on a night like tonight, Meg knew that the cul-de-sac bustled with people who loved Jess and who had come especially for him. She grinned in acknowledgment of this fact, and felt a rush of affection for her boyfriend. It erased any unease that troubled her at Mrs. Langbroek's confident assertion.

That boy is going to marry you some-day . . . People had said as much before, though it was usually behind Meg's back and it usually drove her insane that they tried to write the story of her life without her permission. But tonight, for some reason, she didn't mind being the future Mrs. Jess Langbroek. She didn't mind the glitter of his ring on her finger. It will fade, she rationalized. It always did.

"You look smug."

Meg didn't have to turn to know that Dylan was standing at her elbow. The air around him was marked with his presence — the scent of his skin, the sweep of his shoulders, the mild aura of discontent that emanated from him as if nothing ever quite suited him exactly as it should. Meg knew every note, every nuance, though it pained her to keep a running catalog, even if it was against her will.

"I'm not smug," she said, irritated that he had interrupted her reverie. But her skin shivered at his proximity. "I'm content."

"You look self-satisfied."

She tilted her chin to glare at him.

"And there's no reason you shouldn't be pleased with yourself." Dylan was obviously amused. "It's a big day for your boyfriend."

The barbed provocation irked her. "He's your friend," she reminded him.

"We're not quite as close."

"I'm not in the mood," Meg muttered and stepped away without excusing herself.

Dylan followed. "Hey, I was just teasing. Why so sensitive? We used to joke around all the time."

"That was a long time ago."

"Far away," he agreed with a glint in his eye. "But not forgotten. At least, not for me."

It wasn't the first such bewildering conversation that Meg had had with Dylan over the years, and she was tired of trying to read between the lines of his riddles and games. There had been times that she was sure his cunning flirtations were intended to tempt. There had been times when she almost broke Jess's heart over the thin hope that Dylan had finally decided she could be more than a friend. But nothing ever came of their increasingly perplexing interactions, and Meg eventually gave up and settled back into the routine of remaining in motion, of following where Jess was so willing to lead, because there was no reason not to.

"Tonight is about Jess," she said with a sigh, hoping that her tone would be enough to convey how very much she wanted Dylan to leave her alone.

He didn't get the hint. "Then what?" he probed. "Then Jess will be gone and what will his girl do?"

"I'm not . . ." Meg trailed off because it wasn't something she could dispute. She was Jess's girl and all of Sutton knew it, whether or not she particularly liked the distinction. Arguing the finer points of Dylan's connotation was futile. "You don't understand," she finished, narrowing her eyes coolly.

Dylan backed off, palms up and a wry smile on his face. "Chill out," he warned her. "All I'm asking is, do you know what you've gotten yourself into?"

"What in the world are you talking about?"

He glanced around to make sure that no one was bothering to listen in on their conversation. Satisfied, he leaned in a bit closer to Meg and said just above a whisper, "I told you to be careful with Jess."

"And you were wrong. Jess has never been

anything but the perfect gentleman. The perfect friend. The perfect boyfriend." She drew out the final delineation, rubbing it in and hoping that Dylan was, even the tiniest bit, jealous.

But he didn't seem jealous. He seemed angry. "You're an idiot, Meg," he told her, forgetting to lower his voice like he had earlier. "I never took you for that. I thought you were smart, independent, different from other girls. But you're exactly the same. You just took a little longer to grow into your stupidity."

Meg lunged at him in fury and stood on tiptoe so she could look him straight in the eye. "I have no idea what you're talking about, but you're being a total —"

"He owns you," Dylan interrupted before she could say the words that boiled on the tip of her tongue. "Or at least, he thinks he does. I just hope it's not true."

He backed away. Meg stumbled a little, losing her footing when he wasn't across from her, holding her in place with a band of tension between them as inflexible and hard as steel.

"You're wrong," she said softly.

Dylan shrugged, trying to act as if he didn't care. But Meg could see the tendon in his jaw cut a severe path along his chin and down the side of his tan neck.

"You're wrong," she said again.

"I know what he wrote on your ring."

Confusion stopped Meg cold, but before she could question him, before she could make him explain what he meant, Dylan was gone. He weaved through the crowd, brushing people out of his way, and jumped in his brother's hand-me-down truck. It roared to life and sped around the corner, out of sight.

There was nothing she could do but watch him go.

The rest of the night, Meg felt sick. Her fingers tingled, her stomach clenched, each breath she took felt hard to come by. She was grateful that nobody pressed her when she moved food around on her plate, and even more thankful that everyone gave her a wide berth. Of course, she assumed that their careful distance was maintained because they wanted to give her room to grieve Jess's impending departure. Whether or not everyone's impressions were true was irrelevant as far as Meg was concerned. At least they were leaving her alone.

It wasn't until the last car pulled out of the cul-de-sac and the last porch light went off that Meg realized what had been plaguing her all night. Her throat was clenched, her jaw sore, and when Jess slipped his arms around her waist and kissed the nape of her neck through the soft screen of her hair, an unexpected sob escaped her lips and surprised her so much, she choked on the sound.

"It's okay," Jess murmured, turning her gently around in his arms so he could hold her close.

Meg didn't know why she was crying, but she was too overwhelmed to be discerning. Instead of trying to gather herself, she dug her fingers into Jess's back, clutching great handfuls of his shirt and holding on as if it was all she could bring herself to do. It was.

"Shhhh." Jess urged. "Don't do this now. I've never seen you cry before. Not once."

"Never?" she gasped.

"Not even when we were little kids. Not when you hurt yourself or someone teased you or you were embarrassed . . . I think you're getting softer with age."

Meg's tears had eased enough for her to be insulted by Jess's blithe observation. She tried to extract herself from his embrace, but he wouldn't loosen his arms from her waist. "I'm not soft," she sniffed, resting her palms on his chest, her forearms snug and tight between them.

"I never said that." There was a mischievous glint in his eye. "I said softer. Like the difference between granite and slate."

Her eyebrows lifted in confusion.

"Trust me." Jess laughed. "You're still hard as stone."

She still wasn't sure if she was being insulted or not and she expressed her displeasure by knuckling away her tears and trying to wiggle out of his grip again.

"I love you," Jess told her, smoothing his offense with a kiss. And though it was something that he had said many times since the first night he worked up the courage to utter the words, it still sent a little shiver through Meg. But she said it back because it seemed wrong somehow not to. It seemed wrong not to acknowledge the gift of his love without reciprocating in kind.

They kissed. They held each other. They said good-bye. When Jess finally pried himself away and backed a few steps from her, moving reluctantly, slowly, as if waiting for her to stop him, Meg realized that she hung in limbo. She was suspended between a beginning and an end. A new start and a history that, if not rich, was at the very least significant, lasting. It was too much to just walk away from, and she jogged after him and threw her arms around his neck. She kissed him, hard. Then she turned around and walked away, refusing to take one last look back.

When she had made it to the shelter of her bedroom, Meg shut and locked the door behind her. The bed was rumpled and inviting, the wingback chair she had stolen from the basement appealingly draped with pillows. But Meg sagged with her back against the closed door and slid all the way to the ground, pressing her knees into her chest. She wasn't crying, not anymore. And yet, she trembled as she slipped off Jess's ring.

In the four months that she had worn his token of appreciation, his thank-you, she had never once taken it off. From the moment he placed it on her finger, it remained untouched. It had never crossed her mind to look at it, to turn it over in her hands.

Now, with Dylan's words humming in her ears and her lips still warm and bruised from Jess's insistent kisses, she studied the gold band as if it contained every secret she'd ever longed to know.

I know what he wrote . . .

She studied it from every angle. Tried it on every finger so she could see how far it would slide down. Felt it over and under, letting her fingertips explore every edge and smooth place, every angle. And finally, when there was nothing else left to discover, she held it up to peer inside the band.

One little word made her feel both cheated and beloved. One word changed everything.

MINE.

13
LUCAS

Lucas stayed at work later than usual, scrolling through dozens of pages of missing women reports. He started out reading them all, but by the time he had swallowed a handful of horror stories like bad medicine, he started to create a sort of method to tame the madness. Though he didn't know an exact height, Lucas had seen the body and was sure the woman in the barn had been fairly tall. Therefore he only read profiles that matched a specific height — between five-six and five-ten. The woman had also been wearing a dress, so it was easy to rule out the countless entries that documented blue jeans or skirts or shorts. Or swimming suits or pajamas. And there was a record for a missing woman in a sheet, swept from the earth like a fallen angel found. The thought made Lucas feel scalded and violent. Like he could atone for all that had happened with the righteous vengeance of his own misplaced wrath. He was angry. But he didn't know who to be angry with.

By the time he gave up and put his computer to sleep, Lucas had a scribbled list of nineteen women that matched his rather vague criteria. They ranged in age from fifteen to forty, and they were, sadly, just the very tip of the iceberg. He had also managed to spare a few moments to research the ring, and while he was almost certain that the distinctive leafed design was a Black Hills gold creation — a style that was both ubiquitous and immediately recognizable in his corner of the Midwest — there was no company with the initials MKD that dealt in Black Hills gold.

After the last few days, he had to admit that going home to Jenna and Angela felt like a mild form of torture. He wanted to call Alex and disappear in the bottom of a glass. Lucas wasn't sexist and he wasn't much of a drinker, but he needed his friend and he needed a beer. There was no way around it.

As he made the short drive home, Lucas planned to pop into the house, quickly change his clothes, and then take off under the premise that he wanted to give the girls some time alone. Girl time. They liked that, right? It sounded good, even to him. It would seem gentlemanly, when the truth was, chivalry was the last thing on his mind.

But when he pulled into his long driveway, his house seemed fuller somehow, bursting at the seams, from the uneven patchwork of windows to the crooked screen door, and bustling as if a party was going on inside. All the lights were on in the kitchen, and through the frame of the leaded picture window in front of the table, he could see Jenna and Angela silhouetted inside. The fall evening was already darkening, and although a cool breeze made him zip up his light jacket, the transom was open above the sink. Music poured out from beneath the whitewashed sash.

Music?

And laughter, Lucas realized as he approached the back door. He turned the handle carefully, but he didn't need to be wary of disturbing anyone. The beat that danced from the sound dock on the kitchen counter was loud and frantic, and his wife's laughter was pitched to match.

"You're crazy!" Jenna shouted over the din.

The music was definitely not from the Hudsons' collection, and from his vantage point in the mudroom, Lucas could see that the iPhone plugged into the sound dock was hot pink. Obviously Angela's. If he was right, the melody was Latin, and the sway of Angela's hips betrayed a pretty fantastic attempt at salsa, even to the untrained eye. The two women bopped and shimmied around the kitchen, apparently in the throes of a one-on-one lesson.

"It's all in your hips," Angela coaxed, grinning so wide that Lucas was sure he could have counted each ivory tooth. "You have to swivel them. Try figure eights. Draw figure eights with your hips."

Apparently Jenna wasn't catching on, because Angela threw up her arms, sashayed over to the dark-haired beauty, and put her hands on Jenna's waist, coaxing her to swing in rhythm to the music. They stumbled and giggled and tried again.

And then, against all odds and against her very nature, Jenna gave in for a moment. It was almost as if Lucas could see an invisible weight slide off her shoulders like a heavy garment. The dark cloud of her worries pooled around her feet and she closed her eyes. For a handful of seconds in the warmth and harmony of the kitchen, she danced. She really danced. Like no one was watching her. Like she didn't have a care in the world.

A lump rose in Lucas's throat, and though

he tried to swallow it away, the thickness remained. It filled his chest and bubbled up against his tongue, where it threatened to suffocate him with the beautiful understanding that the wife he loved still existed. She was spinning before him.

All thoughts of running away with Alex for the night evaporated. She was here, and he wasn't going anywhere. "Thank you," he breathed. And then he did the unthinkable. He clapped.

The sound of his heartfelt applause didn't carry in the noisy room. But after a few particularly enthusiastic spins, Angela suddenly looked up and gasped. The smile melted off her face and her arms dropped ungracefully against her sides. Jenna froze, too, her hands raised above her head and one hip cocked at an angle. She stared.

"What in the —"

"You caught us," Angela chirped, interrupting Jenna and bounding over to the iPhone to kill the music. She forced a slight smile, and though she seemed flippant about Lucas's abrupt appearance, he could tell by the set of her jaw that she was still angry with him. The nonchalance was for Jenna's sake.

And Jenna? Lucas's gaze shot to her. She was straightening out her shirt, pulling at the tails of the gray cotton blouse and refusing to meet his eye. The apples of her cheeks were stained pink.

Making Jenna blush was no small feat. In another world, Lucas would have laughed and leaped into the kitchen. He would have caught his wife around the waist and kissed each of her rosy cheeks in turn. But she was already turning away from him, and the line of her shoulders seemed to underscore the distance between them.

"You snuck up on us," Jenna said, clearing her throat almost shyly.

Lucas shook his head. "I did no such thing. All I did was come home."

"You're early."

"Actually, I'm late," Lucas said, pointing to the clock on the stove.

"Oh, no!" Jenna threw herself across the room and yanked open the oven door.

For the first time since he entered the house, Lucas became aware of something other than his wife. The air was filled with the scent of garlic and onion, olive oil and tomato sauce. "Smells fantastic," he murmured. "What are you making?"

"Burnt garlic bread," Jenna sighed, setting a tray with two long loaves of crusty French bread on the counter.

"It's not burnt," Angela consoled her. "It's toasty."

Jenna handed Lucas a wooden spoon. "Give the sauce a stir," she said, and turned back to the bread.

Standing between Jenna and Angela, Lucas wondered how much the younger woman knew about the battleground that was his marriage. It hadn't occurred to him until he was lifting the lid off a pot on the stove that maybe his presence was unwelcome in his own home. It wasn't a very nice thought.

But the aroma of Jenna's homemade sauce made his mouth water and slowly erased any thoughts of Alex and a numbing drink or two. He even found it hard to care whether or not Angela could see how far his relationship with Jenna had unraveled. The marinara was bubbling and hot, dotted with yellow cherry tomatoes that she had left whole. As he stirred the wooden spoon through the thick contents of the oversized pot, he wondered: When was the last time they had enjoyed a meal together? When was the last time it was homemade? He almost said something about the irregularity of their family meals and how nice it was to come home to a from-scratch supper, but he changed his mind at the last second.

"How about I set the table?" he offered instead, replacing the lid and reaching for a stack of plates from the cupboard.

Jenna sliced the bread and Angela drained the noodles while Lucas put the table together. He grabbed clean glasses from the dishwasher, then had a better idea and abandoned the etched tumblers in favor of three pristine wineglasses that he and Jenna rarely used. He had to wipe them with a towel because they were dusty, and almost gave up on his plan when he couldn't find a corkscrew anywhere. But Jenna reminded him that they had a cheap one in the picnic basket.

When they were all sitting down, steam rising from the heaped serving platter between them, Lucas produced a golden bottle of unlabeled wine and proceeded to butcher the cork as he tried to open it.

"That looks like moonshine," Angela said.

"Close enough," Jenna said with a smirk. "Another gift from one of Lucas's patients. She brews a pretty powerful homemade wine."

"I don't think you brew wine," Lucas said, finally managing to extract the cork.

"Whatever."

"What is it?" Angela asked. "There are no vineyards around here."

"Dandelion."

Her nose wrinkled. "Ugh."

"That's why we've never tried it before."

"You're experimenting on me?" Angela said, looking unimpressed.

"No, I think Minnie Van Egdom is experimenting on all of us." Lucas measured out a little in each of their glasses and raised his hand in a toast.

"We don't toast," Jenna reminded him.

"Come on, it'll be fun."

Though she rolled her eyes, Jenna reluctantly raised her glass and Angela followed suit. But when the light sparkled off the three crystal goblets, Lucas realized that he had no idea what to say. What was there to toast? Angela wasn't in town for a casual visit, and things between Lucas and Jenna were as icy as ever. Catching Jenna as she danced so carelessly had loosened something in Lucas, and he had forgotten, if only for a moment, the impossible situations that they were each stuck in. It all came rushing back as the women across from him waited in skeptical expectation for his words of celebration and ceremony. He wished he had never brought out the dandelion wine.

Lucas swallowed. "Uh, to life," he stumbled. "To our lives. May they be . . . more than we imagined."

Jenna gave him a funny look, but she lifted the glass to her lips and tasted. "Not bad," she said, taking another sip. "Not bad at all."

They all agreed that the wine was, if not good, at least drinkable, and the pasta simply defied description.

"I've never tasted better," Angela declared, and although Lucas lamented the whole-grain capellini that his houseguest had insisted on buying and mourned the absence of meatballs, he had to agree. Even a vegetarian version of his wife's secret recipe was impossible to beat.

"Your best effort yet," he complimented Jenna, hoping that she'd catch the wink he threw her way. But she had already begun to sink back into herself, to pull the folds of her heavy cloak tight around her where she could hide behind an impenetrable wall of stony detachment. Lucas knew that it was all an act — that Jenna excelled in the art of self-preservation. But it didn't matter, she merely nodded at his praise.

"I did it for Angela," Jenna said. "I wanted her to have a nice, home-cooked meal."

"I get home cooking from time to time," Angela assured them. She spun the tines of her fork through the tangled noodles on her plate. "Or, I guess I should say I used to."

Jenna gave her a look of such genuine compassion and query that Lucas was shocked at how quickly his wife's countenance could change. In anyone else, the transformation would ring false, but Lucas was only reminded of what an excellent social worker his wife had become. Strength and empathy and resolve and capability seemed to emanate from her in a subtle fog of understanding. All she had to do was soften her face like that and he longed to tell her his darkest secrets. He knew Angela felt the same way when she went on without being asked to.

"My boyfriend's parents used to invite me over a lot. They had this incredible mansion in the hills . . . Every Sunday after church we'd go there for a big, formal meal."

"Church?" Jenna wondered, her tone both uncharacteristic and indicative of her surprise.

Angela laughed. "Yeah, you know, the place where I used to go with you when I was a kid? The brick building with the bells and the pews and the boring sermons?"

Lucas watched his wife to gauge her response, but her features had gone blank. "We don't really go anymore," he explained.

"What?" Angela looked dumbstruck. "But you guys loved it. You actually believed all that stuff."

"Still do." Lucas shrugged a little and took a big bite of pasta so he had an excuse not to elucidate further.

"But you quoted scripture, and prayed around the table like *Leave It to Beaver . . .*"

"Just because we're taking a little break from church doesn't mean we've given up on God."

"Maybe it means He's given up on us," Jenna muttered. Then she diverted the conversation back to where it had started without leaving room for discussion. "So, what happened to your boyfriend and Sunday dinners with the folks?"

"Oh, we broke up."

"I'm sorry."

Angela smiled ruefully. "Don't be. We weren't meant to be." She put quotes around the catchphrase with her fingers and sighed. "He came from a big, happy, functional family, and I just didn't fit in. You know, I read somewhere that if you don't learn love at home, it's hard to learn it elsewhere."

Lucas opened his mouth to object, to console her in some small way so she didn't look so cheerless, but at that moment Jenna put her foot on his under the table and pressed down in warning. He held his tongue.

"And," Jenna began, "do you believe that?"

Looking back and forth between the two of them, Angela contemplated the answer. "No," she said finally, "no, I don't think I believe that. At least, not entirely."

Jenna didn't comment on her answer in any way. She just nodded as if she understood, then passed the Caesar salad to Lucas for a second helping. He hadn't even asked for it and felt a thrill of connection that she could still read his mind when it came to the little things.

There was a lull around the table then as the ladies pushed their plates away and sank back into their chairs. Lucas didn't think the silence was comfortable exactly, but it wasn't uncomfortable either, and he was grateful for that. As he chewed, he tried to come up with something to say, a question to ask or a funny anecdote from his day that would keep everyone around the table a little longer. It wasn't the night that he had envisioned, but there was beauty in it, moments of peace that were worth the awkward pauses and the unsettling presence of Angela Sparks at his table. Again. After all these years. It was almost enough to make him forget about the woman in the barn, the ring in his pocket. Almost.

But before he could think up something interesting to say, Angela came up with a question of her own.

"Say," she grinned, tapping her fingers on the table as if the thought had just occurred to her, "speaking of big, happy, functional families, what about you two? I thought you guys would have a mittful by now. Where're all the Hudson rug rats?"

It felt to Lucas as if all the light, all the pleasure of their shared meal was sucked out of the room. Just like that the garlic smelled too sharp, the incandescent bulbs above the table were too bright, the music that they had turned on before sitting down was too loud. There was dressing-soaked lettuce in his mouth, but it was hard to swallow. He had to remind himself to chew, to be careful with his teeth, because they wanted to grind the insides of his cheeks. No, no, no, he silently moaned. Don't do this.

He struggled to choke down the romaine and rush to Jenna's rescue. They had agreed on a preplanned answer, a quick and easy way to put off overzealous well-wishers and people who seemed to think that a husband and wife couldn't possibly be a family until children were involved. Lucas was still trying to remember the words, the exact thing he was supposed to say, when Jenna spoke up.

"Actually," she said slowly, "there was a baby. A little girl. She was stillborn."

That wasn't what they had planned.

Angela gasped, a little intake of horror and grief that Lucas couldn't quite decipher. Was she aghast at their loss? Or ashamed that she had ever been so tactless as to ask the question in the first place? Maybe both. "I'm sorry, Jenna," she croaked, reaching across the table for her mentor and friend. "I'm so sorry, I didn't know."

"We named her Audrey," Jenna said. "She's buried behind the church where we used to take you." Then she slid her chair back and stood with as much dignity and composure as a queen. "Lucas, I'd like you to clean up the kitchen."

He couldn't stop himself from reaching for her hand, but she ignored his gesture. "Of course . . ." he began, but she swept out of the room without giving him another glance.

Jenna didn't come downstairs for a long time, and Lucas knew that she was in the unfinished nursery. Audrey's heart had stopped beating at thirty-eight weeks, full term, and Lucas and Jenna had long been rejoicing in her as if she was already theirs. From the day a pink plus sign appeared in the window of the pregnancy test, they considered themselves parents. A Mission-style crib in blond pine had been set up in a small room painted cornflower blue. There were pink daisies springing out of the base-boards and yellow chiffon curtains trimmed in eyelet lace. A handful of pink and purple pajamas already dangled in the closet on tiny hangers. It was the hangers that Lucas later couldn't look at, though why their miniature design broke his heart, he never could understand.

While his wife mourned in solitude, Lucas cleaned the kitchen. He knew from experi-ence that Jenna wanted to be alone, that she would resent any intrusion into the private hall of her pain, where she hung memories and regrets like pictures on the wall. She didn't visit there often, but when she did, she liked everything to be in its place, every edge of sorrow to be sharp and ready so that she could reach out a finger and bleed.

It killed Lucas. He hated the way she clung and moped and grieved without end. Wasn't two years enough? Shouldn't she be moving on by now? Though Jenna lived a normal, productive, mentally healthy life most of the time, there were moments when it seemed as if Audrey had died yesterday instead of years ago. Worst of all, she had let what happened come between her and Lucas. And she still visited the nursery. Not often, but it was too much all the same.

As Lucas cleared the table and scraped leftovers into the garbage can, Angela worked wordlessly beside him. She had looked stunned when Jenna left the room, but a warning glance from Lucas kept her in her seat when it seemed like she would jump up and race after her friend.

"It's okay," Lucas told her. And those were the last words between them for nearly twenty minutes.

But when Lucas hung the towel through the handle of the refrigerator door and turned to give the room a last once-over, Angela finally found her voice.

"How long ago?" she asked.

"Just over two years."

Angela nodded once. "She doing okay?"

No, Lucas wanted to say. Isn't it obvious? Instead, he tried to arrange his lips in a slight smile, a token of reassurance that everything was all right. It didn't work, but he didn't feel like baring his soul to Angela;

he'd rather lie. "We're doing fine," he said. "I think you just caught her off guard."

She nodded again, but this time it was clear that she didn't believe him for a second. "I'm sorry I brought it up. That was really stupid — really insensitive of me."

Lucas shrugged. "When you're dating seriously, the question is always 'When are you two going to get married?' As soon as you're married it changes to 'When are you two going to have kids?' It doesn't stop until you have a child to show for it. It's inevitable."

"You must hear it all the time."

"Not as much as we used to. For the most part, people know what happened and they leave us alone."

"What about Jenna's grandma, what was her name? This must be hard on her."

"Caroline passed away last April. She had Alzheimer's, but she remembered that Jenna had a baby. She just forgot that Audrey didn't live."

Angela put her hands to her cheeks and moaned, a little cry of sympathy that made Lucas want to crawl out of his skin. He moved away abruptly, leaving the kitchen in darkness and flicking on a lamp in the adjoining living room. Grabbing the TV remote from the coffee table, he flopped on the couch. Though he could feel Angela slink into the room behind him, and though he knew he should ease her discomfort in some small way, he did his best to ignore her.

The truth was, he was furious with her for showing up at all. Ever since she'd appeared in his driveway, everything had gone wrong. His theories about Jim Sparks, his disregard for the past, even his tenuous hold on his wife, were all in ruins because of Angela. It was so much easier when he could mourn her as the broken woman beneath the floor of the barn.

I ached for you when you were gone, Lucas thought. And then he was horrified with himself. What was he doing? Wishing that Angela was dead? That she hadn't escaped her nightmare of a life and started over fresh, halfway across the country? No, he concluded. I don't want her dead. I just want answers. Whatever they may be.

Out of the corner of his eye, Lucas saw Angela curl up on the love seat and pull a blanket over her lap. He wanted to be alone. A part of him wanted to tell Angela that she should leave, she could spend the night in Jim's house; he and Jenna needed time alone. But that would be downright cruel. Asking Angela to go back there would be like asking her to return to the scene of a crime. Which it was, except that the crime Jim committed against Angela was never accounted for. Instead of saying anything, he found ESPN and turned up the volume. An hour of SportsCenter would do much to ease his mind.

But he only got to see a few minutes of football highlights. Jenna came downstairs shortly after he had settled on the couch, staring blindly at the glowing screen. When he heard her on the steps, he spun to watch her, his eyes seeking her face as if he could read the sad story of what she had gone through in the gravity of her dark features. But she refused to meet his gaze. Instead, she walked slowly into the room, one foot in front of the other as if each step took effort, and put out her hand for the remote. He passed it to her without complaint. Then she sank into the rocking chair, and flipped through a dozen channels until she found a rerun of *Gilmore Girls.*

"Something for the ladies," Jenna said, her eyes fixed on the TV.

Nobody said another word for the rest of the night.

14
MEG

Meg continued to wear Jess's ring, in spite of what it said, and even though the boldness of the etched claim made her want to slap him across his perfectly dimpled cheek. She chose to take for granted the assumption that deep down, the boy she had grown up with didn't mean to upset her, to claim her with the imprint of those four loaded letters. It's innocent, she told herself. It's meaningless. A joke, a misguided term of endearment . . . She could almost make herself believe it.

The real reason Meg kept wearing the ring was that it was an indelible part of her, as much a part of her personal landscape as an engagement band on the finger of a bride-to-be. Of course, the little woven band wasn't an engagement ring, but everyone would have noticed its absence. From her parents to her friends, there would be questions to answer, and she simply didn't want to explain what Jess had done. It was too complicated. So she endured the bold claim engraved inside the ring, and with him so far away, it wasn't too hard to ignore.

For the first week or two of college, Jess called every night, filling up an hour or more with small talk about his classes, his professors, his geeky roommate from somewhere in Wyoming. Meg half listened, and used the other half of her brain to finish homework or arrange her CD collection according to her newest whim: by genre, album, or artist. She had inherited Bennett's boxed set of the entire collection of The Smashing Pumpkins when he moved out and forgot to take it along, and she liked those albums organized by virtue of the emotion they invoked. For some reason she found her fingers on *Mellon Collie and the Infinite Sadness* more often than not when Jess called.

But it didn't take long for his phone calls to taper off. Meg couldn't help but silently rejoice that his attention was shifting elsewhere. And then she missed him in the very next breath.

School was a good diversion as Meg teetered between the waxing and waning of her feelings, or lack thereof, for Jess. She threw herself into her academics with honorable abandon. And when that wasn't enough, she tried to coax the girls' PE coach into letting her start an intramural lacrosse league. Talking with Jess on the phone one night, she had happened across a History Channel special on the Native American origins of lacrosse, and decided that as an inhabitant of the Great American Plains, she'd instigate a Sutton-sized revival of the aggressive sport.

The answer was a very adamant no.

But Mrs. Casey was willing to stand behind powderpuff football, which Meg happily agreed to — providing they drop the detestable designation "powderpuff."

"But that's what it's called," Mrs. Casey argued, right after she pointed out that pastel pink T-shirts would be the perfect complement to the Sutton blue-and-white.

"It's appalling."

"It's tongue-in-cheek."

"It's patronizing."

Mrs. Casey pursed her lips and was about to put her hand on Meg's shoulder when she realized that that would be patronizing. "Okay," she said instead, giving in. "Fine. Whatever you want. What do you want to call it?"

"Girls' Football League," Meg said, as if the question was downright ridiculous.

"You do realize that powderpuff — I mean, girls' football — usually consists of one game, right? Junior girls versus senior girls in one flag football game. No real stakes — bragging rights only."

Meg sighed. "Is there a handbook or something?"

"No."

"Then we can do whatever we want."

Throwing up her hands, Mrs. Casey laughed. "And what exactly do you want, my dear?"

Meg chose to ignore the slight condescension and said: "A weekly scrimmage, maybe two a week, with as many girls as we can convince to sign up."

"Teams?"

"If there are enough girls, we'll make two or three teams. Otherwise we'll pick jerseys every game and switch it around."

"Where will you play?"

"The football field."

"The coaches will never allow it."

"The soccer pitch?"

"The boys' and girls' teams are already fighting over it."

Meg thought. "We could use the city soccer field. You know, the one right beside the baseball diamonds? They only use it for summer rec anyway."

282

Mrs. Casey nodded. "It's your job to call and get permission."

"Okay. One last thing . . ." Meg paused, trying to slide a final question under the radar, but there was no way to soften her request. "Tackle?" she said quietly.

"Absolutely not. Touch or flags, and I mean it, Meg Painter."

Meg's football experiment exploded. She was the match that sparked the fire, but the flames spread more quickly than she had dared to hope or imagine. The unofficial Girls' Football League collected the leftovers, the girls who hadn't made the cut for the school soccer or basketball teams, or who weren't cheerleader or dance squad types. Meg had to admit that she was surprised by some of the girls who did show. A few of them traded in heels for tennis shoes, and wore lipstick that got smeared as they sweated out their frustrations on the soccer pitch turned football field.

Within the first two weeks of rather disorganized play, there were at least forty young women gathered on the field after school twice a week. Games were scheduled for Tuesdays and Thursdays at four, just enough time to change clothes, grab a snack, and run a few warm-up laps. The rules were modified as they went along, and the girls customized the game according to their desires. No helmets, pads, or cleats. Only eight players per team allowed on the field. And as far as the girls were concerned, there was no such thing as a penalty for an ineligible receiver downfield, pass interference, or grounding the ball. The idea was to keep the game moving and the ball in play. They could even justify the occasional occurrence of unnecessary roughness.

Mrs. Casey's "no tackle" rule lasted less than ten minutes into the inaugural game.

It was a mess at first, all aggression and estrogen and awkward ball handling. But Meg wasn't about to let her pet project fall to pieces, so she made an executive decision one afternoon and told everyone to line up. She counted the girls off to threes, and the unofficial trio of the Girls' Football League was formed. The teams took turns squaring off against each other, and captains emerged without too much fuss. Best of all, they picked ridiculous team names in mockery of the original powderpuff moniker. The Pigskin Barbies bought T-shirts in an alarming shade of electric fuchsia, the Broken Stilettos wore black, and Meg's team, Riot Girls, donned a tie-dyed blaze of orange and red with the sleeves ripped off.

It was all an attempt at satire, a self-mocking flippancy that made them feel at once connected and competitive. In making fun of themselves, and each other, it gave them permission to laugh — and then to take each other down when they squared off on the field.

Meg loved every minute of it. Much to her surprise, she discovered that she had a mind for strategy, and could often see the field laid out before her like a chessboard. She instinctively knew which players were tired or distracted, and after she called an unprecedented blitz on the Pigskin Barbies' quarterback, her team never questioned her judgment again. She had been granted the role as team captain by merit of the fact that she had formed the league, but when she started calling winning plays, she earned the title.

By the time the weather began to turn and the girls had to play in sweatshirts and stocking caps, the Girls' Football League had acquired a certain notoriety in the community. They were mildly infamous, for Mrs. Casey dropped any school ties with the rogue association, and some parents decided to forbid their daughters to play. But no one ever got hurt beyond a sprained ankle or a twisted knee, though one freshman had to have a couple of stitches after she tripped over her own two feet and split her lip on her bottom teeth. There were enough unbiased bystanders to assure her parents it was a no-fault accident.

The GFL even began to draw a small crowd of spectators, and the more enthusiastic fans (mostly boyfriends of the players and girls who were too chicken to play) made signs in support of their favorite teams. Some even went so far as to invent ludicrous cheers. Meg's favorite was a rousing chant of "Riot Girls" that ended in a triumphant, feral growl. It made her laugh, even though no one was cheering for her in particular.

Once, as she was sprinting off the field in the middle of a game, Meg's gaze momentarily left the scuffle of players and did a quick scan of the small crowd that had gathered. She was stunned to find the outline of her father, standing with his arms crossed, at the very top of the berm around the city soccer pitch. She knew that he had to have left work early in order to catch her game, and a little trill of anxiety rushed through her. Was he angry? Would he make her quit? But when she locked eyes with her dad, he smiled wide and did jazz hands just for her benefit. She could almost hear him

say it, "Jazz hands!" And though she should
have been embarrassed by his little display,
it pleased her more than any moment she
had yet experienced in the GFL.

Greg Painter never did say anything to his
daughter about the game that he witnessed,
even though a pileup had left one girl fighting furious tears and another with shallow
pools of blood in her scratched palms. Meg
took his silence as acceptance, maybe even
quiet approval, and she read pride in the lay
of his hand on her back before she slipped
into bed that night.

And though Meg loved her Tuesday and
Thursday diversions with unadulterated joy,
there were times when she wondered where
it had all come from. It wasn't in her nature
to be overly self-analytical, but little whys
seemed to float on the clouds of smoke that
billowed from her football fire. Meg knew it
was all more than the fallout from a History
Channel documentary.

She could try to convince herself that she
had always been a bit of a tomboy and that
she had always loved football. Both true,
but it was more than that. The league wasn't
merely a hobby, nor was it a feminist statement — although the GFL did exude a
certain paralleled sense of strength and
femininity — and Meg wasn't the sort to

287

fuss about gender issues too much anyway.

And yet, after a hard game, when she stood beneath a scalding spray of water in the shower, there were only two things that Meg thought of: how much her muscles ached, and why she did it — what drove her to run with the Riot Girls.

Jess, she thought more often than not. I do it because I'm furious with Jess. Or because I miss him. Or because I just plain don't know what to do with him. Or without him.

Then, halfway through a game against the Broken Stilettos, when the snow was just beginning to fly in southwest Iowa, Meg was confronted by a second unexpected spectator at the soccer pitch, who turned all her theories about her own self-flagellation upside down.

The Broken Stilettos were up by a touchdown, and there was less than a minute left in the game. The Riot Girls' quarterback had just been sacked, third down, and their only hope was a Hail Mary, a play the Catholic girls underscored with a heartfelt recitation of that prayer from across the line of scrimmage.

Meg was quite possibly the best wide receiver in the entire girls' league: tall and lanky and fast, impeccably proportioned for the perfect last-minute play. But nothing was ever quite perfect in their legendary league. When the center snapped the football to their quarterback, Meg took off like lightning, weaving through black T-shirts as she worked her way to the sidelines and far down the field. She didn't look over her shoulder; she didn't pause to see what was happening behind her. She just ran. The plan was for her to come up at center field and turn for the pass. The truth was, none of the girls were good enough to pull off such an elaborate play, but they had nothing to lose.

When she was within ten yards of the goal line, Meg realized with a burst of adrenaline that she was alone. No one could keep up with her — her crazy play could actually work. She tried not to smile, but there was a grin on her face as she turned, and through the fifteen bodies crowding the field, she could just make out her quarterback. The girl still had the ball, and as Meg watched, she threw it. It wasn't a terrible throw, but it was off to the right. Meg tried to gauge the distance as she ran to receive it. But as she lifted her fingers to pluck the ball out of the air, she felt a rush like wind around her. She skimmed the football with her fingertips, but instead of rising to meet it, she felt herself yanked down. And then the wind was knocked from her lungs as a snarl of bodies fell over her, elbows and knees and angles in all the wrong places.

The Black Stilettos screamed and congratulated each other on their first win against the Riot Girls, dancing victory jigs that rivaled the show-offs of the NFL. Meg was left on her back in the cold grass, hard chips of snow the size of pinpricks falling against her hot face and melting on her cheeks. She closed her eyes.

"You okay?"

Even though she wasn't hurt, Meg fully expected her teammates to come and lift her off the ground. But the soft query was not from one of the girls. Her eyes flashed open.

"Dylan?"

He was standing over her, dressed in a thick, corduroy jacket with the collar turned up. His hands were bunched in his pockets, but when she said his name, he took them out and cupped them around his mouth to blow warmth into his palms. "Good game," he said. The corner of his mouth was tweaked in amusement.

Meg grunted and rolled onto her hip, pushing herself up and swiping at the dead grass and leaves that sprinkled her back like confetti. "Thanks," she said dryly, trying not to look at him. But as much as she didn't want to admit it, as much as she wanted to just walk away and go lick her wounds with her trounced teammates, her heart beat an irregular rhythm with him so close. She caught sight of a couple of the Riot Girls making their way toward her, but she gave her head an almost imperceptible shake and they paused, confused. When she didn't make any move toward them, they gave up and walked back to the sidelines and the rest of the team.

Though she couldn't exactly pinpoint why, Meg both wanted and didn't want to be alone with Dylan. She saw him all the time — in the halls of Sutton High, around town, at school events — but she usually avoided him as if they were strangers with no shared history at all. He seemed more than happy to do the same, and yet from time to time she'd look up and find his gaze on her. The way he watched her was unsettling, and even when she caught him in the act, he didn't look away. Instead, he'd hold her eyes for a moment, then tilt the edge of his mouth in a half smile of profound amusement and wait until she broke the tenuous connection between them. Meg didn't want to be so feeble, but she was always the first to turn away.

It infuriated her, although even as she resented him for teasing her, there was something in Dylan's look that always left her wanting more. It was as if he had things to say, words that were poised on the tip of his tongue, and if Meg could only catch him at just the right moment, she could unlock all the secrets that hid behind the curve of his lips. She wanted to know. She was dying to know.

"You've got quite the racket going on here," Dylan said, turning to survey the girls as they walked off the field.

"I'm not conning anyone," Meg assured him, eyes flashing.

"These girls believe they're actually accomplishing something," he argued.

Meg exhaled hard through her nose. "They are. We are. We're getting out a little aggression."

"Girl power to you," Dylan joked.

"You're an idiot."

"Hey."

Something in his voice made her look up.

"I'm giving you a hard time. It actually looks like fun. You guys are brutal. I'd pit you against Sutton's team if they didn't all have a hundred pounds on you." He laughed then, and it was such a genuine sound that

Meg felt a smile tickle at her own mouth. For a split second she saw the GFL the way the rest of the world saw it: as an entertaining diversion. She was happy to make people smile. But then the moment faded as quickly as it had come and she was left feeling cold and tired, with the beginnings of a killer headache thrumming against the base of her skull.

"I'm glad you enjoyed it," she said, turning to go. "I need a shower."

She meant for her statement to be taken as a dismissal, but Dylan fell into step beside her.

"I'll give you a ride home," he said.

Meg faltered, shocked by his offer and more drained than she realized, but Dylan shot out a hand to steady her.

"You okay? There were a lot of girls on top of you."

"I'm fine."

"Are you sure? You stumbled there a little. Could be a concussion."

"It's not a concussion."

Dylan winked at her. "Didn't think so."

She yanked her arm out of his grip and picked up the pace, but he kept up easily. The snow was falling harder now, the flakes growing in size as the precipitation made the transition from icy sleet to soft snow. It was just beginning to crown the grass, draping the brown blades with strands of white so clean and delicate, Meg almost hated to ruin it with her footprints.

"Slow down, tiger," Dylan tugged on the back of her sweatshirt. "My truck is in the opposite direction."

Meg watched the rest of the girls straggle toward the parking lot and raised a fist in solidarity at the few who were sneaking glances her way. When she could see their smiles across the field, she allowed Dylan to steer her away from the crowd and toward the pickup he must have parked on the gravel road behind the sports complex.

"This your first game?" she asked, trying to make conversation.

"Nope."

She shot him a dark look. "I've never seen you here before."

"I sit there," he told her, pointing in the direction they were headed. The berm around the field rose higher at the south end, creating a gentle hill that ended in a row of live oaks that were easily as old as Sutton itself: linking arms, Meg and Dylan couldn't encompass the girth of the massive trunks. "I've got a bird's-eye view," Dylan said.

"So you like to see but not be seen?"

"Something like that."

They walked in silence the rest of the way, Meg painfully aware of the way their shoulders brushed from time to time, the familiarity, even after all these years, of his presence beside her. She wanted to close her eyes and take his hand so he could lead her to the truck. She wanted to feel the brief encounter, to be wholly in it as it happened instead of worrying about where to put her feet and when. In an effort to control the revealing nature of her uncensored thoughts, she folded her arms around her and kept her eyes fastened to the ground.

The falling snow had gathered into an early winter storm by the time they reached the truck, and Meg was trembling in her sweats. Dylan yanked open his door and ushered her inside, letting her slide across the bench seat so she didn't have to run around the large vehicle. He didn't look at her as he turned the ignition, but once the engine caught, he made no move to flip on his headlights or put the transmission in gear. Tinkering with the vents, he directed them at Meg and turned the heat on high.

"It'll be warm in a sec," he informed her.

"Thanks." Her voice seemed strange somehow, small and distant, and Meg held herself tighter to ward off the cold.

"Here" — Dylan started to unbutton his coat — "you don't have a jacket. Take mine."

For some reason the offer made Meg blush crimson. "No, no, I'm fine."

But he shrugged it off and handed it to her anyway. When she wouldn't take it, he draped it over her and tucked the collar in around her neck. "What?" he joked. "I have to force chivalry on you?"

She gave him a tight-lipped smile.

"You haven't even had a chance to cool down. You could pull something that way."

"Since when do you worry about me?"

An indecipherable look swept across his features. Dylan's eyes were at once sad, angry, confused. Did she sense a trace of hurt? But he masked his emotions quickly and laughed. The sound was hollow in the cab of the truck. "No one needs to worry about you," he agreed. "You can take care of yourself."

Meg nodded, half wishing that he'd strap on his seat belt and drive away, and half wishing that the snow would fall endlessly and they'd be stuck on the deserted road on the very edge of Sutton. If not forever, at least long enough to work out whatever needed to be worked out between them.

Apparently Dylan was just as torn because he made no move to do what he'd promised, to drive her home.

They sat in the truck, watching the snow outside the window as it collected all around them. Any remnants of daylight were gone, and the storm had rendered the landscape utterly still and dark. To Meg, it felt like they were alone in the world. She knew there were things she should say, questions she should ask, but the longer they were quiet, the more the quiet made sense. She sat beside Dylan until she was warm enough to tilt his coat to one side. It slipped off her shoulder and she placed a warm hand on the seat beside her.

"You're not wearing Jess's ring."

Meg looked down at her left hand as it rested on the ripped seat of Dylan's truck. There wasn't even a faint line where the ring had been. There was no evidence that she had worn it at all. She wanted to tell him that she took it off for football, only because they had instigated a "no jewelry" rule, but the air in the cab was charged and living. How could she talk when she couldn't breathe? So she stared at her fingers, willing the answer to materialize between them, to make sudden and obvious sense, so that Dylan wouldn't wonder at her inability to speak.

"You took it off," he said again, tumbling

the words like the sides of a Rubik's Cube, and all at once everything changed. The act of removing the ring was no longer passive; it was active. She had removed the ring. It seemed to make all the difference to Dylan.

Meg wasn't entirely surprised when she felt the tip of his finger draw a line from her ear to her chin. But his touch burned all the same, white-hot and tingling, and she stifled a shiver in the dark truck. She closed her eyes as he said her name, again and again and again, until his lips found hers and his whispers sighed their way into her mouth. It was what she had been waiting for, and she kissed him back, arching her neck for the warmth of his tongue and not stopping to think of the consequences.

15
LUCAS

"You don't like her here, do you?"

The question was so fraught with potential disaster that at first Lucas tried to ignore it. He busied himself by putting his toothbrush and toothpaste away, then gave the bathroom counter a quick swipe with the hand towel. The way Jenna hovered in the open bathroom door made him feel oddly exposed, like he was back in college and had to share personal space with relative strangers. They didn't use the bathroom together anymore, Jenna smoothing on makeup with a foundation brush while he shaved over the sink. Now they slipped into the intimate space in shifts, almost secretively, as if they had much to hide. Lucas hadn't closed the door to brush his teeth, but for a moment he wished he had.

"I'm glad she's okay," Lucas finally managed, and it was a close approximation to the truth.

He had expected Angela to leave as quickly as she had come, but one week after seemingly materializing out of thin air, she was still claiming his couch as her own. Even after the debacle of their attempt at a happy family dinner, Angela seemed content to dwell amid the thick and stifling hush that had settled over the Hudson house. Coming home from work in the evenings, Lucas had the feeling of wading into a shallow body of still and stagnant water. It was calm, but it was heavy and depressing just below the surface. He set his jaw, tried not to breathe too deeply, and leaned against the bathroom counter since Jenna was blocking the door.

"What is it about her that you can't stand?" Jenna said softly.

"Nothing," Lucas said. "I can stand her. I stand her just fine." Actually, he was surprised that Jenna could stand their houseguest. After all, Angela had more or less committed treason by bringing up Audrey, even if inadvertently. And though Jenna didn't know what Angela had done in a manipulative moment at the age of eighteen, couldn't she feel the tension between her houseguest and her husband? The unspoken guilt that filled their interactions with shared shame?

"Well, I think it's obvious you have something against her."

"I don't have anything against Angela," Lucas said, but he suspected that what Jenna really wanted was a confession. "It's just hard, having her around. I mean, we don't have an extra bedroom, she's practically a stranger . . ."

"She's practically a family member."

"That was years ago. We thought she was dead, remember?"

"Well, it's pretty obvious she's alive."

"I just don't understand what she's doing here."

Jenna turned her head to look down the hallway, and although Lucas couldn't see her face he knew the expression it held.

"At least we didn't have to go to a funeral," Lucas said, assuming that his wife was as grateful as he was that Angela decided to have Jim's body cremated and forgo a traditional ceremony.

"That's heartless."

"I didn't mean it that way."

"I think she skipped an important part in the healing process." Jenna sighed.

"That's what she's doing here? Healing?"

"She's saying good-bye. She's making amends."

He didn't get why Angela had to use their

couch as home base for coming to peace with her past, but he was wise enough not to say as much. Instead, he let the silence stretch until Jenna drew her own conclusions.

"But she has to be doing something, doesn't she?" Jenna eventually said, her voice suddenly thick with sarcasm. "It wouldn't be enough for her to simply take it all in, work through her past and her relationship with her father in whatever way she feels necessary."

"That's not fair."

"It's perfectly fair. You're a fixer, Lucas, you're hardwired to mend things. But some things just can't be fixed."

"Angela can't be fixed?"

"Don't be dense." Jenna turned away from him and started toward the attic stairs.

Lucas flew out of the bathroom behind her. "Why do you want to fight?"

Jenna stopped with her hand on the doorframe of the tiny alcove that opened on the staircase. Her head drooped a little. "I don't want to fight."

"Yes, you do. Stop picking fights with me, Jenna." Lucas was surprised to discover that he was angry, but the fine specter of sorrow walked hand in hand with his fury. "Don't you want to make this work?" he asked, his voice cracking.

Jenna looked down.

"Have you given up completely? Because I'm not ready to give up." Lucas closed the space between them and took Jenna by the arm. His touch was gentle, but she flinched as if he struck her. Maybe she was afraid that he would kiss her again. Maybe she hoped he would.

"What happened between us?"

When Jenna looked up at him, her eyes were filled with tears. They were wide, and so stark with pain that Lucas's fingers tightened on her arm.

"What?" he whispered, drawing her close. She fought his embrace for a moment, but then she softened into him, giving in as he curled his arms around her and held her close.

"You have no idea what I've been through," Jenna breathed against his chest.

Lucas drew back and lifted her chin with his finger, forcing her to look at him. "Unless there's something that you're keeping from me, I know exactly what you've been through. I went through it, too. Remember?"

"It's not the same," she said, closing her eyes. Tears leaked down her cheeks, and Lucas had to suppress the urge to kiss them away.

"I know we deal with things differently, but that doesn't mean we have to suffer alone. I understand, Jenna. Audrey was my daughter, too."

"I lost two daughters, Lucas. Two. You can hardly even acknowledge what I lost when Angela left."

"She's back now," Lucas said. "Doesn't that help? Doesn't that change everything?"

Jenna dropped her forehead against his chest and squeezed him hard for the span of a single heartbeat. "Yes," she whispered. "It changes everything. It makes me realize just how far apart we are." And then she wiggled out of his grip and escaped up the stairs two at a time.

When Lucas woke in the morning, the scent of snow hung about the house in foglike wisps of winter. It was too early for snow, experience had taught him that it would be weeks yet before the first flakes began to fly, but apparently Creation had missed the memo because a lingering chill haunted the Hudson home. The windows were old, the walls poorly insulated, and as Lucas descended the stairs into the living room, he cursed himself for not making the improvements that Jenna had suggested last year. At the time, stretching the rotting siding through one more season seemed frugal. Now he just felt cheap. And cold.

The ladies were huddled in the kitchen around a stainless steel teapot that was just beginning to simmer on the stove. Jenna was a caffeine addict, but since Angela had moved back in, she had followed the younger woman's health-conscious lead and hadn't been indulging her early-morning coffee fix. For the reunited duo, breakfast consisted of nothing more than decaf organic green tea infused with jasmine, although Lucas suspected that Jenna still perked herself an entire pot of the black stuff at work and happily dipped into the box of doughnuts that seemed to perpetually adorn the reception desk at Safe House. Jenna was not a green tea sort of woman. And Blackhawk was not a green tea sort of town. He wondered where Angela had bought the smelly leafy stuff in the first place.

"Coffee on?" Lucas asked in greeting, unexpectedly warmed by the fact that he could see a couple inches of dark liquid in the smoky glass pot. He had tossed and turned all night, thinking of Jenna, dreaming of her in brief snatches of sleep, and he prayed that after their tiny breakthrough the night before, she had dreamt of him, too.

"No." Jenna wouldn't meet his gaze, but she turned from the stove and narrowed her eyes at the coffeepot in accusation. "That's probably left over from yesterday."

Lucas couldn't stop his chest from knotting a little, but he went to empty the soupy sludge without complaint. "What's your day look like?" he asked, tossing the question to no one in particular. The kitchen seemed frozen; he chipped away at it with words.

For a moment, the only sound was the rush of the faucet as he filled the carafe and the shrill whine of the teapot just beginning to scream. Then Jenna pulled the pot from the stove and Angela took the lead by answering, "I'm going back to the farm. Same old, same old."

Lucas was tempted to ask her what she did there, how she could spend hour after hour sifting through the rubble of her father's depressing life, but after his conversation with Jenna the night before, he didn't dare.

"And I'm doing the same thing I do every other day," Jenna spoke up. "I'm working."

It was obvious from her tone that his innocuous question had annoyed her, but Lucas couldn't figure out why. He was only trying to be polite. To make conversation. To defrost the air before it became so cold that even his breath formed icicles.

Angela cleared her throat and perched carefully on the very end of a chair, holding her mug of tea in both hands before her as if it offered a certain protection. From what, Lucas couldn't begin to guess. He found her stance peculiar somehow; the shrinking violet pose didn't fit her at all. "Say, Jenna," Angela started, looking at the jade-tinted contents of her cup, "could you drop me off at the farm on your way to work?"

So she wanted something. Thus the ingenuous downturn of her pale eyes.

"Sure. Why?"

The girl shrugged one cashmere-clad shoulder. Lucas doubted she could afford such a sweater on a coffee shop manager's hourly wage, but he was grateful at least that the garment she wore was her own. It was a vast improvement over his favorite dress shirt.

Angela swirled the contents of her cup and deigned to answer Jenna's question. "I need a ride because I walked home yesterday and left my car there. I needed a little time alone."

Jenna didn't respond, but Lucas's eyebrows shot up. Jim's farm was nearly four miles out of town and yesterday had been brittle, enough to make him dig through the cardboard box that contained his winter paraphernalia so he could find a pair of Thinsulate gloves. The wind alone would have been enough to convince anyone who needed a little alone time that privacy could be achieved in the comfort of a warm car. Women were impossible to understand.

Then again, Angela's frigid trek wasn't entirely out of character. She had, after all, hiked miles to leave Jim's farm before. Lucas was mostly upset that he hadn't been observant enough to pick up the profundity of her distress. It had to have taken a lot of inner turmoil to convince her to strike out across the frigid Iowa landscape with nothing but her two feet to carry her. Of course, he had noticed yesterday that her rental wasn't in the driveway when he came home from work, but he'd assumed that Jenna had told her to park it in the garage. A clinging frost had crisscrossed the windows like an uneven sprinkling of confectioner's sugar the last several days in a row, and he had meant to offer Angela the garage as a begrudging courtesy. He felt a twinge of gratitude that Jenna hadn't beaten him to it and he still had a chance to prove to her that he was trying.

"I'll bring you." Lucas heard the words as if he had not said them, and was startled to find the women staring at him with an almost palpable curiosity. He quickly re-arranged his features. "I mean, Jenna works on the opposite side of town, and my clinic is only a few miles from your dad's farm. I mean, your farm. I mean, it's not far away." Lucas swallowed. Was it Angela's farm now? He should have just shut up when he had the chance.

Remarkably, Jenna was smiling at him. It was a little smile, to be sure, faint and one-sided, and yet more than enough to make Lucas grin back like an overeager schoolboy. That was exactly what he had wanted: for Jenna to see that he was trying. Her approval was well worth the cost of a quick car ride with Angela.

"I think that's a good idea," Jenna said. "It'll give you two a little time to catch up."

"Sure," Angela consented.

"Besides, I need to run." Jenna upended her full mug of tea in the sink and gave Lucas a little wave good-bye as she passed. It was brief, perfunctory, but she did it all the same. It carried him through a quiet, standing breakfast, a quick tooth brushing, and even the tedious task of scraping off the windshield of his icy car.

Lucas didn't regret his absentminded offer until he was actually cocooned in his car with Angela, no way out. He had scratched through the frost to create a peeking hole in the windshield and two matching portholes in the windows of his hatchback. A thin morning light drifted with aimless abandon into the interior, making Angela's skin glow gray and infusing Lucas with a sense of fleeting melancholy, as if it was all a dream. Maybe it was. Maybe Jim dangling from the rafter, the sad body beneath, and the ring that he still transferred from pocket to pocket as if it were a talisman of great value were all part of a strange, indecipherable nightmare.

In the week since Angela's appearance, Lucas had spent so much time trying to learn more about the ring, the body, the untold story of Jim's barn floor secret. He stayed up late at night researching reports of missing persons and wading through the never-ending mire of tragic stories that seemed doomed for obscurity. His little list of nineteen missing women grew to nearly a hundred as his personal search party crossed state borders to include South Dakota, Minnesota, and Nebraska. Lucas red-starred any reports that mentioned a ring, though he never came across a single record that included reference to a Black Hills gold ring.

And when he tired of staring at the familiar glow of the computer screen, Lucas spent hours at the library searching newspaper archives for anything that caught his attention. The Blackhawk paper boasted a column that chronicled visits from out-of-town relatives and friends, and Lucas scoured these seemingly trite paragraphs looking for clues.

Everything turned up empty, like a trio of magician's cups with the prize secreted away where Lucas could never dream to find it. The futility of it all made him want to turn the ring over to Alex. Maybe the police chief could do something with it. Maybe Iowa DCI would be able to tap into their resource pool of forensic scientists and crime scene investigators and come up with some case-breaking lead. But Lucas clung to one thin hope that stopped him from giving up his piece of purloined jewelry: Maybe the ring didn't belong to the woman, maybe it was Angela's, and it rightfully belonged to her.

When Angela sank into the car and clicked her seat belt, Lucas was a tangle of contradictions. He resented her; he was grateful she was alive. He found her beautiful; he thought she was repulsive. He longed to give her the ring and learn once and for all if it was hers; he dreaded the idea of admitting what he had done. With a frustrated sigh, he turned the key in the ignition.

"What do you do there?" Lucas asked, out of the blue.

"What do you mean?" She didn't sound irritated, but it was hard to tell.

"At the farm. What is there to do? It can't be a fun place to be."

Angela snorted. "Very perceptive, Lucas. No, it's not fun. Not at all."

He backed out of the driveway slowly, rolling down his window so he could stick his head out and see where he was going. It didn't bother him that she was being snappish. He waited.

"You know what I'm doing," Angela finally offered as they pulled up to the only stoplight in all of Blackhawk.

"I do?"

"I told you. In your office that day. I'm trying to prove that Jim didn't kill anyone."

"Good luck with that."

"You're being asinine."

"Good word."

"You can be such a jerk."

Lucas glanced at her out of the corner of his eye. "I'm sorry," he said after a moment. "I'm just trying to understand."

"No you're not," Angela grunted. "You've already decided that Jim's a murderer. You think that I'm wrong, that I'm being ridiculous, and now your only goal is to make me see things your way. It's not a formula, Lucas. You can't apply a twelve-step program to my situation."

He was stunned silent. Did he really do that? Had he bothered to listen to her at all? Did he even want to understand? The questions seeped from his mind as quickly as they formed. He was trying to help. All he ever did in any and every situation was try to help. It was what he did. It was who he was. A swift defense sprung to his lips, but before he could voice it, Angela continued.

"I bet you've never done anything crazy. I bet you've never even skinny-dipped or drag raced or copied a paper in college. I bet you've never followed a passion to its conclusion because you simply couldn't imagine doing otherwise."

Passion. For Lucas the word was unexpectedly loaded and immediate. It brought two things to mind simultaneously, and they fought for foreground in his consciousness. Jenna. The Woman. The latter had begun to slowly unearth herself for Lucas, to rise above the shroud of details that seemed to

313

cloak her in mystery so that she was no longer reduced to simply the bones, the pitiful dress, the ring. She was still unnamed, but it seemed cruel to say so, for she bore a name to someone even if the only way that anonymous person could remember her was in generalities. Daughter. Sister. Friend. Beloved.

Didn't passion, at its root, come down to a burning desire to know? I want to know you. I want to know how. I want to know why.

Yes, Lucas knew passion.

They turned off the paved road and crushed gravel beneath the tires of Lucas's car. Each ping of sand and rock against the undercarraige made him cringe, but the tightness in his chest had nothing to do with his vehicle. He could feel Angela's gaze on his face as surely as if she had laid a cool palm on his cheek. His hands began to sweat, but he didn't know why.

"You're wrong," he told her, refusing even a peek in her direction. "I know passion."

"I never said you weren't passionate," Angela assured him. He thought he could detect a hint of humor in her voice. "I said I couldn't imagine you following a passion to its conclusion. There's a big difference."

Though he wasn't entirely sure what she

meant, Lucas felt a pinch of self-reproach twist behind his ribs. For a split second he was sure that Angela knew about the ring, that she was referring to the cowardice of carrying it around in his pocket like some sort of charm. But she couldn't know, and in a small avalanche of understanding, Lucas realized she was referring to Jenna. To its conclusion . . . What was that supposed to mean? Of course he'd follow his wife anywhere. Of course his passion for her would last until the bitter end. His heart began a dizzying downward spiral. The end? Of what? His marriage?

"I don't know what you mean," he said quietly.

"I didn't expect you would."

When Lucas pulled into the long driveway of the farm, he was repulsed at the sight of all the yellow tape, draped everywhere, almost decorative somehow, like hopeful ribbons tied to trees as if their cheering presence alone could coax a soldier home. But Jim wasn't coming back, and Lucas wondered if Angela had ever considered this place home. The flapping strips would have felt like an affront, a downright mockery of all that had happened if they hadn't been emblazoned with the sobering words: PO-LICE LINE DO NOT CROSS.

"Can't you take that down?"

She shrugged as if it didn't matter. "You know, I would have been done here a long time ago if I hadn't spent my first three days chatting it up with every Tom, Dick, and Harry who thought he had something to contribute to the case. They don't. Have anything to contribute, that is."

"And you do?"

She gave him a shrewd look as she unbuckled her seat belt. "I'm systematically going through every scrap of paper, every unpaid phone bill, every forgotten corner, in search of some sort of a clue. I don't know what I'm looking for, and I'm not finding anything, if that's what you mean. But, I'm not going to stop until I do."

"Didn't DCI already do that?"

"Yup. But they don't know my dad."

"How long will you let this thing drag out?"

"As long as it takes."

Lucas was flummoxed. "Are you kidding me? You have a life in California. A good life. You love it there. You hate it here."

"Right on all counts," Angela acquiesced, but the rigid line of her narrow back told him that she wouldn't give up until she found what she was looking for.

"You're crazy."

"No, although I'm doing something crazy."

"Why?"

She squeezed her eyes shut and put a hand to her forehead as if she was offering a prayer for patience. "You're a broken record, Lucas."

"I try."

"To understand, right?"

"Always."

"I'm going to try one more time," Angela said, waving her finger as evidence of this final attempt at explanation. There was a trace of a smile on her face, but when she tried to muster the right vocabulary to encompass the breadth of her desire to know what had happened beneath the floor of her father's barn, she frowned. Lucas watched as she aged in the span of a heartbeat. All at once she seemed very tired, and though her face was still soft and unlined, she looked old beyond her years. "I don't want to live like this for the rest of my life," she whispered, her voice failing her.

"Like what?"

"Like the unloved daughter of a murderer."

Her admission sucked the air out of the overheated car. Suddenly Lucas was hot, and he reached to turn down the heat and put the transmission in park. He thought about cracking open the window, but it seemed insensitive. He wondered if she would interpret the action as an insult, as if he didn't want to breathe the same air as the daughter of a coldblooded killer.

"You're not the daughter of a murderer," Lucas comforted her, but there was no erasing what seemed to be, for all intents and purposes, the truth.

"You're right," Angela asserted, lifting her chin slightly. "I'm not. And that's exactly what I'm trying to prove."

Although he couldn't claim to get it, Lucas felt a wave of pity build in him like the overpowering rush of a rising tide. He fought to keep the emotion buried deep in his gut where it couldn't spill out into his face because he knew that if Angela caught a whiff of his pitying sympathy she'd hate him forever. His features remained stony. She could never know that his heart broke for the little girl she was and the fragile woman she had become. And she could never know that he had the audacity to consider her fragile.

Lucas wanted to help — didn't he always? But there was nothing he could say to soothe the unending sting of her personal history. In fact, words eluded him entirely.

Neither of them spoke, but Angela didn't make any move to get out of the car, and the two of them sat side by side, staring out the windshield, for what felt like a very long time. Lucas squinted at the gloomy landscape before him — the wiry trees, the long brown grass, the broken edges of the neglected farm that bespoke the disregard it had endured — and was quietly surprised when an answer of sorts seemed to present itself.

He could help her.

It was with a sense of embracing the inevitable that Lucas dug his fingers deep into the pocket of his wool pants. There was a certain fatefulness in the air, as if everything that had happened before was for the benefit of this one moment, and he experienced an instant of profound peace as his forefinger hooked the thin, gold band. Lifting it to the muted light of the car, he held it out to Angela.

She glanced at the ring. Glanced at him. Back to the ring. "You're giving me a ring?" she asked, incredulous.

"It's not yours?" he said, breathless as he waited for her answer.

"No."

Lucas exhaled. "Then yes, I guess I am giving you a ring."

"I don't think that's appropriate."

"All right, I'm not giving you a ring," he muttered. "At least, not like that." He waved it at her, teasing her with it. "Take it."

"No."

Lucas groaned. "Would you please just take it? You have no idea how hard it is for me to pass it on to you."

Angela put her palm out for the ring and Lucas dropped it into her hand. She closed her fingers around it for a second, then plucked it out with the thumb and index finger of her other hand. "It's pretty," she said, studying it. "It's Black Hills gold, right?"

"I think so."

"And you bought it for Jenna?" Angela framed her inquiry with a hard, skeptical look. "You want me to tell you it's nice? To tell you it's a good pick for her? I don't really know her taste."

"It's not for Jenna," Lucas dissented. "It's for you."

"I don't want it —"

"It's yours," he interrupted, refusing to take it back.

"I don't want it."

"Yes, you do. It's your clue."

16
Meg

As they kissed, the snow blanketed the world around them, softening the edges and hiding their indiscretion behind a modest veil of soft gray-white. It seemed to Meg as if a dam had burst, and knowing that Dylan was here with her now was a furious erosion of all that had come before. Their failed friendship and the years of distance between then and now dissolved when his lips met hers; they admitted without uttering a single word that this was what they had wanted all along.

Meg drank him in, leveled by the urgency of her need for him and the raw longing that made it almost impossible to tear herself away. Finally, she thought, catching the fabric of his shirt in her fingers. "I've waited so long," she mouthed against the warmth of his neck. And though she didn't allow herself the luxury of the words, everything inside her acknowledged: This is good. This is right.

"Where did this come from?" Meg whispered when they finally forced themselves to break away from each other.

But Dylan didn't answer. He rubbed his head as if massaging away a headache, and turned to peer out the windshield with the mystified look of a dreamer waking from a deep sleep. His forehead was creased, his eyes slightly narrowed, but when he put the truck in drive to take her home, he reached for her hand. Holding her fingers as if he hoped to crush them into his own, to make her a part of himself through pressure alone, he made the agonizingly short trek from the soccer pitch to her parents' driveway. The drive was silent, but Meg's head hummed with the thrill of what had happened, the whir of song inside of her lending a surreal quality to the night.

By the time Dylan pulled into her driveway, they had separated, but Meg still tingled in the place where his hand had pressed hers. She felt intoxicated, heavy-limbed but light-headed, and she asked him again, "What just happened?"

Dylan didn't say anything at first. He sat staring straight ahead, both of his hands white-knuckled on the wheel and his face carefully expressionless. If she hadn't known him so well, Meg would have imagined that he was angry about what had happened, what he had allowed himself to do. But she knew his aloof stance had nothing to do with regret. He simply couldn't bring himself to look at her. The air in the cab of the truck was vibrating with the possibility of what might be. Meg could almost feel his hands around her waist, in her hair, tracing the curve of her ear as if he was actually touching her instead of just thinking about it. The electricity between them was compelling enough to make her knot her hands in her own lap and sit with her back pressed to the passenger door, far away from him because she couldn't trust herself to be close.

After the ferocity of their moments alone, it was sobering to be in her driveway. Her mom and dad were behind the bamboo shutters in the living room, and Jess's parents were at their backs, sentries across the cul-de-sac who could destroy the unexpected sanctuary of the truck that now held their secret. Meg was grateful for the dark sky and the curtain of snow that continued to fall and fall and fall.

"I've wanted to do that from the minute I first saw you," Dylan said, answering the question Meg had forgotten she asked.

"You were too young to want something like that," she blurted, her eyes sparkling.

"Nah," he responded, grinning. "Romeo and Juliet were like, what? Ten?"

Meg laughed and kicked his leg with the toe of her muddy sneaker. Even if someone was looking out the window, they wouldn't be able to see that contact. "You did not just compare us to Romeo and Juliet. That is so lame."

"Girls like that kind of stuff," Dylan shrugged, hiding a brief grin. He pulled his hands from the steering wheel so that he could study them in his lap.

"You know me better than that."

He moved his chin a fraction of an inch and stabbed her with a look so naked and honest, she was convinced that he had just given her a glimpse past every fear, false vanity, and pretension. It took her breath away. "Yes," he said. "I know you better than that."

Meg blinked and turned to look out the windshield. "Why?" she asked again.

"Why what?"

"Why now? Why not back when I . . ." She almost said, "fell in love with you," but she stopped herself before the words slipped out. Though she was heady from the cling-ing astonishment of his kiss, the last thing she wanted to do was admit that she was, in fact, in love with him and had been for years. But if he noticed her abrupt suppression, he didn't let on. Meg fumbled to continue. "Why not before?" She didn't finish the question, but her thumb felt absently for the ring that usually circled her finger. A little tremor of surprise flowed through her when she realized that it wasn't there, and she had to remind herself that she had taken it off for football.

"Why not before Jess had his way with you?" Dylan asked, watching her with an unmistakable glint of bitterness in his gaze.

Meg glared at him. "It's not like that," she snapped, furious that he would dare to accuse her.

"Relax," Dylan said. He braved a moment of contact, sliding his fingers across the bench seat so he could tangle them in her own. He held her hand for a moment, then squeezed hard and let go, wrapping his palms around the steering wheel again where it was safe. Or, at least, safer. "It's all about timing, Meg. Always has been. Getting close to you is like trying to catch the wind. Either I tried to grab too early, or I closed my hand too late. You always seemed to slip right through."

She considered his explanation for a moment, and though it seemed feeble, she accepted that a nugget of truth might reside in it. "But there's more to it than that," she said.

He nodded once and seemed to struggle with his thoughts for a few seconds. "It's brutally honest," he finally admitted.

"I'm a tough girl," Meg assured him.

Dylan sighed and passed his hand over his face. "What do you expect, Meg?"

"What do you mean?"

"Where do you see us in five years? In ten?"

"College," Meg said slowly. "Then . . . I don't know. Why does it matter?"

"Do you see us together?"

The question hit Meg hard. Together? Somewhere, deep down, the answer was a real and living thing, a dream that she held in a place so secret she wondered where it had been hiding. Yes. She thought it almost instantly as hope blossomed in her chest. Together. Aren't we perfect together? But Dylan's eyes were unfolding a different story entirely.

"Come on, Megs. You think we'd make it? You with your perfect little life and white picket fence?"

"We don't have a white picket fence," Meg huffed.

"Whatever. Your life is still perfect. You have a bright future, a daddy and mommy who love you. A big brother who'll probably discover the cure for cancer . . ."

"Bennett isn't that smart."

Dylan laughed, but it was a dry, humorless sound. "We'd never work. Not seriously anyway. We could . . ." he shrugged. "Do this. But I didn't think that this was what you wanted."

Meg wasn't entirely sure what *this* was, but she was absolutely certain that Dylan was trying to let her down easy. That he didn't feel for her the same way that she felt for him. Something inside her fragmented, broke into a million tiny pieces and shivered the detritus of her shattered wishes all the way down to her toes. But she couldn't stand the thought of crying in front of him. Instead of breaking down, she got angry.

"So what exactly is this, Dylan?" Meg half shouted, thrusting her index finger back and forth in the space between them. "What are we? Have you been using me all this time?"

"Using you?" Now Dylan was mad, too. "How have I used you? How have I ever used you? I have done everything in my power to respect you — even when being honorable was the last thing on my mind."

"How noble," Meg muttered.

"We're friends, plain and simple. Always have been. That's all we could ever be — and you know it."

Meg crossed her arms over her chest and glared out the slushy windshield. "I have no idea what you're talking about."

"How many times have you come to my house?" Dylan asked, changing tactics so quickly Meg's head spun.

"What?"

"Just answer the question."

Meg didn't have to think about it, but the answer was so surprising it took her a moment to spit it out. "Never," she whispered, realizing for the very first time how strange that sounded. Why had she never been to his house? She knew where it was, of course, and she had stood on the doorstep many times, but she had never seen beyond the shag carpet of the wood-paneled entryway.

"Never," Dylan repeated, as if that answered everything. He put both hands on the steering wheel, and out of the corner of her eye, Meg could see his knuckles slowly turn white. "Didn't you ever stop to wonder why I never invited you in? Why I never really talked about my own life?"

"Dylan, I —"

"My dad was a meth head," he interrupted. "Do you even know what that means?"

"Of course," Meg managed to squeak out.

"I told you my parents were divorced, but I didn't tell you why. Whenever you asked me about my family or my past or about living in Arizona, I told you Phoenix fairy tales and changed the subject."

"That's not my fault." Meg was reeling, but she managed to feel a flicker of exasperation, too. She had never asked him to shield her from the nasty bits of his past, his life. If she had known, would it have changed anything? "You could have told me the truth."

"The truth? How do you think an ugly story like that would go over in sweet little Perfect Town, USA? There's a church on every corner and standards so high you all practically kill yourselves trying to reach them. Do you think your parents would let you hang out with me if they knew that my dad died of an overdose five years ago, and that they had to fish his body out of a gutter?"

Meg felt all the air in her chest leave in a rush. She was left panting on the front seat of the truck, wondering how she could love him and hardly know him at the same time.

"My life is nothing like yours," Dylan said. "And my dad is just the tip of the iceberg.

We came up here to try and get away from it all, but Sutton isn't home. We don't belong here. I don't belong here."

Meg tried to reconcile the Dylan she knew with the bleak narrative he was painting. She could feel the angst rolling off him like waves of summer heat, shimmering and indistinct with the pain of all the secrets he still held. "But you're not your father. You're nothing like that," she said.

"No. But that doesn't change anything, does it?" He turned and caught her chin loosely in his hand, rubbed her jaw with his thumb. "Do you think your parents would let you date me if they knew that my mom still drinks to forget? That my brother got kicked out of school in Arizona because they found weed in his locker?" He searched her eyes, leaned in a little closer. "The only reason I didn't get kicked out, too, is because they didn't find mine."

"Dylan . . ."

He shook his head as if he could read her mind. "That's not me. At least, not anymore. But, still." His gaze was earnest, almost pleading. "I did the best I could, but I more or less raised myself. Why do you think I always liked hanging out at your house so much?"

Meg turned her face into his hand and

closed her eyes. She wanted to kiss his palm, to press a gift inside it so that he would know just how much he was worth. How much she loved him for who he was. But she didn't dare.

"I'm not going to college," Dylan said, dropping his hand. "I have no idea what I want to do with my life. No clue where I'll go after graduation. Seriously, Meg. What can I offer you?"

"Does it have to be all or nothing?"

Dylan gave her a wry look. "You think we could have a few casual dates? Hang around a bit and then call it quits?"

"My parents would understand," Meg started, but Dylan cut her off.

"It would never work," he said again. "I don't fit in your world, and you don't fit in mine."

"That's the stupidest thing I've ever heard."

"But it's true. You belong with someone like Jess. Not Jess, mind you. He's a moron. But you'll find yourself some handsome scholarship recipient, graduate college summa cum laude, rise to the top of your field, have a few adorable babies, and live happily ever after."

"And you'll . . . ?"

Dylan arched one eyebrow, but his eyes

were heavy. Sad. "I told you. I have absolutely no idea. And I can't take you with me. You'd wake up one day in some cheap trailer with a job as a gas station attendant and a hangover, and hate me for ruining your life."

They were silent for a few long minutes, and in that small span of time, Meg realized that at least in some ways, Dylan was right. She had lived a sheltered life, and though she hated to admit it, there was a set of unwritten rules that she was expected to follow. Her parents did have plans for her, and as much as they liked Dylan, she knew that they considered him a bit of an outsider. Broken family, a bit rough around the edges. A bit too good-looking. A bit too dangerous. Meg's life was supposed to be simple and clean. Dylan's baggage wasn't something they would want her to shoulder. And they didn't know the half of it.

But even as Meg's heart broke, she became aware of the fact that she also had plans for herself. She didn't know what her future held, but it sparkled bright and fresh and just out of sight, the merest whisper of all that was to come. A promise. She was surprised that Dylan could see it. And stunned that he couldn't imagine it for himself.

"Hey," Dylan said before she could muster the courage to speak. "It's okay. You're still my girl. You're just my sometimes girl. Sometimes I have you, sometimes I don't. It's enough." He didn't say "for now," but the limitation was implied. "You know, Meg, I'm really sorry. I never meant for this to happen."

"You regret kissing me?"

His bittersweet half smile slipped a little, and it was so perfectly lopsided, Meg had to repress the urge to kiss the down-turned corner until it righted itself. But the mood in the truck had changed, and though every inch of her body still prickled with the desire to slide next to him and bury herself in all his angles and lines, she made herself sit very, very still.

"Some people just don't fit," Dylan told her. "Whether we like it or not, I don't think we were meant to be."

After a long moment, Meg nodded, sealing an agreement that tore her heart to make. She didn't know exactly what Dylan expected from her, from them, but she was willing to suspend all her doubts if it meant that maybe, sometimes, at least more than this one time, they could share the furtive refuge of a moment like this. "Okay," she whispered, because it seemed the only thing to say.

"Okay."

They breathed in harmony for a long minute, then Dylan stuck out his hand in an imitation of the hapless greeting he had extended when he pulled her down behind the raspberries. It recast everything. Made light dark. "Friends?" he asked.

"Friends," she agreed, but the word was harsh against her tongue, sour and thick with yearning that she swallowed whole.

Maybe it should have been easy to go back to the way things had been, but in the days and weeks after giving in to the irrepressible pull of each other, Meg had a very hard time reverting to same old, same old. Passing him in the hall at school, it was almost impossible for her to stop herself from touching him in some small, hidden way. She turned her palm out and brushed his arm, keeping her face blank and her eyes fixed straight ahead as she felt the cord of muscle beneath his warm skin. Or she would alter her path a bit and brush past him on her way to what she now considered some inconsequential class. Their hips would touch, their shoulders, elbows, legs, it didn't matter. But wherever she touched him, she would burn in the spot for many minutes after he was gone.

Her skin felt tight, constraining, as if the girl inside was not the same as the one who had existed before Dylan changed everything with a kiss. She hated herself for each display of weakness, loathing the way that he had somehow separated her from everything she believed herself to be. The worst of it was, she couldn't read him. She was no more aware of his desires and intentions than she was able to decipher her own. Everything was foggy and indistinct, muted by the overwhelming fact that she ached to be with him, no matter the personal cost.

It didn't help that Dylan kept coming to her football games. He sat beneath the oaks, tucked far away and out of sight unless you knew what, or whom, you were looking for. Meg looked. She inspected the hill for him with an increasing urgency that bordered on desperation. The inner turmoil contributed to the passion of her game, but the mental clarity that had kept her team on a winning streak was muddled and dark. The Riot Girls started to lose, and Meg found that she didn't care. After the clock ran out, she tried to be cool, nonchalant, encouraging her team and quickly sending them on their way. "I have a ride," she would admit when pressed. "An old friend." She hoped her face didn't betray the agony that word inflicted.

And though she wanted to run when the rest of the girls turned toward the parking lot, Meg forced herself to cross the field slowly. Arms wrapped tight around her, chin tucked low, head down, so she didn't have to watch him watching her come.

Sometimes they didn't even make it to the truck. Sometimes he caught her chin and tipped it toward his own face, tasting her with little kisses as if she was something to be savored.

"I'm sweaty," she complained, pulling away.

"I don't care."

It was always the same. A dance of their own invention that had a certain careful choreography, even though everything felt haphazard, quick and wild in its bewildering intimacy. She demurred, he chased, and they gave in to each other for as long as they dared. Until they had to pretend that nothing had ever happened and go back to the status quo of their normal lives. But there was nothing remotely normal about their clandestine relationship or, in fact, any area of their lives, when the days seemed to center around the next possible time they might find to be alone.

As November wore on and the end of the Girls' Football League approached, Meg began to feel restless. The girls were starting to complain about the cold, and the football games were no longer well attended by either players or spectators. But Meg was afraid to pull the plug on the league because it meant her stolen moments with Dylan were numbered. In the end, the choice wasn't hers to make: the Pigskin Barbies announced the date of their last game against the Riot Girls and called it the championship.

Nobody contested the unorthodox conclusion to the GFL, and Meg actually smiled when she heard. She couldn't help thinking of the girls as her girls, and she was happy to imagine that the league had been a bright point in their fall, maybe even in their entire high school experiences. It certainly seemed to have emboldened them.

A large crowd gathered for the final game, bundled in football blankets and waving extra team T-shirts over their heads as makeshift pennants. When the league champions had been decided once and for all, everyone was supposed to go home and shower, then meet at Giovanni's, the only pizza place in Sutton, for a victory dinner.

It didn't really matter who won; the victory belonged to every one of the forty-two girls who participated in the full, unsanctioned season. Everyone was coming: players, fans, parents who thought the girls were plucky and admired their charming audacity. It was the perfect end to the season, but the plan filled Meg with both excitement and dread because, although she was looking forward to celebrating the success of the GFL, she was terrified to have her last postgame encounter with Dylan.

The early snow had melted and the day of the championship was cold but not unbearable. Meg's breath came in short bursts anyway, as if the temperature was well below zero and it caused her physical pain to inhale. She told herself that it was because she didn't want the football league to end, and she tried valiantly to keep her head in the game. But though she strived to focus on leading her team to victory, the Pigskin Barbies won by a touchdown. Then there were screams and hugs and chaotic piles of girls on the field as they rejoiced in the weeks of their self-made glory. Some girls even cried, and Meg didn't begrudge them their tears. She just hugged them harder and smiled wide to make up for their tear-streaked faces when someone from the sidelines shouted, "Say cheese!"

It was all much, much more than she had ever dared to hope or expect when she had walked into Mrs. Casey's office months ago. Meg should have reveled in the success, taken a few moments to relish the sights and sounds around her, to enjoy the triumph of the GFL that had, in a few short months, become iconic in Sutton. But her heart was already over the berm at the end of the field, she saw herself holding Dylan for what she feared would be the last time. After all, it wasn't like he could just start coming over to her house or pick her up after dark to take a long drive down a deserted road. It wasn't like she could break up with Jess and let Dylan make an honest woman out of her, so to speak. Dylan had made that perfectly clear.

Meg stayed on the field, pasting a grin on her face for countless photographs and shaking hands when the girls wanted to introduce her to their parents, until the last stragglers found their way to the parking lot. Then she picked up the football that all the girls had signed with a permanent marker She crossed the field with a strange hollowness in her gut, a sense of foreboding that made her petulant and short-tempered as she approached Dylan's shadow against one of the naked trees.

"You were awesome," he said when she was close enough to hear the low rumble of his voice.

"We lost."

"Doesn't matter."

She shrugged to show him that it didn't matter to her either.

Dylan's gaze shifted beyond her, and she saw his eyes narrow as he tried to make out the parking lot. It was already too dark to see across the expanse of field. "I'll miss watching you," he told her, seemingly buoyed by the fact that they were alone.

"Whatever." Meg broke away from the line of trees and started down the far side of the small hill in the direction of Dylan's waiting truck.

"Hey," he soothed her, snaking an arm around her shoulders and giving her a little squeeze. "What's up with you?"

"This is wrong."

"The end of your infamous Girls' Football League?"

Meg squinted at him in the descending darkness and saw that he knew exactly what she was talking about. She spelled it out anyway. "Us."

He nodded. "I know."

"What do you mean?" Meg asked, stepping out of his one-armed embrace.

"What do you mean, what do I mean? You're the one who said this is wrong."

She bit her lip. "Wrong because I'm still supposedly dating Jess? Or wrong because . . ." She couldn't finish. Or maybe she didn't want to. It was too hard to admit that what he was playing at she had hoped was for real. Kind of like the Girls' Football League. "Forget it."

Some of the tenderness that Dylan had exhibited the first night in his truck had disappeared with the advent of their less than conventional friendship, and he gave her a playful shove. Meg knew there were terms for this sort of thing, this thing that they were — Friends With Benefits, FTMO, Friends That Make-Out — and they all sickened her to the point of actual, stomach-clenching nausea. When Dylan leaped in front of her and spun her off her feet with a laugh, Meg gritted her teeth and pushed him away.

"What?" Dylan looked surprised, maybe a little hurt.

"This is wrong."

"You already said that."

"It's not . . ." She fumbled, trying to encompass everything she felt in one perfect word, something that would fall from her lips like a bomb and explode with meaning at his feet. "It's not honest," she managed.

"So tell Jess. Or stop seeing me."

But Dylan had missed the point entirely. It was true that she wasn't being honest with Jess — his phone calls were becoming increasingly uncomfortable for her, and it felt wrong to wear his ring, even though she didn't dare take it off any longer than the span of her football games. And yet she was more concerned about being honest with herself. She hated the lies that she was telling herself: That everything was okay. That Dylan's kisses were meaningless. Fun. A diversion, like the GFL and her entire ruse of an autumn.

"What do you want, Meg?" Dylan demanded, but his eyes were wide and dark and, she imagined, sad.

She opened her mouth and closed it, trying to come up with a way to explain all that she felt and the hurt of having him in bursts. But in the end, she didn't know what to say to him.

They got into the truck in silence, and she didn't slide across the seat to hold him like she usually did. He turned the key and revved the engine just a little higher than necessary, then drove her home without another glance, without a single remark to ease the tension between them, though the air was filled with all the thoughts they refused to voice.

When he pulled into the driveway, Meg sat in the truck as if in a trance, her mind swirling with things unsaid, years' worth of confessions, and what felt like a lifetime of emotion that she had pressed deep and tried to ignore. Now she pictured herself pushing it all back, using her hands to force it down and down, into the dark places that had healed when Dylan's kiss loosed the chains and set every unspoken hope free. But the sea of emotion had grown in the short weeks of their so-called affair, and she knew their furtive romance was the sort of quiet crime that could leave a graveyard of broken hearts in its wake. Her palms overflowed with the breadth of it all. It spilled between her fingers and trickled down over the seat where she had believed, for a moment at least, that everything could change. Didn't he feel it?

But Dylan must not have felt it. He must not have known what it meant to Meg to leave him like she did, wordlessly, without a kiss to ease the parting or even one last touch. He didn't even say good-bye, and neither did she.

17
Lucas

Lucas spent the morning unhinged, blowing in the wind, as if one of the screws that held him together had finally slipped loose. He felt like that more and more these days: undone; falling apart in places that he wondered if he would be able to fix. He had been wrong about so many things. It was disconcerting.

Thoughts of Angela and the ring underscored every moment of the long hours before his lunch break. Had he done the right thing? It was the question that seemed set on continuous play in the sound track of his life. Always there, always demanding more than he was able to give.

"Do the right thing," Lucas's father had said, repeating his own personal mantra as if it was enough to keep his son on the straight and narrow. And Lucas did as he was told. He lived life clean and simple, trying to keep people and circumstances in careful order within the world that he so painstakingly constructed around himself. Jenna was an aberration. So was Angela, the ring, his fixation on the woman in the barn. Was it a fixation? An obsession? Or had he, like always, just hoped to do the right thing?

When lunchtime finally rolled around, Lucas locked himself in his office and riffled through his notes about the missing women. Their names slipped beneath his fingers as he fanned the pages, their stories blurred into one long lament. It felt so hopeless, so completely impossible to find one single, forgotten woman out of thousands who had vanished that Lucas was ready to throw the entire heap into the garbage can. He couldn't save Audrey. He couldn't save his marriage. And he couldn't save this broken, nameless woman.

The stack of papers made a dull thud at the bottom of the plastic recycling bin. Lucas stared at the top sheet for a moment, then shifted a pile of old envelopes off the edge of his desk and watched them flutter down to obscure the evidence of his research. He felt a brief stab of hope that Angela was doing better with the ring than he had done with the missing women.

The ring. Suddenly Lucas was gripped by the certainty that he hadn't looked into it enough. He hadn't given the piece of jewelry much attention — mostly because he harbored the hope that it was Angela's until the moment she dismissed that notion. But maybe it wasn't a common Black Hills gold ring at all. Maybe the ring was the key, not the woman.

It felt strange not to have the ring in his pocket, and he battled a brief regret that he had given it to Angela. MKD could stand for dozens of different things, but it was possible that if he could trace the origin of the ring, he could find out who had bought it. Or, at the very least, where her story began.

A few minutes later, Lucas tore a sheet of paper fresh from the printer and shot Angela a text as he swung out the clinic door. He would fly out to the farm, maybe ask Mandy to rearrange his schedule a bit for the afternoon . . .

But he didn't make it out of the office parking lot.

"We're playing today," Alex told Lucas, slamming his car door just as Lucas dug his keys out of his pocket.

Caught off guard by Alex's sudden appearance, Lucas shook his head determinedly and folded the piece of paper in his hands. Stuffed it into his back pocket.

"Racquetball? Is that today? Can't do it. Too busy. Too much going on."

In spite of their hectic schedules, Lucas and Alex tried to meet at least once a week to play racquetball. It began as a way to work off a little aggression, a midweek release that kept them fit and focused. When Angela showed up in town, Lucas begged off their regular court date for a week. Alex let it slide once, but apparently he wasn't going to forgive a second time.

"I'm not taking no for an answer," Alex grunted. He threw a duffel bag at Lucas, and the nylon bundle slammed into his chest.

"Uncalled for." Lucas glared at the police chief, but it was hard to be mad at Alex. Especially since he was trying to be a friend.

"Shorts, T-shirt, tennis shoes . . ." Alex ticked off all the necessary items on his thick fingers. "I even remembered your ugly brace thingy."

"It's a safety strap for my glasses," Lucas told him, bending to retrieve the duffel. He unzipped it to make sure that Alex hadn't tampered with anything.

"My condolences."

"Because I wear glasses?"

"I wouldn't be caught dead in that ridiculous stretchy doodad."

"Doodad?"

"Four-eyes."

"You're infantile," Lucas complained. "And you have glasses, too, in case you've forgotten."

"Shhhh!" Alex shot Mandy a quick look. She had pulled into the parking lot during their exchange and was making her way slowly toward them. "I don't want Mandy to know I'm not perfect in every way."

"Let me refresh your memory," Lucas said in a stage whisper. "You wear bifocals. For reading. Because you're an old man, Kennedy."

"Shut up."

"He's old," Lucas told Mandy, jerking a thumb in Alex's direction and shaking his head as if it was a sorry thing indeed.

Mandy laughed. "You two are worse than kids. You're worse than my boys, and they're downright primitive. Neanderthals, I swear."

Alex winked. "Caught me."

"Stop flirting with my nurse."

Mandy consulted her watch. "You've got just under an hour," she said, ignoring Lucas's comment. "Have fun."

Lucas grabbed a handful of his friend's shirt and dragged him toward his car. "Fine," he said, certain that if he refused Alex would know that something was wrong. "Let's go."

"You're playing? It's because I packed your duffel, isn't it?"

"You got my bag out of the trunk of my car. Remind me never to leave my keys in the ignition again."

"Oh, but you didn't. I used the extra set you hide in that magnetic case under the wheel well."

The lone racquetball court in Blackhawk was in the basement of the community center. A heavy, double door opened on a low, narrow hall with a popcorn ceiling that more likely than not boasted enough asbestos to turn their lungs black with cancer. The lighting was limited to sparse sunlight that filtered through the frosted-glass window in the door, the floors were sticky, and the walls seemed to ooze a shade of orange that always made Lucas feel like he was descending into the belly of a beast.

It was a far cry from the streamlined, modern gyms that Lucas enjoyed during his school years, but there was something masculine and inviting about Blackhawk's version of a fitness center. Since it was so decrepit and unkempt, Jenna and her ilk avoided it as if it were some seedy bar. But for Lucas, it was veiled in mystery, dark and secretive — the perfect place to say things that couldn't be voiced in the comfort of a warm kitchen or beneath the glow of a sunlit sky. Over the years, he had admitted many things to the concrete walls of the racquetball court. And Alex, always the friend, promptly forgot them the moment they emerged from the dark.

Sometimes Lucas thought of the racquetball court as his own confessional, and Alex was as tight-lipped as a priest. It was healing somehow to say aloud the things that ate him alive, and then forget that they had ever been given breath. No matter what Lucas voiced — I don't think I want another baby; I think something's wrong with Jenna; I think something's wrong with *me* — Alex let it bounce off him like the ball careening from wall to wall. The police chief returned each hit with a deadly slice of his racquet but offered little commentary on all the winged words that the good doctor loosed. Yet when Lucas missed the ball, or tried to hide things that his friend knew he needed to say, Alex was merciless. Occasionally he even aimed for Lucas's back instead of the front wall, and the welts he inflicted had nothing to do with punishment and everything to do with distraction.

Lucas knew that Alex's presence at the clinic and his insistence on playing in spite of everything that had happened was all about turning his head. If Alex had a personal motto, it would be "Let it go," and the chilly court seemed to echo with that mantra as he warmed up. He was all fire and jazz, bopping across the court like a man ten years his junior. It made Lucas laugh, and that was the point.

"Thank you," Lucas said when he was queued up in the service zone, ball in hand.

"For what?"

"Getting me out of the office." Lucas bounced the ball and caught it, then surveyed Alex as he stood center court, ten feet behind the short line. The police chief was squatting, arms out and ready, paunch hanging over the waistband of his shorts. "You got me out of the office, remember?"

"Shut up."

"You look ridiculous, by the way."

"Serve the ball, moron."

The play was fast and frenzied, and though Alex managed to maintain a lead, it was slight. He had a killer backhand and could put a spin on the ball that had the capability of leaving Lucas with rubber burn if he got in the way. Though he couldn't hit as hard, Lucas was faster and willing to dive for balls that were out of his reach. All said and done, they were pretty evenly matched.

As they sprinted and lunged, cracking the ball off the walls in their echoing cave with dizzying speed, they spat out conversation in bursts of ricocheting dialogue.

"How's she doin'?" Alex grunted.

"Angela?"

"Yeah."

"Good." Lucas rallied a low-flying service.

"Jenna?"

"Fine."

They played in silence for longer than usual because the presence of the Woman was heavy and unspeakable between them. Alex had nothing to contribute but conjecture and frustration, and Lucas hardly trusted himself to acknowledge the company of her ghost while maintaining the lie of omission he had guarded since taking her ring. But halfway through the first game, the space was so filled with her presence, it began to feel like a stifling tomb instead of a racquetball court.

Lucas took a deep breath and dove in. "Tell me about the investigation."

"You know I can't."

"That hasn't stopped you so far."

Alex sighed. "Nothing to tell. You know that. The dental records were not a match; the body isn't Angela. So that's a dead end. It's not like there's some dental record database that we can consult."

"There isn't?"

"Dentists keep dental records," Alex reminded him. "The only way we could find a match is if we could find the woman's dentist."

"And you'd have to know who she is to figure out who her dentist is."

"You see our dilemma."

"What else?" Lucas asked. "There has to be more that can be done. More tests or something."

"What would you suggest? There are no fingerprints to match, no evidence that survived the years between the crime and our discovery of it, nothing identifying on the body at all."

Lucas cringed inside. Opened his mouth to say, "There is . . ." But he couldn't do it. Though Lucas had a hard time imagining that he had much in common with Jim Sparks's long-lost daughter, there had been some unavoidable thread of commonality in the car earlier that morning, a mere suggestion that was compelling enough to make him feel safe handing her the ring and confessing exactly where he had gotten it. But standing in the sobering reality of the derelict racquetball court, his friend across from him looking skeptical and frustrated,

Lucas's confusion was compounded. He hoped Alex couldn't read the doubt in his face. And he hoped that his furtive research of less than an hour ago would turn up something. Anything.

"Do you know how many people go missing every day?" Alex questioned.

After all his research, Lucas had a pretty good guess. But he shrugged and played dumb.

"Two thousand three hundred."

"Are you kidding me? Do you mean worldwide?"

"In the U.S. alone. The National Center for Missing Adults tracks about forty-eight thousand active cases."

It was a staggering thought. She, whoever she was, was nothing more than a number in the midst of those statistics. A small white hand waving in surrender — but who could see it among the press of people? Lucas felt something coil deep in his abdomen, a cool snake of regret that curled up in some hidden place where guilt took quiet root.

"The interviews?" Lucas asked hopefully.

"Ongoing."

"Forensics?"

"Her neck was broken. Badly. But they're having a tough time determining exactly what could have caused that sort of damage. There are a lot of potential scenarios."

Lucas tried not to let his mind consider the possibilities. "I thought you found buckshot in the barn," he said.

"There was some. But it's impossible to date and scattered everywhere. Jim was probably shooting at pigeons. She didn't have any gunshot wounds."

They broke for a sip of tepid water from the antiquated drinking fountain after Alex won the first match by two. Lucas thought they were on safe ground, well past the perplexing conversations about Angela, Jim, and the body beneath, but Alex didn't seem to agree.

"Seriously," the police chief asked, leaning against the fountain as Lucas bent for a drink. "What's up with Angela?"

Lucas stood. Swallowed. "What do you mean?"

"For starters, why's she still here?"

"Collecting evidence."

"Evidence?" Alex pulled up his nose as if the very thought was ludicrous. "She's a kid. What's she gonna find?"

"She's hardly a kid."

Alex swept his hand as if batting away the reminder. "Sorry, she's frozen in time for me. But that's irrelevant. We've scoured that house. She's not going to find anything."

"Look, she's going through his papers with a magnifying glass, but I don't think she's found anything," Lucas said. "Jenna believes it's nothing more than a way for her to deal with what's happened. She's putting her story to rights, then she'll go back to California and leave it up to DCI."

"It's always been up to DCI."

The second match was a fast game, too frenetic to allow much room for conversation. Lucas threw himself into the game with complete abandon, and managed to squeak out a win near the end when Alex was breathless and unable to keep up with his partner's intense pace.

"I guess you let me win?" Lucas asked after Alex lunged for the ball on game point and missed.

"Nah. Fair and square," he conceded. Lines of sweat made twin trails down the sides of his face and he was breathing heavy, but he smiled all the same. "Good thing I have one more chance to redeem myself."

They paused for one last drink break, even though it meant that their final game would most likely have to be cut short. But as soon as Lucas threw open the glass door of the racquetball court, he heard the distinctive ring of his cell phone. When he bought the phone a year earlier, Jenna had downloaded a hip-hop tune and set it as his ring tone for a joke. It made her giggle every time he got a phone call because it was so incongruous with his straitlaced personality. Lucas hated the obnoxious tune, but it was a small thing that made his wife happy. It was worth it. And he probably would have ignored it when it rang in the middle of the match, favoring a quick drink and a final, tiebreaking game, if Alex hadn't covered his ears and complained.

"That's downright painful. Answer it or turn it off!"

Lucas dug through his duffel and grabbed the phone. It was Angela.

His heart thudded dully, but he tried to act natural. "Dr. Hudson," he said.

"Oh, that's so formal. Hello, Dr. Hudson. Do you sign your letters like that? Does it say Dr. and Mrs. Hudson on your address labels?"

"Angela. Come on."

"You recognize my voice. That's sweet."

Lucas felt Alex's eyes on him and he tried to turn his back to his friend discreetly. "Where are you?"

"I'm at the Central Café. Did you know they have free Wi-Fi here? Seriously. I was blown away."

"Uh, can I call you back later?" Lucas

357

asked, peeking over his shoulder at Alex and arching one eyebrow as if to say, "Crazy girl."

"No," she said so forcefully Lucas pulled the phone away from his ear. He quickly replaced it, afraid that Alex would be able to overhear their unexpected exchange. "No, you can't call me back," she continued. "I followed your text and I actually found something."

Lucas drew a shallow breath. "What do you mean?" He wanted to race up the stairs and have this conversation in private, but then Alex would know beyond a shadow of a doubt that something was up. Instead, he tried to relax his shoulders, look nonchalant. "What about it?"

"You were right. It's not Black Hills gold. There's no MKD in the Black Hills gold market."

"I know."

"There's Stamper, that's STMP, and Black Hills Designs, that's BHD, and Landstrom's — I can't figure out if they have a logo — but no MKD."

"I know." Lucas braved another peek at Alex and wasn't surprised that his friend had settled himself against the wall, arms crossed over his chest so he could observe the entire one-sided interchange. The two men smiled at each other thinly. "So what?" Lucas said, turning his attention back to the phone.

"So I kept refining your searches."

"Are you sure this can't wait until later? I'll be home around suppertime."

"No," she said as vehemently as before. "I'll cut to the chase: I found it. A jewelry company called Matthew Kane Designs."

Lucas went still as he waited for her to continue. "And?" he prompted.

"And he's an independent jeweler in Omaha, Nebraska. He specializes in earth-themed jewelry . . . leaves, branches, trees, flowers . . . Lucas, I went to his website and his stuff looks just like the ring you gave me."

There were a dozen things Lucas wanted to ask her, but every question seemed to give too much away. In the end, the only thing he could safely say in front of Alex was: "Uh, good. That's good. Let's talk about it tonight, okay?"

"You're not alone," Angela surmised, dropping her voice. "Okay, I get it. I'll let you go. But this is it, Lucas. And you need to take the day off tomorrow. I made an appointment for us with Mr. Matthew Kane himself. You're my fiancé and we're shopping for engagement rings."

A little moan of surprise escaped his lips before he could contain his shock. He tried to cover it with a forced cough and said into the phone, "Uh, okay. Great. Thanks for calling. We'll see you later." He clicked off before she could say another word.

Lucas held the phone for a moment, pretending to change one of the settings as he attempted to come up with a convincing excuse for his bizarre chat with Angela. When he finally turned back to Alex, he could tell by the police chief's face that no matter what he said, the man leaning against the wall would be utterly unconvinced.

"Found something?" Alex asked, arms tight across his chest, well-defined muscles in his forearms bulging. He was soft in some places, fit in others, and he liked to pretend he was intimidating even though he knew he was anything but.

"It's, uh, personal. A personal discovery. She's making peace with her past."

"Lame, Lucas. You can do better than that."

Lucas raised his hands, palms up, and struggled for words. "I don't know what to say. It's complicated."

"I'll bet."

The two men stood silent for a moment, staring at each other without the benefit of words to soften the sudden edges between them.

Lucas moved first. "You know, I'd better get going. I have an appointment at one and I really need to shower."

"Yup," Alex nodded, reaching for his own duffel bag and slipping the head of his racket into the open zipper. "We'd better get going." He brushed past Lucas on his way to the stairs, but stopped in the archway of the narrow hallway, blocking the way up. "I need you to promise me something first."

"Okay," Lucas said without hesitation, but he wondered if it was a promise he'd be able to keep.

Alex leveled a finger at his friend's nose. "You'd better promise me that you'll be careful with the Sparks girl. I don't know what's going on, but I feel trouble in my bones."

"There's no trouble, no trouble at all."

They both knew he was lying.

18
MEG

Meg wasn't ready to see Jess when he came home at Thanksgiving.

There was no closure in the wordless good-bye that had happened in the cab of Dylan's truck, and in the interim Meg and Dylan hadn't exchanged a single word. But that didn't mean that she didn't think about him all the time — nearly every minute of every day, as if he was a part of her, as natural as her breath, as close as the air on her skin. It was downright painful to see him in the halls at school; her chest clenched, her pulse quickened, and try as she might to ignore that he was there, when he walked away he took pieces of her with him, bit by bit, little by little, until she felt as if the wind blew through the holes he left behind.

Meg wanted to talk to him, but she didn't dare. Part of her was afraid to hear what he had to say, and the rest of her was terrified to see him face-to-face, for fear she'd fall to pieces. She wasn't the sort of girl who crumbled, but then again, until her indiscretion with Dylan, she hadn't considered herself the sort of girl to cheat on a man who loved her, either.

Strong. She was strong. She had to be.

But as the end of November approached, she didn't feel strong. Not at all. For the first time in nearly three months she was going to see Jess, and everything was supposed to be the same between them. It wasn't. Everything felt different. It was as if they had never happened, or if they had, that her time with Dylan had negated any good thing that passed between them.

Confession fell hard upon her shoulders. As much as she wanted to shrug it off and pretend that they were okay, the memory of Dylan pressed her down with such a staggering weight of physical guilt that she wasn't sure she would be able to stand up beneath it. She feared she'd see Jess and he'd know, really know. She felt like her mistakes with Dylan were altering enough to leave her a different girl entirely. Branded somehow. Changed. And it just had to be visible, as identifying as a letter emblazoned across her chest.

"Are you excited?" Linda asked a few days

before Jess was scheduled to arrive home for the holiday.

"For what?"

Linda gave her daughter a searching look. "For Jess to come back."

"Of course."

But Linda was shrewd enough to know that Meg's answer didn't come close to the truth.

"Long-distance relationships are hard, aren't they?" Linda's expression invited her daughter to open up, but Meg avoided the question and refused to turn away from the book she was pretending to read. She had been on the same page for twenty minutes.

"You know," Linda began, settling onto the arm of the couch where Meg had stretched out. "You're young, honey. You don't have to stay with the same boy forever. It's not like you have to marry Jess."

"Mom."

"I'm just saying: it's okay if you don't want to see Jess anymore. I mean, you're still just a girl, Meg."

"Okay, fine."

Linda braved contact, laying a tentative hand on her daughter's arm. "You all right?"

"Yeah. Fine."

"Okay." Linda nodded.

"Okay."

But the older woman must have suspected that Meg was far from okay, because when Bennett came home for Thanksgiving break, the night before Jess was scheduled to arrive, Linda resorted to drastic measures: she sent her son in to spy. Meg knew her brother's presence at the door of her bedroom was far from innocent because he cheerfully announced it in greeting.

"I'm here to spy," Bennett blurted without preamble, edging the door open with his toe and staring at Meg as she sat cross-legged on her bed.

She was stiff and miserable, fed up with trying to find a comfortable position when she was agonizingly aware of all her uncooperative angles and lines. Nothing felt quite right, inside or out, and when Bennett showed up in her doorway, she gave up trying and stretched her legs in front of her with a defeated sigh. She sat like that, legs akimbo, arms limp beside her, and watched him walk into her room and close the door.

They weren't close, not really, but his absence had allowed their faltering relationship to reach a new plateau of understanding. He still avoided her when he came home for breaks, but they acknowledged each other. When Bennett left for college and she had him in small doses, Meg found her brother more tolerable. As Meg matured, Bennett uncovered more redemptive qualities in her personality. He even passed on his English Lit books when he thought she would like them. More often than not, she did.

Meg groaned, watching her brother make himself at home in the wingback chair that sat in a corner of her room. "She's resorted to spying? That's low."

"Nah, I think that's what moms are supposed to do. It's in the handbook."

"There's a handbook?"

"Sure."

"Can I have one?"

"I think they hand them out when you actually become a mom."

Meg yawned, shaking her head from side to side as if to clear it. "Not a mom handbook, a handbook for me. I want one for my own selfish reasons."

"They don't make one for that."

"Who's they? I think I hate them."

"Hear, hear."

"Welcome back, by the way." Meg tossed a pillow at him. It was as close as they got to sibling affection. It was enough.

In reply, Bennett caught the pillow, fluffed it, and crammed it behind his head. Leaning back, he closed his eyes and kicked his legs up onto the bed.

"So, tell Brother Bennett what you're doing that's got Mom all in a fuss."

"Brother Bennett? That's disturbing."

"What you call me is irrelevant. You're just supposed to spill your guts and then I'm supposed to report back to Mom."

"That's heinous."

"Pretty much." Bennett opened his eyes long enough to wink at her. "I can't say I care all that much about the soap opera of your high school existence, but I can promise you that I'd never rat you out to Mom."

Meg studied her brother intently. "Thanks."

"That's just common decency, Meglet."

"All the same."

"Tell you what. I'll just take a little snooze in your chair, then when I wake up, I'll tell Mom we had a stellar heart-to-heart. It's all top secret, blah, blah, blah, but the bottom line is, you'll be fine. That way Mom won't be too upset about her poor baby girl to make her famous corn bread stuffing for Thursday."

"It all comes down to stuffing for you?"

Bennett gave a little moan at the thought. "The promise of that stuffing kept me going this fall, I'll have you know."

They sat in the bedroom in silence for

several minutes, and when Bennett's breathing lengthened, Meg was sure her brother had done exactly what he said he'd do and was asleep. She leaned back herself and stared at the ceiling, at the orange peel texture and the matching handprints that she had put beside the light fixture when she jumped on the bed after eating Doritos. Her mother had been furious about the greasy marks, but Meg loved the five-pointed stars of her small hands. They were her own constellation; iridescent symbols poised to hear her nighttime wishes.

"So?" Bennett's voice startled her so much she jumped.

"I thought you were asleep!"

"Come on." Bennett opened one eye and frowned at her. "You're not gullible, Meg. Don't pretend like you are. It's unbecoming."

His comment was deflating somehow. "I don't feel like myself these days," she admitted. And though he didn't prompt her in any way, Meg found herself wanting to say things to him. "I'm confused."

"Obviously."

She wanted him to ask, to ease the words out of her with careful questions and subtle nudges, but he closed his eyes again and said no more. Meg took it upon herself to continue. "I'm confused about Jess."

"You're a kid. What's there to be confused about? Break up with him."

"I don't know if it's as simple as that."

Bennett sat up straight, glowered at her stupidity for a moment, then rearranged himself on the chair, legs over the wide arms and lower back cushioned by the pillow that had formerly bolstered his messy bed head. "Of course it's as simple as that. You're what, sixteen?"

"Seventeen. Just. Thanks for remembering my birthday, by the way."

"No problem. Anyway, as I was saying, it's easy. You're a kid."

Meg made a warning sound in the back of her throat. "Stop calling me a kid."

"Sorry. Habit."

"Break it or get out of my room."

Though Meg wasn't schooled in the finer points of her brother's evolving character, for a split second she thought she could see something soften in his gaze. "Why isn't it easy?" he asked.

"You're taking a psych class, aren't you?" Meg countered, narrowing her eyes at him with an almost palpable skepticism.

"I am! I tried empathy there. Did it work?"

"No."

He snapped his fingers in mock disappointment, then consulted his watch and moved to stand. "I think Mom will buy that we've had a meaningful heart-to-heart. It's been long enough, wouldn't you say?"

"Sure."

"It's been real, little sis."

She watched him go, but when his hand was on the doorknob and he was a heartbeat away from slipping out, Meg blurted: "Dylan and I . . ." She didn't finish, but Bennett stopped.

"You slept with him?" he asked without turning around.

"No," Meg whispered, shocked. "No, of course not. Nothing like that."

"At least you're not entirely stupid," Bennett sighed, and turned to lean against the back of the door and survey her. "But something happened, and this is why you're confused about Jess."

"Yeah."

"A little love triangle."

"Look, Jess is like family. I don't want to hurt him."

"That's not a reason to stay with someone. Besides, if there's something going on between you and Dylan —"

"There's not," Meg interrupted. "Nothing is going on between us at all."

Bennett stretched, bored of their circuitous conversation. He could almost brush his fingers against the ceiling, and rising to his toes, he tried. "Whatever," he said, his head tilted up. "Do whatever you want. But just between you and me, Jess's a good guy. It's Dylan I'd worry about if I were you."

Bennett's unexpected candor startled Meg, but it didn't help her unravel the mystery of her heart and what she wanted. In some ways, it only confused her more. She tried to write it off as the clinging remnants of sibling rivalry, but something about Bennett's words sunk deep. In the end, she found herself no more or less prepared to meet Jess when he came home from college for his first real break.

Meg knew that Jess would be pulling into town around suppertime, and though she didn't wait by the window for the first hint of his arrival, she was painfully aware of each sound, each trace of irregularity in the descending dusk outside. Cars drove by intermittently, neighbors put out their recycling bins for the waste department pickup in the morning, and mothers called their kids out of the cold for supper, baths, and bed. But no one pulled into the cul-de-sac until the Painters were putting a light meal on the table.

Looking up from the loaf of bread that she was slicing, Linda caught the tilt of her daughter's head and glimpsed the unmistakable glow of headlights through the drawn shades. "He's home?" she questioned carefully.

It seemed to Meg that her mother was trying to gauge her reaction. "If that's him," she said. She didn't know if she should appear nonchalant, even uninterested, or if her mother expected a girlish squeal and a race to the front door. Either way, she feared the slight tremor in her voice gave away the tempest of emotions that fought for precedence inside her. All at once she was furious with herself. What was she afraid of? "I'm guessing he'll go home for supper and then come over here later," Meg supposed aloud, and she was thankful that this time her voice was steady.

She lifted a salad bowl from the counter and carried it into the dining room at the back of the house as if everything was perfectly normal, as if her heart wasn't trying furiously to beat out of the confines of her chest. It was doubtful that Linda bought her deception, but at least Meg had an hour or so before she had to face Jess. Maybe she could pull herself together by then.

But her hour of reprieve turned out to be

less than a minute. Meg heard a quick volley of knocks on the front door, a characteristic staccato of familiarity, followed by the anxious click of a handle being turned and the sound of Jess's voice as he called into the house, "Anybody home? Can I still do this?"

There was a marked pause in the air, a feeling that the entire house was holding its breath in anticipation of the next words that would be spoken. Meg tried to conjure up something to say, something that was neither cold nor too welcoming, neither false nor startlingly accurate. But Linda was the first to speak, and the warmth of her tone as she stepped out of the kitchen and into the foyer hit just the note that Meg had feared.

"Jess Langbroek. Of course you can still do that. You've been doing it since you were five years old. You're family," Linda said warmly. "You belong here."

Meg listened to her mother and her boyfriend with the reassurance of the kitchen between them and knew that Dylan was right. Jess — or a boy just like him — did belong in her home. Great family, stable background, promising future. Things had been simple between her and Jess because they followed a fixed pattern, provided a framework that she hadn't even known she was working within.

And yet, she didn't love him.

What could she possibly say to him? In the end, it wouldn't have mattered if she had rehearsed a script for weeks in anticipation of his arrival. Her mind was blank, her heart so frozen, she was sure she could feel the ice in her chest crack and splinter with each muffled beat. She set the salad bowl on the table and took a deep breath, tugging on the edges of her sweater to straighten it.

"She's setting the table," Meg heard her mother say. Then there were footfalls and laughter about bits of hurried conversation that she couldn't make out. And before she could expend a moment's worry about how he would respond when he saw her, Jess was standing in the archway between the kitchen and dining room.

He materialized out of a three-month absence taller, broader, older. If her eyes weren't failing her, his hair was darker, and his eyes, too. It seemed to Meg that wisdom had imparted a deepening of more than just his mind. There was a hopeful half smile on his face, as if he was returning to a place full of memories and rich with a life that he looked back on with fondness and expectation. It seemed to her that he longed to find everything as simple and unchanged as he remembered, even though he was not the same man. Meg stood rooted to the ground as she watched him emerge from what felt like the ancient past, and wondered if she was everything that he had waited for.

Jess's gaze took her in slowly, from the crown of her pony-tailed head to the un-painted toenails of her bare feet. She felt self-conscious, exposed beneath the daring search of his inscrutable blue eyes. She found herself looking at the floor, at the faded white cotton of his mismatched socks as he approached. He had taken off his shoes at the door and something about the closeness of that act, the permanence — I'm here to stay — made her heart catch in her throat.

When their toes touched, Jess slid into her in a deliberate reproduction of the night of their first kiss, wrapping his arms around her with such gentleness that Meg felt herself melting into his embrace against her will. The ice that had been her petrified heart fell one drop at a time and seemed to pool around their sweetly mismatched feet and rise until Meg wondered if she could drown in her own invisible tears. But Jess didn't appear to notice her hesitation as he pulled her tight against his chest, and instead of pressing her head against him, he let his own forehead sink to rest on her shoulder. It was an act of unaccountable surrender.

"Oh," he exhaled against her collarbone. "I've missed that. I've missed you."

Meg felt herself tighten around him, her arms cinching around his neck as if she could never be convinced again to let him go. Her fingers spread into his hair, pulling his head down against her and holding it there with a ferocity she hadn't realized she felt. Her chest was empty and hollow, cavernous in its need for air that could never hope to fill the gaping space. She opened her mouth, closed it. Opened it again and whispered against his ear: "I'm so sorry."

19
LUCAS

The afternoon passed quickly for Lucas — too quickly, because although he couldn't help but worry unendingly about what awaited him at home, he was dying to know more about Michael Kane Designs.

It seemed to him that the entire three-pronged predicament of the Woman, the ring, and Angela was nothing more than a misunderstanding, a kindness gone wrong. He had extended his hand in empathy, a touch of commiseration that, while admittedly tinged with an almost desperate need to know what had happened and why, had spiraled out of control. And now that his touch had become a lifeline, it could not be retracted. For better or worse, he was, body and soul, a part of this thing.

But while he was electrified by Angela's discovery about the unique design of the ring, he was uneasy about Jenna's inevitable reaction. He tried to speculate how she would feel. Betrayed that he hadn't told her what he had done? Angry that he had dared to do something so foolhardy and illegal? Hurt that he had shared his trespass with Angela, a virtual stranger to him and someone he didn't like all that much, instead of her? Probably all of the above and more. Jenna had always surprised him with her unpredictable reactions.

When Lucas blew into the kitchen, he found Angela alone at the table, draped over the hardback chair as if she owned the place, long hair pulled up in a slipping ballerina's knot and jeans rolled up to her knees. One leg was tucked snug against her chest, foot flat on the smooth seat beneath her; the other leg arched over empty space like a bridge, heel resting on the edge of the varnished pine table and toes splayed with a tissue woven over, under, over, under, like the first row of a flimsy, handwoven blanket.

She was painting her toenails iridescent red, a color that shone like the hood of a new car and sparkled, even from across the room, with flecks of glitter. Lucas looked down at his own wool socks, the heavy pants that hung in a clean, straight line from his hip to his heel, and wondered, Why? Who would see the decorated feet, glistening with ten perfect points of ruby like drops of fresh-spilled blood? But he didn't whisper a word.

Instead, he called, "Jenna home?" though it was obvious to him that she wasn't. The house lacked a certain gravity, as if even the walls knew that nothing was quite anchored without her.

Lucas hesitated in the doorway, uncertain in spite of his earlier impatience, because it felt faintly inappropriate to walk in on Angela in the act of painting her toenails. Her feet were bare before him, the pale skin almost intimate as she cupped her arch, a whisper of pink tongue visible between her lips as she concentrated. And though she had certainly heard him come in, she didn't look up or acknowledge his presence in any way. Lucas felt as if he should leave, or at the very least, avert his eyes.

But then Angela finished her pinky toe, capped the tiny bottle, and turned. "No," she said, her gaze as layered and shiny-hard as her nail polish. She seemed focused to Lucas, at once determined and triumphant as if she knew what she wanted and it was well within her grasp. He fumbled to say something, to ask another question, but she smiled suddenly and the strange spell was broken.

Lucas let go of a stale breath. "Where is

she?" he asked.

Angela shrugged. "Working late. I stopped by her office this afternoon and she told me not to expect her back until seven."

Lucas wished for a moment that he had stayed at work, but as quickly as the thought arose, it evaporated, a wisp of steam that left an unexpected relief in its wake. He could talk to Angela honestly, uninterrupted. Without the phantom of his wife's growing disappointment hovering over him.

As if Angela could read his mind, she commanded, "Ask me."

"What?"

She rolled her eyes. "That is quite possibly the most annoying expression in the world, Lucas. Don't act so stupid. Don't act like I've caught you off guard. You know exactly what I'm referring to."

"I don't know what you want me to ask," he said flatly.

"Use your imagination." Angela smirked.

Lucas crossed the room slowly and passed around the table so he could stand opposite her. But he didn't move to sit down, and Angela seemed annoyed again. She kicked out the chair in front of him with one of her newly manicured feet, bumping him just below the knees with the lathed edge of the sturdy seat.

"I hope you didn't just make me smudge my polish," she complained. Then she indicated the chair with a flick of her chin. "Sit. We have lots to talk about."

Lucas sat reluctantly. "Tell me about the ring," he said.

"That's not a question, but it'll do." Angela grinned, a sudden fierce expression that had nothing to do with joy. She demanded: "Tell me you're dying to know. Tell me it's all you thought about all afternoon."

"If that were true, it would have been very unfortunate for my patients."

Angela blinked. "Are you sure you took the ring from the barn?" she asked after a moment. "I can't believe you did it."

"Neither can I," Lucas admitted. "And I think I made a huge mistake. I shouldn't have taken it and I shouldn't have given it to you."

"Too late for that, isn't it? You want to know, Lucas. I know you do. You're the one who set me on this path."

He did. It was no use denying it, even if good sense continued to wage war in his heart and mind. "Convince me," he muttered. "You've got five minutes to make me believe that I did the right thing in committing a felony."

"Is it a felony?"

"No." Lucas sighed. "I very discreetly asked one of my patients about it, a retired sheriff."

"And? What's going to happen to you?"

"He figured my allegedly fabricated scenario would result in a fine. Maybe a theft charge. But it could be dropped if I returned the ring. It would depend on whether or not the investigators decided to press charges."

"And me?"

"I guess you're an accessory."

Angela shrugged. "I'm okay with that."

"We don't even know if it's her ring."

"Of course it's hers," Angela said, dismissing his reservations with an irritated wiggle of her fingers. "It's not my mother's — he gave all of her stuff to Goodwill after she died. And it's not mine. There were no other women in Jim's life."

"That you know of."

Angela glared at him. "It's hers. I know it." Apparently sick of wasting time on the legal particularities, she blurted, "It's an original. Michael Kane is an independent jeweler who specializes in one-of-a-kind creations. Michael does his own designs, but he also allows clients to describe, draw, or invent their own wearable art using a CAD program. No piece of jewelry is ever duplicated."

Lucas laid his hand palm up on the table and Angela placed the ring in it without further comment. It was a unique piece, and though he could see why the original design struck him as distinctly Black Hills gold, there was a difference. The leaves were bigger, less detailed. And they arched off the band, creating hollow spaces and undercuts that seemed too detailed for the pretty but distinctly cookie-cutter charms he had seen before in neat jewelry store displays.

"How long has he been in business?" Lucas asked.

"Over twenty-five years."

"What makes you think he'd remember this ring?"

Angela flashed him a sly smile. "He keeps records. I asked."

Lucas felt a thrill, a sudden burst of adrenaline that forced him to acknowledge that Angela's discovery was huge. Michael Kane Designs could hold the key to the Woman's identity.

"Did you ask him about it? About this ring?"

She shook her head, a little wrinkle appearing between her eyes. Picking up the glass bottle of her gleaming polish, she tapped it on the surface of the table in a soft staccato of muted frustration. "He told me that most of the private designs are strictly confidential. Apparently people don't want their creations copied."

Lucas blew a hard breath between his teeth. "Then what in the world makes you think that we'll learn anything about this ring?"

Angela continued the careful tap-tap-tap of the bottle, studying the fruitless movement, brow furrowed in concentration. It seemed like she wasn't going to respond to Lucas's question, but finally she palmed the small vial and fixed him with an unwavering look. Her eyes were clear and dark, the gray-green color of a river stone, and equally immovable. Then, as he watched in growing discomfort, the corner of her mouth curled the tiniest bit, presaging a change that overtook her beautiful face like a slow sunrise. The smile that she gave him was both innocent and hungry, ingenuous and cunning.

"He'll tell me whatever I ask."

Lucas didn't doubt her.

Though Lucas had serious reservations about Angela's half-baked plan to interrogate the designer of the ring, the sheer simplicity of her scheme and her determination to follow it through impressed him. Before he had a chance to excuse himself from the impulsive trip to Omaha, Angela categorically dismantled all his watertight arguments.

Like a child playing her parents off each other, Angela confessed to already bringing up the topic of Lucas's short departure with Jenna on the phone. She didn't provide too many details, but Lucas got the impression that the reason she'd masterminded for needing him on the two-hour drive to the small Midwestern city was something that tugged at Jenna's already frayed heart-strings. What was it this time? A subtly communicated need for a father figure? A faint suspicion on Jenna's part that Angela's tough exterior was nothing more than an elaborate ruse? That inside the controlled, attractive exterior dwelled a sad little girl who longed for stability and love? Either way, it seemed Jenna didn't even pause to question it. According to Angela, his wife not only granted her permission, she seemed eager for Lucas to make the trek with the confused young woman.

"We're going to see my father's lawyer," Angela explained, filling Lucas in on the story she had constructed.

He sighed, hating the thought of lying to

his wife, but now that things were falling into place, he could feel the pull of the Woman's mystery as if it was anchored deep inside. The thought of knowing was intoxicating enough to cloud his vision, even though he believed himself duty bound to deny it. "Why would Jim have a lawyer from Omaha?" he asked, forcing himself to try to poke holes in Angela's plot.

"You know he didn't trust anybody here. Besides, my mom grew up in a little town a few miles northwest of Omaha. My grandfather did all his business there. It's plausible that my father would follow suit."

"It's plausible."

"No, it's possible. And we just made it so. Act as if it's true."

Lucas gave a barely perceptible nod. "Why isn't Jenna taking you?" he asked.

"She didn't offer." Angela avoided his eyes. "And she didn't question it when I asked for you to escort me."

He knew that Safe House was currently sheltering two young women, and that Jenna was all but drowning in the mire of their complex problems and the complications of a pair of frightening boyfriends. "She's very busy," he told Angela.

"That works out just fine for us."

Lucas didn't know how to respond.

Amazingly, getting a day off work proved almost as easy as convincing Jenna that Lucas needed to go. Though his schedule was already nearly full for the following day, Angela persuaded him to call Mandy and beg the long-suffering nurse to clear his agenda.

"I need a personal day," Lucas croaked into the phone, thankful that his aversion to lying caused his voice to crack as if he really was in desperate need of a little time off.

"You haven't taken a day of vacation in two years!" Mandy exclaimed so loudly he had to pull the phone from his ear. "No sick days either! Are you sick?"

"No," he confessed. "I'm not sick. I just . . . I need this."

There was a long silence on the line.

"Mandy?"

"Yeah."

Lucas took a deep breath. "You'll do it?"

"Of course I will. But next time it would be nice if you planned your personal day a bit in advance."

"Thanks, Mandy. Reschedule everything you can, and be sure to give the patients who need to be seen to —"

"Don't tell me how to do my job."

"Okay." He paused. "Thank you."

"You're welcome."

Lucas clicked the phone off and covered his eyes with a damp hand. Stifling a little groan, he said, "I can't believe you orchestrated this. It feels wrong."

Angela turned from the counter where she was preparing vegetarian wraps for a late supper. Jenna would be home in minutes, and while her impending presence made Lucas's stomach knot, Angela was leaning against the counter with natural ease, slicing a cucumber into papery rounds like a gourmet chef. "Look," she muttered, pointing the tip of her knife at his forehead in mock threat, "Jenna's fine with it, Mandy's fine with it, and you owe this to me."

"I owe you?"

"You're pretty free and easy with your false accusations," Angela reminded him.

It saddened Lucas a little to think she might be proven wrong. "I'm not sure my entirely reasonable assumption that Jim killed you makes me liable to you," he muttered.

"And her. You owe it to her." Angela set a fist on her hip and narrowed her eyes at Lucas. "You took her ring and now you don't want to follow through? You started this, I'll remind you. And you're going to finish it."

"I'm following a passion to its conclusion?" Lucas said wryly, quoting their earlier conversation in the car.

She winked. "Exactly. We're in it together, whether you like it or not."

"Where does that leave Jenna?"

Angela's expression turned serious. "You want to tell her?"

"What makes you assume I haven't shared the ring with her already?"

"You haven't."

It bothered Lucas that she was so certain. "Maybe Jenna would understand. Maybe she'd support us. Or even . . . help."

"She'd try to talk us out of it. She might even contact someone about the ring, with or without our consent."

It was true. Jenna had a very finely bordered sense of justice, and though Lucas's own understanding of right and wrong was usually just as harshly defined, the Woman was blurring all his careful boundaries. He didn't want to give up the ring and he didn't want Jenna to, either. Even if it seemed like the right thing to do. Maybe black and white weren't quite as distinct as Lucas had always imagined them to be.

"You're right," he finally sighed. "But if this proves to be a dead end, if Michael Kane Designs has nothing to offer us, we need to turn in the ring ourselves. This woman deserves that."

Angela considered his words for a moment, head tilted as she studied the sharp tip of the knife blade. "My dad didn't kill her, he didn't kill anyone."

It was the first time that Lucas had heard her refer to Jim as her dad. He didn't agree with her, but he also didn't want to give her a reason to jump on the defensive. "If we can't prove that," he said, trying to placate her, "maybe someone else can."

She nodded once. "Okay." Then her eyes glittered and she turned to carve a red onion in half with one well-aimed sweep of her wide blade. There was a quick snick of sound followed by a dull thud as the length of the knife embedded itself in the worn butcher block. Her shoulders seemed stiff with defiance when she added, "But I have a feeling about this."

Lucas didn't want to admit it, but he did, too.

20
MEG

Jess let Meg go without a fight. It was in him, she could see fire in his eyes. But the flames died quickly, quenched by something inside her that spilled out so soft and slow she wasn't even aware of its stealthy departure until it was too late. It wasn't tangible or quantifiable, but it was real, and the unspoken words between them silently acknowledged the truth: Meg was not in love with Jess and probably had never been. The realization made him go pale, and she reached a hand to warm the marble of his cheek.

He jerked away.

"I'm so sorry," she whispered.

"You said that already."

They stood facing each other in the dim, cold light of the porch. It wasn't where Meg would have chosen to talk, nor when, but her inadvertent apology in the dining room began something that she couldn't stop. It was a hapless admission, a thought she hadn't meant to give voice to, but once the words slid from her lips, they opened a spreading fissure along the length of her ongoing lie and it all leaked out.

There was nothing more to say. Jess seemed to understand this as Meg's hand fell slowly back to her side. He helped to widen the distance between them by taking a deliberate step back. His face was steely, a chiseled study in hurt, and he didn't even attempt to temper himself for her benefit. Though he had spent the last two years of his life trying to make her happy, he did nothing to ease the agony of the moment. And then, apparently before he could change his mind, he spun on his heel and walked away.

Meg opened her mouth to call after him, but what was there to say? Good-bye? Not like this, she thought. It can't end like this.

"Your ring," she blurted, twisting it off her finger though it was strangely painful to do so.

"Keep it," he called, not even pausing to look over his shoulder. "I don't want it."

"But . . ."

Jess turned at the car, and she struggled to read his eyes in the shadows. His chin was severe, his gaze black and hidden beneath the line of his heavy brow. For a second Meg thought he was waiting for her and she took a step toward him. She stopped cold when out of the darkness he said, "I loved you."

The slam of his car door cut the lingering sweetness of his confession with a sound of harsh finality.

Meg had no idea that it would hurt so much to hear him say it like that. Like his love was already gone.

After having them both, it was difficult to have neither. She was suddenly a map without borders, peppered with holes, directionless. And although she tried to ignore their absence, Jess and Dylan left jagged cracks in her heart that simply refused to fill. She tried to push things deep into the gaps, to smooth them over with friends, classes, and another season of the Girls' Football League, but as Jess and Dylan continued to take pains to remove themselves even further from her life, Meg felt their loss in all the hidden places that had refused to heal.

Jess switched to an out-of-state school for his sophomore year of college and took an internship at a law firm in Minneapolis so he wouldn't have to come home during the summer. While his decision could be considered an investment in his future, Meg felt sure that it had much more to do with severing his past. And when Dylan graduated from Sutton High, he impulsively joined the Air National Guard and left for boot camp at Lackland Air Force Base in San Antonio, Texas. She didn't even know he was leaving until he'd already been gone a week. Meg was heartbroken, but she also felt a grain of satisfaction that Dylan, who had felt so directionless, was doing something.

When it became obvious that the girl Meg had been was long gone, Linda finally asked her daughter, "What do you want?"

"I don't know," Meg confessed.

"Maybe I should ask, 'Who do you want?' "

It was a fair question, for after their breakup, Meg had admitted that her seemingly platonic relationship with Dylan was more complicated than she first let on. Jess had asked how she could have lied. After the initial shock and suffering that filled his days after Meg's apology, Jess embraced his fury and didn't keep secrets about what had transpired between her and Dylan. All the same, she didn't want to field such inquiries from her mother. She forced a smile, but the expression faded fast and never reached her eyes to make cheerful creases. "Both," she murmured.

Linda laughed at her daughter's attempt at humor, but Meg hadn't been joking. "They're both good boys," Linda said as if it was a matter of making a decision between two equally appealing choices. But if it were that easy, Meg would not have found herself lamenting the fact that it was no longer her choice to make.

"Good boys," Meg echoed, because her mother expected a response.

"But I think it's best we leave this all in the past." Linda patted her daughter's knee soothingly. "There are plenty of fish in the sea."

Meg groaned. "That's a terrible expression."

"And it's a big sea."

"Now you're mixing your metaphors." Meg forced a chuckle for her mother's benefit, and knew that when Linda walked away, it was with a feeling of accomplishment. They had talked, they had laughed, she had come to her senses — supposedly a surefire recipe for success. But it was banal, and it didn't work.

Though it took Meg a long time to find her equilibrium again, she earned a perfect

4.0 average in her senior year. Part of her academic success was the direct result of the disentanglement of her heart and mind. No more was she drawn in two opposing directions. No more did she have to hate herself for feeling one way while acting another.

But as the months went on, a new awareness began to emerge. Not only was Meg's life less complicated, it was more hers again. She felt like herself. She was more relaxed in her own skin, more aware of her wants and needs and able to balance herself when things didn't quite work out as she planned. Without realizing that she was doing so, or even that she had stopped in the first place, Meg began again to make her friends laugh, banter with her teachers, eagerly try new things. She wasn't who she had been, nor would she ever be again, but she was well on her way to redrawing the map that had been irreparably damaged.

"I've missed you," Sarah told her one night.

And in a flash of understanding, Meg knew that she had indeed been missing. "It's good to be back." She grinned.

"You are never allowed to date again."

Meg laughed. "That's a bit harsh, don't you think?"

After Meg graduated with honors and received acceptance letters from her top four choices for university, the world seemed once again set before her, a prize for the taking, a treasure to be plucked. There were long conversations about where she would go, what she would do. Veterinary medicine since she loved animals and was strong in the sciences? Education, given that she had a way with kids? Maybe marketing because, as her father loved to tease, she could sell oceanfront property in Iowa.

In the end, Meg opted for none of her family's preferred futures. Instead, she found a job online with AT&T in a little community on the coast of California. A part of her was determined to prove Dylan and his accusations of her perfect, pre-arranged life wrong. But even more than that, she wanted to find her own path. To step off the road that had been paved before her and make her own decisions about all that was to come. She told her parents the day after graduation and left the week after that.

"Where will you live?" Greg demanded, his daughter's announcement as raw and tender as a fresh wound.

"I found a roommate online."

"Online?" The word might as well have

been a vulgar curse.

"Her username is Kate24, but she told me I can call her Katie."

"Her username?"

"She's a good person, Dad. I checked it out online and she's legit."

That seemed to mollify him a little, but Linda still sat shell-shocked and silent behind him. "How will you afford rent?" Greg continued, rubbing his eyes as if he couldn't bring himself to look at her.

"I have money saved," she said quietly.

"College money."

"I only need a little. Just enough for travel costs and the first month of rent."

"And after that?" Greg demanded.

"I'll go back to school in a year. I just —"

"No, I mean what will you do after that money runs out?"

"I told you: I already have a job. I'm going to be a retail sales consultant for AT&T. It sounds fancy, but basically it means I'll be —"

"A cashier at a cell phone store."

"You don't have to make it sound that bad."

"It is that bad."

"Dad —"

Linda suddenly interrupted. "Megan Elise Painter. Don't. Do. This."

There was an urgency in her mother's words, a purpose that thwarted Meg's best attempts at remaining calm and collected. "I have to do this," she whispered around the rising lump of emotion in her throat. "I need a year off. I have to be away."

The steadfast silence that met her declaration was unnerving.

"I have to," Meg continued, trying to make them understand. "Besides, I was accepted at Cal Poly. Either way, I'd be in California."

Linda's mouth dropped open a little. "It's not the same. School and a job at a cell phone store are not the same thing."

Meg knew then that it was no use trying to make them understand. Not now. Maybe not ever. But that didn't ease her own growing need to go.

There was a book on the coffee table in the Painters' living room, a hardcover copy of E. M. Forster's *A Passage to India*. Meg had never read it, and the book had languished there for as long as she could remember, unread, but fat and imposing and beautiful with its dust jacket watercolor rendering of an alluring foreign landscape. The pastels were ethereal but distinct, impressionistic but hinting at a certain long-lost clarity, as if the painting merely represented the remnants of a dream already fading. It gave Meg a sense of isolation. Of an absence — her own? — but somehow the awaiting void was comforting, almost peaceful, as if all expectations had been stripped away.

She took the dust jacket with her when she left.

And although she departed without blessing, Meg felt blessed when the sun shone bright through the rear window of her car as she headed west. And when the mountains of Colorado began to rise in an imposing line of purple on the far-flung horizon, Meg's cell phone beeped a text message from Bennett: *You'll be fine.*

It had to be so.

Greg and Linda didn't have much say in Meg's self-imposed exodus, but they made sure that she was cared for on the journey. She wanted to go alone, and they let her, but they insisted that she stop along the way. Interstate 80 was the most direct route, requiring no back-road turnoffs, potential detours, or confusing twists through unfamiliar territory. They didn't have friends or family along the approved itinerary, but Linda appealed to the ladies in her quilting circle and unearthed an aunt in Cheyenne and a retired pastor and his artist wife in

Reno. Meg was scheduled to spend a night with each, and she reached her required destinations on time and cheerful, leaving behind her such an impression of spirit and maturity that her hosts called their Sutton connections and raved about "that lovely girl."

It was only when Reno was a speck in her rearview mirror that Meg felt really cut loose. It was behind her, all of it, and there was no going back to the way things had been. In one breath she lamented the loss and embraced all there was to come, no matter where life took her from here. No matter what it held.

The address of her new apartment was printed out with careful, handwritten instructions on the passenger seat, but when Meg got close to the coast, she ignored her predetermined destination and followed the signs to the nearest beach.

It was the perfect day to begin again. The sun was casting lazy rays in the sort of casual warmth that made coastal life seem so carefree and spontaneous, so undemanding. Meg could imagine herself here, barefoot and laughing, beside a friend or two, maybe a small collection of people who made her feel like the sun shining down on them was more than a happy coincidence.

She grinned at the thought, and when she parked her car in the little rock-sand lot behind a small rise that obscured her view of the ocean, she was so excited that she forgot to lock the doors.

The Pacific itself was immense. Blue so pale in the late-afternoon light that as dusk approached, the water blended seamlessly with sky until all were one. Meg stared at it until her eyes hurt, trying to distinguish the line where the white-capped waves became clouds and wishing that she could see beyond the curve of the earth to the places where islands began to rise out of the sea.

She wasn't even aware that she had stepped out of her sandals until her toes were nipped with cold at the very edge of the surf. It was such a pleasant thrill, so delightfully bracing and vital that she rolled up her faded jeans to the knees and waded in as far as she could go. Her pants were soon soaked by the waves, but she didn't care. She would have shed them altogether if she had been alone. But there were people walking on the beach: an elderly couple, a group of kids that didn't look quite old enough to be unsupervised, a woman with only her small dog for company. Meg waved at them and considered it a good sign when they waved back.

Just as she was about to drag herself from the water and go in search of her new room-mate and, hopefully, friend, Meg felt some-thing hard beneath the heel of her foot. It was embedded in the sand, but as she tried to pin it against the ocean floor, a wave slid backward off the beach and tried to pull it free. There was an erosion of sand, a splash as another tide sweeping in collided with the wave as it left, and Meg thrust her hand beneath the water, drenching her shirt with a blotch of wet that matched the damp on her jeans and emerging triumphant with a shell in her hand.

It was faultless, a fanned scallop in alter-nating stripes of buttercream yellow and salmon with two perfect triangles bordering the tip. Inside was a shimmering, silvery pink so delicate that it felt almost inap-propriate to gaze upon its exposed beauty. She turned it over in her hand, dragging her fingernail across the ridges and wonder-ing what had happened to its mate. It was half of a whole, but it seemed perfect to her.

Later, Katie would tell her that the shell was a heart cockle. Common. Boring. Certainly not a treasure to display on her nightstand as if it was some precious trinket. But ordinary or not, it was exquisite to Meg, and without knowing why she did it, she lifted the shell to her mouth and tasted the salt of the sea. The ribs were a pattern against her tongue, a vibration of the distance it had traveled. A reminder of away. Meg palmed the shell and pocketed it, and it never left her bedside after that day.

Three months later, the little heart cockle stood watch when Meg's cell phone rang with an unfamiliar number.

"I miss you," the caller said.

Meg had to admit that in many ways she missed him, too.

21
LUCAS

A chilly wind moaned through the hushed street, but Omaha's Old Market still bore some signs of a warm and prosperous summer. Brown geraniums in hanging baskets drooped heavy heads in desolation, withered petals whispering free to create sad mosaics on the brick-lined street. Windows still clung to posters announcing outdoor concerts, art festivals, and craft fairs, and somewhere a forgotten wind chime sang a tune that seemed elegiac, a lament for the sun and laughter that had undoubtedly filled the quaint neighborhood only weeks before.

The unassuming storefront that quietly announced Michael Kane Designs was tucked between a high-end furniture boutique on one side and a smoky record store on the other. Lucas stood in front of the frosted glass that obscured the interior of the jewelry store and surveyed the street with a wary eye. He and Jenna had made the trek to Omaha's picturesque historic district many times in their first few years in northern Iowa. They missed the bustle of Chicago, the noise, the people. And though Nebraska's biggest city was tiny in comparison to the metropolis they were accustomed to, it was a relief to sit at one of the outdoor tables of the little coffee shop on the corner and bask in the presence of people. The scent of Indian food mingled with the earthy sweetness of their steaming lattes, fresh-baked sourdough bread, and cut flowers from the florist down the street. Lucas could picture Jenna there now, swirling the contents of a stoneware mug and lifting it two-handed to her lips while her eyes absorbed the colors, the lights.

They were sure they had marked every nook and cranny, every unexpected fountain and ivy-draped, crumbling path. But in all their wandering through the narrow streets, delighting in the kite shop, the one-room museums, the unexpected mall behind a modest-looking single-pane door, they had never chanced upon the little store marked with three letters linked in curling calligraphy: *MKD*.

"How long did you say this store has been around?" Lucas asked as he watched Angela trace the monogram with a manicured finger.

"Mr. Kane told me on the phone that this was his twenty-seventh year."

"I don't remember the place," he mused.

"Well, just because he's been in business that long doesn't mean that it's all been in this shop." Angela gave him a strange look. "Besides, who made you the keeper of the Old Market?"

Lucas shrugged. "I'm not. I just don't like being caught off guard."

"That's one of your problems."

"I think this used to be a pottery store . . ."

Angela rolled her eyes but tucked her hand in the crook of his arm with an indulgent smile all the same. "Come on, honey," she cooed, batting phony doe eyes at him. "Act like you love me."

Lucas still had serious reservations about her plan that they play a happily engaged couple, but before he could restate his protest, Angela swung open the door with her free hand and pulled him inside.

A bell over the door caroled their arrival with a trill of light notes before it fell back against the aged wood in an unharmonious jangle. There, it seemed to say. I've done my job. Standing on the threshold and glancing quickly around the small store, Lucas realized that everything else had that same tired quality. There were two lighted display cases with smudged glass and more than one spent bulb. And the hardwood floor wore a groove down the center from all the feet that had crossed it in the century since it had been laid. Looking up, away from the dilapidation of the once-lovely floor, Lucas caught sight of a crystal chandelier, impressive in its size and the cut of the glass, but covered in a film of dust so thick the light it produced was meager at best. Other than the floor, the glass counters, the chandelier, there was nothing at all in the room. No pictures on the walls, no cash register, no chair. Nothing.

Except a door directly opposite from where Lucas stood with Angela's hand still warming the curve of his elbow. It appeared unnaturally short, as if he would have to duck to enter the dark recess behind the retail space, and it was covered with a red brocade cloth like he would have expected to see at a French opera house. From behind this curtain there was the rattling sound of a thick, smoker's cough, followed by a husky "Be with you in a sec."

"Mr. Kane?" Lucas whispered, looking down at Angela's upturned face.

She shrugged and fixed a smile to her lips

as if it was an accessory she could take on and off.

The curtain moved and an elderly man stepped from behind it, inclining his head in what appeared to be a courteous greeting, but Lucas saw the low beam of the lintel brush the mop of his thick gray hair as he passed. "Hello, hello," he called, and though his face was deep-set with un-numbered crags, his crinkled eyes were warm and friendly. The smile he offered them was genuine, if only a bit hesitant, as if he had endured the slight of many browsers who merely glanced at his goods and left. "What can I do for you?"

Lucas took a breath to speak, but Angela gave his arm a hard squeeze and gushed, "Are you Mr. Michael Kane?"

The old man looked confused for a minute, but then he straightened the collar peeking from beneath his brown sweater and gave an almost shy nod. "That's what they call me."

Angela let go of Lucas and rushed forward with her hand outstretched. "Oh, it's so nice to meet you, sir. I'm a big fan of your art."

"My art?"

"Your jewelry. You are the designer, aren't you?" She swept her hand to indicate the meager displays behind her, the same ones

409

that she and Lucas hadn't even taken a moment to glance inside.

"Yeah, it's mine."

"Well, I just love what you do. It's understated but exquisite, the perfect balance between —"

"She's enthusiastic," Lucas interrupted, coming up behind Angela and forcing himself to put his hand on the small of her back. His fingers hovered over the fabric of her coat, not quite daring to press against the curve of her body. He didn't want to put himself in the middle of the situation, but he thought Angela was laying it on too thick. She might be disarmingly beautiful and irrefutably charming, but he got the impression that if she didn't cool it a little, Mr. Kane would disappear into the rabbit hole behind his diminutive store and not come back.

Lucas cleared his throat and forced a smile. "We're, uh . . . we're engaged. And I told her that she can pick out the ring."

At this, Mr. Kane shrugged and pursed his lips apologetically. "I don't work with diamonds."

"Oh, I don't want a diamond," Angela assured him. "I'm familiar with your work. I've been to your website."

Mr. Kane nodded proudly. "My grandson

designed that. As for me, I don't know how to turn on a computer, much less surf the spiderweb." He seemed as pleased with his own lack of technological skills as he was with his grandson's obvious expertise.

Angela threw back her lovely head and laughed, tickling the back of Lucas's hand with the curled tips of her glossy hair. He yanked away and tucked his fingers deep into the pockets of his coat. "So," he began, fumbling. "How does this work?"

Mr. Kane took a few steps into the store and moved behind the display case along the wall. "I have a few samples that you may browse through," he told them, indicating the meager offerings beneath the glass. "But I specialize in custom-designed jewelry. Most people have an idea of what they want when they come in."

Lucas followed Angela's lead and bent over the counter, pretending to study the pieces inside.

"I have my own on-site gemological laboratory," Mr. Kane said, launching into a well-rehearsed speech about the finer details of his business. "And I work directly with a manufacturing facility that features a complete casting room as well as four jewelry benches. I oversee the entire process, and when the piece is cast and assembled, I personally set the gems and do the finishing."

"Satisfaction guaranteed," Angela quipped, looking up at him through the soft curtain of her hair. It cascaded over her shoulder and glowed like white gold in the muted light as she bowed over the glass.

Mr. Kane smiled gently and nodded. "I like my customers to be happy."

They had only been in the store a few minutes, but Lucas could already tell that Mr. Kane was enamored with his alleged wife-to-be. It was almost impossible to discern the exact reason for her magnetism, but Lucas suspected it had something to do with her disquieting mix of forgotten innocence and beauty, her easy smile but somehow burdened eyes.

"Does anything strike your fancy?" Mr. Kane asked, still watching her as he opened the sliding door of the cabinet with a tiny gold key. The movement was instinctive, as if he had done it many, many times.

"They're all very pretty," Angela told him, straightening up. "But I did actually have something in mind." She unzipped her purse and pulled out a cream-colored box from deep inside. Easing off the cardboard lid, she fished around in a shallow bed of cotton until she emerged triumphant with a delicate ring between her thumb and fore-finger.

"I know all your designs are original," she said, "but I just love this."

Mr. Kane squinted at the ring in her hand and she offered it to him without pause. Lucas held his breath as the older man studied it, wondering if he'd recognize the piece, if he knew its rightful owner. He both dreaded and anticipated the implications of that possibility. Was she close? Would he be able to give them a name for their mysterious Woman? And, either way: Where would they go from here?

A full minute unraveled as Mr. Kane studied the ring from every angle. He tsked at the broken stone and tried to use the filed point of his fingernail to dislodge some stubborn dirt, but in the end he gave up and a certain satisfaction settled itself over his features. "It is pretty, isn't it? Even so abused."

"Beautiful."

"But I didn't make it for you," he said.

Lucas's heart stumbled in his chest.

"I would have remembered if I made it for you," Mr. Kane continued, unaware of Lucas's silent reaction. "May I ask where you got it?"

Though Lucas wanted to ignore the jeweler's question and demand to know who had commissioned the piece, he swallowed his questions and served up a portion of the story that he and Angela had agreed upon in the car. "We found it."

"We were hiking in the Black Hills when I saw something glitter in the dirt just off the path." Angela gave the tale flesh, crinkling her nose at the false memory of finding such a treasure in the dust.

"She liked the design, so she googled your initials and voilà. Here we are." Lucas waited, skin prickling as he prayed that Mr. Kane would buy their fabricated story. But the old man didn't seem suspicious. He merely smiled blandly and handed the ring back to Angela.

"Well," he said, "no two pieces are the same. I can't duplicate this one."

"I don't want you to," Angela assured him. She held out the ring and indicated different points along the gold band. "I want a small topaz here, princess cut, and one leaf on either side of the stone. Oh, and I'd love it if you could make the band look like a branch. Can you do that?"

"Certainly," Mr. Kane said, apparently warming to the idea of a new project. He leaned forward, eager to look more closely at her proposed alterations. "And what about your fiancé?" The old man met Lucas's eye and winked conspiratorially. "Are you happy with her creation, sir?"

Lucas tried not to look painfully uncomfortable. "Whatever will make her happy," he murmured, sounding like a fool.

But Mr. Kane didn't notice or didn't care. Though his store was situated in prime retail territory, Lucas doubted the old-fashioned jeweler entertained much business as of late. Maybe his styles were considered out-of-date. Maybe people preferred buying tennis bracelets from sparkly emporiums with gentlemen in well-pressed Italian suits. Whatever the reason for his noticeable lack of current success, Lucas did not like Angela's taking advantage of Mr. Kane's situation by stringing him along in the hope of a lucrative sale.

He was just about to call Angela off, to make some excuse about their present inability to commit to a commission, when she reached into her purse again and took out a sleek leather pocketbook. She snapped it open and counted out a few denominations, then laid them on the counter in front of Mr. Kane. Five crisp, one-hundred-dollar bills fanned across the glass. "How about we consider this a down payment?" she purred. Pulling a homemade business card from another compartment in her wallet, she placed it on top of the money. "This is my information. Call me if you need anything and we'll settle the account when the ring is finished. You do ship, don't you?"

"Yes, of course," Mr. Kane said, obviously flustered by her decisiveness and the money on the counter.

"Is it adequate?" Angela demurred, intentionally misreading his hesitation. She reached into her wallet again, but Mr. Kane shook his head firmly.

"It's fine," he said. "Perfect, in fact. The topaz . . . ?"

"A half carat should do it," Angela smiled, discerning his question before he asked it.

Mr. Kane tapped his fingers against the display case in what Lucas surmised to be quick calculation. He picked up the five hundred dollars and smiled doubtfully. "This should be just under one-third?"

It was apparent that he didn't want to startle her with the estimated amount, but Angela smiled and stuck her hand out to seal the deal. "I can't wait to see it," she said.

Lucas was incredulous, but the money was legit and so was her card. Mr. Kane was holding it carefully, reading the fine print, and Lucas scanned the address upside down. Angela Webb, San Luis Obispo. She had just bought a ring from Michael Kane Designs. He almost leaned down to breathe a question in her ear, but Angela wasn't done yet.

"I'm so happy to be working with you, Mr. Kane," she said.

"Please, call me Mike."

"Mike," she amended. "But there is one small thing I would like you to do for me."

"Anything." He grinned.

Angela held up the ruined ring and gave her features a doleful cast. "I'd like to find the rightful owner of this ring. I'm sure she's beside herself that it's gone. Do you know who you made it for?"

Mike looked hesitant. "I don't remember who commissioned it."

"But you told me that you kept records."

Stunned by her boldness, Lucas watched Mike's expression shift slightly. The older man seemed to be wrestling with himself, but either he was giddy from his recent sale or he was smitten with Angela, because he shook his head indulgently and wagged a finger at her like she was a naughty child.

"You're the one who called me."

Angela tipped her chin in acknowledgment.

"You're early. I didn't expect you for

another hour."

"We were eager to meet you," Angela hummed, still working him.

"Well, I don't normally share my records. They're my own personal scrapbook. I like to keep track, you know."

"But you will share, just this once," Angela coaxed him. "It would mean so much to me to be able to return this ring."

He balked. "The ring may have changed hands, or the contact information might be obsolete. What if they threw the ring away on purpose? Maybe they don't want it anymore."

Angela laughed. "We both know that's not true." She gave the jeweler's forearm a gentle squeeze, but Lucas could see that her gesture was unnecessary. He had already made up his mind.

"Give me a minute," Mike sighed. "I'll see what I can find."

When he had disappeared behind the curtain, money and business card clutched firmly in his hand, Lucas spun on Angela and gave her a hard look.

"What?" she whispered, smirking.

"You just bought a fifteen-hundred-dollar ring if his estimation is right. I hope you don't expect me to fork over the difference, honey."

"I'm buying it for myself, sweetheart. Jim wasn't rich, but he left me all he had. I see this as a gift to myself. A present in precelebration of proving my father's innocence. After all, he's getting the records!"

Lucas couldn't stop the wide smile that broke across his face. He knew that she was wrong about her father's innocence, but he didn't care. They were actually going to learn something! A name, an address, maybe more.

Mike came back only a few minutes later, clutching a three-ring binder that was bursting at the seams. It was spread open in his arms with approximately half of the slick pages on one side and half on the other. Lucas wondered what gave the sheets their wan glow, but as Mike approached, he realized that the binder was filled with plastic page protectors, each seeming to house just a simple leaf of paper.

With an air of unmistakable pride, Mike said, "The ring is my design. Someone bought it off the rack, so to speak."

"What do you mean?"

"Well, most people come with a design in mind, but this one is all mine. In addition to custom designs, I make my own pieces and sell them in the store."

Lucas and Angela leaned in, studying the

pencil sketch that had been affixed with scotch tape to a piece of white paper. The lines were confident, the shading perfectly subtle. In addition to being a master jeweler, Mr. Kane was an artist. In just a glance Lucas could tell that it was indeed the ring he had found with the Woman. "Who bought it?" he demanded, surprising himself. "There's no information here."

"Patience, patience," Mike warned. "I keep details on the back." He flipped the page over with a flick of his wrist.

Lucas could see a yellow invoice in the pocket behind the picture. He craned his neck to catch a name, a telephone number, anything, but before he could make sense of the scrawled writing, Mike slapped a palm on the sheet.

"I don't feel right giving out personal information." Angela gave a sad shrug and took the small box out of her purse. "I'll leave this with you, then. You'll contact the owner, won't you?"

Mike wrinkled his forehead at the thought. It was evident he found the idea of playing the part of an unwilling detective distasteful. "I don't really have time to track down strangers," he sighed, "but maybe just this once."

There was a hushed moment as Mike's

finger trailed the smudged invoice. He had written in pencil and the lead was obscured in some places. Lucas sent up wordless prayers and crossed his fingers for good measure. "Got something to write with?" Mike finally asked.

"Mm-hmm." Angela produced a pen from her purse and positioned her hand to scribble the information on the lid of the jewelry box.

"Looks like the person who purchased it was a Mr. Jess Langbroek." Mike blew an amused breath between his teeth and glanced up at them. "Bought it just over a decade ago for a hundred fifty dollars."

Angela and Lucas were supposed to be entertained at the bit of trivia, but the jeweler's joke backfired on him, because suddenly he realized that Angela might not appreciate buying a similar ring at such an inflated price. "It had an opal," he rushed to explain. "A very tiny stone. Flawed. And that was ten years ago . . ."

But Angela couldn't have cared less. "Do you remember him?" she asked, trying to sound nonchalant. Lucas could detect the slight strain in her voice, but he was convinced Mike didn't notice a thing. "Was he young or old?"

Mike lifted one shoulder toward his ear,

seemingly relieved that Angela wasn't going to make a stink about his prices. "I've had hundreds of clients, ma'am. I have no recollection whatsoever of a Jess Langbroek."

"Is there an address?"

He gave her a shrewd smile. "Can't say I'm comfortable giving out that kind of information. He's more or less local, I'll tell you that. But if you're serious about finding him, you're going to have to do the rest."

"A telephone number? An e-mail address?"

"Nope," Mike said, heaving the book closed and laying his hands on top of it with a decidedly protective air. "Anything else I can do for you folks?"

Lucas watched as Angela slid the jewelry box back into her purse and dazzled the man across from them with another of her luminous smiles. "No," she purred. "You've been so helpful. Thank you." And then she leaned over the counter and kissed him lightly, European style, on each cheek.

As they left, Lucas had no doubt that when Michael Kane bothered to recollect their unusual visit to his store, the edges of his memory would be blurred by the brilliance of the woman who had brushed his stubbly wrinkles with her kiss. The fact that they had solicited information about the ring would be completely overshadowed by the fond impossibility of her.

During the brisk but silent walk back to the car, Lucas could feel the excitement bounce between them, a red-hot ball of energy that made him want to shout. But they contained themselves, remembering even to walk close in case the jeweler chose to watch them retreat. When they were behind closed doors, however, all their careful calm erupted in a disbelieving frenzy of celebration.

"We have a name!" Angela shrieked.

Lucas grinned. Without thinking, he raised his hand palm out and Angela slapped it in triumph. The smack of their high five echoed through the car, and she hit him again and again, pounding at his hand with her fists until he laughed and told her that he was a pencil pusher, not a boxer. "My patients would appreciate it if you wouldn't damage the goods."

She smiled at that, a wide, toothy look of delight that slowly faded into something softer. There was a moment of utter stillness in the car, and then Angela dropped her eyes and reached for his hand. This time, she wove her fingers through his, and when he didn't immediately pull away, she pressed the tangle of their twined knuckles to her lips. In a heartbeat, she was beyond the barrier of their hands, breathing against his cheek, her lips grazing the spot where the corner of his mouth fell into a shallow dimple.

Spurred out of immobility, Lucas jerked his fingers from her grip and banged his head on the driver's-side window of his frost-covered car in his rush to get away. He brushed his cheek with his thumb, trying to erase the evidence of her lips, and then clutched his hands in his lap as if she had stung him with her tender kiss. He didn't know how to react, what to do or say, and his mouth slowly opened and closed in a caricature of a dumb fish.

"I'm sorry," she whispered, her quiet voice cracking. "I didn't mean to do that. It was an accident."

"An accident?" Lucas exclaimed, much louder than he meant to. "An accident is something that just happens, that sneaks up on you, that you can't stop."

"Yeah," she murmured. "Exactly."

"Exactly what?"

Angela covered her face with her hands and moaned. "Are you really that stupid, Lucas? 'Cause I'd rather not spell it out for you."

"Spell it out for me."

Sweeping her hands through her hair, she ducked her head and sighed. Then she took a deep breath and gathered the strength to look him straight in the eye. "No. Some things are better left unsaid."

Lucas felt his jaw drop but couldn't seem to lift it.

"Oh, come on." Angela rolled her eyes. "It's your run-of-the-mill victim transference. Isn't your wife a social worker? Don't you talk about these things? My daddy didn't love me and I never had a strong male role model . . ." Her words were bitter, and as Lucas watched, her eyes filled with angry tears. "You're a great husband, Lucas. You love your wife. You're gentle and handsome and kind. You were the first man in my life who wasn't completely messed up. And I've always wanted to be a part of that. A part of something whole and healthy."

"I'm not . . . whole and healthy. I'm messed up," Lucas said, surprised to hear himself speak.

Angela managed a thin smile in spite of the wetness shimmering at the corners of her eyes. "Yes, you are," she agreed. "Very messed up. Just like the rest of us. And I'm not really in love with you. Not anymore.

you."

"You were in love with me?" Lucas stammered.

She snorted and carefully dabbed at her eyes with the tips of her fingers. "You are so clueless."

"You just told me that you're in love with me!"

"Was," Angela corrected. "I was in love with you. Or I thought I was. Maybe I'm still getting over it a little. Maybe I'll always be getting over it."

"I don't get it."

She gave him a wicked half grin. "I was in love with Jenna, too."

"You're a lesbian?" Lucas croaked.

At this, Angela laughed so hard, the tears that had threatened to spill streamed down her cheeks.

"You're not a lesbian?"

"No," she finally assured him, still chuckling. "I mean that I loved the both of you. Like parents in a way, but you weren't old enough to be my parents. And like mentors, I suppose, because all my life I wanted to be just like you. And sometimes I loved you like friends, and sometimes I loved you because you were the only people that God put in my life to love me back. Get it?"

Lucas nodded. "I think I do." He paused, bit the inside of his lip. "But you . . ."

"Tried to seduce you?" Angela finished. She picked at a buckle on her purse and avoided his eyes as much as he tried to evade hers. "I'm sorry," she said after a moment. "Old habits die hard, and it's difficult for me not to try and gain the upper hand in any situation by using what I've been given. My body, my face, my charm."

He pondered that for a moment. "Well," he said eventually, "someone certainly thinks highly of herself."

"You made a joke!" Angela applauded him. "That was funny, Lucas. Well done."

"I'm a funny guy," Lucas protested. "I make jokes."

"No, you don't."

"Sometimes."

"Rarely. Admit it, you're uptight."

Lucas frowned. "I prefer 'conscientious.' " He chanced a peek at Angela and saw her narrowing her eyes at him with an almost palpable skepticism. Raising his hands in defeat, he said, "Fine. You caught me. I'm uptight. But it's just because I want to do the right thing."

"How do you know what the right thing is?"

"It's pretty obvious, isn't it? I'm quite sure

you have a conscience, too."

Angela nodded. "And yet you took the ring."

"Character malfunction." Lucas sighed, trying to be droll.

But Angela didn't laugh. Instead, she dug in her purse and produced the box that held the ring. Flipping open the top, she plucked it out with her thumb and forefinger and offered it to Lucas. "Maybe it's not always about being right," she said softly, watching his face with a look he couldn't quite decipher. "Maybe, sometimes, it's about being good."

"There's a difference?" Lucas said trying to lighten the mood. He accepted the ring and stuck it in his pocket without looking at it.

"It wasn't right to take the ring, was it?" The question was rhetorical; Lucas didn't bother to answer. "But if this name leads us in the right direction and we figure out who she was, that would be a good thing, right?"

Maybe. Maybe not. Did they have any idea what they were getting themselves into? Had he paused for even a second to consider the implications of his selfish, impulsive act of potentially damning theft? If he had known that taking the ring would lead him to a parking lot in Omaha where a woman ten years his junior would reach across the car and tempt him, again, would he have taken it? Lucas shivered, suddenly aware of the cold, and reached to start the car. "I get it," he said, "but I'm not in the mood for a theological debate with you."

"It's not theology."

"I'm not in the mood for an ethical, philosophical, existential, metaphysical, or theological debate with you." He pressed his lips together in a smile of finality. "Look, I think we've lost sight of our goal. We got excited, we went a little crazy, but we're okay now. It's been enlightening." He paused, his hand on the gearshift and his countenance declaring the subject closed. "We okay?"

Angela held her tongue, and since Lucas didn't want to think anymore about what had happened, he chose to interpret her silence as assent.

"Good," he said, looking over his shoulder and putting the car in reverse. "Because my mystery woman is ready to be named."

Lucas started when he felt her hand on his arm in spite of what they had just been through. His stomach sunk a little, but when he turned to confront her, Angela's eyes were wide and serious, her expression earnest.

"Your mystery woman already has a name," she said. "It's Jenna. I wouldn't forget that if I were you."

Because Lucas didn't know what to say, he didn't say anything at all.

22
MEG

Meg liked her new roommate. Katie was the antithesis of a California girl, with jet hair and skin the color of the ivory-rose underside of the shell Meg had found on the beach. She was also the most self-assured person Meg had ever met, but her confidence made her selfless and friendly, quick to smile and happy to forge her own path in life.

Katie wore jeans when it was ninety degrees, but occasionally forgot to don shoes when she left the apartment. Her lips were striking, no matter the time of day, in a shade of cheap Revlon lipstick that reminded Meg of apples, so shiny and smooth, it seemed a reflection played off the pout of her ample mouth. Best of all, her long arms and the soft curve of her shoulders and upper back were resplendent with a rabble of tiny butterfly tattoos in the colors of a pastel rainbow. Meg often looked at her friend and was overwhelmed with a feeling of serenity, as if the girl was so gentle, so safe, she collected fragile, winged wonders around her.

Though Meg felt neither fragile nor winged, it seemed a gift to find herself rooming with a young woman who made her experience a sense of unexpectedly deep peace.

In addition to adoring her roommate with a wide-eyed awe that Meg had rarely known, she also liked the mindless simplicity of her job, the tiny apartment she shared with Katie, and the West Coast in general. In some ways her arrival felt like a homecoming, like she had finally found the place where she was always meant to be.

Only a few weeks after Meg arrived, she saw a poster advertising surfing lessons on the bulletin board in the back of the AT&T store, where she was, as her father had predicted, little more than a cashier. She didn't hesitate to rip off one of the short tabs that broadcast the instructor's name and cell phone number, and a few days later she found herself lying on a rented long board and paddling out into an ocean that seemed endless as she left the shore farther and farther behind. Turned out, she was quite possibly the world's worst surfer. But she liked to ride the waves all the same, and a photo of her wet-suit-clad self being all but consumed by a white-capped wave was the first thing she sent to Jess when he called her and they started talking again.

"I miss you in my life," he told her. "We've been friends for, what? Twenty years?"

Meg laughed. "I haven't even been alive that long."

"Ah," he mused, dismissing her observation, "but we were friends when you were in utero. When you were little more than a wish. Though I had hoped you'd be a boy."

"Sorry to disappoint."

"I think it worked out better this way."

Meg found herself looking forward to his calls, anticipating them as a tenuous but necessary connection to the life she had once led. A life that was so far behind her she wondered sometimes if it had existed at all. And while she had initially been skeptical about their interaction, Jess calmed her fears quickly and assured her that his intentions were completely platonic.

By the time the holidays rolled around, it seemed that everything between them was back to the way it had been before the garage kiss and the years of confusion that followed. They were back to being almost-siblings, close in a comfortable, familiar way that required little maintenance. And when they realized that Meg could only come home for Thanksgiving and Jess wouldn't be able to make it back to Sutton until Christmas, they shrugged off the loss and continued their long-distance friendship without pause.

They shared phone calls, quick, one-line e-mails, and a haphazard assortment of postcards and letters that they both saved, but neither told the other that there was a growing stack of correspondence like collected evidence of their renewed affection.

Jess was in his third year of college, prepping to take his first stab at the LSAT and trying to boost his résumé and personal statement essay with an undergraduate internship at a recognized law firm in Minneapolis. And Meg was loafing in California, finding herself, though she hated to succumb to such unimaginative clichés. She sometimes wondered if Jess really had time for changeable lines of their undefined relationship, or if he was seriously interested in pursuing, even casually, a girl who was content for a season to take surf lessons and peddle cell phones. But just when she was ready to admit that their interlude was over, she'd pick up the phone and he'd be waiting on the other end. Or she'd find a postcard in the mail, something strange and silly, like an image of the Mary Tyler Moore statue gracing the corner of Nicollet and Seventh in downtown Minneapolis. She immediately scrounged up a pair of go-go boots and a trench coat, and had Katie take her picture as she threw a borrowed hat into the air.

She never knew that Jess stuck the photograph to his wall with pushpins, right next to the glossy image of a tiny, drenched Meg smiling openmouthed at a wave as it towered over her.

More than a year after Meg left Iowa for the sunny balm of Central California, Jess talked her into a late-summer rendezvous in Sutton.

"The last week in August," he announced one day when she picked up the phone.

"What are you talking about?"

"Let's go home," Jess suggested, a smile in his voice. "I haven't seen you in . . . how long has it been?"

"Two years? Two and a half?" Meg guessed, trying not to remember too clearly the circumstances under which she had last seen him. The dining room. The porch. The good-bye as he slammed the door to his car. Her heart sunk a little at the memory. It still stung to know that she had hurt him.

"That's too long. And I need a break. I haven't been home since Christmas."

"I haven't been home since Thanksgiving."

"You've always been independent," Jess teased. "But your mom would love it if you'd schedule an unexpected trip home. What do you say?"

Meg hedged a little, humming into the phone as if it was a difficult decision to make. In reality, she had already made up her mind. "Only if I can find cheap tickets," she finally acquiesced.

"I already checked. There's a sale on."

"I'm starting school the last week in August."

"You are? Where? What are you studying?"

"Cal Poly," Meg said, a smile in her voice. "I promised my parents I'd only take a year off, so I guess it's time. And I have no idea what I'm studying. One thing at a time, thank you very much."

Jess laughed. "Fine. We'll meet in the middle. One last hurrah before you're buried in books."

Meg bit her lip and held the phone away from her ear, staring at it as if she could see Jess in the little screen if only she concentrated hard enough. But the LCD display offered no hints, no advice. It was black, asleep. She sighed and cradled it against her cheek.

"Okay," she said.

"That's my girl."

Meg's hand tightened on her phone in uncertainty, but his inflection was light, joking. He was being patronizing in a good-natured attempt to provoke her. She let it go.

They scheduled a long weekend, arranging it so that Meg could fly out early in the evening on a Thursday after work, and head back to California late the following Sunday night. That way she only had to take off one day of her nine-to-five, Monday-through-Friday routine at the AT&T store, where she had worked hard to earn such cushy hours. She ended up swapping her day for a couple of crummy evening shifts, but she figured the inconvenience was worth it for the chance to see Jess again.

"I thought you broke up with him," Katie wondered out loud as Meg packed and repacked for her short trip.

"I did."

"But now you want him back?"

"No. I want to know if I might want him back," Meg tried to explain, but she only ended up confusing herself. "Maybe. Someday. I don't know."

Reaching over to take a pair of shorts that Meg had unceremoniously deposited in her carry-on and folding them along the seams, Katie filled in the blanks. "But you and Jess have been talking,"

"For a year now," Meg admitted. "And I like it. He's a good friend. Always has been."

"A friend."

"Yeah."

"But he loves you?"

"He did."

"Does he still?"

Meg contemplated the butterflies that seemed to be migrating down Katie's arm. "Is that new?" she asked, pointing to a lavender beauty with saffron-tipped wings.

"No. You're avoiding the question."

Sighing, Meg turned back to the haphazard pile of clothes on her bed. "Does he still?" she repeated, almost to herself. "I don't know. I guess that's what I'd like to find out."

"What about Dylan?"

The question stilled Meg's hands. Although she had dated casually since coming to California, and she had hidden nothing about her past from Katie, his name still startled her a little. It was like stepping into the ocean before her surfing lessons — brisk and surprising, even though experience should have taught her what to expect. Now, hearing his name poured out so casually between them, Meg wished she'd been more tight-lipped. She didn't feel like being interrogated. What about Dylan?

"I don't know," she confessed, hoping that her roommate couldn't sense her irritation. "Dylan's out of the picture. Has been for a long time."

Katie didn't press her further, but it was suddenly obvious to both of them that just because something was in the past didn't mean it was buried.

But their conversation didn't dampen Meg's spirits too much. She tried to focus on what had been set before her, this gift of reconciliation that she hadn't dared to hope for when Jess pulled out of her driveway more than two years before.

The plane ride halfway across the continent held a certain delicate anticipation, as if a world of possibility might unfold itself before her when she landed. It seemed inevitable to her, a wish that was sure to be granted, and try as she might to picture it otherwise, her life seemed poised to unfurl at her feet as she stepped from the airplane. The fact that Jess had promised to pick her up from the airport only heightened the sense of beginning, the strange feeling that this was a trip for second chances. For starting again.

When Meg finally crossed the threshold into Gate A7 of Omaha's Eppley Airfield, she had to force herself to walk at a normal pace. It wouldn't do to let Jess see her coming, face lit up as if she couldn't wait another second to correct past mistakes, as if she couldn't wait another second to see him. That was part of it, but Meg was more anxious to explore the life she had left behind, the future she had forfeited when her mistakes made her believe that away was the only option. Where Jess fit into all of that she didn't yet know, and she didn't want the weight of it all to rest on his shoulders before she even had a chance to make sense of how she felt. He wouldn't understand.

In the end, Meg needn't have expended such worry. Jess was nowhere to be seen, but Linda Painter stood grinning at the top of the gently sloped hallway when Meg stepped from behind the glass of the security station and out of the terminal.

"Hey," Linda called when Meg was close enough to hear. The sound was a soft endearment that encompassed everything from "Hello" to "I love you" to "I miss you." She folded Meg in a hug, and the girl

440

could feel the intake as her mother breathed in the scent of her skin. Squeezing tight, Linda exhaled, then pushed away and held her daughter at arm's length. "You cut your hair."

Meg fingered the uneven fringe of her new pixie cut. It was tousled and messy, almost boy-short. Katie made her tuck it behind her ears to show the pretty line of her jaw, and she did that as her mother watched, smoothing the cropped tresses behind the new collection of tiny studs that arched along the top of her ear. If Linda noticed, she didn't say anything. "My roommate did it," Meg said, trying not to sound self-conscious though she meant both the haircut and the piercings. "Do you like it?"

Linda's eyes sparkled. "It suits you. I'm glad I got to be the first to see it." She reached for her daughter's bag and Meg handed it over without complaint.

They walked in silence for a few moments, back to the escalators that would take them down to the short-term-parking garage. Meg used the opportunity to attempt to formulate a question that didn't seem too disappointed, too forward, but Linda anticipated her daughter's inquiry before she had a chance to voice it.

"Jess's stuck in Minneapolis," the older

woman said, crinkling the corner of her mouth in sympathetic disappointment. "Some legal thing that I don't completely understand, but I do know that he's in court when they were supposed to settle something quietly. People are greedy." Linda clucked, unable to resist adding her own commentary. "They always want what they don't have."

Meg held her tongue. She doubted that Jess was stuck in court because of greed — the firm he interned for practiced mostly criminal law — but her mother's uninformed assessment struck a chord all the same. Suddenly her high hopes for fresh starts and new beginnings felt avaricious. Wasn't she happy? Wasn't her life satisfying and simple and everything she could want? After all, she was only nineteen years old. In spite of what she had known, what she had felt or believed she felt for the two boys who had consumed so many years of her life, her days were so soft with green, she wondered for a moment if she had lived at all.

Shaking off her unwieldy thoughts, Meg linked her arm through her mother's and grinned. She was thankful for Linda's presence and the flash of wisdom it had inspired. The fence she had been sitting on abruptly felt unnecessary, pretentious, and contemplations of love lost and unrequited were unnecessarily solemn for a whirlwind retreat in the place she still considered home. It was better this way. Better to see Jess on less intense terms.

"I'll see him tomorrow, right?" It wasn't a question so much as a reassurance to her mom that she was happy to see her and far from heartbroken that Jess wasn't able to keep their unconventional date.

"He was going to leave first thing in the morning," Linda informed her.

"I'll look forward to seeing him then."

But Meg never did see Jess.

"I'm sorry it worked out this way," he apologized over the phone, when it became apparent that he wouldn't be able to sneak away for even a day.

"I don't get it," Meg countered, trying to keep her voice neutral and whine-free. "Aren't the courts closed for the weekend?"

"Yeah, but we're up to our eyeballs in research. Turns out, our client wasn't entirely honest with us. Imagine that."

Meg grunted.

"We have a lot to do to be ready for court on Monday morning."

"So . . ." she drew out the word, trying to

picture the boy she had grown up with in this new world, this self-contained universe of almost film-worthy importance — for some reason the court scene from *A Few Good Men* looped continuously in her mind's eye. Jess seemed to hold the key to some stranger's sad life. "So you're some big hotshot lawyer now, huh?"

Jess laughed. "Mostly I get coffee and pull files and nod. I'm still an undergrad, remember?"

"Still sounds important."

"Nah," Jess demurred. "But if I hope to boss some puny little intern like myself someday, I need to be here."

"Okay," Meg said because there was nothing else to say. It wasn't like he needed her permission. "It was a nice thought all the same. Maybe we'll see each other in another couple of years."

"Thanksgiving?" Jess asked.

"Christmas this year."

He moaned. "Maybe I'll have to come to California sometime."

"Maybe."

Meg was about to click off the phone when something dense and unspoken in the silence between them made her pause. There were so many things left unanswered, so many possibilities that had been postponed, or worse, surrendered with this one small stroke of fate. For a moment, she saw her life as a collection of coincidences, a haphazard map filled with random twists and turns that would have been wholly different if she had slept in late once or twice, listened to her mother's warnings, said no. Or maybe yes. She felt like this telephone good-bye was permanent, an opportunity missed that could never be recaptured again. It made her brave.

The query bubbled up and out of her so quickly, she was stunned by its unchecked urgency: "Why did you write that on my ring?"

There was no need to explain. Jess knew exactly what she meant. "I wondered how long it would take you to ask," he said, all trace of humor in his tone spent. Instead, he sounded tired, and Meg imagined a certain bittersweet edge to his words. "I kept waiting for you to notice it and ask, but when you never did, I just assumed that either you weren't very observant or you just plain didn't care."

"It made me angry," Meg admitted, and realized as she said it that it seemed small to her now. Insignificant and immature. She almost wished she could take the question back.

"I kept waiting for you to ask, for a chance to explain. I guess it's too late now."

"I'd like to know."

There was a long stillness during which the only thing Meg could hear was their breath in quiet harmony. She was about to laugh it off and pretend they'd never followed each other down such an old and winding road when Jess broke the peace between them and disclosed the secret that she hadn't even known he kept.

"It's not literal," he said. "I never meant for you to think that I considered you mine. In fact, quite the opposite. Remember when we were kids? All the backyard games and the bikes and skateboards and basketball . . ."

In spite of the uncertain pound of her heart, Meg smiled at the wealth of memories they shared. "Of course."

"Even then you were larger than life. Little Megan Painter, tougher than the boys, braver than kids twice your age, steady and confident and fearless."

She almost opened her mouth to tell him that even if she appeared to be the girl he described, she didn't always feel that way. The person she let the world see was not necessarily the young woman inside. But he continued before she had a chance.

"I think I loved you when you were still in diapers. Is that possible?"

Meg laughed. "Not likely. But I was a cutie."

"Still are," he declared, and Meg wasn't at all surprised by his boldness.

"You haven't seen my new haircut."

"I'd like to, but that's irrelevant. I was trying to tell you a story here. If I get sidetracked, I'll lose my nerve."

"Go on."

He drew in a long breath and let it out slowly. "Like I was saying, it doesn't mean mine like I think I own you or something. I guess it's ironic — I claimed you knowing I could never claim you because you don't belong to anyone. Because I was eighteen and believed I was in love."

"Okay . . ."

There was a beat or two of silence. Then Jess tried again. "Right before my grandma passed away, we all went around her house with pieces of masking tape and put our initials on whatever we wanted to keep. It was our way of setting aside the things that meant the most to us. Of saving them. It was hard when you flipped over something special and found someone else's name already on it."

"What did you put your initials on?" Meg

asked, because he didn't need to explain it anymore. She understood.

"A pair of my grandpa's wooden shoes. He wore them around the house when I was a kid."

"I can picture them," Meg said, smiling. "You kept them on your desk. I didn't know they were your grandfather's."

But Jess was already over the shoes. "Do you still wear the ring?"

The question stopped her cold. No. No, she didn't wear it and hadn't since she'd slid it off her hand and tried to offer it to him when they broke up. But she had kept it close, in a little canvas pouch where she stored her makeup, and her fingers would sometimes brush along the cool ridge of the cut leaves.

"Don't answer that," Jess split her reverie with a hurried command. "I shouldn't have asked. It doesn't matter anymore. Besides, we never really had a chance, did we? You loved Dylan even though I was right there in front of you. Heart in hands, as it were."

"I didn't love Dylan," she retorted without wondering if what she said was true or not.

"You acted like you did," Jess said softly. "But hey, this is all ancient history, right? We've grown up. Left our childish ways behind . . ."

And with that, everything was neatly shelved away, out of reach and beyond discussion, for a line had been drawn between what had been and what would be. It felt to Meg that Jess left no room for overlap.

"Wish I could have seen you," she said, her throat tight though she couldn't quite pinpoint why. Her mother was right, people always want what they don't have.

"Me, too," Jess echoed.

When they said good-bye, something felt different, and Meg sat clutching the phone for many long minutes in the solitude of her childhood bedroom. Then she got up and went to find the makeup bag that sat like a visitor on the counter of the bathroom she used to consider her own. At the very bottom, beneath the shiny tubes and pretty glass bottles that comprised her meager drugstore collection, she found the ring lying in wait.

She didn't look at the inscription again. She didn't have to. But she did hold the narrow band to her face, admiring the cut of the flowers, the iridescent, rainbow-colored glow of the opal. Then she slipped it onto the index finger of her left hand. It still fit.

Meg passed the remainder of her trip

enjoying the little things and forcing herself to take what she had been given, to accept it at face value and not permit her heart to expect more. Her mother's pancakes were a gift, and the sound of her father whistling in the morning. There was the familiar but untraceable scent of fresh linen that graced the Painter home, and the way her bed had sunk to fit every line and curve of her body. The days were long and hot, but the evenings fell gently, cooling the air with a mellow, soft breeze that stroked her skin as she sat on the deck, mom on her right, dad on her left. They watched the stars come out, lighting the overgrown bramble of raspberry bushes like a string of fading Christmas lights, and talked about things that were pleasant and safe, as comforting and wholesome as butterscotch candy on Meg's tongue. They discussed her childhood. College classes that would start in just a couple weeks. The tomatoes that hung like heavy jewels from the twining plants just off the edge of the deck.

It was a time of hard-earned peace, and maybe it lulled Meg into a place of calm acceptance, a sense that everything was okay, had always been okay, and would work out all right in the end. And if life was not going to deal her a happily-ever-after, then at least it would be filled with enough joy to make everything well worth it. It already was.

Linda dropped her daughter off at the airport late on Saturday. It was an evening flight that would deposit Meg on the West Coast drowsy and red-eyed, but for once Meg wasn't leaving behind a mother with matching bloodshot, tear-filled eyes. It felt right that she was going and they both knew it.

"Love you, hon," Linda said, leaning over the console to give her daughter one last parting hug.

"Love you, too." Meg shouldered her backpack and swung open the car door. Catching her mom's outstretched hand, she gave it a good-bye squeeze. "See you at Christmas."

"Don't forget to send me a wish list."

"It's August."

"I know! I'm already way behind."

Meg laughed as she grabbed her carry-on out of the backseat. "I'll work on it on the plane."

"Brilliant." Linda powered down the passenger window so she could wave as she pulled away, and blew a final kiss through the opening before merging with the traffic that flowed through the drop-off area.

Meg watched until her mother's taillights disappeared around the corner, then she set off down the median between the two wide lanes separating drop-offs from pickups and commercial vehicles from private ones. The airport had been under construction for as long as she could remember, and it had encouraged her parents to dispense with the drawn-out good-bye routine involving short-term parking and handholding through the check-in line. Nowadays she didn't even have to go to the ticket counter. No checked luggage and a preprinted boarding pass meant she could show up an hour before her flight and breeze through security hassle-free.

But though she could go through the steps blindfolded, Meg always battled a little anxiety right before a flight. What if she had misread the departure time? What if her flight had been postponed? What if it took an hour to get through security?

Meg was so focused on getting to the revolving door beneath the United sign that she didn't hear him calling her. His voice was nothing more than one more thin layer of suffocating noise adding to the chaotic symphony of people and cars and announcements crackling through the tinny loudspeakers. But then he said her name again, Megan Elise Painter, all of it, as if he was reading from a roll sheet and she had no choice but to say in obedience, "Here I am."

At first she didn't see him. She turned a slow circle, scanning faces for someone familiar, but she didn't recognize anyone among the crowd of evening travelers. The sky was dark, the sun all but set behind a wall of impenetrable clouds, and a tower of shifting slate that climbed the horizon as if it lived and breathed cast shadows that played off faces like light on water. A storm was coming, and Meg doubted for a moment that her flight would take off at all. Forgetting the sound of her name as it had sliced through the sticky, humid air only a handful of heartbeats ago, she spun on her heel to enter the airport and check a departure board.

But then he called her one last time, and she stopped dead in her tracks.

She knew his voice, familiar and foreign, strange but intimate, and it pulled her, took her by the shoulders and spun her around. She couldn't stop herself from searching for the face she still knew, the features her unconscious traced in midnight dreams.

This was no dream.

He was parked beside a swath of crumbling concrete, the driver's side of his pickup nearly brushing against the orange pylons that sectioned off a particularly messy phase of the unending airport improvement project. He had left the truck on, and the engine growled like a sleepy beast well past its prime. Meg knew that truck. Knew the hand that rested against the hood, the dark eyes that scanned the crowd of travelers swelling in and out of the airport terminal. She was supposed to be leaving, hopping on a jet plane and disappearing off the edge of the known world, but here before her stood a reminder of who she was. Who she had been.

Meg wondered for a moment if he was allowed to be there at all, if airport security would rush over and tell him he had to move before she had a chance to decide if she wanted to see him or not. But even as she contemplated the simplicity of walking away, she knew that it was far from simple. It was the sort of decision that tasted like forever.

Forever. The thought made her heart seize, her chest feel tight. She knew she should turn around, but she couldn't bring herself to do it. There was an instant of complete immobility, a few seconds during which the world seemed to sputter, gasp, and start, and Meg stood rooted to the ground as if she had been planted there before the beginning of time. Then something in his face changed, and she knew that he realized she had seen him. Her fate was sealed.

He grinned at her. A slow-moving, all-encompassing smile that started at his lips but didn't end there. His joy seemed to envelop the rusted lines of his truck, the space between them, her. The force of it hit her at the same time a cool wind lifted from the south, a quick exhalation of air that carried with it the scent of rain and the first few rumbling notes of thunder in the distance. Meg didn't mean to, but she smiled back. And when she crossed the drop-off lane to meet him, his name was waiting on her tongue, sweet and warm and begging to be whispered. To stitch together the small span of space between them.

To bring her back to a time before everything had changed.

23
LUCAS

It wasn't hard to find Jess Langbroek. Lucas did a quick search on his phone and came up with a half dozen possibilities that he quickly whittled down to one. There was a dentist in New Jersey and an artist in a small town in the Netherlands, as well as a handful of women named Jessica who went by Jess. But the man they were looking for was Jesse Elliot Langbroek, a presidential scholar and the resident of a small town that was only a forty-minute drive from Omaha.

"Sutton, Iowa," Lucas said, showing Angela the address on the LCD screen of his phone. "But the information is a decade old. Jess Langbroek graduated from high school ten years ago. He's probably long gone by now."

"There's nothing more recent on him?"

"Not that I can tell. Maybe he goes by Jesse now. Or his middle name."

"Well, we have to go," Angela said, leaving

no room for discussion. "We're less than an hour from knocking on the door of the guy who bought the ring. Her ring."

"I'm familiar with the ring," Lucas assured her. "I stole it, remember? But you're jumping to conclusions. He could have moved. She could have given it away. It could be a dead end, Angela. You need to consider that possibility."

"It's not. I'm sure of it."

"This article is about his presidential scholarship. We don't even have an address."

"I do." Angela held up her own phone. There was a Yellow Pages entry for a Donald and Gayle Langbroek at 439 Ninth Street Circle NE, Sutton, Iowa. "It's kind of an unusual name. There's only one Langbroek family in Sutton. His parents? Definitely a relative."

Lucas rolled his eyes, but the truth was that even without her prodding, he would have taken the road to Sutton instead of the interstate home. His heart was thumping a fast, irregular rhythm at the thought of being so close to where her story began. "Fine," he said. "I'll call Jenna and let her know we won't be back for supper."

But Jenna didn't answer her cell, and Lucas was forced to leave a short, strangled-sounding message that he was sure crackled with the guilt he felt over his blunder with Angela in the car. Had she kissed him? Had he let her? Had he just cheated on his wife? Again?

Although men were supposed to belong to some sort of womanizing boys' club by virtue of nothing more than their gender, Lucas had never joined. He had no idea how to handle the lingering effects of Angela's almost-kiss and her subsequent confession. I love my wife, he thought, and he felt the need to say it aloud, to make it true by forcing Angela to hear the words. But underneath his instinctive reaction, he felt something living and insistent poke through the cracks of his carefully constructed pretenses.

When was the last time that Jenna had looked at him the way Angela did in the car? Had his wife ever looked at him like that? It was an unsettling thought, and Lucas was convinced that he could feel doubt growing like an eager weed as it raised jealous fingers toward the sun. Jenna had always been quiet, a bit of an enigma, a puzzle to be solved. But throughout their courtship and most of their marriage, he had considered her inscrutability to be one of her more intriguing qualities. At what point had her admirable autonomy become a liability? A root of uncertainty that, he had to admit, deep down made him question everything?

"You're going to miss the turnoff if you don't slow down," Angela said, tapping her window to indicate the hidden road that intersected the highway they were on. "That's the way to Sutton."

"How do you know?"

"Sign, genius."

Lucas flicked on his blinker and stepped on the brakes hard enough to make their seat belts lock. He hid a smug smile when Angela gave a little gasp.

"Thanks for the heads-up."

Though he hadn't been paying much attention to the drive, the road to Sutton required his full attention. They had climbed from the flatlands of the Iowa prairie to what he knew from hearsay were the rippled mounds and sheer ridges of the Loess Hills. The brown fields had given way to burr oak forests, their gnarled branches bent and arthritic. As the car wound through unfamiliar terrain, the smoky sunset of a gray sky was obscured by the soft curve of hills and the trees that grew in abundance. Lucas found it all rather pretty in an ominous, enchanted sort of way, as if the world had shifted to envelop the fable of the Woman and lend a sense of folklore to her tragic story.

"These are silt hills, you know," Angela said, sounding more like a tour guide than the troubled woman he knew. "In some places the silt is ninety feet deep. The only other place in the world that exhibits loess to such a dramatic extent is somewhere in China."

"I had no idea you were so interested in geology."

"I'm not," she muttered, turning her face from him so she could look out the window. "Jim and I didn't take vacations, but once a year he sobered up enough to make the two-hour drive to DeSoto National Wildlife Refuge. It's a state park that borders the hills."

Lucas tried to imagine Jim hiking trails or baiting a fishhook for his ponytailed daughter. No matter how he attempted to frame the picture of a happy father-daughter duo, it didn't work. "That's nice," he finally said. "Sounds like a happy memory."

"He went deer hunting and left me in the visitor center for hours on end," Angela said dryly. "I read the natural and cultural interpretive exhibits so many times, I swear I still have them memorized."

By the time they pulled into the city limits

460

of Sutton, the sun was nothing more than a remembrance on the horizon, a trace of thin and wavering light that pressed the clouds like a watermark. It was close to supper-time, and Lucas could see the lights on in nearly every house they passed. The windows glowed golden and welcoming, and the quiet scene was so peaceful and invit-ing, it was hard to absorb the fact that they were about to disrupt a stranger's solitude with questions about a woman long gone. Lucas couldn't imagine what awaited them behind the door of one of these houses. He pulled over to the side of the wide residential road and put the car in park.

"What are you doing?"

"Stopping," he said. "We can't just drive up to this address and knock on the door with no plan whatsoever. What are we going to say? What are we going to do if Jess Lang-broek is still living there?"

"Be happy?"

"Be serious. If he's still there — if he lives at this address, we could be on the verge of changing his life."

Angela chewed her bottom lip, looking for once like she didn't know where to go from here. "I don't know, Lucas. But we've made it this far. We can't stop now. I say we stick to the story we told Mr. Kane: we found the ring and now we're trying to return it."

"What if he smiles, says thanks, and takes the ring?"

"We won't give it to him."

"He bought it, Angela."

"For someone. It's a woman's ring — quite possibly a dead woman. We'll demand to see her. There's no other way."

Angela's slapdash plan was so full of holes, Lucas felt his resolve leaking away like water from a sieve. But she was right: they had made it much farther than he imagined they'd go, and it seemed cowardly, almost irresponsible to turn around now. He sighed in resignation, and drove the final blocks in silence, determining to let Angela and her cunning charms take the lead when they rang the doorbell.

The small cul-de-sac was easy to find as they neared the outskirts of town. A green sign announcing the street was situated directly below a streetlamp that flickered to life just as they approached. It seemed fortuitous, and Lucas pulled into the empty drive with a fledgling sense of anticipation. Maybe, just maybe, everything would work out exactly the way they hoped. Easy answers. Black and white. Right and wrong outlined so clear, so stark and obvious there was no room for second-guessing.

There were only three houses in the circle, and the largest bore the numbers *439* in wrought-iron scrollwork above the brick garage. An old basketball hoop with a bent rim and the shredded remains of what used to be a net stood sentry beside the driveway, but it seemed obvious to Lucas that the structure was a relic. No bikes, children's toys, or youthful paraphernalia littered the yard, and there was a distinctly old and unused feel to the dark house. No lights illuminated the windows.

"I don't think anyone's home," Lucas said, but Angela already had her car door open. "It's dark," he called. "I don't think —"

The car door slamming cut off his unasked-for observations.

Lucas wondered if he should join her, but it was all over before he had a chance to make up his mind. Angela jogged up the driveway, her feet falling lightly, her long hair swaying with every stride. She seemed eager as she flew up the three short steps to the front door, and she rang the doorbell with the open palm of her hand, as if she had to do it quickly and decisively or risk losing her nerve. Then she took a step back and waited, fingers looped in her front pockets, elbows akimbo, head cocked in expectation.

Nothing happened. She reached for the doorbell again. Waited. Rang it two more times before Lucas stepped from the car and called, "No one's home, Angela."

She threw up her hands and cursed, forgoing the bell to knock loudly on the door one last time. When the echo of her pounding faded and not even a drape had rustled in the house, she slunk down the steps with her shoulders rounded and walked at a snail's pace back to the car.

"Get in," Lucas told her. "It's cold."

"This can't be a dead end," Angela moaned, slumping in the car and pulling the door shut weakly. She had to reopen and shut it twice before it latched properly. "I had such a good feeling about this."

"Me, too," Lucas admitted.

Her eyes widened with a hungry look and she sat up straight, fixing him in a desperate stare. "Let's stay. We'll find a motel and try again later. In the morning. Whenever. It doesn't look like an empty house. Someone's got to live here . . ."

But Lucas was already shaking his head. "We can come back."

"Stay," she begged. "I'll call Jenna. I'll explain that we're held up . . ."

The thought of Angela calling his estranged wife to explain an overnight stay chilled Lucas's blood. No matter what he felt about their relationship and how it had changed over the years, he couldn't stand the idea of giving Jenna any reason to mistrust him. Not now. Not when his marriage dangled by little more than a fragile strand of broken promises. "No," he said, the tone of his voice enough to wipe the hopeful look off Angela's lovely face.

She glared at Lucas, startling him with the whiplash of her emotion. Then she blinked and the anger was gone. Gentling her features, she said, "I'm starving. Let's find a place to grab supper and then we'll head back to Blackhawk."

"But before we leave, we'll swing by here one more time," Lucas said, completing her scheme for her.

Angela nodded, a triumphant assurance in the dip of her head because she'd known that Lucas would agree to this one small request.

"Surely someone will be home in an hour or two." Lucas grimaced a little to show her just how long-suffering and patient he really was. But the idea sounded good to him, too, and as he mentally reviewed their short trek down Sutton's historic main street, he remembered seeing a pizza and sandwich joint that made his mouth water in spite of the situation. "We didn't have lunch, did we?"

"I'm still working off a cup of tea."

Lucas did a U-turn in the cul-de-sac and headed back toward the shops. "There was a —"

"Pizza place just past the gas station," Angela finished. "I bet they have hoagies."

He laughed. "You're a vegetarian," Lucas reminded her.

"Maybe I'm in remission." She pouted, crossing her arms over her chest. "It's hard being in the Midwest and sticking to my diet. Instead of sushi bars you have greasy spoons. Instead of multigrain muesli you have . . ." She fumbled, waving her hands in aggravation. "You have Mrs. What's-her-name's homemade blubber bread."

"Mrs. Van Egdom. And I believe it's banana bread."

"Whatever. I'm in a shitty mood. Don't mess with me."

Lucas knew better than to ignore that warning, and he drove straight to the small restaurant without provoking her further, even though it would have been a good outlet for his growing tension.

Giovanni's didn't have a parking lot, so Lucas parallel-parked in front of the small restaurant, even though the painted lines were so faded, he couldn't make out where one space began and another ended. He didn't worry about tickets in Blackhawk because Alex was known to tear up citations for people who he believed deserved second, third, and fourth chances. Lucas was one of them. But Sutton was an unknown entity, and as he left his car at the curb, he hoped any cop would see the out-of-county plates and be gracious.

While the exterior of the restaurant featured the same unimaginative brick as the rest of the shops on Sutton's main drag, the interior was a different story altogether. Giovanni's was too unapologetic to be cliché, and as Lucas took in the red-checked tablecloths, the faint strains of accordion music in the background, and the old black-and-white vintage photos vying for space on every wall, he knew without being told that a proud immigrant family owned and operated what seemed to be Sutton's only restaurant. The place was nearly empty, and for a moment Lucas was surprised. But then he remembered that it was barely five o'clock and people were likely just getting off work. Besides, if the large sign over the takeout counter was any indication, it appeared most people preferred to dine at home.

"Two?" An apron-clad waiter approached Lucas and Angela as they stood in the doorway, absorbing their surroundings.

"Yes," Lucas said, smiling at the friendly-looking man. He had olive skin and dark eyes, and his glossy hair was slightly longer than the current style and parted down one side with a ruler-straight line. The owner's son? Lucas silently guessed.

"Is a booth okay?"

Lucas nodded, and the waiter grabbed two menus from the hostess stand before leading them to a table next to the frosted window. As Lucas slid onto the bench, he noticed a faint, cool vapor coming off the glass, but he didn't mind because someone had cranked the heat in the restaurant and it was so warm he was already shrugging out of his lined coat.

"Here you are." The waiter pulled a long-handled lighter from the pocket of his apron and lit a white candle in the center of the small table. Lucas fought an urge to blow it out; it felt too intimate, too datelike. But before he could come up with an excuse to extinguish the flame, the waiter offered him a bifold menu and began to point out the specials. "Tonight is spaghetti night, all you can eat, with breadsticks and Caesar salad — all homemade, of course. We also have an assortment of subs, meatball is very popular, and we're famous for our pizza. Can I start you off with something to drink?"

Lucas ordered a Coke, Angela bottled water, and the waiter left them to study their menus.

"I already know what I'm having," Angela announced, closing her menu and turning it facedown on the table in front of her.

"Salad?"

"The spaghetti special," she corrected him. "With a meatball. But if you breathe a word of this to anyone, I'll be forced to kill you in your sleep."

"As a doctor, I have to admit that I'll be glad to see you eat something more substantial than tofu for once. You look anemic to me."

"Thanks."

"I'm just saying."

Though most of the tables at Giovanni's were empty, it took a long time for their waiter to come back. Since they didn't want to talk about the thread of anxiety that stretched between them, linking them to each other and to all that had happened and was about to happen, Lucas and Angela studied the homespun menus, commenting on the mosaic of photographs that covered the front and back and pointing out interesting portraits to each other.

There were fuzzy black and whites that bore creases from age and showcased the smooth faces of unsmiling young couples. Some photographs highlighted important events in the history of Sutton: a group of men standing around a brand-new fire engine that bore the town's name, a handful of people cutting the ribbon on an unmarked building, a still life of the Welcome to Sutton sign surrounded by wild pink roses. And a few pictures seemed more recent. Angela was drawn to one on the front cover of the menu, a group of girls standing on a brown field, faces and arms muddied with dirt, a scuffed football held high between them.

"You like our Girls' Football League?" the waiter asked, a grin in his voice and a Coke and water in hand as he seemingly materialized out of thin air.

Angela smiled. "Is that what this is? I love powderpuff."

"Oh, no, no. They didn't play powderpuff." His lips still curled as he remedied her false assumption, but there was something sad in his eyes that stopped Angela from questioning him further.

Lucas ordered for both of them, ignoring Angela's scowl and requesting two specials that appeared in half the time it took the waiter to bring their drinks. The breadsticks were hot, the salad served family-style in an oversize bowl, and the pasta was thick and saucy and steaming.

"It's not as good as Jenna's," Lucas commented when there were only a few lone noodles left curling on the bottom of his plate.

But Angela wasn't listening. In spite of her self-professed hunger, she barely ate, electing instead to play with her food and sneak regular peeks at the phone on her lap. Lucas knew what she was doing; he could feel the frantic energy shivering off her as minutes ticked by on the digital clock she kept consulting, but he wasn't about to let her frustration unnerve him. He didn't know what, if anything, awaited them at the empty house they had so recently left, but he did know that they would approach it a second time on his terms. His way.

"You're going to stay in the car," he told her.

Angela's head popped up. She looked startled. Almost scared.

"I don't think you can handle this," Lucas

continued. "You're too emotionally invested. I'm going to the door this time."

"No way," Angela spat. "Absolutely no way."

"You don't have a choice." Lucas held his fist above the table, keys clutched in his palm. "We're not going back if you don't agree to this."

Angela's glare was white-hot and deadly. "I hate you."

"I'm sorry you feel that way," Lucas said, but his tone was perfectly flat and unemotional. He realized with a start that he sounded exactly like a father weathering a teenage daughter's tantrums. He smiled. "Regardless of your feelings for me, the fact remains: we're not going back unless you swear to stay in the car until I tell you otherwise."

"No."

"Then it's back to Blackhawk." Lucas threw a few bills on the table and stood abruptly. He grabbed his coat off the hook on the end of the booth and was halfway to the door before Angela stopped him.

"Fine, I'll stay in the bloody car," she hissed.

"I thought you'd see things my way." Lucas offered her his arm, but she batted it away and swept out the door before him. It slammed shut, disturbing the air and leaving the faint scent of perfume and warm skin in her wake. It smelled like fear to Lucas. But he didn't mind her anxiety.

For the first time in a very long time, he felt completely in control. Capable of handling whatever storm their rookie sleuthing had stirred up. And he could definitely sense dark clouds on the horizon.

Lucas squared his shoulders and followed Angela out into the night.

24
MEG

The storm came slowly, flirting with the horizon as it danced, two steps forward, one step back. Clouds swirled like ink in dark water, and lightning rumbled menacingly in the distance. Dylan kept the air conditioner on low to ward off the clinging insistence of the humidity, and though Meg welcomed the sharp edge of cold that whispered from the vents, she couldn't stop shivering. When Dylan saw her trembling, he offered her a blanket that he had wedged beneath his bench seat. She declined, convinced that it wouldn't stop her from quivering anyway.

"I can't believe I'm doing this," Meg said more than once as Dylan's truck ate up the miles on the interstate.

"Why not?" he laughed, reaching a hand across the seat as if to touch her. But it felt like a lifetime had passed since they had enjoyed that sort of freedom, and he wrapped his fingers around the gearshift as a tangible alternative. "The Meg I used to know wouldn't think twice about embarking on an adventure like this."

She didn't bother to tell him that she wasn't the girl he used to know. "Are you sure you want to do this?" she asked instead, leaning forward to catch his eye even though he was driving.

"Sure," he said with an attempt at an indifferent shrug. "Yeah, why not? Besides, we're kind of stuck now. Your plane is scheduled to leave in fifteen minutes. Even if we could make it back to Omaha in time, they'd never let you on board."

Meg put her hands to her mouth to stop a wave of panic that made her stomach lurch. What was she doing? Had she no sense? A part of her wanted to demand that he turn around this very instant, that he take her home. But then, as she watched the dim lines of his profile, Dylan stole a look at her out of the corner of his eye. In the glow of the dashboard lights, she could see the raw joy in his face, the delight at the unexpected gift of her presence. The entire situation was downright absurd, and yet, here he was beside her, smiling the same smile that she hadn't even realized she dreamed about until she saw it again, in the flesh, directed at her.

He was here, wasn't he? Wasn't there a certain beauty in that? Wasn't there something pure and special in the serendipity of their meeting and the doors that it so astonishingly opened? Dylan had surprised her again. What could she do with that but count it fate? Maybe it was more than that. Maybe it was a gift.

Meg shook her head to dispel the doubt that continued to fog her mind with a cloying sense of surrealism. "I can't believe I'm letting you drive me across the county," she said.

"It's going to be fun," Dylan assured her. "A reunion. Old friends. For old times' sake."

"I'm going to miss work."

"Bah," Dylan scoffed. "What's a couple of days? Call them in the morning and explain you've been delayed. They'll understand. Besides, how long can it take to drive to California? I'll fuel up on coffee and energy drinks and go through the night. Or we'll take the scenic route. Haven't you always wanted to see Yellowstone?"

"Well, yeah, but —"

"But what? This is the chance of a lifetime."

"I start school in —"

"Two weeks. You'll be fine."

476

"You're sure you won't be missed?"

"My classes start the same time as yours, and I had Guard last weekend. No roommate to worry, no plans . . . I crash where I want to and wander at will." Dylan winked at her, obviously fond of his life and his freedom.

It was an invitation to ask, and be asked, to go over the details of their lives like the intricate chapters of a mysterious book. They passed the minutes talking, filling up every potentially awkward pause with chatter that was anything but mundane. For Meg, those first interactions in the cab of Dylan's truck were the deliberate wanderings of an explorer happening upon the same secret haven twice. What had changed? What had stayed the same? What had survived the process of his growth and maturation and yet remained as a faint indication of the boy that he had been?

"Tell me something different," Meg entreated. "Where have you been? What have you really been doing since I saw you last?"

"I already explained everything," Dylan said. And it was true. In the last hour and a half they had spent together in his pickup, they had been over it all, from basic training to active duty to some sense of constancy in the 114th Fighter Wing. But Meg made him tell it again and again, and every time he repeated the particulars of his life, she learned a little more. New details emerged like planks on a bridge that they were gradually building to span the gap of all the years between them.

By the time the first raindrops began to splatter on the windshield, Meg felt as if she knew who Dylan was and where he had been. Or, at least, she knew a part of it, and it was enough to make her believe that the rash decision she had made in the drop-off lane at Eppley Airfield had been a good one. Maybe it hadn't been the wisest choice, but in getting to know Dylan again, she believed that it contained the potential for good all the same.

In the years since their separation, Dylan had wandered wider and ran even farther than Meg. He spent nine months in Kuwait and another two rebuilding some small town in Oklahoma where a tornado turned everything within a three-mile radius to matchsticks and tinder. When he decided to settle in one spot long enough to build a career in the Guard, he hoped to join the 161st Air Refueling Wing in Phoenix, Arizona, but he found the weather unbearable and the jobs too limited. A superior noticed his gearhead tendencies, the way he loved to tinker with systems and repair anything he could get his hands on, and suggested that Dylan try tactical aircraft maintenance and put his subconscious preoccupation with mechanics to good use.

"I specialize in F-16s," he told Meg proudly, and she grinned at him like she knew what an F-16 was.

"Look at you," Meg said. "You were the boy with no plans. No future."

He gave her a wry look. "It's not glamorous, but I like it. I work on engine maintenance, hydraulics, and other systems . . . It's what I'm going to school for."

It sounded impressive, but Meg was even more affected by how he could be so familiar and yet so changed. Dylan appeared larger, taller, wiser. His characteristically unshorn hair was buzz-cut, and all his lines were defined, as if someone had taken a razor and done away with any edge that hinted at even the slightest softness. And yet, in spite of all he had done and seen, in spite of where he had been and the way it erased his ability ever to truly go home again, he was still Dylan. His eyes were still a door that seemed to open just for Meg, taking her in, glittering at her with some singular understanding that made her feel known.

I love you, she thought, marveling at the realization that seemed so obvious in retrospect. I always have. But as quickly as it tripped across her heart, Meg quashed the skip of emotion. She chalked it up to the storm, the circumstances, the past that circled between them like a specter.

"How did you find me?" she asked for the third time, to give herself something else to focus on.

"We've been over this." He laughed. But she knew he'd tell her. She could see that he wanted to say it as much as she wanted to hear it, as if going over every particular could only lend depth and substance to what had already been set in motion.

"Come on," she coaxed.

There was a moment of silence, and then he said, "I came for you."

"How did you know?"

"I ran into Sarah picking up gelato at Giovanni's. She said I'd just missed you."

"You were in town . . ."

"Just passing through."

"But your family lives in Arizona," Meg said, wondering aloud. She hadn't realized until now that there was no reason for Dylan to be in Sutton at all. He wasn't visiting relatives or hanging out with old friends. Meg had gotten the impression that Sutton was not the high point of Dylan's past.

"They moved back the year after I graduated. We haven't had contact with anyone from Iowa for years." The corner of Dylan's mouth tipped in a wry smile. "I guess we weren't suited for Midwest life after all."

"I'm not sure I am either," Meg said. "But if you've cut ties to Sutton, what were you doing back?"

"The guy I bunked with in Kuwait lives in Minneapolis. We hung out for a few days, and on my way home I decided to swing through my old stomping grounds."

Meg shook her head. "It's crazy. We were so close and we almost missed each other." The coincidence was delicious, whimsical, and romantic. And yet it seemed both mysterious and fateful that the weekend she had planned to rekindle something with Jess, providence intervened and gave her Dylan instead.

"I was looking for you," Dylan confessed. "I wondered if I'd see you walking down the street with Jess. Maybe pushing a stroller."

Meg punched him in the arm. "Barefoot and pregnant? That's how you pictured me? Jess and I are ancient history, and babies are the last thing on my mind."

"You have no idea how glad I am to hear that."

"What's that supposed to mean?"

"Jess is an idiot."

Meg flicked his arm with the back of her hand. "No, he's not. He's a good guy. It's not his fault you never had the courage to ask me out."

The truck went strangely quiet. Meg looked over to see the harsh angle of Dylan's chin, the way he clenched his teeth in an attempt to bite down on whatever had so suddenly infuriated him.

"What?" Meg didn't want to be afraid of him, but the cab of the truck was dark and all at once he was foreign, intimidating.

"He owned you, Meg. For all intents and purposes, you were property of Jess Langbroek."

"That's not fair."

"It absolutely is. He staked his claim on you."

Meg fumbled for words. "That's insane."

"We were such kids," Dylan said, shaking his head. "When I think about it now it makes me sick, but back then it was big, you know? I believed him, heart and soul."

"What are you talking about?"

"Jess assured me I wasn't good enough for you. And he swore he'd tell everyone all the Reid family secrets if I ever forgot that."

"That's blackmail."

Dylan laughed. "Hardly. We were, like, fifteen. It's ridiculous, really, but we were trying to start over in Sutton, and I couldn't stand the thought of my mom having to suffer through all those small-town rumors." He shrugged. "Not like it made any difference at all. People knew who we were. What we were."

"I didn't."

"I guarantee your parents did. It's why there was no weeping or gnashing of teeth when I slipped out of your life."

"I can't believe he did that," Meg fumed, trying to get her mind around everything Dylan had said. "I can't believe he's the reason . . . All those things you told me, they all came from Jess?"

"He was trying to protect you." The words came slowly, but Dylan seemed to mean them. "And he was right about a lot of things. I didn't know who I was or where I was going. We both believed you deserved better."

"I don't know if I can ever forgive him."

Dylan swallowed hard and seemed to consider something for a long moment. Then he reached across the seat and grabbed Meg's hand as if he needed to feel the touch of her skin. Now. He said, "Jess loved you in his own way."

"But you came for me." To Meg, that one truth meant everything. It erased all that had come before. It left room for all that was to come. And though there were a lot of things that she would still have to deal with, it was enough for now to let go.

"When I heard that you were on your way to the airport, I figured I was too late."

"But you came."

He laughed. "Doing eighty. And when I pulled up at the airport . . ."

"There I was."

"The rest is history."

No, Meg thought, it's yet to happen. But she wouldn't let herself think that, and she buried the hope deep, rebuking herself for indulging foolish dreams.

She would have liked the road to go on forever, the night to stretch until the mystery of their shared past — what they had been and what they could yet be — was as real and tangible as the shell she still kept on her nightstand. But the storm had other plans, and as the rain fell heavier and the lightning became too infrequent to ignore, Dylan turned on the radio to try to catch a weather report. He didn't have to wait long for an assessment of the current conditions, because the first station he found was running a recording of the emergency broadcast system.

"It's a thunderstorm warning," Dylan told her as if she couldn't hear for herself. "Fast accumulation, hail the size of golf balls, and winds up to sixty miles an hour."

The rain was starting to pelt the windshield in an onslaught so fierce, Meg was convinced it was hailing. And then, as a peal of thunder spun into a flash so bright there seemed to be a moment of daylight in the truck, she saw pebbles like frozen snow ping off the hood of the truck, and she knew it was hailing, with worse to come.

Usually, Meg wasn't concerned about a storm unless the word *tornado* was attached. But as the rain continued to fall and fall and fall, already rushing over the interstate an inch deep and pouring into the ditches, she felt a moment of fear.

"What should we do?" she called over the noise of wind and water.

Dylan was clutching the wheel in both hands and didn't take his eyes off the road to address her. "I don't know," he half shouted. "We're still a good forty miles from Sioux Falls, and I don't think we can make it that far before the brunt of the storm hits. It seems like we're driving straight into it."

"We can't just pull over," Meg cried. "What if it floods?"

Squinting at a roadside sign that was all but obscured by a veil of water, Dylan's shoulders squared. "I know where we are. My corporal lives close to here. Maybe we can make it to his place."

"It's the middle of the night!"

Dylan risked a quick look at her. His eyes were hard and serious. "You got a better idea?"

"A hotel? A motel?"

"Have you seen anything like that recently?"

They took the next exit, and although Dylan assured her the farm that would be their refuge was just over ten miles away, it felt like it took an eternity. The rain was falling so hard now that they could barely see past the rusty hood ornament of Dylan's pickup, and even though the windows were rolled up tight, rainwater gushed down the inside of their doors and made shallow puddles on the floor. When they turned off yet another abandoned blacktop to risk the perils of a gravel road that looked more like a quick-moving stream than a safe passageway, Meg almost screamed in frustration. She wanted to ask Dylan if he had any clue whatsoever of where they were or where they were going, but she held her tongue. She didn't want to hear him admit that they were lost.

Just when she had given up hope of their ever finding sanctuary from the storm, Dylan hit the steering wheel with his open palm and whooped. "I found it!" he cheered, and they pulled into a lane that Meg assumed led to the farm they had been searching for.

The house was in complete obscurity, but when lightning flashed, Meg could make out the shape of a hulking barn on their left. She also caught sight of a heavy metal fence blocking the driveway a heartbeat before they crashed into it.

Dylan saw it, too, and slammed on his brakes at the last second, nosing the gate with the bumper of his truck. The whiplash stunned them both silent, and as the engine stilled for the first time in hours, they became aware of the full fury of the storm that raged outside.

"The barn," Dylan yelled, grabbing Meg's hand. "I don't see any lights on in the house, but I don't think we'd make it there anyway. Can you run to the barn?"

In spite of the situation, Meg mustered an indignant scowl. "Are you kidding me?"

Raising a skeptical eyebrow, Dylan indicated her attire with a sweep of his gaze. The sundress and sandals that were so perfect for a leisurely plane ride to her temperate home in California were laughably inappropriate for the current state of affairs they found themselves in.

"So I'll get wet." She shrugged. "You will, too."

He squeezed her hand, then let go to reach under the seat and grab the blanket that he had stored there. "Slide out my side," he instructed. "We'll make a run for it. The hail has stopped for now. Hopefully it won't come back until we've made it to the barn."

Meg nodded.

"On the count of three. One, two, three!" He threw open the door and dragged her out, slamming it behind them.

Meg landed in a puddle so deep, it lapped at her ankles and splashed the hem of her dress. The rain was a sheet of water, heavy and dense, and she hunched her shoulders against the unanticipated weight of it. Even so, she was soaked from head to toe before Dylan began to pull her in the direction of the barn.

"Come on!"

They stumbled and almost fell, the mud and gravel and water dragging at their feet, sucking one of Meg's sandals off before she could bend down and refasten it.

"Leave it!" Dylan shouted, feeling her pause and presuming the reason when she reached for her ankle. "We'll find it in the morning!"

She obeyed, and they scrambled over the slippery fence together. Then Dylan wove his fingers through hers and they ran headlong for the barn. Using bursts of lightning to measure the distance to their destination and adjusting accordingly, they crisscrossed the lawn in breathless abandon, sprinting for shelter as if their lives depended on it. In less than a minute they reached cover by the aging building, and Meg huddled in the slight protection of the eaves as Dylan lifted the heavy latch. He pushed Meg into the sagging refuge and followed, but there was no way to secure the door from the inside, so he put his back against it and stood drenched and panting in the darkness.

The barn was stuffy, the air musty and stagnant, but to Meg it was a blessing because it was dry. She could feel water dripping off her fingertips, her dress, the tendrils of hair that clung to her forehead. Raising her hand to smooth away the worst of it, she pushed her hair out of her face and was tempted to shake herself off like a dog. A flash of lightning lit the barn and she caught sight of Dylan looking at her, a rakish grin on his face.

"I'm soaked," she complained, but against all odds, her voice melted into laughter.

He started to laugh, too, then he reached for her in the darkness and drew her bit by bit into a wet embrace. Her resistance was halfhearted, and when Dylan took her wrists and secured them around his waist, she held him. Their clothes were clinging and heavy, their arms and legs splattered with mud that they had kicked up as they ran. But Meg didn't really notice those things. Instead, she was aware of Dylan's arms around her, the hot exhale of his breath, his saturated T-shirt against her cheek, and beneath that the furious beat of his heart. She shuddered, but not because of the storm.

When she finally lifted her face to his, he crushed her against him, pressing her lips as if he was drowning and her kiss was hope and air and life. He cupped her face in his hands, drinking her in, and she explored the firm curve of his back with her fingers, walking up each rib with a tenderness that made him tremble beneath her gentle attention. As she traced the line of his collarbone, she wished she could wrap her hands around the permanence of those bones and never let go. She would hold him, no matter if he changed his mind again.

Meg had no doubt that if he had been able to see more clearly, Dylan would have carried her deeper into the barn. As it was, they had to make do with stumbling around in the dark hand in hand. A cursory search of the ground floor revealed a wasteland of junk and old farm machinery, but Dylan soon bumped into a wooden crate that they could prop against the door to hold it closed. Their next discovery was a ladder, and they climbed it one rung at a time into a forgotten hayloft.

The hay was moldy and sparse, the second floor leaky, but they didn't care. Dylan still clutched the blanket he'd taken from the car, and even though it was soggy and smelled like dust, he spread it on the dirty floor. Then, fingers trembling, he reached for Meg.

"You're soaking," he said, barely brushing the place where the strap of her sundress had slipped off her shoulder.

"So are you." Meg took a step closer and put her hand on the very center of his chest so that she could feel his heart beat beneath her palm.

There was nothing frantic about the way they undressed each other. Nothing quick or thoughtless. There couldn't be. The world was nothing but wet clothes and warm skin, whispers and sighs, secrets that the barn would always keep. They curled together in the hay, the points of their bodies touching like an imperfect reflection: forehead to forehead, nose to nose, hand to hand. When she exhaled, he breathed, and sometime during the long, long night, they fell asleep.

Meg woke in darkness, her muscles cramped and her shoulder blades numb and tingling where they poked against the wooden floor of the haymow. But even with her body aching, she couldn't stop her lips from forming a faint smile because she remembered where she was and who was lying beside her.

She squinted at the roof of the barn, trying to gauge the soft gray lines of morning that creased the drooping peak like strokes of blurred charcoal. By the hint of pale light that filtered through the narrow slats, Meg guessed that it was getting close to six o'clock. Not quite sunrise, but from the absolute quiet and the fact that she could already make out subtle shadows in the colorless barn, she believed the sun would rise over a clear sky. The storm was over.

Sometime in the night, she and Dylan had

rolled out of the blanket, but she could still feel the thin wool beneath her and his arm like a pillow cradling her neck. She didn't want to wake him, but she was too stiff to suffer the entanglement of their bodies for another second. Holding her breath, she tried to slowly shift away.

"You awake?" Dylan asked, his lips suddenly against her forehead.

"You're not asleep?"

"Haven't been for a long time." He moved a little so that Meg could stretch, but when she rolled onto her side, he followed her, circling his arm around her waist.

"What've you been doing?"

"Watching you. Listening to you breathe. Did you know that you snore?"

"I do not!"

Dylan laughed. "No, you don't. At least, you didn't last night."

"You mean this morning." Although she loved him wrapped around her, Meg felt the first niggling touch of guilt tumble down her spine. She had abandoned her life on a whim only to find herself a fugitive in some stranger's barn. It was scandalous, but the excitement of what they had been through had yet to wear off completely. She squeezed her eyes shut and was suddenly aware of her skin, Dylan's bare leg against hers, and the fact that there was nothing at all between them but air. Meg reached for the crumpled pile of fabric that was her sundress. It was still damp, but she sat with her back to Dylan and pulled it over her head anyway.

He didn't try to stop her, but he brushed his hand against her thigh, sweeping away bits of hay that clung to her skin. When Meg didn't protest, he sat up behind her and kissed the nape of her neck, smoothing his fingers across her shoulders and down her arms, and she tingled in all the places he touched.

"Dylan, I —"

"Don't," he interrupted. "I'm sorry. I didn't mean for this to happen." He wrapped his hands around her waist and carefully spun her around so that they were face-to-face. "But I don't regret it. I know this sounds crazy, Meg, but I'm yours. I always have been, and I always will be."

Meg covered his mouth with her own before he could say more, and against her lips he whispered, "I love you." She said it back. *I love you.*

As Dylan trailed his fingers down the length of her arm, Meg didn't think anything of his lazy wanderings. She enjoyed his touch and had to fight the urge to arch and encourage more, when he picked up her hand and gave the ring on her forefinger a gentle twist.

"You still wear this?" Dylan asked.

She wasn't sure if he had noticed it before or if his discovery of Jess's ring was recent. Either way, she could detect a suspicious edge to his voice, though he tried to sound nonchalant.

"I haven't for years," she said, wishing she had remembered it and wrenched it off. Especially after all that Dylan had confessed.

"Why do you have it on now?"

Meg pulled back, glad that the shadows still obscured his features. If she couldn't see him clearly, he couldn't see her. She wasn't sure that she wanted him to know that as of only yesterday, things with Jess had been anything but resolved. Should she downplay it? Or tell the truth?

"Jess and I have been talking," she finally confessed. "I was supposed to meet him in Sutton this weekend."

"You came home for Jess?"

"Not just for Jess," Meg said, regretting that she hadn't simply told him that she thought the ring was pretty and considered it an accessory.

"But you've been talking. About what?"

"About us," she whispered then rushed to

495

explain. "I thought you were out of the picture, Dylan. We haven't talked in years. And Jess . . ."

"Has always loved you."

"Yeah."

"So have I."

Meg was quiet for a long moment. "You haven't always made that very clear."

He still had his fingers wrapped around the ring, and when he started to slide it off her finger, she didn't complain. "Can I now?" he asked. "Can I make it clear?"

She fell into his kiss willingly, and when he took off the ring and pressed it into her palm, she curled her arms around him and felt the unencumbered candor of her bare hands. The absence of the ring was like a weight lifted. There was nothing between them now.

"I'll be back in half an hour," Dylan said, lacing up his shoes. "I'll go gas up the truck, grab some cheap coffee, and we'll hit the road. Sure you don't want to come?"

Meg yawned and blinked long. "I need to charge my phone," she murmured, ignoring his question unintentionally. She was too sleepy to think straight. "I forgot to do it last night, and it was dead when I got to the airport. My parents are probably freaking out that I haven't called them yet."

"We'll find a restaurant off the interstate and you can plug it in there." He brushed a kiss across her forehead. "Go back to sleep. It's obscenely early."

From between half-closed eyes, Meg watched as Dylan studied her for a moment. She could only begin to imagine what he was thinking. What she must look like. Hair mussed, eyes dark from lack of sleep, sundress ruined. But she could feel the expectation of all that was to come radiating off her in waves. She was so hopeful it hurt, and the only balm to ease the shame of her fairytale dreams was that Dylan seemed just as optimistic.

He tipped her chin and kissed her one last time, deep and thoughtful, as if he could taste her soul on his tongue. Then he pushed himself up reluctantly, picked his way to the edge of the loft, and disappeared down the ladder with a wink.

Meg sighed and stretched, pointing her fingertips and toes before cradling her head in her hands. Curling into herself, she marveled at Dylan, at the way, after all these years, they fit. Fear trembled deep inside her, but she also knew that nothing good could ever happen without risk. She had risked much, and she was ready to rest in the knowledge that Dylan was a chance worth taking.

Bathed in light, Meg dozed, slipping in and out of daydreams where her life took on the surreal quality of blurred edges and fairy-tale perfection.

When Meg startled awake, the barn was silent but for the shallow gasp of her own breath. She held herself perfectly still for a moment, straining, listening, but there was nothing to hear. Dylan? His name whispered across her lips, but it wasn't him. He had just left, hadn't he? Meg willed herself to calm down, but something dark and unreasonable was rising in her chest. And in the split second before the barn door crashed open, Meg knew.

She knew that she wasn't alone.

Her heart stopped, then stuttered back to life when she heard a heavy shuffling like an aged man walking with a laborious, uneven stumble.

"Who's there?" The shout rose from beneath her, and the strong voice didn't match the feeble swish and thud of his approach. Worst of all, the man who called out into the dim, predawn light did not sound curious. He sounded furious. "I said: Who's there? Show yourself!"

As Meg scrambled off the blanket and

huddled in a crouch, she heard a strange, metallic clack that seemed oddly familiar. The sound buzzed at the brink of her memory, flirting with some ancient memory, but before she had a chance to place it, an explosion rocked the barn. Desiccated bird droppings and a decade of grime fell like soft snow where dozens of tiny holes punctured the rotting roof above them.

Meg was too dazed to scream. She threw herself backward, crawling on hands and knees to a pile of stacked bales that required her to climb if she wanted to go any farther. Turning her back to the straw wall, she slunk down as far away from the edge as she could get.

Meg's knees were scraped and bleeding from her frenzied attempt at escape, and she could hear someone scraping around down below, bumping into things and cursing as he came. The insults that he flung at her were meaningless compared to the sound of his gun being cocked a second time.

"Who's there?" the stranger yelled again.

"It's all a misunderstanding," Meg breathed to herself. The stranger must be enraged, and rightly so, considering that she and Dylan had taken refuge in his barn without his consent. She was trespassing.

How could he know that she meant no harm? A terrified chuckle rose from somewhere deep inside, but there was no mirth in the slight sound. She sat up straighter as if she was straining to see over the edge, and mustered the courage to yell, "Hello? Please, don't shoot. My name is —"

A second report burst through the floor in front of her, sending buckshot scattering like the hail that had bounced off the ground the night before.

This time, Meg screamed. And tried to stand. "No!" she shrieked. "You don't understand!"

There was a terrible confusion of noise from below that made her limbs go numb and her steps falter. But she kept going, frantic for the chance to see him, to make him hear her voice before he did something they would both regret. She believed that he wouldn't shoot her — she had to believe that — and it gave her the rush of adrenaline she needed to stop her legs from buckling. For a second, she thought she could hear the unmistakable sound of the gun being cocked a third time, but it was drowned out by the sound of her own heartbeat pounding in her ears.

Meg was intent, blinded by the conviction that it was all a horrible mistake. All she could think was: If he could only see me, if he could just see me . . .

But then something snagged at her foot and she tripped, plunging headlong as the shotgun fired a third time. There was blackness and distance and a feeling like falling.

Then pain.

Something was hot against her chest, but she was aware of a cold and spreading numbness that wasn't alleviated even slightly by the heavy blanket Dylan had obviously tucked around her. Dylan? She tried to say his name, but the vowels and consonants wouldn't form, and all she could do was exhale.

One long, low breath passed her lips like a wordless whisper. Like a cry in a foreign language filled with love and longing and loss. It floated and fell, a wisp of damp fog that dissipated into shadows tinged gold, shadows that were just beginning to fade.

To be shot through with light.

25
LUCAS

There were lights on in the house.

Lucas could see the warm glow from the windows of Number 439 even before he turned down the street. The air seemed different somehow. It was blushed and expectant, charged with possibility.

"You promised," Lucas reminded Angela as he pulled into the driveway and put the car in park. She was leaning forward, her hands on the dashboard and her neck craned toward the house as if she could pierce the blinds with the intensity of her stare. He half believed she could. "You promised."

It was pointless to wait for Angela to respond, so Lucas threw open his door and crossed the driveway. She didn't follow, and he was both grateful and surprised.

Lucas took the steps at a deliberate pace, and paused on the porch. He was so close. So close. Adrenaline made him feel invincible, ready for whatever he would face behind the gilded front door. But he knew he had to handle the situation with a level head. He inhaled in a deep, steadying breath and rang the doorbell. There was the muffled sound of footsteps, the metallic clack of a lock, and then the door swung open wide.

She stood a full head shorter than Lucas, a slightly built woman with pretty, steel-colored hair and a sweet face creased by innumerable laugh lines. "Can I help you?"

Lucas didn't give himself even a second to think. To stop and consider what he was doing and why. "Hi," he said, trying to look honest and affable. He stuck out his hand and she shook it without pause. A small-town woman accustomed to friendly neighbors and the occasional Jehovah's Witness, whom she would undoubtedly invite in for tea and cordial religious debate.

"My name is Lucas Hudson. I'm actually looking for someone who may or may not live here. Is this the Langbroek residence?"

"It is," she said, now with a hint of wariness.

He grinned. "This is a total long shot, but does Jess Langbroek live here?"

"He used to." The woman seemed to relax. "You one of Jess's friends? He meets so many people . . ."

"Yes," Lucas latched onto the bit of information she unknowingly provided, trying to scrabble together a believable story. He hadn't really thought about what he would say if someone answered the door. "Old friends. Actually," he thought of the Woman, "we have a friend in common."

"I don't suppose it's Dylan Reid, now, is it? Because he's in town, too. Can you imagine that! Two of Jess's old friends popping in on the same day. Dylan stopped by this afternoon. He was looking for Jess, just like you."

"Dylan Reid?" Lucas sifted the name, trying to come up with a connection. It seemed odd that he and Angela weren't the only people looking for Jess Langbroek. But he came up blank.

"Oh," she waved her hand dismissively. "Someone he knew in high school. I had forgotten that Dylan even existed until he showed up on our doorstep. But you are definitely not familiar. You didn't go to high school with Jess, too, did you?"

"No, ma'am."

"Thank goodness. My memory's not as good as it used to be. Would you like to come in for a cup of coffee?" She stood back to let him in, and down a short hallway, he could see a cozy living room and the flicker of a television. "My husband is in the shop, but I'll call him in. We like meeting Jess's friends."

"That's very kind, but I'm in a bit of a hurry. We were just passing through and thought we'd stop." Lucas jerked a thumb over his shoulder and watched as Mrs. Langbroek took a glance at the car. By some miracle, Angela was still in the passenger seat, silhouetted in the glare of a floodlight that had clicked on when Lucas pulled up.

The older woman smiled. "She's pretty. Looks a lot like the girl that Jess and Dylan used to fight over. Long blond hair just like that. Such nice cheekbones . . ." She shook her head quickly, her smile faltering as she tried to bury whatever memory had dimmed the light in her eyes. Or maybe she was trying to dig it up. She seemed disoriented for a moment. Flustered. But she steadied herself and said, "No matter. If it's not a cup of coffee you're after, what can I do for you?"

Lucas could hardly believe his luck. "A phone number?" he asked. "An address? Jess and I lost touch and I'd really like to track him down and say hi."

If Mrs. Langbroek was surprised that Lucas couldn't simply e-mail or Facebook Jess

505

to ask for that information, she didn't show it. Lucas felt a rush of affection for a generation that wasn't shackled to the god of technology. It probably never crossed her mind to wonder about Lucas's inability to locate his so-called friend by more savvy means than driving to his hometown.

Mrs. Langbroek insisted on writing down Jess's information, and while she was scrounging in the hall desk for a piece of scrap paper and a pen, Lucas gave Angela a tentative thumbs-up. She snubbed him by turning her head to look out the far window, but he knew that she'd be pleased with the success of his operation. Even if she wouldn't admit it.

"Here you are." Mrs. Langbroek pressed the paper into Lucas's palm and gave his hand a squeeze. "I'm sure Jess will love to hear from you. He might be a big-shot lawyer, but he's lonely, you know? It's hard to see your kids lonely. I wish he'd find a nice girl and settle down . . ." she trailed off, and Lucas gently extracted his hand from hers. Things were getting just a tad too personal, and he was eager to leave Mrs. Langbroek to her memories. It felt disingenuous to lead her on in this way. He hated himself a little for lying to her.

"Thank you very much," Lucas said,

inclining his head in the slightest of bows.

"Well, you're very welcome. I was happy to give his number and address to Dylan, too. Maybe you three could get together and reminisce about the old days."

Bemused, Lucas took a small step backward and glanced at the paper in his hand. The address was in Minneapolis, and there were ten digits in what looked like a legitimate phone number.

"Thanks again." He nodded once and headed back toward the car, but he wasn't halfway there before Mrs. Langbroek stopped him.

"I almost forgot!" she called, waving him over. "Could you give this to Dylan when you see him? He left it here this afternoon."

"Pardon me?"

"Here . . ." she crossed the space between them at a light jog and handed Lucas a cell phone clip. "I probably won't see him again, but you can give it to him when you boys get together."

"But —"

"I don't even know what it is!" She laughed, breathless and cheerful as a new grandma. "But you must be staying at the Gaslight Inn, too. Just pop it on over to his room. I'd really appreciate it."

Lucas didn't know what to say, so he

didn't say anything at all. Instead, he pocketed the clip and accepted the unexpected hug that Mrs. Langbroek gave him. She smelled faintly of cinnamon.

"You two are sure on friendly terms," Angela grumbled when Lucas slid into the driver's seat. Mrs. Langbroek was standing in a dim circle of porch light, waving at the car as if Lucas was a beloved friend instead of a complete stranger.

"What can I say? I bring out the best in people."

Angela snorted. "That's nice and all, but we didn't come here so you could make friends with an elderly lady."

Lucas held up the slip of paper, and Angela snatched it out of his hand. "It's Jess Langbroek's phone number and address," he explained. "And I got it cheap."

"What's that supposed to mean?"

"All we have to do is return this phone clip." He dug the accessory out of his pocket and passed it, too, to Angela.

"You're joking."

"Some friend of Jess's left it at her house this afternoon. He's supposed to be staying at the Gaslight Inn." Lucas gave Angela a sidelong look. "We drove by it on our way into town. It won't kill us to drop it at the front desk on our way out."

Angela didn't say anything.

The air in the car was alive, volatile. Angela was sparking with energy as she squinted at the paper in her hands. It was too dark to read anything, but Lucas understood her desire to stare, to cement the reality of what they had uncovered. She was doing the same thing he was: trying to imagine where it would lead them.

When he pulled into the parking lot of the Gaslight Inn, Angela wrenched open her door before he could stop her.

"I'll do it," she called over her shoulder. "Back in a sec."

But she didn't even know his name. Lucas turned off the car with a sigh and followed her into the lobby of the shabby hotel.

The room was small, but it was lit up like Christmas, strung with tiny lights that blinked on and off in a rhythm Lucas was sure could cause seizures. There was a ratty couch, a table with outdated magazines, and the shadowy entrance to a small pub across from a middle-aged man behind the check-in counter. He was looking at Angela as if she was a present to be unwrapped. Lucas was glad he'd come along.

"What's his name?" Angela asked, turning to Lucas. The cell phone clip was already on the counter between her and the man, who was openly gawking.

"Dylan something or other."

The desk clerk blinked a few times and tore his attention away from Angela. "There's only a couple people staying here. I think the guy you're looking for is in the bar."

"Can you just give him the clip?"

"He's right in there." The man gestured, and turned his gaze back to Angela. "Do it yourself."

Lucas pushed a hard breath through his nose and reached over Angela's shoulder to snag the clip. "Fine," he snapped, waiting for Angela to back him up and annihilate the desk clerk with a single wicked look. But she wasn't paying any attention to their exchange.

Instead, her eyes were fixed on an unfamiliar man as he walked out of the bar behind them. Lucas couldn't see his face — the man was looking over his shoulder — but he was wearing jeans and a light Columbia windbreaker that seemed too insubstantial for the deepening cold. His hair was dark, yet sand-streaked at the crown, as if he spent a lot of time in the sun. Squinting at his back, Lucas tried to place the swagger, wondering if he knew the guy. Angela obviously did, or thought she did, because she took a few steps toward him.

He watched Angela muster a stunning smile then call, "Hey!" just as the man reached for the door handle. The stranger turned and looked straight at her. Even at a distance, Lucas could tell that this was no case of mistaken identity — the set of his features in the second he caught sight of Angela was enough to betray that he was exactly who she thought he was. In the blink of an eye, his look flickered from bland disinterest to shock to what Lucas interpreted as fear. Reaching for Angela, Lucas almost put a protective hand on her elbow, but he couldn't bring himself to do it.

"I thought it was you," Angela said, her smile faded but intact as she considered his curious response. "I'm Angela," she added, touching her fingertips just beneath her collarbone. "You probably don't remember me. It's been years . . ."

Something in the man's eyes caught fire. "Eight years, to be exact."

Lucas noted with alarm that the man across from him was breathing hard and his chest had started to heave with the gasping effort. "You okay?" Lucas asked, taking a step forward to put himself between Angela and the stranger. "You don't look so hot."

But the man ignored him. "What happened?" he said between clenched teeth. His attention was directed over Lucas's shoulder, and he fixed Angela with a gaze so filled with loathing, it seemed to drain the air of warmth. "What happened?" he repeated, low and lethal. And then, he suddenly shouted it: "What happened?"

The room went absolutely still. Lucas could feel blood rushing in his ears, and he felt rather than saw Angela take a step backward. He already had his hand on his phone, prepared to dial 911 or at least threaten to, but before he could do anything at all, Angela whispered from somewhere behind him, "I don't know. I swear to you, I have no idea."

Time seemed to stutter and stop. Then, all at once, the man from behind the check-in counter yelled a string of angry, indecipherable words, Angela let out a slow, sad moan, and something that could only be described as agony settled over the stranger's features.

Without warning, he whipped around and put his fist through the wall beside the door.

26
LUCAS

"You're lucky the entrance is framed in dry-wall and not brick," Lucas said as he wrapped the stranger's hand in a cool, damp towel from the bar. "Your knuckles will turn nice and purple, but you don't need stitches and your metacarpals seem fine." He sounded detached and analytical, even in his own ears, but this was familiar territory. In the midst of the chaos and drama, he was doing something that made him feel distinctly grounded: he was ministering to an injury. Fixing something. Or, at least, doing what he could.

The man tried to pull away, but Lucas had his fingers spread over the fine bones of the back of his hand, and he pressed the bruised cluster of scaphoids at the base of his swollen palm with his thumbs. The stranger sucked in a quick breath and met Lucas's gaze for a second. "I'll make it," he said.

"Oh, I'm sure you will. Why don't you go

get yourself cleaned up a bit, and then we can have a little chat in that corner booth." Lucas indicated the nearly empty restaurant with a nod, leaving no room for discussion or disagreement.

In the moments after Angela reintroduced herself to the young man and everything disintegrated, Lucas found himself picking up the pieces of a situation that he couldn't begin to understand. The desk clerk had rushed over, Angela had plastered an uncharacteristically ineffectual smile on her face, and the inscrutable stranger had extricated his hand from the ruined wall. The bartender threatened to call the police and then Angela's bravado failed and she burst into tears. It was absolute mayhem for a few minutes until Lucas took the reins.

He had talked the bartender out of calling the cops by explaining it was a personal situation and offering to pay for the damage himself, and within seconds, it was obvious to everyone involved that Lucas was the man in charge of this unexpected rendezvous. Even Lucas, who had felt somewhat benign and useless up until now, considered his role pivotal — as far as he was concerned, no one was leaving until he was satisfied that everything had been laid bare.

While the stranger made his way to the

bathroom, Lucas led Angela to a booth in the corner of the motel bar.

"His name is Dylan," Angela said as Lucas slid in opposite her. "He might not be the man that we're looking for, but I think he's tied up in this somehow." Although she wasn't crying anymore, she was dabbing at the corners of her eyes with her ring fingers. She patted delicately, but in spite of her careful ministrations, she looked frayed at the edges. Absolutely terrified.

"Dylan Reid? The same guy who was at the Langbroeks' today looking for Jess? Who is he, Angela?"

"I don't know," she said. "I have no idea who he is."

"What do you mean you have no idea who he is? Obviously you know who he is."

"It's not like that." Angela picked at a loose corner of laminate tabletop. "I met him. Once. I'm just good with faces, I guess."

"What do you mean, you met him? Where? When? What makes you think he has anything to do with the ring and our missing woman?"

"I met him eight years ago." A wry smile shadowed her mouth for a split second before it was eclipsed by a frown. "It's too big of a coincidence, don't you think? Do

515

the math, Lucas. What happened eight years ago?"

Lucas didn't have to do the math. He already knew. "You disappeared."

Angela lifted a shoulder. "And he took me."

"What do you mean, he took you? Are you trying to tell me you were kidnapped?"

She actually laughed. "You can be so dense. Of course he didn't kidnap me. Dylan gave me a ride to the truck stop. I knew him for fifteen miles. I wanted him to take me farther, but he wasn't interested." She sounded miffed, even after all these years.

"I thought you hitchhiked."

"I did. Once I got to the interstate."

"Why didn't you tell us about him?"

"I didn't think he was important. Trying to explain about the stranger at the farm just complicated the story."

"What complicated the story?" Dylan had appeared at the edge of their table, and he hovered over them, leaning into their conversation yet poised to flee. His head was tilted toward them, but everything about his demeanor suggested that he longed to run. Even his hands were twitching at his sides.

"Sit down," Lucas said, trying to sound kind. He wasn't feeling particularly benevolent, but it was apparent that their journey had led them here. To a seedy bar with a nervous stranger. Or, not quite a stranger.

Since the table was a booth, Dylan didn't seem to know where to sit. Angela was centered in the middle of her bench and Lucas wasn't immune to how awkward it would be to encourage Dylan to slide in beside him. After a moment of hesitation, Lucas motioned to one of the hardback chairs at a neighboring table. Dylan took the hint, pulled the chair over, and slouched at the head of the table.

"What happened?" Dylan said, repeating the refrain that had spun him into such a frenzy earlier. He seemed deflated somehow, defeated, and he studied the white towel still wrapped around his injured hand as he asked the question with quiet fervor. "I just want to know what happened."

"Wait a second." Lucas looked from Angela to Dylan and decided that neither of the people in front of him were well suited to handle whatever lay before them. "I need to know a few things before we dig into this. First off, introductions. We've established that you know Ms. Angela Sparks."

"Webb," Angela interrupted.

"Ms. Angela Webb." Lucas inclined his head. "And I'm Lucas Hudson. Who exactly are you . . . ?"

"Dylan Reid."

"Okay, Mr. Reid. It's obvious that the two of you are acquainted, so how do you know Ms. Webb?"

As Lucas watched, Dylan looked up at Angela from beneath a fringe of hair that was too long to be stylish. All at once Lucas knew that his unkempt appearance was not something he cultivated to emanate an aura of casual indifference. Instead, the ragged edges that made Dylan appear roguish and handsome were actually evidence of a man who lived on the knife edge of sanity. There was something off about him, something wild and almost feral. Lucas sat a little straighter in his seat and surreptitiously pulled his cell phone from the holder at his hip.

"We met at my dad's house," Angela supplied when Dylan declined to answer. "I came home one day and he was there."

"You know Jim Sparks?" Lucas asked, leaning forward to catch Dylan's eye. He didn't mean to use the present tense, but Dylan didn't react. Were Dylan and Jim still in contact? Did he know that Jim had hung himself?

"He was my corporal," Dylan said. "Years ago. I'm not . . ." he trailed off, cupping his

518

hand at the base of his head as if he was nursing a migraine. He sighed. "I was discharged from active duty. I haven't thought about it in a very long time."

Lucas ignored that piece of personal information, though he tucked it away for later. He didn't know much about the military, but he was rather certain that even discharges that were not labeled dishonorable often bore a stigma. There had to be a reason to be let go. He said, "But you served with Jim?"

Dylan nodded.

"I'm sorry to be the one to tell you this, but I'm afraid Corporal Sparks is dead."

"I heard it on the news."

Lucas tried to hide his surprise. Although even the national stations had included a little piece about the mysterious suicide-homicide in obscure Blackhawk, Iowa, it wasn't attention-worthy. There was always another bizarre case waiting in the wings to take the momentary spotlight. And yet, anyone with access to CNN, and who actually cared to listen, knew that Jim Sparks had hung himself in his barn. It wasn't shocking that Dylan had heard. Still, Lucas couldn't help feeling on edge.

The bump and jolt of their awkward conversation ground to a halt. A dozen questions spun like spokes on a wheel in Lucas's mind, but he simply didn't know where to start. It was too bizarre, too convoluted, and he was hardly an interrogator. What made him think that he could make sense of any of it?

All the same, the ring was out of his pocket and clutched in his fist before he knew what he was doing. Maybe Dylan didn't have anything at all to do with their impossible quest, but the man's strange, emotional reaction to seeing Angela had sparked a flame between all of them that slowly smoked and flickered. There was something going on, and the only thing Lucas could think to do was provoke whatever sleeping beast crouched so dangerously between them.

"I'm assuming you know also about the body buried beneath the barn," Lucas said. "A young woman. She hasn't been identified yet."

Dylan passed his hands over his face but didn't react.

"We don't know who she is, but we believe that she left a clue behind."

When Lucas held the ring up, he knew he had struck pay dirt. Although it didn't seem that Dylan's face could get any paler, he blanched, and all the fight seemed to drain out of him as if someone had pulled a plug in his resolve. He cursed. Again and again, his mouth formed words that flowed out of him in a bitter lament of regret. By the time he put his forehead on the table in sur-render, Lucas was so confused he didn't know if he should call the cops immediately or put a consoling hand on Dylan's back.

"You recognize the ring? Is it hers?" Angela's voice was raw with hope.

Dylan didn't nod, but he whispered, his words barely audible: "What did he do?"

"What do you mean?" Lucas pressed. "What did who do? Jim?"

"He didn't do anything," Angela hissed. "You did. And now you're trying to use his death to cover up whatever heinous crime you committed in our barn! Who was she?" Angela was half standing, towering over Dylan as if she would beat the answers out of him. "Tell me, you sick bastard!"

Lucas reached across the table and caught Angela by the shoulders, thrusting her back down in her seat. He had no idea what was going on, but the bartender was starting to look at them as if he doubted the wisdom of his earlier diplomacy. "Get ahold of yourself," he said, and his voice carried so much authority that Angela crossed her arms over her chest and contented herself with boring holes into the top of Dylan's head with her glare.

"Oh, God," Dylan breathed, the name an incantation, a blessing, a curse. "I shouldn't have left her. I should have taken her with me. I should have —"

"Dylan." Lucas gripped his arm firmly to stun him out of his reverie. "Please. Start at the beginning."

When Dylan got back to Jim's farm the morning after the storm, the bench of his beat-up truck was littered with offerings for Meg. There was a box filled with rainbow-sprinkled doughnuts, crullers, and something that looked like a chocolate daisy. A cardboard cup holder held four different kinds of coffee — from straight black to a French vanilla cappuccino that had frothed from a giant machine — because when he was standing in front of the beverage counter, Dylan realized that he didn't know what Meg liked to drink. He couldn't stand the thought of returning to the farm without exactly the thing she would have longed for, so he bought everything the gas station had to offer.

In addition to his culinary purchases, Dylan had also bought a tube of toothpaste and two toothbrushes, deodorant that smelled like roses, a couple packs of gum, a comb, and a six-pack of water bottles. He didn't remember until after he had paid that both he and Meg had overnight bags under the Tonneau cover in the bed of his truck. Surely Meg had her own toothbrush and deodorant, just like he did. But he shrugged off his own foolishness and enjoyed the feeling of buying something for her, of the somehow chivalrous gesture of picking out the toothbrush that would clean her sweet mouth.

The farm was quiet as Dylan pulled into the muddy drive, and the morning sun was slanting through the trees as if to highlight the damp beauty of the waking world. Because the gate was still closed, he parked in the same spot he had the night before, grateful that most of the water had already seeped into the fertile ground.

Glancing at the clock before he turned off the engine, Dylan felt a little stab of worry at how long he had been gone. The belts had squealed a bit when Dylan started the truck that morning, and at the gas station, he had pulled around to the mechanic shop and taken a peek beneath the hood. The alternator belt was wet, but there was nothing that he could do about that except let it dry out naturally. However, while he was at it, Dylan figured he'd better check the oil and make sure the spark plugs were dry. Everything seemed to be in decent working order, but the quick trip to town he had promised Meg had turned into nearly two hours. He was anxious to get back. To see her.

Dylan left everything in the truck and hopped the fence into Jim's yard. It was strange to retrace his steps to the barn in the light of day. Surreal to remember the desperation of the night before, the way Meg stumbled beside him, the unexpected refuge they had found. Dylan glanced over his shoulder at the decrepit house and wondered if Jim was even around. Should he stop and say hello? Or grab Meg and go? Jim's alcoholism was common knowledge on the squad, and Dylan had witnessed Jim turn violent on more than one occasion. Maybe it was best to just leave.

Ten steps from the sanctuary of the barn, Dylan heard a door slam behind him.

"Who the hell do you think you are? Get off my property!"

Dylan wheeled around, hands in the air. "Sir! Corporal Sparks, sir!" Dylan's voice snapped to attention and boomed across the space between them. "Private Reid, reporting for duty." It was a ridiculous thing to say. No one called Jim sir, neither his rank nor his character warranted it. But as soon as Dylan saw the shotgun in Jim's hands, he knew he had said the right thing. The tip of the gun wavered as the drunken man regarded Dylan through slitted eyes.

"It's me," Dylan said, trying to sound nonchalant though his heart threatened to throb right out of his chest. "I brought you home a couple months ago. Remember? After we had a few too many at the Rooster?" It wasn't *we* who had a few too many, and it wasn't just a few. But Dylan wasn't about to split hairs.

The nose of the gun dipped a little lower and Dylan took a few wary steps toward the sagging porch of the house. Jim was dressed in a pair of faded jeans and a white T-shirt that was more gray than white and bore yellow stains beneath the arms distinguishable even from a great distance. He looked homeless. Homeless and sick.

"I know this is really unexpected, Corporal Sparks, but my girlfriend and I got caught in the storm last night." A twitch of surprise at how natural it felt to call Meg his girlfriend made the corner of Dylan's mouth curl. It was fine, for now. He wanted to call her more than that. But he couldn't think about that with crazy Jim before him. Dylan tried to focus. "We were in a bad way, sir, and when I realized how close we were to your farm, well, I figured we didn't really have a choice. That was quite the storm we had last night."

Jim still hadn't said anything, but a cloud seemed to pass over his face. He put the gun down, propped it against the porch railing, and sat down heavily on the top step. Dylan was afraid for a moment that he would slip right off the edge and smash his head on the cracked cement of the sidewalk, but Jim righted himself and heaved a congested sigh. "Get the hell off my property, you son of a bitch."

"I will. I will right now, sir, but I have to get Meg first. She's still sleeping . . ."

Dylan was already several paces away when something about the grotesque way Jim cleared his throat made him turn around.

"She's not here," Jim said.

Dylan froze, uncomprehending. "What do you mean, she's not here?"

"Are you deaf? I said she's not here. She's gone."

It felt like flashbulbs were going off in Dylan's head, and he stumbled over a patch of uneven ground. Jim's words didn't make any sense, and yet a dark feeling seemed to descend over the farm, a faint awareness that everything was not as it should be. Dylan shivered.

"What do you mean, she's gone?"

Jim shook his head in disgust. "You really are the stupidest . . ." He trailed off, spilling the last of his tirade down his own chest like liquor he forgot to swallow. He looked up suddenly. "She left you. How hard is it to get that through your thick skull?"

"Meg wouldn't leave me," Dylan said. He sounded hoarse, even in his own ears. "She wouldn't. Not now." He glanced around the farm, barely taking it in. "Where would she go?"

Jim shrugged. "It's what women do," he slurred. "They go. They up and leave you."

"No." Dylan shook his head, and found that he couldn't stop shaking it. "No. She wouldn't. She didn't." He spun around and ran for the barn, calling her name as he went. "Meg? Meg!" Bursting through the barn door, he shouted into the stillness, but even before he climbed the ladder to the haymow, he knew the barn was empty.

There was nothing on the wooden platform but the blanket where they had fallen asleep twined together. He could still smell her skin. He could still feel the weight of her head on his chest. Dylan stumbled uncertainly to the edge of the open haymow and scanned the barn as if it held the secret of Meg's disappearance. There was nothing to see. A soft mound of loose, fresh hay on the ground beneath him. An old plow. A cluster of rotting bee boxes.

"She's gone." Jim sounded out of breath, and he leaned on the frame of the barn door as if he doubted his own ability to stand upright.

"You keep saying that," Dylan whispered. It didn't matter that Jim couldn't hear him. He didn't care.

He wanted to scream. He wanted to throw things and hit someone and jump from the brink of the ledge where he found himself teetering, toes curled over the edge. He wanted to do it all again. He wanted to take it all back.

For a sharp, agonizing moment, he wanted to die.

His heart broke, but in mere minutes, he learned that a broken heart can turn into a bitter heart before it even has the chance to grieve.

"I don't believe you!" Dylan screamed. But the truth was, he did. He could feel that Meg was gone as surely as he could feel the crumpled corner of the blanket when he stumbled over it and almost tripped. A rush of vertigo made him lightheaded, and Dylan fell backward onto the dusty planks of the haymow and sat with his head in his hands for what seemed like the remainder of his miserable life. But when he looked up, it was still morning. Jim was still framed in the door of his cursed barn.

Dylan scrambled to his feet, leaving the blanket and the memories it held. He half slid down the ladder and landed hard on the packed floor of the barn. "I'm going to find her," he rasped, his throat sore from dust and heartache.

"Good luck," Jim said. Up close, Dylan could see that the older man's eyes were red-rimmed and haunted. He couldn't focus on anything for more than a second, but he met Dylan's gaze once. And in that one look was a lifetime of hurt and anger and regret and hell. Dylan thought for a moment that Jim was going to vomit at his feet, but instead he doubled over and pulled something from the pocket of his jeans.

"She had this." Jim tipped the object into Dylan's outstretched palm, but as soon as Dylan realized what it was, he dropped it into the dirt at their feet. Meg's ring felt like it had the power to burn. It was a slap to the face, a cruel reminder. A burden he had no desire to carry.

"I don't want it," Dylan said.

He was too broken to realize that Jim's words didn't make sense. She had this. Not, "She gave this to me." Or, "She wanted you to have it."

Maybe, if Dylan had been listening, he would have known.

"So you left?" Lucas could hardly choke out the question, he was so absorbed in Dylan's tale. It was heart-wrenching. It was wrong. And it was wrong that Dylan had just hopped in his truck and driven away.

"Of course not." The telling had obviously exhausted Dylan, and he pinched the bridge of his nose between trembling fingers. "I drove up and down the gravel roads for hours. I traveled the route between the interstate and back half a dozen times, and stopped at every gas station and truck stop within a thirty-mile radius. I figured she couldn't have gotten too far."

"And you just, you just trusted Jim? You believed him that Meg had left?"

Dylan paused before answering. "Yes. And no. I did at first. I mean, she was gone. And I was so shocked and hurt, I wasn't thinking straight. But I came back late that afternoon and parked in a field driveway about a mile from the farm. I circled back and combed his property. Looked through the groves and outbuildings. Tried to find something that would tell me where she had gone. What had happened to make her leave."

"But you didn't find anything."

Dylan scoffed. "I'm no detective." Then all at once his face crumpled, his gaze darting back and forth as if he was scanning the interior of the barn in his mind's eye. "But there was fresh hay on the ground."

"So?" Angela sniffed. "It was a barn. There was lots of hay."

"I wasn't gone that long," Dylan said, ignoring Angela. "He wouldn't have had enough time to bury her. But he hid her. It must have been so simple . . ."

"You're insane."

"Something happened. He covered her." He spoke evenly, logically, but his hands trembled on the table. "I looked everywhere except beneath my own nose. If I had just looked. I should have . . . I should have known . . ."

"You should have known that my dad killed your girlfriend in cold blood?" Angela's fury was so unexpected, Lucas started. He had almost forgotten that she was there.

"Nobody said that," Lucas said calmly.

"Dylan didn't say that. We don't know what happened. I'm starting to think we may never know exactly what happened."

"He just implied that my father shot a young woman and covered up the murder."

Dylan didn't say anything, so Lucas stepped in again. "She didn't die of a gunshot wound, Angela. She died of a broken neck."

"An accidental broken neck? A broken neck that apparently my father felt the need to cover up?" Angela was working herself into a lather. "Are you telling me that you believe this shit? He's lying through his teeth, Lucas! *He* killed her and dumped her body in our barn, and now he's trying to frame my father! Why would Jim do that?"

"Maybe Jim woke up drunk and realized that there was somebody in his barn . . ."

"How?" Angela asked.

"The door was open," Dylan said. "I didn't bother to shut it when I left for town. Maybe he heard me start the truck that morning. It screamed to wake the dead." He swallowed hard, apparently conscious of his role in alerting Jim to the trespasser in his barn.

Lucas didn't need to remind Angela about her father's history of violence. In the years before he closed in on himself and more or less lived the life of a hermit, Jim had accumulated a long list of misdemeanors, including an aggravated assault from a bar fight that landed one man in the hospital overnight. And Alex had been down to talk to him on more than one occasion about his fondness for chasing teenagers off his property with a loaded gun. There were rumors of undiagnosed PTSD from events that Lucas could only begin to guess at, but he knew that the death of Jim's wife and a stint in the Middle East had to have left indelible marks. The truth was, trying to untangle the gnarled rope that was Jim Sparks's life was like attempting to undo a constrictor knot: impossible.

But, knowing what he knew about Jim, could Lucas believe that the fractured man had gone too far the morning that Meg died? Could he have snapped and done something that he regretted, and then tried to cover it up? That, Lucas decided, was sadly, and distinctly, possible.

"Angela." Lucas said her name softly because she still looked ready to flay Dylan alive. "Jim had Meg's ring. It was tucked inside his suicide note."

It wasn't proof of anything, but it was enough to poke a hole in the hot bubble of Angela's rage. She sagged a little, and bit her bottom lip so furiously Lucas was afraid she'd puncture the skin.

"What happened that night?" Lucas asked, directing the question at Angela. He already knew the answer.

"I left," she whispered.

"And can I presume that you were telling the truth about everything? The fight, the whiskey bottle, the final straw?"

It took her a few seconds, but she nodded. Her eyes were tortured, and Lucas could tell that she was drawing the same conclusion he was.

"I was there." Dylan studied Angela as if seeing her for the first time. "It was dark, and I had come to the farm one last time."

"Why?"

Dylan was still staring at Angela when he said, "I was trying to . . . get rid of Meg's things. Her overnight bag and her carry-on. The toothbrushes that I had bought and the doughnuts. All of it. I threw it on the porch because I couldn't stand to have it in my truck. And Angela was just stepping out the door."

"He wouldn't take me any farther than the truck stop," she muttered.

Dylan shook his head. "I couldn't."

Something struck Lucas. He reached across the table and grabbed Angela by the wrist. Waited until she gathered the courage to look him in the eye. "You just spent days scouring his house, Angela. They're there, aren't they? Meg's bags."

"There were no bags," Angela hissed.

Lucas thought for a moment. "He dismantled them. There were strange clothes in your closet, weren't there? Stuff you didn't recognize, but that DCI would simply assume was yours."

The fact that she wouldn't answer was affirmation.

After a minute Lucas said gently, "It works, Angela. His story works."

Angela's eyes flashed and she turned on Dylan. "Why didn't you step forward when Meg turned up missing? Her parents had to have filed a missing persons report. If you're so innocent, why didn't you tell them your story?"

"I've spent the last eight years running as far as I could from any connection I ever had with Meg. When I left Sutton, I didn't look back. I didn't really have friends in Iowa besides her, and I worked hard to keep it that way."

"That's very convenient." Angela sniffed.

"I'm not proud of it." Dylan hung his head for a moment before lifting it to gaze out the darkened window. "I feel like I've lived half my life trying to forget Meg Painter. And after she left me, I didn't want to know about her happy ending and how she had reunited with Jess."

"Jess Langbroek?"

"How do you know Jess?" Dylan asked suspiciously.

Lucas held up the ring. "We did a little investigating. He was the person we were looking for. Not you." Suddenly Lucas remembered his visit with Mrs. Langbroek and the cell phone clip that had brought them to the Gaslight Inn and Dylan. He had pocketed the clip in the midst of the uproar, and as he fished it out, he felt deeply indebted to Mrs. Langbroek and the part she didn't even know she had played. He slid the phone clip across the table and Dylan caught it. "You left this at the Lang-broeks'."

Dylan fingered the plastic accessory but didn't seem to register what it was or where it had come from. His mind was on Meg. "I thought she was with him all this time," he whispered. "I had no idea Meg was missing until I saw that piece on the news about Jim."

"And you put it all together." Lucas realized he was still holding Angela's wrist, and he released her belatedly. She rubbed her forearm as if smoothing away the evidence of his fingers.

"Parts of it. Enough." Dylan's shoulders rounded and he sank into himself. "I came to see Greg and Linda — her parents. To tell them what I know."

Dylan didn't have to admit that he had never made it to the Painters'. His shame was palpable. He must have considered the Langbroeks a sort of stand-in, a step between him and the people whose lives his story would change forever. Lucas noticed a slight tremor in Dylan's hand, and wondered what caused the involuntary motion. Fear? Horror at finally learning the ugly truth? Or did Dylan medicate himself to forget? He didn't smell like booze, and he didn't seem like an addict. But Lucas was all too aware that there were many different ways to numb the pain. Some more subtle than others.

Lucas studied the ring that he had slipped on his pinky, taking in the curve of leaves and the cracked opal, the iridescent beauty split down the middle. He had spent his life striving to do the right thing. To help people. To promote justice. But after hearing Dylan's tale, he couldn't see clearly enough to determine what that was. He couldn't help thinking of what Angela had said in the car only hours before: Maybe it's not always about being right . . . It's about being good. Maybe this time what was right and what was good were not the same thing.

Dylan would be questioned mercilessly, maybe even suspected of a role in Meg's death — Angela certainly seemed convinced of his guilt. His life would definitely never be the same. And maybe that was the point. As Lucas looked between the two of them, he accepted that everyone had to be held accountable for the things that they did — and didn't do.

"It's not my story to tell," he said eventually, and he slid the ring off his finger and handed it to Dylan.

Angela gasped, but Dylan accepted the ring without pause. He seemed grateful to hold it again, and for one of the first times in his life, Lucas couldn't predict far enough ahead to assume an answer. Black and white didn't seem so clear.

"Thank you," Dylan said, and when he began to cry, Lucas had to look away. "Thank you, but it's not mine. It never was." He closed his fist tight around the ring for a second, then released it onto the table, setting the gold into a spin that Lucas stopped with the weight of his palm.

Dylan had made his choice.

"Okay," Lucas said, picking up his cell phone. "I've got a call to make."

Alex was beyond livid, but Lucas didn't care.

While they waited nearly two hours for the DCI team to arrive, Dylan found his way to an empty booth and laid his head down on the table, face turned toward the wall. His arms arched over his head like he was trying to hide himself from the world, and Lucas wondered, from the slow, deep way he breathed, if he was crying. Lucas knew that kind of grief. That kind of crawl-out-of-your-skin, kill-me-now, I-can't-stand-it grief. He had seen Jenna curled into the same ball the day they buried Audrey.

Lucas wanted to tell Dylan how sorry he was. How deeply he felt the younger man's loss, and how he knew what it was like to believe you that had been forsaken by the world. By a cruel God who didn't care and refused to help. Though it wasn't logical, Lucas fought an urge to touch the top of Dylan's bowed head. He raised his hand a little, maybe to hold it out for a handshake, maybe to raise it in condemnation. Or blessing. But Dylan never saw the offering of the doctor's outstretched hand because he wouldn't, or couldn't, lift his head. Lucas dropped his arm to his side and turned away without saying anything.

Be with him, he thought. Lucas whispered it over and over again until the words bloomed of their own accord and the final hour of their vigil before the authorities burst in grew into a prayer of the sort he hadn't spoken in years. It was a balm to his soul, a comfort that made Angela's fury and Dylan's sorrow seem bearable somehow. Like small, black remnants of fabric that only made the mosaic more beautiful. Hadn't he learned that long ago? That the light shines brighter because of the darkness around it? Though it seemed impossible, Lucas felt hope in the wings. For himself. For Jenna. Even for Dylan. There was a certain expectation, a hint of lingering promise that he was just beginning to remember.

When Alex finally arrived, Lucas was ready for him.

After giving their statements and being interviewed for longer than Lucas felt necessary, Alex begrudgingly gave Lucas and Angela permission to go home. It sounded like heaven to Lucas, like some faraway fairy-tale land, and his heart nearly burst at the thought of leaving the sorrow of Dylan's story behind. But it wasn't something you simply walked away from.

In the moment before they left him, Lucas caught Dylan's eye and tried to smile. It didn't work, not completely, but something passed between them all the same. An understanding, if nothing else.

"What are you doing here?" Lucas asked Dylan, though he had already admitted that he had followed the newscast of Jim's suicide and the unidentified body in the barn back to Meg's hometown. DCI established that his next stop would have been Blackhawk and the last place he had seen her alive. He just hadn't made it that far.

"I came here to find her," he whispered.

But Lucas knew that was only half of it. Dylan had also come to let her go.

27
LUCAS

Angela didn't have much to say on the way home. She sat curled against her door, arms wrapped tight around her abdomen and head tilted toward the window as if she couldn't get far enough away from Lucas. As if she longed to peel away the glass and hurl herself into the night as it careened by.

Lucas attempted conversation more than once, but there was nothing he could say. Her father's absolution had been swapped so quickly for a guilt Angela had never anticipated. Who could blame her for not being able to absorb it? He knew that any anger she clung to was the result of a lifetime of disappointments, accumulated like dust in an abandoned corner of her heart. Deep down, she had hoped to hear that her story was nothing but a misunderstanding: that the man who stole her youth and plagued her adulthood was not who she always believed he was. Didn't she deserve a fairy tale?

And yet, there was something redeeming in Jim's final years, in the way he cared for his daughter long-distance even though he couldn't bring himself to do it when she still lived beneath his roof. His watchfulness was a small thing, but it bespoke a depth that Lucas hadn't known Jim possessed. It held a quiet tenderness. It hinted at regret and hope and recompense for sins that could never be repaid. But at least he had tried.

Somehow, it made Lucas believe in the power of small things, the intangible kindnesses that communicated love in a language people rarely stopped to hear.

"It's okay," Lucas wanted to tell her. "He loved you in his own way." But he knew that she didn't want to hear it. Not right now. He prayed that someday, when there was enough distance between the life Angela had inherited and the hopes she'd attached to it — those impossible dreams that she couldn't have stopped if she tried — she'd look back and know that her father had done what he was capable of. It didn't make up for anything, but maybe amid the ruins of her past there remained a door, even a window, that opened on forgiveness.

By the time they drove up to the Hudsons' house on the edge of a sleeping Blackhawk, Angela had petrified: she was as hard and implacable as the furious woman who had stood in his kitchen nearly two weeks before and swore she would clear her father's name. After watching her soften, risking stability to believe in something with no guarantees and allowing herself to hope, it killed Lucas to see her so undone.

"I know that this isn't what you wanted," Lucas said, chancing her wrath in an effort to coax her to talk a little. He thought it would be good for her to let at least some of it out. "But your dad tried to make amends. In his own way, I think he was asking for forgiveness."

"He was a small man," she muttered through clenched teeth. "Spineless and pathetic and weak. He made himself strong by preying on the frailty of others. I should have known. I don't know what I was expecting."

A miracle, Lucas thought. You wanted to rewrite your story, swapping the evil father for a broken and misunderstood man you could love in retrospect. In spite of his earlier feelings for Jim Sparks, Lucas could admit that the man who hung himself in his barn was exactly those things: a collection of loss and failure that would never overcome the sum of all its shattered parts. Lucas just hoped that his daughter wouldn't spend her life paying for the sins of her father.

"Go home," Lucas told Angela gently. "Go back to the life you had and leave this all behind."

"I intend to."

"Just leave your bitterness here."

"So now you're a counselor?" Angela scoffed. "Advise me, O wise one. How exactly should I deal with all of this?"

"Look, I'm not trying to condescend. I just —"

"What? You just what?"

"I want good for you."

Angela didn't say anything in response, and Lucas sat staring out of the windshield at his shadowed home. "She died that day," he said after a moment. "Meg did. But your life began. Don't forget that." As he watched, the first few flakes of the year began a spinning descent to the earth below. He had to squint to make them out, but within minutes, the air was sparkling, resplendent in waves of soft-strewn white like a gift of tossed confetti. It seemed victorious somehow, a halfhearted celebration in honor of all they had learned.

The woman beside him had gotten what

she wanted, but it came at a cost. So had Dylan. So had Meg. They had all paid for wanting what they didn't have and for going to any length to get it. Was it narcissistic to take what hadn't been given? Was it unpardonably selfish to expect things that had never been promised? How could people account for their carelessness? Their hasty decisions and wild impulses born out of thinly veiled self-interest?

Suddenly, with the snow falling and his house framed in a glowing globe of early winter peace, everything was thrust into sharp perspective for Lucas. The air outside was cold and draped with points of snow like accumulating evidence of all the things he had overlooked. Dylan and Meg and Angela weren't the only ones who had paid dearly for wanting what they didn't have, who had forfeited the happiness they could have known for the sake of hollow dreams they couldn't. So had he. This wasn't about Jim Sparks or a crumpled, forgotten body in a wasted barn. It wasn't even about uncovering the truth.

"It's snowing," Angela said.

"I know," Lucas choked out. He was so anxious to flee the car, he felt stifled, claustrophobic. Desperate to find Jenna.

If Angela noticed his impatience, she

didn't seem to notice. She said slowly, as if she was trying to measure his response, "I'm leaving."

"Okay."

"Right now."

Lucas didn't try to talk her out of it, though he guessed she wanted him to. He didn't try to stop her. The decision was hers to make and for once in his life he was going to forget about doing the right thing and focus on doing what he needed to do. For himself. For Jenna.

Angela's bag was packed in ten minutes, her things hastily thrown in with no regard for the mess she would have to deal with when she got back to California. It was as if she couldn't get away from Blackhawk fast enough, and though Lucas didn't blame her — in fact, he couldn't wait for her to go — he held on to the hope that it wouldn't always be this way. That they would meet again, under different circumstances, and the good of what they had shared would outweigh the bad. He wanted to wake Jenna and share the moment with her, to point out the possibility with the same anticipation that made his heart rise at the sight of snow.

But Angela didn't want to say good-bye to Jenna.

"Just give her a hug for me," the young woman said, huddling in the chill of the entryway.

"You don't want me to wake her?"

"It's almost five o'clock in the morning. You never wake someone at such an ungodly hour unless it's important."

"Saying good-bye isn't important?" Lucas questioned, half hoping she'd change her mind and half wishing that she wouldn't.

Angela forced a smile, and already there was the faintest trace of humor there. Of warmth. She wouldn't be cold forever. "Jenna's important to me," she said. "But don't wake her. Tell her I love her. Tell her I'll call her soon."

"We'll see each other again," Lucas finished for her. She didn't argue.

For some unexplored reason, Lucas felt brave, and he strode purposefully toward Angela and pulled her into his arms. It was a brotherly hug, laced with the shelter of a father and the solidarity of a friend. He could be a bit of all three to Angela, and although they had endured their share of relational confusion, he determined that tonight was a fresh start. A chance to step back to the place they should have always been.

"Take care of yourself, okay?"

"I will," she whispered against his chest.

He watched her get into her car and pull away, wondering where she would drive. Back to Sioux Falls to catch an early-morning flight? To Omaha and the place where Meg had stepped into a truck instead of onto a plane? Or maybe she would follow the path that Dylan and Meg had hoped to take: through the Black Hills and Yellowstone and the canyons of Nevada. A honeymoon of sorts turned into a requiem. Whichever way she decided to wander, he hoped it would take her where she needed to go.

Lucas's own journey consisted of climbing a few stairs, but the distance seemed much greater.

The door to the attic was closed, and in all the time that Jenna had been sleeping there, Lucas had respected her privacy and never once opened it. Now, with his palm cold on the handle, he felt a thrill of anticipation. He was storming the tower for her, breaking all their unspoken rules to lay his soul before her. And there was no guarantee that she wouldn't walk away.

Jenna was curled up in the double bed, tucked in a fetal position that took up exactly half of the mattress. Lucas instinctively knew that the other half was for him, but it seemed that there was no welcome in the space she saved, only habit born of routine and preserved through practice. But for once he didn't feel sorry for himself. He simply crossed the expanse of hardwood floor between them and slipped out of his clothes, tracing with his gaze the outline of his wife as she lay beneath the sheet in the soft glow of light from the window.

Crawling in beside her, breaking all the unwritten rules of their so-called separation, Lucas slid across the bed until he was cocooned around her. He buried his face in her hair and draped his hand across her narrow abdomen. For some reason he could never understand, she hated to have him touch her bare stomach, but this morning he didn't care. He curled his fingers beneath the curve of her waist and pulled her tight against him, enveloping her as if he longed to take her in, to make her a part of himself.

Jenna was awake and he knew it.

"Did you do it?" she asked into the darkness, abandoning any attempt at subterfuge.

Lucas kissed the back of her head through a tangle of dark hair. She didn't flinch or pull away. "Do what?"

"Have an affair with Angela?"

"No."

"Did you want to?"

"Did you want me to?"

Jenna made a noise of disgust and tried to pry his hand from her waist. But Lucas refused to let go. He wove his legs through hers and held on for all he was worth.

"I did not have an affair with Angela," he told her, his mouth close to her ear. "I did not want to have an affair with Angela. But I think you wanted me to."

"That's ridiculous."

"I think you wanted me to do something terrible so that you would have an excuse to finally leave."

Jenna breathed slowly in and out, in and out.

He considered her silence an invitation to continue. "We grew apart every day, a little more and a little more, until suddenly we woke up one morning, strangers in bed . . . I don't know you anymore."

"I don't know you," she echoed.

"Why?"

Lucas meant the question to be rhetorical; he didn't expect her to answer. It hung in the space between them, covering the long history of all they had been through and obscuring it beneath a blanket of regret. Did it matter why?

But apparently it mattered to Jenna. "We lost our baby," she told him, replying to his muttered inquiry with a sob that told him just how close her pain still was. How real.

"I'm so sorry," he whispered, holding her tighter, willing her to cry. "I'm so, so sorry."

"Don't you miss her at all?"

"Of course I do."

"Doesn't it kill you?"

"Yes."

"No, it doesn't," she sputtered. "You have no idea what I've been through, how much it hurts. It feels like I was the only one in this marriage to lose a baby." Jenna tried to wriggle out of his grasp, but he refused to loosen his hold on her. After struggling for a few moments, yanking desperately at the iron of his hands, she gave up and gave in to gut-wrenching sobs, the likes of which he hadn't heard for years. It was as if everything she had bottled up since they put Audrey's tiny casket in the ground was all at once bubbling to the surface. He rocked her as she wept.

"I haven't been there for you," he murmured against her neck. "I didn't give you what you needed. I wanted you to get over it, to move on, to start again. I wanted to fix you."

"You want to fix everything." She sniffed, wiping the back of her hand against her eyes, her nose.

"You used to like that about me."

"Until you started trying to fix *me.*"

"I just wanted things to go back to the way they had been."

"Everything changes, Lucas. Audrey changed me. Angela changed me. I can't be the person I was when you married me."

"I know."

"No," she told him. "I don't think you get that at all."

They lay there in silence for a few moments, Jenna's quiet whimpers creating an undertone of loss in their dark room and Lucas's heart keeping pace with the furious racing of his battered mind. He knew what he wanted, but he didn't know how to get there from here.

"What did happen? Where were you last night?" Jenna finally asked, still wiping tears, though her voice had a characteristic edge.

"I stole a ring," he confessed, starting at the beginning.

"Excuse me?"

"Remember the body? The woman in the floor of the barn?"

"Of course."

"I found her ring in the barn. And I took it."

Jenna gave a little gasp and wiggled around to face him. This time, he let her go. "You did what? That's a crime, Lucas. A felony . . . I don't know. But you stole, you tampered . . ."

"I know."

"Why?"

"I couldn't have articulated this at the time, but I think I took it because I wanted to make it right. I was failing us, but this seemed like something I could do. I could take what was broken and make it new."

"I can't believe you did that."

"I know." And then, with his wife facing him in the dim light of a newly snowy world, he began to tell her everything.

Jenna listened willingly enough, and Lucas thrilled to the intimacy of sharing his story with her. At some point he reached out to touch the line of her slender arm with his fingers, and when she didn't pull away, he felt a rush of affection fill his chest. Maybe there was hope for them after all.

Lucas's story faded as the world began to slowly fill with morning light. The snow was still falling, Lucas could tell by the accumulation that continued to deepen on the outside window ledge. He loved the sight of all that white, the sky turning dove-gray with clouds that seemed a comfort. And his heart leaped and stumbled as his wife regarded him across their rumpled bed.

"I don't know what you want me to say," she admitted finally, holding his gaze.

"You don't have to say anything."

"I have to say something. One of us does. You crawled into my bed after months of avoiding it. And now you've just told me that your life for the past few weeks has been a lie."

"I'm sorry."

But she didn't seem angry. "You've already said that."

"I know."

Jenna stared at him hard, and he tried to fill his eyes with every hope and longing that he had secreted away in the years that came between them. He wanted her. He always had. All he needed was to hear her say it, too.

"What do you want?" he asked, his heart thick and suffocating at the back of his throat.

She sighed and closed her eyes. "I don't know. But I don't think your little story is enough to make everything okay. This isn't a fairy tale, Lucas. I'm no princess."

He didn't know what made him do it, but he leaned over and kissed each of her eyelids in turn. Then her forehead, her nose, her cheeks. Her mouth. Just once. A sweet, soft kiss. "Yes, you are," he said.

Jenna smiled a little, a thin, sad smile that accused Lucas of being naive. Foolish. He didn't care.

"I love you," he told her.

She didn't say it back, but she didn't leave either. Lucas knew that it was a start. Nothing more. It didn't erase all they had been through or negate the hard work that they would have to do to get back to the place they had been. But it was something. It was real. And in that moment, with light on their shoulders in a blessing of a new day, it was everything he wanted.

It was a beginning.

EPILOGUE:
LUCAS

Lucas stepped out of the car into a bright, spring morning edged with cool. Behind the cobwebbed veil of lifting fog, everything had sharp edges, winter-hardened corners, biting lines. But today was another start, a softening of the world that had seemed chiseled from ice for months on end. Lucas lifted his face toward the sun. It slanted between high bursts of clouds like dollops of whipped cream and filtered lower through ground-clinging mist in wisps of pulled cotton. It was a promise of more to come.

Leaving the car door open, Lucas stretched, spreading his arms overhead to loosen stiff muscles that rebelled against the early-morning, two-hour drive. Though the spring sunrise was a balm, his heart twisted at the sight of a loose knot of people near the top of a tree-lined hill. They marked his destination, and though he had imagined himself ready to face what awaited him there, he wasn't so sure anymore.

"Do you want me to wait for you?" Lucas asked, leaning down to peer through the driver's-side door. He hoped Jenna would say yes.

"No, you go ahead," she said, nudging him. "I'll join you in a few minutes."

He nodded.

"You okay?"

Lucas studied his wife, loving the whisper of concern in her voice, the quiet under-standing in her dark eyes. Loving all of it, actually. The tint of her lipstick, the way she reached a hand to brush a stray hair from her cheek, the cream of her shirt collar against the curve of her neck. "I'm fine," he told her. "No, better than that. I'm good. I'm going to be good."

Jenna smiled, gifting Lucas with an expres-sion that filled the space between them. That gave him strength.

It was enough.

He took the bouquet of yellow daisies she handed him and waved good-bye before starting up the hill through the dewy grass. His feet left a trail in the budding sea of bottle green, a path that marked his progress from the haven of his car to the small congregation of people that clustered around a center he couldn't quite see. There were maybe a dozen people gathered, not much more, and Lucas was struck by the intimacy of their circle. He felt for a moment that he didn't belong; that his presence was an intrusion, an unwanted interruption in the midst of their quiet counsel. He almost turned back.

But then a woman looked up and noticed his unhurried progress from the gravel parking lot. She was an older, more somber version of the young woman in the photograph he now kept on his desk — a gift that seemed extraordinarily poignant — and when she raised her hand to him in greeting, Lucas's reaction was physical.

It was a blow to see her. An unanticipated slap of grief and sympathy, and, surprisingly, some sudden and overwhelming sense of completion. A sense that this had to happen, and Lucas knew it when he saw her press her outstretched hand to her lips and close her eyes against the quick rush of tears.

They met at the crest of the hill, and though tears continued to spill in crooked trajectories down her cheeks, she smiled. "You must be Lucas Hudson," she said.

"It's nice to meet you, Mrs. Painter."

"Call me Linda." She stretched out a hand in welcome, then thought better of it and pulled him into a hug. "Thank you," she whispered against his shoulder. "Thank you so much."

"I didn't —"

Linda cut him off, squeezing his upper arms as she backed away from their embrace. "You brought her home. I will never be able to thank you enough for that."

"I wish . . ." But Lucas didn't finish.

A man with salt-and-pepper hair and a neatly trimmed goatee to match came up behind Linda and placed a protective hand at the small of her back. "Hello, Lucas," he said. His eyes were sad and lined, but there was warmth there all the same.

"Gregory," Lucas surmised. They shook hands like old friends, and Lucas's throat thickened with emotion at the earnest press of the older man's strong grip. There was much contained in the steady pressure of his fingers. "I'm sorry," Lucas choked out, overwhelmed. It was excruciating to finally stand before Meg's parents with nothing to offer but belated condolences. "I'm so, so sorry . . ."

"No apologies," Greg shook his head even as he fought tears. "Not today. We're here to celebrate Meg's life."

"And we want to thank you for what you did," Linda interjected. "For bringing her home to us."

"But," Lucas protested, anxious to deflect their gratitude, "but I didn't —"

"No apologies and no buts. It happened the way that it happened for a reason. And we're thankful for that. Besides, today isn't about why. It's about remembering."

"Remembering," Lucas echoed, though there was nothing for him to remember. And yet he was anxious all the same to meet her, to know the daughter, friend, and woman that had earned a corner in his heart. She deserved her own set of memories.

The ceremony was unofficial and sprinkled with a fine mixture of laughter and tears. They seemed to split the difference — laughing at a shared story one moment and crying the next. But there was no bitterness in it, and Lucas was happy that he had skipped the funeral and come instead for the private farewell, even if he felt like an outsider looking in.

"We're glad to have you," Linda whispered to him on more than one occasion.

Lucas decided his discomfort was worth it for the sake of the pale but genuine smile that she regularly directed at him.

When it was all over, he stepped forward to the fresh grave and bent before the bare swatch of earth that split the new grass like a wound. "Grace and peace to you," he murmured, hoping that Megan Painter could hear his greeting, his good-bye. He wasn't sure what he believed heaven to be, but if God in his graciousness granted small requests, he prayed that this wish would come true. He added his bouquet to the others, marveling at the sunburst of gold that somehow made her burial ground beautiful.

Near Meg's grave was a small table with a mosaic of framed photographs, and when Lucas lifted the one of a ponytailed toddler, Linda asked: "Do you have children?"

He couldn't help the hesitant smile that pulled at the corner of his mouth. Running his thumb over the face of the grinning, gap-toothed Meg, he replaced the picture and turned toward the parking lot. She was halfway up the hill, eyes wide and hopeful as she came. Indicating Jenna as she approached, Lucas nodded at the child in his wife's arms with unabashed pride. "That's my wife," he said. "And the little girl, that's Mia."

"You have a beautiful family," Linda told him. "How old is your daughter?"

Usually Lucas was cautious, quick to explain that Mia was their foster child, and that though they were fostering to adopt, nothing was ever certain until the final documents were signed. But he didn't want to bog Linda down with details, so he said, "Thank you. She just turned three."

"A precious age."

"Yes, it is."

Linda hugged Jenna when she was close enough to touch and got an armful of Mia in the bargain. The little girl squirmed and reached for Lucas.

He lifted her from Jenna's arms. "Did you have a good nap in the car?" he asked, tucking her in close and laying his cheek against the soft sweep of her fine hair.

Mia didn't say anything, just nuzzled her head into the warm crook of his neck with a familiarity that took his breath away. If he hadn't already lost his heart to her a million times over, it would have melted yet again. A few more months, and she would bear his name in addition to his heart.

Jenna and Linda were talking, huddling within the hushed tones of friendship that women in grief speak fluently. It was hard to watch them, but healing, too, and Lucas wasn't surprised when Linda put her arms around their little trio in a gesture that seemed rich with motherly wisdom and support.

"Don't fall asleep," Linda warned, her

voice gentle but her eyes fierce.

Jenna's confusion was unmistakable in her even gaze.

"We were sleeping in Eden," Linda explained. "But we didn't even know it until it was gone." She sighed, her voice breaking. "Paradise lost."

Lucas reached for his wife's hand and held it tight. "Is it?"

"Is what?" Linda smiled crookedly, tilting her head to match the bittersweet angle of her lips.

"Is it really lost? Forever?"

The older woman closed her eyes. Sighed. "It comes back. Little by little. A bit at a time. Like waking up after a long, deep sleep."

"Good morning," Lucas said, dipping his head in blessing.

Linda lifted her eyes, looked around. The sun was starting to burn off the remnants of morning mist, and as it hit the dew unfettered, the drops of water shone like diamonds in the grass. Behind her, people were laughing softly. A bird chirped overhead. "Yes," she finally agreed. "It is a good morning."

Though Mia had clung to Lucas during the introductions and quiet conversations, she wiggled to get out of his arms as they walked back to the car. He dropped a kiss on her forehead and complied, depositing her in the grass with such care she might have been a made of crystal. And maybe she was.

Mia was changing. Slowly. The first month had been hard. And the second. Neglect had made her quiet and insubstantial, a mere shadow of a little girl. She was slight in every way, feather-thin and wispy, made of nothing more than lightness and air. And yet there was something heavy about her, too, grounded, and she seemed older than her scant three years. But Lucas now knew the sound of her laughter, and though it came hesitantly, it came. He smiled at her, chancing a fatherly touch by smoothing his fingers along the heart-shaped curve where her blond-brown hair met her forehead.

Mia looked up at Lucas, pulled her brows into a solemn line, and said, "Swing me."

They did. Lucas held one tiny hand, Jenna held the other, and they descended the hill with Mia suspended carefully between them. Flung forward, she pointed her toes toward the sky. And when her feet kissed the ground, they lifted her again and again, sweeping her up and up, helping her to fly.

ACKNOWLEDGMENTS

Sleeping in Eden took me more than ten years to write. When I first put pen to paper and started the arduous process of trying to capture the stories of Lucas and Meg, I was a twenty-four-year-old high school English teacher who loved words. I didn't make it very far before life got in the way of my storytelling, and in the decade between, I quit teaching, became the mother of three gorgeous boys, moved to a different country, cofounded a nonprofit organization, and published several other novels. But *Sleeping in Eden* is where it all began — when Jim Sparks hung himself from a rafter in his condemned barn, when I wrote that very first sentence, something inside of me changed. I knew I wanted to be a novelist.

Over the years I wondered if this book would ever see the light of day. And I worried that if it did, I would never be able to remember and personally thank all the people who played a role in its unfolding. I find myself in that humbling situation today. I'm going to name names, I'm going to try, and if I've forgotten you in the telling, please know that your contribution is no less sweet. From the bottom of my heart, for your love and support and wisdom and encouragement, thank you.

Thank you to Todd Diakow, for being the first person to read the first sentence. And for telling me that someday, somehow, it would be published. You were right.

Thank you to Danielle Egan-Miller, Joanna MacKenzie, and Shelby Campbell, the incomparable ladies at Browne & Miller. You've read this book so many times you could probably quote entire passages in your sleep. You went above and beyond.

Thank you to my family and friends for reading so many different versions of this story, and for telling me time and again that it was your favorite. That it made you cry. That you couldn't stop thinking about it. I clung tightly to those words, especially when *Sleeping in Eden* felt beyond redemption.

Thank you to Rebekah Nesbitt, Beth Adams, and Amanda Demastus for fixing and polishing and tightening. You helped me see things I couldn't. This book is so much better because of you.

Thank you to Bruce Gore for designing such a gorgeous, evocative cover for the original publisher's edition. After so many years of dreaming what it would look like, I'm thrilled with how you made it come alive.

And thank you to my boys, Aaron, Isaac, Judah, and Matthias. Always and forever. None of this matters without you.

READING GROUP GUIDE

INTRODUCTION

Dr. Lucas Hudson is filling in for the town's vacationing coroner on a seemingly open-and-shut suicide case in Blackhawk, Iowa, when he unearths the skeletal remains of a young woman in a barn. Lucas is certain that they belong to a local girl, Angela Sparks, whom he and his wife, Jenna, had presumed had run away from her neglectful father years ago. Jenna has never recovered from Angela's disappearance, and Lucas becomes driven to solve the mystery of the victim's identity, both to bring Jenna some closure and to save his faltering marriage.

Years before Lucas ever set foot in Blackhawk, Meg Painter meets Dylan Reid in nearby Sutton, and the two quickly become inseparable. Their relationship turns turbulent when Jess Langbroek, Meg's older neighbor, takes an interest in her. Jess is the safe choice for Meg, stable and loving, but

571

Meg can't let go of Dylan and the history they share no matter how hard she tries. Caught in a web of jealousy and deceit she can't control, Meg's choices in the past collide with Lucas's investigation in the present.

TOPICS & QUESTIONS
FOR DISCUSSION

1. "Blackhawk was nothing to write home about, situated in the proverbial middle of nowhere" (p. 28). Discuss the setting of *Sleeping in Eden*. What role, if any, does the remote landscape of the novel play in the temperaments of its characters?

2. Discuss Meg Painter's initial encounter with Dylan Reid on the Fourth of July during a neighborhood game of Bloody Murder. To what extent does their conversation anticipate the nature of their relationship?

3. "Maybe it was [Angela's] innocence that drew Jenna in. Maybe it was her undeniable beauty or her deep silences or doleful eyes. Whatever it was, it wasn't long after meeting the small, seemingly parentless, grubby Cinderella that Jenna was beyond smitten" (p. 53). Compare and contrast how Jenna and Lucas Hudson feel about Angela Sparks, the adolescent girl they befriend.

4. The eight-year-long unexplained absence of Angela Sparks contributes significantly to the deterioration of Lucas and Jenna Hudson's marriage. Why doesn't her return serve to mend their union?

5. "It was a ring. And if [Lucas's] assessment was right, it was real gold, though grimy and neglected and discolored. The piece of jewelry looked sad lying there, like a dejected attempt at intimacy, an artifact of love that had long faded" (p. 62). Why does Lucas feel that Jenna is entitled to conceal the crime scene ring from the police? What does his ethically questionable decision suggest about his character and his feelings for his wife?

6. When Lucas examines a newly pregnant patient at the clinic, he has a revelatory experience listening to her unborn baby's heartbeat. How does his longing for a child compare to that of his wife? How does their grief over losing Audrey affect their relationship?

7. Why does Lucas invade Jenna's privacy by accessing her computer without her permission? What information does he hope to find? To what extent is his behavior justified?

8. "[Looking] at Jess's face was like peering into a mirror. The way [Meg] felt for Dylan was the way Jess Langbroek felt for her" (p. 176). Why does Meg stay in a relationship with Jess, despite her reservations, when it is Dylan whom she truly loves? How do Jess's possessive feelings toward Meg complicate their romance?

9. How does the return of Angela Sparks affect Lucas Hudson? Given the troubled nature of her relationship with her father, why does she feel compelled to clear his name? To what extent do Lucas and Angela have the same motivation in their search for the identity of the woman in the barn?

10. How does the novel resolve the questions around the body in Jim Sparks's barn? To what extent were you surprised by the explanation for Meg's death? Discuss some alternative possibilities raised by the events of the novel.

11. What do Lucas Hudson and Meg Painter have in common as protagonists? Your group might want to discuss the way each character is affected by their romantic interests, their willingness to rebel against the status quo, and their individual ethics. Which of the parallel narratives did you find

most gripping and why?

12. Meg Painter's love triangle with Dylan Reid (the handsome stranger from the wrong side of the tracks) and Jess Langbroek (the handsome neighbor who knows she's the right one for him) captures some of the dynamics of romantic love that characterize adolescence. To what extent did these relationships remind you of others you know, either from personal experience or from other novels? Did you find yourself rooting for one of the male suitors, and, if so, which one?

13. " 'We were sleeping in Eden,' Linda explained. 'But we didn't even know it until it was gone.' She sighed, her voice breaking. 'Paradise lost' " (p. 564). What does this exchange between Meg Painter's mother, Linda, and Lucas Hudson mean to you? In what ways are you sleeping in your own personal Eden?

14. Near the end of the book, Lucas realizes that everyone must be held accountable for the things that they did — and didn't do. What do you think this means? What sins of omission did the characters in this book commit?

A Conversation with Nicole Baart

1. *The narration of* Sleeping in Eden *alternates between the stories of Lucas Hudson and Meg Painter. Did you write each narrative separately, or did the novel come to you in a linear fashion? What drew you to these characters in particular?*

It took me over ten years to write the stories of Lucas and Meg, and it was a very messy process. The novel came together much like a thousand-piece puzzle: one tiny bit at a time, and only with the help of friends, family, agents, and editors who were willing to get down on the floor and search for missing pieces!

The story was sparked in my mind when the body of an unidentified woman was found near my hometown. I couldn't stop thinking about her. My heart ached for her and for the people who missed her — and who had no idea that she had been found murdered in a ditch in Iowa. She started to come to life in my imagination, and she was very different from who I expected her to be. She was spunky and vivacious and interesting. The sort of girl who tempted fate simply by being her amazing self. And, of course, with a heroine so charming, I had to find someone who would fight for her.

Someone who would feel the pull of her story deeply enough to set aside his own common sense and do everything in his power to right the unimaginable wrong that had been done to her. That someone was Lucas, and like Meg, he was a total surprise! These two characters absolutely gripped me. So much so that I was willing to write and rewrite this book over and over again for an entire decade.

2. *Dylan Reid's and Jess Langbroek's feelings for Meg Painter create the perfect romantic triangle. To what extent did you intend for your readers to support either suitor, as in a "Team Dylan" or "Team Jess" scenario?*

I didn't intend for my readers to pick a suitor for Meg, though I love the idea of "Team Dylan" and "Team Jess" T-shirts! I'd wear them both, depending on my mood.

Honestly, in writing Meg's love triangle, I was trying to explore the nature of women and why we seem to be perpetually drawn to the "bad boy" when someone strong and stable and perfect is often right there in front of us. I've experienced this phenomenon personally, and I know many other women have, too. It's a common story, but one that bears repeating because it can't be explained no matter how hard we try. The human heart is simply too complicated to be reduced to something we can dissect and predict. To that end, Meg's story isn't so much prescriptive as it is descriptive. I didn't want my readers to feel a certain way, and I hope that people end up supporting both Dylan and Jess. I'd love for readers to personally explore why they were drawn to one character over the other. Ask yourself the questions: What past experiences shaped my response? What do my reactions indicate about me and how I view relationships? I love taking the opportunity to dig deep and know myself better, and I feel like I learned a lot through my own personal reactions to the characters of Dylan and Jess. I love them both for very different reasons.

One last thought on this issue: Did you notice that Lucas embodies both the male stereotypes? He's a safe, responsible, level-headed guy, but he ends up doing something totally questionable and rebellious. I think sometimes we'd like to pigeonhole people, but the truth is, we are incredibly complex — and capable of truly astonishing things.

3. *There are a number of "lost" girls in this novel — Angela Sparks, Audrey Hudson, Meg Painter. How did you anticipate this pattern echoing across the overarching narrative of*

the book?

I actually think Jenna Hudson could be added to the list of lost girls in this novel. She's lost in a different way, but aren't we all? I guess that was kind of the point as I continued to develop these characters — to explore the idea that we are all, in a myriad of diverse ways, lost. At least, we often feel that way.

Someone once said that fear and desire keep the world in motion, and though I don't necessarily agree with that, I do think that most people make decisions based on those emotions. We seem to always be running to something or away from it, and many of us get lost along the way. All of the women in *Sleeping in Eden* were tangled up in the contradiction of their own fears and desires, and it led them to some very solitary places, both literally and metaphorically speaking. As for Audrey, I think her loss is central to the book. She symbolizes everything that Jenna wants and can't have, and echoes back Meg's story and the precious young life that is longed for and lost in her narrative.

4. *Lucas Hudson's ethics in* Sleeping in Eden *are questionable. Given the ready temptations of Angela Sparks, why doesn't he surrender*

to more base instincts?

He loves his wife. Period. It bothers me that men are often portrayed as cheating scumbags when most of the men I know are hopelessly devoted to their wives. In fact, in my experience, the stereotype is often flipped on its head: most of the marriages that I've seen break up are because the wife no longer cares to make it work. Of course, that's a gross overgeneralization and I'm sure there are lots of statistics to disprove my sentiments, but just once I wanted to read a story about a man who fought for his woman. Not a fairy-tale, knight-in-shining-armor-saves-the-fairy-princess story, but a gritty, real, heart-breaking story of a bad marriage and a rather bitter, unlovable woman who nevertheless is deeply, truly loved by her faithful husband. Even when he is sorely tempted. As for Lucas's ethics, he takes the ring because he believes that it will soothe Jenna's broken heart and offer her some closure and peace. Everything he does, he does for her, and the ethics of it seem minimized to me somehow in the light of how far he is willing to go to do good by her. What would you do to save your marriage? How far would you go for love? Lucas is tested against those questions time and again in *Sleeping in Eden,* and though he fumbles and struggles at times, I admire him for going so far beyond himself for the woman he loves.

5. *The fostering of a girl in need of a family seems like the perfect solution for the Hudson family. Your book doesn't explain what enabled Lucas and Jenna to overcome their marital problems. Why did you choose to leave this open to interpretation?*

I left their struggle open to interpretation because I didn't think that sort of journey could be summed up in a book — or even in a series of books. Marriage is such a mystery. It's so personal and intimate and sacred . . . And I felt like a bit of a voyeur poking and prodding Lucas and Jenna in their most vulnerable, emotionally naked moments. We see so much of their journey in the book: their grief over Audrey and the divergent roads they take, the way Lucas continues to seek Jenna and she pushes him away. But they have history on their side, and so many shared experiences that knit them together. By the end of the book, I hope it's obvious that they both still love each other and that they have the tenacity to fight through the things that threatened to tear them apart. If love is a choice, I believe Lucas and Jenna choose to love — and Mia is a by-product of that love, not the essence of it.

6. *You're a parent of three children. In* Sleeping in Eden, *you write eloquently of Jenna Hudson's longing for a child. What led you to incorporate this theme in the novel?*

People always ask me how much of myself I put into my novels, and the answer is usually rather vague. But I wrote parts of *Sleeping in Eden* from a very raw and wounded place, and I believe that's evident in Jenna's longing for a baby. Although we never struggled with infertility, my husband and I experienced four miscarriages — two of which took place in the second trimester. Each loss was absolutely crushing, and it destroyed me when people tried to minimize what had happened by saying things like, "Well, at least it was early." To me, the loss was no less. Each time, I grieved for a child. So it was easy for me to pour my heartache into Jenna's character — and to understand how that sort of sorrow could tear a marriage apart. By the grace of God, my husband and I only became closer through our shared suffering. But not every story ends as happily as ours, and it wasn't hard for me to imagine a different scenario. Especially after the birth of our youngest son. My pregnancy with him was high risk, and because I was always steeling myself for bad news, I spent nine months in a state of perpetual stress and numbness. When I finally delivered a beautiful, healthy boy, I wept for days. My mother's heart breaks for Jenna and for women like her. For myself.

7. *You've spoken of "the contrived ideal of what it means to be an author." What do you mean by that? What would most surprise your readers to know about you?*

There's a certain author stereotype. You know the one: We're all quirky and bookish, erudite and narcissistic. We wear jackets with elbow patches, drink coffee by the potful, love cats and tortoiseshell glasses, and live for solitude. And maybe some of those things are a little true (at least, for some of us). But my life is so far from that writer's fantasy! Sure, I write, and I love it and I believe that it's my calling and a profound expression of my soul, but I also do a whole lot of laundry. I change dirty diapers and wipe snotty noses with my sleeve and say astoundingly stupid things. Whenever I get together with other authors, I half expect them to sniff the air and realize that *I'm not one of them.* That I'm not bright enough or witty enough or deep enough to be an Author with a capital *A*. Especially since I sometimes mix up words when I speak and say some insanely dumb stuff. Before I was published, I once told a group of people that I wanted to copulate Margaret Atwood. Uh, yeah. I meant *emulate.* I can't believe I just told you that.

8. *Which of the characters in* Sleeping in Eden *most reminds you of yourself? Were any of your characters modeled on friends or family?*

None of the characters really remind me of myself, but Meg is the girl that I *wished* I was. The truth is, I was a shy little wallflower throughout high school, and I didn't have an athletic bone in my body! I wanted to be tough and brave and strong, but I was skinny and nerdy and quiet. My nose was usually buried in a book, and if someone (a guy!) ever deigned to talk to me, I usually found myself tongue-tied, or worse: mute. But I love Meg's character, her breezy personality and verve for life. I feel much more like her now, and I embrace every challenge and opportunity that comes my way. From backpacking to world travel to participating in a triathlon, I'm up for any adventure. I often say that I'll try anything once. Back then? Not so much.

The only other character that is even remotely based on someone I know is Lucas. This sounds incredibly sappy, but my husband loves me fiercely — and I'm convinced that he'd move heaven and earth for me. When some early readers responded to Lucas's character, they didn't understand why he'd continue to fight for such a moody, grieving woman. But Aaron has stuck with me through some pretty tough times, and even at my lowest (after I lost a baby and didn't get out of bed for a week) he loved me. He called me beautiful and met me in the pit of my deepest need. I am utterly confident in his love.